Praisesurier
- The M   e Series -

"A rip-roaring, romantic adventure that is impossible to put down." - Starred Review

"**A well-written and well-researched story** against the background of early 20th century Mexico." – D. Wells, author.

"This beautifully written novel will have you gripped right from the start." – Melissa Hoskins, author

"**Class intrigue, dynastic maneuvering, and dangerous politics** against growing civil unrest in pre-revolutionary Mexico. Can an unlikely friendship blossom into more? **I couldn't put it down, and nor will you!**" - Jennifer Nugée, Oxford University Press

"A riveting peek into a time of Mexico's history where huge **change, excitement and danger are on the horizon. Hugely engaging characters really pulled me in.**" - Starred Review

"**I fell in love with the characters** and laughed and cried with them all the way on their **exciting journey.** They feel like my best friends. It was **wonderful** to read about this little-known part of Mexican history that happened before the revolution. I cannot wait to read what will happen next." - Starred Review

"A book that will make you weep, rage, and fall in love with an array of **characters so realistic they might step off the page. An excellent debut novel.**" – Jessica Leather, author.

About Rachel Le Mesurier

An exciting new trilogy by British author Rachel Le Mesurier! Rachel is the author of **ARTIE'S COURAGE, A HERO'S HOPE**, and **SOFIA'S FREEDOM**. In the **MUSICIAN'S PROMISE SERIES**, she wants to challenge harmful stereotypes, proving that women can be powerful heroes and that men should never feel ashamed to express their emotions.

Rachel and her family live a quiet life on her home island of Guernsey, where she enjoys teaching sign language, singing, reading, and writing.

Rachel has a degree in English Literature and specialized in literature from other cultures, post-colonial, 19th century, and gothic literature.

In **The Musician's Promise**, Rachel wants to challenge a lot of the harmful stereotypes we still see in today's society.

"Women can be powerful heroes. Men should never feel ashamed to express their emotions." Rachel also says that "even the strongest of people can struggle with mental health - it doesn't make you weak, and it's never too late to get help."

Even though her novel is set over a century ago, the issues that she presents are still very present today. She aims to write characters that readers can identify and empathize, who make the reader think, laugh, and cry as they share their adventures.

Rachel hopes to inspire them to stand up and challenge the same real-world issues those characters face.

When Rachel writes, is because something moved her to tell a story. "Sometimes it's something that has made me laugh or brightened my day, and I want to share that with other people so that they can feel it too. Other times, it's something that has moved me to tears or anger, and I want to bring it to the world's attention so that together we can stand up and change it."

She wants to continue helping people as much as she can, whether that's in the form of advice and support for children with special needs, training assistance animals to help improve people's quality of life, or simply spreading messages of love and tolerance in the world via any means she can.

Rachel often says, "it may seem small, but tiny actions from one person can have a powerful impact on someone else's life in ways we cannot imagine at the time. The little things count!"

Led by strong female characters, **ARTIE'S COURAGE** turns the common damsel in distress trope on its head. Based on real historical events, this thrilling page-turner story of love and courage in the face of adversity follows characters on an emotional journey through laughter, tears, passion, and heartbreak.

THE MUSICIAN'S PROMISE SERIES
- Book 1 -

ARTIE'S COURAGE

A Thrilling Historical Romance Driven by Love and Justice

Rachel Le Mesurier

ARTIE'S COURAGE

THE MUSICIAN'S PROMISE SERIES

*A Thrilling Historical Romance
Driven by Love and Justice*

RACHEL LE MESURIER

Published by
5310 Publishing Company
5310publishing.com

This is a work of fiction. The situations, names, characters, places, incidents, and scenes described are all imaginary. None of the characters portrayed are based on real people but were created from the imagination of the author. Any similarity to any living or dead persons, business establishments, events, or locations is entirely coincidental.

Copyright © 2021 by Rachel Le Mesurier and 5310 Publishing Company.
All rights reserved, except for use in any review, including the right to reproduce this book or portions thereof in any form whatsoever. Reproducing, scanning, uploading, and distributing this book in whole or in part without permission from the publisher is a theft of the author's intellectual property.

Our books may be purchased in bulk for promotional, educational, or business use. Please contact your local bookseller or 5310 Publishing at sales@5310publishing.com.

Artie's Courage Paperback: 978-1-990158-49-0
Artie's Courage Ebook: 978-1-990158-48-3

A Hero's Hope Paperback: 978-1-990158-50-6
A Hero's Hope Ebook: 978-1-990158-51-3

Sofia's Freedom Paperback: 978-1-990158-52-0
Sofia's Freedom Ebook: 978-1-990158-53-7

Author: Rachel Le Mesurier
Editors: Alex Williams, Eric Williams
Cover design: Eric Williams

First edition (this edition) released in March 2022.

For Grandad, whose stories of hope, courage, and revolution inspired this one.

CHAPTER ONE

In all the world, nothing has greater potential to ruin a beautiful day than a missing child. Except, perhaps, two missing children.

Esperanza felt her pulse rising as she checked the back streets, trying not to make eye contact with any of the beggars. Her brothers were not there, nor were they in the plaza or any of the other spots where they often played. She cursed. Her life would not be worth living if news got back to her mother that the boys were missing. She had clearly ordered them not to leave the plaza without telling her, but did they ever listen? How could they do this to her *again*, today of all days, when Esperanza had promised her mother that she would take good care of them?

Today was supposed to have been *her* day. She had been so excited to visit Catalina and tell her the good news, the two of them drinking tea and gossiping in the kitchen while the boys played outside. The plaza had just begun to calm as the cloying heat of the day set in, the stalls of fruit and handmade trinkets packing away ready for *siesta* time. Her brothers had been dancing with their friends in front of the *kiosca* to the tunes of some musician or other, and Esperanza had allowed her mind to drift as she watched them through the kitchen window, listening to the soft, lilting music of the guitar and daydreaming about what it might be like to be the wife of a handsome Don.

Then she looked up, and the boys had vanished.

At first, Esperanza had not panicked. They had probably just gone to the sweet shop, as they often did on the days when they came down to the *pueblo*. However, when she went to chivvy them along, the shop owner shrugged and told her that the boys had already been and gone. They were not with their friends, and she couldn't see them by the stalls or under the trees in the plaza where they sometimes played. They were gone.

She gritted her teeth, trying to work out where to go next. They knew she was only at Catalina's house on the corner if they wanted to go anywhere else. Did they ever listen? Now she was going to be late returning to her mother, and it would only be a matter of time before Louisa got impatient and came looking for them. She would be furious, and Esperanza had neither the will nor the energy to deal with one of her hysterical outbursts today.

She took a turn down the side street towards *Tía* Victoria's shop, hoping that the boys had gotten bored and returned to their mother. It was empty. They weren't at Carlos' jewellery workshop, and there was no sign of them at the bakery, the shoemakers, or any of the other shops on the street. Esperanza's frustration was giving way to fear now. Soon, she was going to have to start asking around, and then there would be no hiding the truth from her mother.

"Excuse me, señor," she begged the nearest man. "You haven't seen two young boys, have you? One is twelve and the other is six, they're my brothers and-"

"Señorita, I've seen two hundred children who match that description this morning," the man snapped back. "I've no time to help you look for yours."

She shot him a dark look, but before she could respond, a child's scream erupted in the surrounding air. Esperanza dropped her basket and ran.

Felipe's voice cried out again from the direction of the plaza, calling her younger brother's name, and Esperanza stumbled over the cobbles towards it. She spotted them immediately. Felipe was standing near the middle of the square, his hands covering his face in fear. A man knelt beside the *kiosca*, restraining a small figure whom she instantly recognized as Miguel.

She could only see him from the back, but she could tell straight away that the man was one of the many street dwellers of Santa Sofia. He was tall and thin, and his thick, dark hair hung in a tangled mop down past the collar of his ragged shirt. His faded trousers were rolled up almost to the knees, held up by a piece of rope which he was using as a belt, and his feet were dirty and bare. One skinny arm was wrapped tight around Miguel's chest to stop him from getting away. Esperanza couldn't see the man's face, but Miguel's features were fixed in an expression of wide-eyed terror, and she watched with horror as the man raised his fist and hit the little boy several times on the back.

The child gave a frightened cry, and at once, his captor spun him around so that their faces were level, speaking to him in a low voice that Esperanza could not hear. Her nostrils flared, and she flew across the plaza with a snarl like a mountain cat.

"Get away from him!" she roared, hurling the stranger to the ground.

The beggar cowered, whimpering like a frightened child as he fell backwards onto the cobbles.

Esperanza paused in surprise, her fist half-raised, her anger giving way to uncertainty. She had expected him to fight or even run, but not this.

Now that she could see him up close, she realized he was much younger than she had expected; more a boy than a man and certainly no older than herself. His face was clean-shaven, his nose and cheeks smudged with dirt. There was something distinctly underfed about him, with his high, pronounced cheekbones and long skinny limbs. Now that she looked at him, it was very difficult to see him as any sort of physical threat at all; he looked as though a strong wind could blow him over. When no further attack came from her, he peered out at her from between his fingers, and she saw a glimpse of large, chestnut-coloured eyes shining up at her through his uncombed hair.

The street boy lowered his hands. His eyes met hers, and a look of shock and wonder passed over his features. They stared at each other, and for a moment, she felt as though time was standing still. Those eyes were so expressive, so familiar somehow, although she couldn't think of where she had seen them before. For a second, she forgot why she was so angry.

A quiet whimper from Miguel jolted her back to her senses, and she raised her fists again with a growl.

"What did you think you were doing, hitting my little brother like that?" she snarled at the boy on the ground, making him flinch again. "What did he ever do to you?"

The boy made no reply. He was still staring into her eyes as though hypnotized, his lips moving soundlessly. Somehow, it was more irritating than if he had chosen to argue with her.

"*Hermana*..." interrupted Miguel through his tears, slipping his sticky little hand into hers. "*Hermana*, he wasn't..."

"Let him speak for himself," she snapped. "Well? What's wrong with you? Can't you speak?"

The boy nodded his head and swallowed, still not taking his eyes from hers.

"Then explain yourself and choose your words well. They may be your last." She flexed her fingers threateningly, trying to intimidate him, but the boy didn't even seem to hear her. He just continued to stare up at her through his long, thick eyelashes, wearing a ridiculous awestruck expression that made her want to kick him.

"Please, *hermana*," interrupted Miguel again. "Don't be cross with him. He was only being kind to me."

"*Kind?*" Esperanza wheeled around to face the child, unsure whether she should be angry at him too for taking the street boy's side over hers. "How is hitting a little child *being kind?*"

"He wasn't trying to hurt me." Miguel's face was tear-stained, his eyes wide and shining. "I was eating my sweet, and it got stuck in my throat and I couldn't breathe. This man ran over and banged me on the back, and the sweet came out."

Esperanza froze for a second, her fists still balled ready to strike, her mind whirring as she tried to process his words.

"It's true," Felipe joined in, putting his arm around his brother. "We were dancing, and Miguel started choking on his sweet. He went a funny colour, and I shouted for help, then this man came running over and saved him."

A strange wave of guilt washed over Esperanza. If what the boys were saying was true, then she had been guilty of a grave error of judgement. No wonder Miguel had looked so frightened if he hadn't been able to breathe. She pictured again how the man had held Miguel, how he had struck him between the shoulders until the little boy cried out with relief, and the more she thought about it, the more obvious her mistake became.

She turned back to the young man, but he had vanished.

"*Señor?*" she called across the plaza, looking around uncertainly for a sign of where he might have gone. "Wait, please... I'm sorry."

"He can't hear you," Felipe pointed out. "You scared him off with all your shouting, and now he's run away."

"Yes, I got that, thank you," said Esperanza through clenched teeth. "I'm sorry. I panicked. I thought he was trying to rob Miguel."

"For what? All he's got is boiled sweets."

"If he wants my sweets, he can have them," Miguel told her earnestly. "I don't want to ever eat sweets again after today." He reached into his pocket and pulled out a little paper bag, holding it up to show her. "He did look hungry, didn't he?"

"*Sí,*" she sighed. "He did. But I didn't think he was after your sweets. I thought... I don't know what I thought. Maybe he was after money or something. I don't know. All I saw was some ragged stranger hitting my little brother. It was only natural to assume that he was trying to rob you. He's a beggar, sometimes they can get desperate."

"He's not a beggar," Miguel argued. "He's a *músico*. We were listening to him playing his guitar before I choked on my sweet. He was nice, he let us dance with him in the *kiosca*."

So that must have been why she recognized the boy. He was the musician who had been playing in the *kiosca* while she was at Catalina's house, the one she had seen her brothers dancing to. All that time, they had been right there in the plaza, if only she had thought to look up at the stage. Still, it didn't explain why she had felt such a jolt of nostalgia when she looked into those chestnut eyes.

"All right, so he's not a beggar," she conceded. "But he's still a street boy. *Mamá* would go mad if she knew you were dancing in the plaza with someone like him. She would never let you come around town with me again."

"Good," Miguel pouted, turning his back on her. "I never *want* to go around town with you again. You're horrible. If he is a street boy like you say, then I think his life is hard enough already, without having mad *loco* girls like you attacking him just because he wears raggedy clothes."

Esperanza's conscience gave a guilty twist. If she had seen a well-dressed man behaving like that towards her brother, would she have still assumed the same thing? Or would she have at least given him a chance to explain? She couldn't be sure. A memory stirred of an argument she had once had with her mother. She had only been around Miguel's age, and Louisa had dragged her home and scolded her for playing with one of the ragged street children. It had taken Esperanza a long time to forgive her mother for keeping her away from her new friend. Her brothers were right; she had jumped to unfair conclusions about the boy in the plaza, just like her mother had that day so long ago.

"I'm sorry, *Gordito*," she admitted, trying to put a soothing arm around her brother. "You're right, I was very mean to that poor street boy, and I'm very sorry for it. I was just so frightened when I saw him hitting you like that. Are you all right now?"

"*Sí*, thanks to him," Miguel sniffled, shrugging her off. "I never want to eat another sweet again."

Esperanza laughed.

"I doubt that your hatred of sweets will last for very long, mi *príncipito*, but still. Would it make you feel better if I promise to watch out for your friend the next time I'm near the plaza and tell him how sorry I am for being mean to him?"

"*Sí*," Miguel sniffled. "You promise?"

"I promise." Esperanza hugged him, and he nodded, brushing the tears from his eyes. "Now, we need to get back to *mamá* and the cart. We're already late, she'll be worried sick. I think maybe it's best that she doesn't find out about this, all right?"

Esperanza knew it would be best for everyone if they all kept quiet. As nobody had ended up harmed on this occasion, there was nothing to gain from troubling Louisa with it.

"*Sí*, all right," Miguel agreed. He ran over to the *kiosca*, pulled out the little paper bag of sweets, and balanced it against the railings where the street musician would see it.

"Just in case he comes back," he explained. "It will give him something to eat."

"I'm sure he will be very grateful," said Esperanza, trying to ignore the tightening knot of guilt in her stomach. "Now, come on. Time to go."

She took her brothers' hands and led them towards the *taverna* on the outskirts of the *pueblo*, where she knew old Rafael would be waiting with her mother and the cart, resolving to put the boy from her mind for now. After all, she had far more important things to think about today. This was the day that her future was to begin, and she had to make sure that she was ready.

She did not see the large pair of chestnut eyes watching her from behind the *kiosca* steps or the smile of wonder on the boy's dirt-smudged face.

As soon as he was sure that the girl and her brothers had gone, he crept out from his hiding place and examined the bag that the little boy had left for him. The child had been right; he had been hungry, although his appetite seemed to have evaporated now.

He had recognized her immediately, even after all this time. Those eyes had always been there in the back of his mind, every day for the last… how long had it been now? Twelve years? Too long, he knew that much. He took a deep, calming breath, trying to stop his hands from shaking. It had been silly to hide from her, although he had not done it due to fear. He had just felt so overwhelmed at seeing her again that he didn't know what else to do. He was aware of how dirty and ragged he looked and had been ashamed of what she must think of him.

Next time, he vowed, he would be more prepared. And there would be a next time. Somehow, he would make sure of it.

CHAPTER TWO

When Esperanza returned home from town, her first job was to help her mother to prepare *comida*. Normally on a Thursday, Louisa would make tamales, Juan's favorite, but since they had begun to mingle with the aristocracy she had been trying new, more sophisticated recipes she claimed were more fitting for people of their heightened social status. Today, Louisa was trying some sort of fancy new recipe involving a lot of shrimps and strong-smelling spices. Esperanza knew this because she had been made to sit next to them all the way home in the cart, and with the combination of the heat, the smell of the shrimps and the rolling motion of the wheels on the bumpy track leading up to the house, she was amazed that she had not been forced to evacuate her stomach over the side. It had come close once or twice.

Even though she was no longer being subjected to that infernal cart, the smell of the raw shrimps continued to torture her stomach. Still, Esperanza knew better than to argue with Louisa when she was in this mood. She left her mother to swear at the shrimps and got to work making tortillas.

"*Papá* is home!" Miguel squealed from outside. The patter of bare feet slapped on the stones as the boys ran to greet their father, and the sound of a man's laughter mingled with the children's high, excited chattering.

Esperanza looked out through the window to see Juan, who was heading back to the house from the direction of the stable. He was filthy, his face and hands splattered with dirt, and mud was caked over his clothing from the soles of his boots right up past his knees. Before he could get to the front door, he was greeted by Louisa's broom, which she brandished in his face like a weapon.

"Don't you even *think* about coming into my nice clean kitchen looking like that!" she screeched, warding him off as though he were a stray dog. "Where on *Earth* have you been?"

"Damn new stable boy," Juan cursed. "I gave him a job because Jorge assured me that he was good. It was a filthy lie. What kind of stable boy is afraid of horses?" He shook his head, grumbling. "He's spent all damn morning chasing the stupid creatures around the field. In the end, I gave up and had to go out and catch them myself. I had half a mind to leave him out there all day and let him learn, but there's a storm coming in, and I couldn't risk it. I've left him to wash and feed them. Hopefully, he can manage that, at least."

"Well, it's a good job that Don Lorenzo didn't turn up and see you like this," Louisa tutted, handing him a cloth so that he could wash his face in the trough of water beneath the kitchen window. "You're mixing with gentlemen now; you need to start behaving like one. That's why you've got farmhands, to do the jobs that don't befit a man of your social status."

"Oh, not this again, Louisa." Juan rolled his eyes, taking off his boots and leaving them by the door. "I've managed to secure a business deal with Don Lorenzo. He hasn't adopted me as his son. There's no need to get carried away with it all."

"He doesn't need to adopt you as his son," Louisa snapped back. "He already has one. One who has taken an interest in your daughter, in case you have forgotten. You never know, if we're lucky, we could find ourselves making another *business arrangement* before the year is out." She picked up a stiff brush and started beating the mud from the hem of his trousers, and Esperanza felt her heart give a nervous little lurch.

"Stop getting ahead of yourself, Louisa," Juan warned. "His son hasn't even *met* my daughter yet."

"Are you saying you don't think he'll like her? She's the most beautiful girl in town."

"I'm saying *she* might not like *him*. She hasn't liked any of the other suitors who have come after her so far. I don't see what'll be so different about him."

Esperanza couldn't deny that both of her parents had a point. People often called her beautiful, just as they did with many of the other girls in the *pueblo*. But Esperanza was different. Her bright, ocean-blue eyes had always made her stand out; they were her blessing and her curse. She had grown used to people staring at her, some because they found her beautiful, but others because their bored, superstitious minds needed a scapegoat for a poor harvest or an outbreak of illness in the *pueblo*. Even as a child, her eyes had inspired terror in the other children, and she had found herself very lonely as a result.

Nowadays though, to her infinite relief, the gossips of Santa Sofia seemed to have put aside their silly superstitions, and she was regarded more as a rare butterfly than a venomous spider. In fact, in the four years since she had turned sixteen, Esperanza had been bombarded with love-struck suitors hoping to impress her. Some of her admirers had been very exciting prospects too, at least in her parents' eyes, but unfortunately, they had all turned out to be *idiotas*.

There had been the rich landowner's son, who had insisted upon serenading Esperanza from beneath her balcony. She had thrown a jug of water over him, with the promise that it would be boiling oil the next time he troubled her. They had not heard from him again. Then there was the wealthy doctor from Santa Juanita who had made an ill-advised joke about how he would like to 'examine' her, and she had slapped him so hard that she had made his nose bleed. They had not heard from him again, either.

The worst had been the young *Capitan* from the *presidio*, with his smart uniform and his handsome face. Esperanza had briefly considered him until one afternoon when he got too bold and tried to kiss her, and she smashed a vase over his head. Her parents had worried that someone might end up arrested after that incident, but fortunately, nothing more had come of it. At least she could never be accused of being a girl of loose morals, even if her manners needed a little work.

"Don Raúl *will* be different," Louisa said with confidence, trying to persuade herself as much as her husband. "He's the son of Don Lorenzo. How could any girl ever hope for a better man? His father owns most of the gold mines in Sinaloa, for a start. And I hear he's extremely handsome."

"You hear," repeated Juan, rolling his eyes again. Louisa moved aside to allow him into the house, and he hung his sombrero on the hook by the door before heading towards the kitchen. "That's the point, Louisa. You don't *know*. You've never met the man. He could have a face like a- *Dios mío*, what's that ungodly smell? Has something died in here while I was out?"

Juan clapped his hand over his nose and mouth as the smell of the shrimps hit him.

"That's your *comida*," said Louisa through gritted teeth. "I'm trying something new. We're having grilled *arrachera*, shrimp, sausage, onions, potatoes and *chiles toreados*."

"But it's tamales day!"

"Tamales are peasant food. It's time we started eating food that is a bit more sophisticated, now that we're associating with a better class of people. I got this recipe from Victoria. She swears that this is the sort of food that her sister-in-law cooks for Don Lorenzo at his *hacienda*."

"Well, Don Lorenzo is welcome to it. I think I'll stick with the tamales."

Esperanza snorted with laughter, and Louisa turned on her with a growl.

"I don't know what you think you're laughing at, young lady. You should be watching and learning. You'll need to be able to cook dishes like this if you want to be considered as a wife for Don Raúl."

"He likes this sort of stuff, does he?" asked Juan, prodding the pan suspiciously. "Watch out if he tries to kiss you, *mija*. His breath will kill you from twenty paces if this is what he lives on."

Esperanza burst out laughing again as Louisa clipped her husband around the back of the head with her palm. He laughed too, flopping into a chair next to the kitchen table and rubbing his head where she had hit him.

"Don Raúl is a very refined gentleman," Louisa reminded them, shooting a haughty glare at her husband. "You only need to look at his father to know that. He is a close personal friend of President Díaz, they fought together in the Battle of Puebla. It would be like being married to the son of the president himself, you would be the envy of every young woman in Mexico. He's handsome, cultured, well-mannered, and a huge supporter of the arts too. The only child of one of the richest Dons and most powerful politicians in all of Mexico." Louisa's eyes twinkled. "I don't need to tell you what a boost this would be for our family, *mija*, to be linked by marriage to such a man."

"I'm starting to wonder if this is really about Don Raúl wanting to marry Esperanza or you wanting to marry Don Lorenzo." Juan wiggled his eyebrows. "I hear that he's widowed and available, Louisa. What a shame you're not."

"Ay, keep speaking to me like that and I soon will be." Louisa swiped for his head again, and Juan ducked away, laughing.

"I'm just saying, Louisa, try not to get too carried away." He sat back, stretching his arms behind his head. "Don Lorenzo has invited us to his *baile*, yes, and it's wonderful that he wishes to introduce his son to Esperanza. But we're a long way off a marriage proposal, they haven't even met yet. Besides..." his expression turned serious. "I hear rumours that the trouble in the cities is getting worse. President Díaz isn't too popular among the people at the moment; it seems that his subjects haven't taken kindly to him having Madero arrested. They're saying that he rigged the election, and the calls for revolution are getting stronger every day. Assuming that Díaz and Don Lorenzo are as close as you say, then this may not be such a wise alliance after all. If the president falls, Lorenzo will fall with him."

"Nonsense," Louisa scoffed. "Do you really think a great man like Don Lorenzo can be frightened by a few angry peasants? What do you think they're going to do, knock him unconscious with the smell of their unwashed armpits?"

"There's strength in numbers, Louisa. I think that Don Lorenzo would be a fool to underestimate the importance of keeping his people happy."

"You worry too much. Say that you're right, and the trouble does come to something. Say that the peasants rise up and take over the cities, take control of Santa Sofia." He tried to interrupt her, but she raised a hand to silence him. "I don't think it will happen, but let's imagine it does. Don Lorenzo still has his estates in Spain, and he has his ships. He can easily take himself back to Europe and live in perfect comfort there until all the nonsense blows over. And if he does, I'm sure that he would, of course, take his family to safety with him. *All* of his family." She gave him a meaningful look.

"I suppose you have a point," he sighed. "You're very quiet about all this, *mija*. What do you have to say on the subject?"

Esperanza wasn't sure, to be honest. The idea of being a great lady sounded lovely in the colourful picture that her mother had painted for her. She would live in a grand *hacienda* and wear jewels. There would be wonderful parties with music and dancing, the best food that any lady could eat, servants to fulfil her every whim. The only problem was the thought of marrying a man she barely knew.

Still, as Catalina had pointed out to her, she ought to consider herself lucky. It was common for a girl not to even meet her husband until their wedding day, and at least Don Raúl was young and handsome. Catalina had grown to love her husband in time; there was no reason why Esperanza couldn't learn to do the same, especially if he was as wonderful as her mother had promised. She just couldn't fathom why such a man would be interested in marrying a farmer's daughter.

"I suppose I won't know how I feel until the *baile*," she confessed. "I'm not sure that I would fit in with people like Don Raúl and his friends."

"Nonsense," argued Louisa. "You could pass for one of the most refined ladies in all of Mexico, if only you tried to behave like one."

Esperanza rolled her eyes, and Louisa scowled back at her.

"See, *mija*, this is the sort of thing I mean," she scolded. "If you stand any chance of attracting a man like Don Raúl, you will need to think far more carefully about your behaviour. You must be polite, obedient and graceful at all times. You must smile at Don Raúl and curtsey to him in the proper European fashion, show him you are just as good as any of those fancy Spanish *doñas*. It'll be good for you to spend time with Don Lorenzo's friends, you can learn from them. A lady can be judged by the company she keeps."

"Ay, that rules us out then," Juan piped up. "Sorry, *mija*, it looks like you'll have to go on your own if you want to impress all the important people. What a shame."

"You're not getting out of it, Juan," Louisa snapped. "You know how important it is that you impress Don Lorenzo and his associates. You need to be on your best behaviour too. The pair of you, you need to realize that you will never fit in with the nobility until you learn to act like them."

"Act. That's the problem, isn't it?" Esperanza scowled. "Am I expected to spend my life pretending to be something I'm not, just to impress a man?"

Now it was Louisa's turn to roll her eyes.

"You're looking at it all the wrong way, *mija*," she sighed. "I'm not asking you to be something you're not. I'm asking you to be the woman you have the potential to become."

"*Mamá...*"

"Hear me out. You could have such a wonderful life, you could make us all so proud. I want to see you achieve that, for all of our sakes."

"I know, *mamá*, but..."

"But nothing! *Dios mío*, child, why must you always argue with me?" Louisa snapped. "I'm trying to talk to you, and all you do is interrupt!"

"I'm sorry, *mamá*, but the shrimps!"

Louisa wheeled around. A thin haze of black smoke was rising from the pan behind her where the forgotten shrimps were burning, little flames licking the sides of the pan while the charred remains of *comida* crackled and smouldered, ruined. She threw her apron up over her face, choking on the smoke, and hurled the pan, shrimps and all, straight out of the open window into the water trough below, where they fizzled and hissed before sinking to the bottom.

Esperanza and Juan watched Louisa with silent apprehension as she stared down through the open window at the remains of her culinary masterpiece, waving her cloth to disperse smoke that still drifted through the kitchen.

After a long moment, Juan cleared his throat. "So, does this mean that we can have tamales after all, then?"

Louisa threw the cloth at him.

CHAPTER THREE

Don Lorenzo's *hacienda* was grander than Esperanza had ever imagined. From a distance, she could see it silhouetted in the moonlight, its high stone archways towering over acres of lush green fields. Trees lined the torchlit path as far as the eye could see, and the wheels of her carriage kicked up clouds of pale orange dust as they rattled along towards the wrought-iron gates. The gardens were filled with more varieties of shrubs and flowers than she had known even existed, their sweet scent hanging in the cool night air. Fireflies glowed among the foliage like tiny stars, their light reflected in the huge, bubbling fountains on either side of the front entrance, making the water look as though it had been enchanted.

As the carriage drew closer, Esperanza could see the guests mingling underneath the archways, laughing and chattering to each other. Could this truly be her home one day? She tried to imagine herself dressed in fine silk and adorned with expensive jewellery, the esteemed lady of this huge estate. She tried to tell herself that she was excited by the prospect, but if she was honest, she just found the whole idea quite intimidating.

Rafael drew the carriage to a stop. Juan hopped down, giving the nearest horse a reassuring pat on the hindquarters before offering a hand to each of the ladies. Lanterns lined the stone stairway leading up to the main doors to the *hacienda*, which were guarded by a pair of uniformed servants. Esperanza gazed up in awe at the ornate stone coats of arms and smooth cherub faces smiling down at her, peering out from the roses and ivy which trailed down the pillars and flickered gold in the soft light.

A servant led Esperanza and her parents through to a large courtyard. It was even more beautiful than she had expected. Tables lined the outer edges of the space, filled with plates of exotic fruit and fresh bread. A wide space in the middle of the courtyard had been cleared for dancing, and a stage decorated with a heavy velvet valance had been erected on one side for two musicians who sat side-by-side on wooden stools entertaining the guests. Soft, lyrical guitar music floated in the air, harmonising with the tinkling sounds of laughter and gentle chattering.

Men stood around discussing business and estates and refilling their wine glasses, looking dashing in their ornate Spanish-style coats, their tall boots shining and elegant lace cravats decorating their throats. They were beautiful, and yet more beautiful still were the ladies, milling about in a rainbow of silk and lace. Gold embroidery embellished their bodices and hemlines, and Esperanza could even see pearls sewn into some of the designs, glowing against the opulent fabric. She felt positively plain in comparison, a moth among butterflies.

Louisa spotted Don Lorenzo, instantly recognizable with his high forehead and handsome nose. She herded her daughter towards him, and Esperanza could almost feel the desperation radiating from her every pore.

"Señora Dominguez." Don Lorenzo bowed his head to kiss Louisa's hand. "I am so pleased that you could join us. And the lovely *Señorita* Esperanza. I hope you had an agreeable journey?"

He and Louisa exchanged pleasantries, regurgitating the same mundane comments and polite enquiries that the poor man must have already endured a hundred times that night. Esperanza tried to force a smile.

"*Señorita.*" Don Lorenzo turned to her, the corners of his eyes crinkling as he smiled. "Allow me to introduce my son Raúl. He is very much looking forward to meeting you."

He beckoned to a handsome man in a red silk waistcoat and jacket who excused himself from his friends and headed towards them, a glass of wine in his hand. The son was the image of his father, with the same aquiline nose and chiselled features. He looked around thirty years old, his skin smooth and his slick black hair free from his father's grey tones, and while they shared the same masculine square jawline, Don Raúl's was framed with a well-trimmed beard. He was around a head taller than his father, with a broad chest and muscular limbs that left Esperanza in no doubt of his physical strength. His most imposing features, though, were his eyes. While Don Lorenzo's eyes were warm and laughing, his son's were as cold as ice, big and black and absent of any emotion. They made Esperanza shiver.

"Raúl, this is *Señorita* Esperanza Serrano Dominguez, the young lady I was telling you about earlier. Does she not have the most enchanting eyes?"

Don Raúl regarded Esperanza with mild interest, looking her up and down in the same way that her father might consider a new horse.

"It is a pleasure to meet you, *señorita*." He bent to kiss her hand, and she responded with a small curtsy. Perhaps it was her nerves, but his eyes looked just a tiny bit out of focus, his words ever so slightly slurred. "Father has spoken most highly of your many virtues."

"Thank you, *señor*. I hope I can do his kind words justice."

Don Lorenzo gave his son a stern, searching look, his lips forced into a stony smile.

"Raúl, I am told that this young lady is the most talented of dancers. Perhaps later on she may be gracious enough to honour you with a dance?"

Raúl bowed.

"That would give me great pleasure, *señorita*. In the meantime, if you would excuse me, I just need to catch a quick word with Don Luis. I beg your pardon." He flashed her a charming smile, kissed her hand again and swept away to join another man in an ornate burgundy jacket, who immediately refilled his wine glass.

Esperanza breathed a sigh of relief. Perhaps it was just her imagination, but something seemed a little unbalanced about his walk. She didn't care, as long as he was walking away from her. Her nerves seemed to have turned her legs to jelly.

Juan had come over and was busy shaking Don Lorenzo's hand, both of them smiling and exchanging cordialities, allowing Esperanza a moment to get her head together. Her father looked nervous, but he beamed as Don Lorenzo took him over to a table to introduce him to his other business associates. A few men leaned across to shake Juan's hand, and one of them poured him a drink. It all seemed to be going well.

"Stay close to him," Louisa hissed, nodding towards Don Raúl. "Don't let him forget about you. Your future depends on it, *mija*."

She floated away after Don Lorenzo, leaving Esperanza to puzzle over how to fulfil such a demanding task against such stiff competition. She was very aware of how the other ladies were looking at her, muttering to each other behind their lace fans and smirking. Judging by the way they were looking at Don Raúl, swishing their skirts and batting their eyelashes at him, she guessed she wasn't the only one out to win the handsome Don's affections tonight. Esperanza couldn't help feeling uncomfortable. A few of the ladies she recognized, but most she didn't. She got a strong impression that they didn't want to get to know her, and she had to admit, the feeling was mutual.

Esperanza steered herself away from Don Raúl's adoring female entourage, choosing instead to see whether she could find anyone of interest on the dance floor. A few couples were dancing, some more elegantly than others, and for a minute or so Esperanza perched on the edge of a fountain to watch them. She loved dancing. She loved the sensation of freedom that it gave her, the feeling of being able to express herself without being reminded that young ladies should be seen and not heard.

She longed to join the swirling figures in the middle of the courtyard, but this was not the sort of place that a girl could dance alone without being considered improper. It was a shame. She often preferred dancing alone over having some lumbering *idiota* weighing her down, as was the case with a few of the couples she could see. She felt a twinge of pity for one lady in particular, whose elderly partner's dance skills were clearly a little past their best. He kept tripping over his own feet, mumbling frightened apologies as he accidentally kicked her and got himself tangled in her skirts, clinging to her like a terrified child. She was trying to be patient with him, but she looked less like a woman dancing and more like a mother trying to teach her toddler to walk. Esperanza gave her an encouraging smile as they passed her, which the woman did not return.

Wishing that she hadn't agreed to come to this *baile* at all, Esperanza scanned the room again for a sign of a friendly face. Her gaze fell on the two musicians on the stage, the only two people she had seen so far who appeared to be genuinely enjoying themselves. Unlike the other men with their ornate European-style jackets, these men were dressed in baggy white shirts and royal blue waistcoats. They each wore a red necktie and matching belt, and both had rolled up their sleeves to keep the loose fabric out of the way of their guitar strings. One of the men looked a little older than the other, with dark eyes and a round, serious face which twitched with concentration as he played, his foot tapping on the wooden stage with each strum of his guitar.

However, it was the younger musician that caught Esperanza's attention. He was slimmer than his friend, to the point that he had needed to wind his belt several times around his waist to keep the ends from dragging on the floor. His long, skinny arms were wrapped around his guitar as though he were holding a child, skilled fingers dancing up and down the fretboard as he plucked the thin strings. He was singing, his tone mellow and sweet to her ears, and Esperanza found herself drawn in by the soft emotion in his voice.

There was something so familiar and comforting about him. She was sure that she had seen him somewhere before, but where? He was handsome in an awkward, youthful sort of way, with high cheekbones and a straight nose. While the older musician beside him looked quite smart, his thin moustache immaculately trimmed and his jet-black hair neatly parted on one side, the younger man's hair hung over his eyebrows in long thick strands, soft and dark and shining. He must have sensed Esperanza staring at him because before she had a chance to look away, he glanced up from his guitar and their eyes met.

At that moment, Esperanza instantly knew where she had seen him before. He was the same musician that she had shouted at in the plaza, the one who had saved Miguel from choking on the sweet. He looked so different with his smart clothes and combed hair; it was no wonder that she hadn't recognized him straight away. But there was no mistaking those big chestnut eyes, so warm and sparkling and full of energy. He froze in surprise at the sight of her, his eyes wide. His voice faltered and his fingers briefly forgot what they were doing, and his companion had to give him a gentle kick to bring him back to himself.

Esperanza gave him a shy smile, the familiar, horrible feeling of guilt forming a tight knot in her stomach again. For the briefest of moments, he looked at her with a mixture of awe and apprehension, but then his face split into a huge grin. He puffed out his chest and resumed singing, his melodic voice seeming to receive a boost of energy at her presence. Esperanza felt the knot in her stomach loosen. At least someone seemed to be enjoying her company tonight, even if she couldn't fathom why.

Sensing that she was being watched, she glanced over at Don Raúl's table, where the laughter appeared to be growing louder. A few of the men were looking at her, Don Raúl included. Their voices were raised in merriment, the drink having loosened their tongues to the point where they didn't seem to care who could hear them. Esperanza tried not to look at them, pretending to be fascinated by the dancers.

"Come on, *amigo*. Have some fun. What I wouldn't give to be the lucky man who all the ladies are chasing after!"

"It's not luck, it's money." Don Raúl's voice was slurring from the drink. "I'm well acquainted with what these girls are after. They're nothing but shallow parasites. Why should I give them the time of day, just because my father has decided that I ought to marry? Do I not deserve to at least choose my own bride?"

"Come on, Raúl. Surely not all of the ladies are as bad as you say. I've seen a few new faces here tonight. Maybe one of them could be the girl you're looking for."

"You'd have thought so, but they're still all hand-picked by my father. See that one over there, in the blue dress? That's the latest silly little *tonta* he's trying to force upon me."

"Isn't she the farmer's daughter?"

"That's the one. Father thinks she would be a good match for me."

All of the men laughed apart from Don Raúl, and Esperanza felt heat rising in her cheeks. They were all drunk.

"At least your children would be handsome, *amigo*. Look at her eyes. Have you ever seen eyes that colour?"

"Ay, there's no denying she's pretty," piped up another voice. "But a farm girl as the wife of Don Raúl? It's a ridiculous idea."

"I know, I know. But you know Father. I'll have to dance with her at some point tonight and get it over with."

"Then dance with her, *amigo*. Have a bit of fun and keep the old man happy. You don't have to marry her. She's a farm girl. She's bound to be too desperate to deny you anything. I'll bet she'll even give you a roll in the hay if you ask nicely."

All the men laughed again, and Esperanza felt her cheeks burn harder. To think, she had believed that wealthy gentlemen would be more refined, more mannerly than the ordinary people she met in Santa Sofia. But even late at night in the taverna, this kind of loose talk about a lady would not have been tolerated.

"You know," Don Raúl mused, "come to think of it, she is rather pretty, isn't she? A little skinny, perhaps, but enough meat in the areas that matter. Good hips."

"If she's as good a dancer as they say, then she'll likely be good at using those hips for other purposes as well."

More laughter. "Sí, you might be right. Maybe I could have some fun with this one."

"Go for it, amigo. And when you get bored with her, let me know. I'd like a turn."

"Wouldn't we all!"

The table exploded with laughter, and Esperanza couldn't take it any more. She turned towards them, intending to push past their table and join her father, but one of the men stood up and blocked her way. They were all still laughing apart from Don Raúl, who was looking at her with an expression of contemplation, his cold eyes hazy from the drink.

"Señorita Esperanza, isn't it?" His voice was cool. "Sit down. Let me pour you some wine."

Esperanza glared at him.

"No, thank you, señor," she said coldly, somehow managing to keep her voice calm despite the anger bubbling inside her chest. "Excuse me, please."

"I told you to sit down."

"And I told you, no."

The men around her stopped laughing. They stared at her in silent awe, their eyes shifting from her stony glare to Raúl's and back again. For a second, the Don looked thunderous. Then, to Esperanza's surprise, he gave a low chuckle.

"Well, well. You are a fascinating creature, aren't you?" he smiled, his voice brimming with amusement. "I seem to have misjudged you. It's not often that people say no to me."

Esperanza didn't like the way that he was looking at her, his cold, unfocused eyes drifting down her body and back up to her face, his lips twisted into an unpleasant grin that made her shudder. She felt her anger ebbing away, replaced by a strong desire to get away from him.

"Come, señorita. I want to see if you really know how to use that beautiful figure of yours. Dance with me." Raúl stood, swaying, and took Esperanza by the hand. She tensed, her eyes darting to where her father sat with Don Lorenzo and his other friends, but they were engaged deep in conversation.

Look up, her eyes screamed. *Help me*. But nobody heard.

"Please, señor-" she begged, but he was not listening, half-dragging her towards the dancefloor by her wrist. She resisted, but Raúl only gripped her tighter, weaving as he walked. She felt panic rising in her chest, a cold queasiness seeping up her spine. Her head was telling her to strike him and run, but her body refused to obey. Smiling faces swam around her, their laughter too loud in her ears. She had no choice but to follow him.

Raúl stopped in the middle of the courtyard, yanking Esperanza around to face him. She gave a cry of surprise and tried to back away, but he only sighed impatiently and pulled her closer.

"What's the matter? I thought you liked dancing?" His words were slurred, and his brows furrowed as he struggled to focus his eyes on her face. "I asked you to dance. Any other woman here would be delighted at such an honour. What's wrong with you?"

There was a hint of threat in his voice, and the sudden sense of tension around them told her that others had noticed too. The people around them had stopped dancing and were standing back to stare at her. She realized that the music had ground to a halt, and a hushed silence was spreading across the courtyard.

"Dance with me, *niña*."

"*Lo- lo siento, señor*. I think I need to sit down, I am feeling a little faint."

He laughed, and she struggled not to grimace at the foul stench of alcohol on his breath.

"*Sí*, I often make women feel a little faint. One of my many talents. Come, I will hold you up. Dance." He grabbed her waist and pulled her roughly to him.

"*Señor*, let me go. Please. I- I can't." Tears sprung to her eyes. Her heart felt as though it had been plunged into cold water, and she didn't know what to do. She had never imagined that it was possible to feel so alone in such a crowded place, yet here she was, completely out of her depth in a desperate situation that her mind was too numb to think a way out of.

"What do you mean, you *can't*?" Raúl growled. His eyes were dark and cold, piercing through her with an expression that made her blood turn to ice. His grip was too tight, his nails digging into her skin so hard that she had to fight not to scream.

"I'm afraid it's my fault, *señor*." A gentle hand touched Esperanza's shoulder, and a voice she recognized spoke softly from behind her. She turned to find herself looking straight into the warm chestnut eyes of the young musician. His face was fixed in a calm smile, although his fists were clenched. "The problem is that I already asked the fair *señorita* for this next dance. While I'm sure she is honoured by the attention of a fine gentleman like yourself, her sense of duty prevents her from breaking her promise to me. Isn't that right, *señorita*?"

He looked down at Esperanza. *Play along with this,* his eyes begged her.

"Sí," she croaked.

"Of course, señorita, I do not blame you for wanting to accept this gentleman's offer instead. I release you from your promise. It's a *contradanza* next, I believe, nice and lively. I am happy to accept the following dance to make up for it..." he winked at Raúl. "Especially as I hear it will be a slow one. In the meantime, I think I'll go and get a drink. I've spotted a fine *tempranillo* over there that I'm keen to try."

Raúl swayed on the spot for a second, his face contorted as he processed the musician's words. Esperanza held her breath.

"No," he said eventually. "I want the slow dance. You can have this one, *músico*. The *señorita* can consider it a warmup. In the meantime, I might try that *tempranillo* myself." He released Esperanza and staggered away through the crowd after the promised wine, leaving her alone with the boy. Her head felt light, and she realized she was trembling.

"Are you all right, *señorita*?" The young musician took her hand turned her to face him.

"What were you thinking?" she snarled, flinching at his touch, her voice shaking as she pulled her hand away. She rubbed at the nail-shaped marks on her wrist from where Raúl had gripped her. "How could you promise him a slow dance with me?"

"I did no such thing. I merely told him that the dance after this one would be a slow one. The rest was all his assumption." The musician winked at her. His voice was warm and low. "I can't help it if he puts two and two together and makes twenty-two now, can I? Besides, you have nothing to fear, *señorita*. I won't let him touch you again. Trust me."

The nerve of the man. Here he was, a street musician barely older than herself, standing in the home of one of the most powerful Dons in all of Mexico and speaking as though he owned the place. Esperanza couldn't help but smile at his confidence. Somehow, something deep inside her did trust him, although she couldn't think why. The remaining guitarist on the stage struck up a few lively chords to signify the start of the next song, and the boy turned and bowed to Esperanza, offering her his hand and looking up at her with those warm, sparkling eyes.

"May I have the honour of this dance, señorita?"

"Sí, I suppose you'd better after that exchange, hadn't you?"

She took his hand and allowed him to guide her in a circle around him, twirling her skirts with her free hand. The boy tenderly placed one arm around her waist and began to lead her in a lively contradanza, spinning her with gentle confidence until she couldn't help but relax. *He is actually good at this*, she realized with surprise as he twirled her around the courtyard with ease, his feet never missing a step. His eyes remained fixed on hers, warm and twinkling as he smiled. People were stopping to watch her again, but this time Esperanza didn't mind. This felt good.

A broad smile spread across her face as for the first time that evening, she started to enjoy herself. The boy grinned back at her. He suddenly spun her away from him, then back in against his chest. She laughed, caught off-guard, but the safety of his arms kept her from falling as they turned together, her flowing skirts wrapping around them both like a cocoon.

Her body felt light. She had always loved dancing, but it had never felt like this before. It was as though everyone else in the room had disappeared apart from her and this boy with his warm smile and his sparkling eyes. Her laughter seemed to spur him on, and he puffed out his chest, twisting his body to guide her in even wider circles with such intricate steps that she had to fight to keep up with him.

She realized with a twinge of disappointment that the music was coming to an end. As the guitarist strummed out his final few chords, the boy twirled her around one last time so that they were positioned right in front of the stage. Then he caught her waist and they plunged together into a low dip, the suddenness of the drop leaving her breathless. He held her against his chest, so close that their faces were almost touching, and she could feel his ribs rising and falling against hers as they both fought to catch their breath.

The crowd around them whistled and clapped, and Esperanza was jolted back to the reality of where she was. She glanced up at the sea of silk and smiling faces all around her, the cheering crowd forming a defensive barrier around herself and the boy. Don Raúl was fighting his way through the crowd towards her, a bottle in his hand and a thunderous look on his face. She felt a flush of panic shoot down her spine.

"Trust me, *señorita*," her musician whispered.

He shot a look at the guitarist on the stage, and Esperanza heard the older man's voice call out over the crowd.

"A toast, ladies and gentlemen, to our gracious hosts! To the great Don Lorenzo and his family, who have so kindly invited us all here tonight to celebrate..."

The crowd turned to look at Don Lorenzo at the far end of the courtyard, and the boy seized his moment. Before Esperanza could protest, he put his hand behind her head and dropped to the ground on top of her, throwing his weight across her body. The momentum rolled them both underneath the stage, the heavy satin valance hiding them from view. Esperanza landed on top of him, her body pressed to his. Her hands gripped the front of his shirt, and she could feel his heart pounding fast through the thin fabric.

"What on Earth do you-" she started, but he reached up and pressed his finger against her lips.

She fell silent as his eyes met hers, the hammering of her own heartbeat thudding loud in her ears. Time stood still as they lay entangled together, holding their breath, their gazes locked on each other. The darkness prevented her from reading his expression, but his eyes were shining. One of his arms was around her waist, holding her tight to him, his other hand still pressing a gentle finger to her lip. Esperanza found herself lacking any will to move.

How long the moment lasted she wasn't sure, but after what felt like an age, she heard the crowd applauding and the music started up again from the stage above them. The boy relaxed beneath her, releasing her waist, and she cursed herself for missing his warmth as she rolled onto the ground.

The boy rolled onto all fours and crawled over towards the back of the stage, gesturing for her to follow. He carefully lifted the hem of the valance, peering out underneath for any sign of footsteps.

"When I give you the signal, we run, understand?" he whispered. "And try to keep low."

She wanted to ask him where they were going, to protest about what people might think if they were seen crawling out from under the stage together. She knew that she should refuse to run anywhere with him for fear of the rumours it may start if they were caught. But somehow, the words stuck in her throat, and against her better judgement, she found herself nodding.

"Now!"

The boy took her hand and sprung out from beneath the valance, pulling her behind him. Staying low, they slipped away behind the stage, ducked through an archway and sprinted together across the open grass towards the stone wall at the opposite end of the garden. The gate was locked, but this didn't seem to bother the boy. He found a foothold in the jutting stone and helped Esperanza over the wall before vaulting over himself, both of them collapsing breathless and laughing in the grass.

CHAPTER FOUR

For a few minutes, neither of them spoke. Esperanza tried to slow her breathing, struggling to collect her fragmented thoughts.

They appeared to have broken into some sort of walled garden. Roses lined the walls, glowing almost silver in the moonlight, their thorns snaking up over the cold stone and stretching up towards the sky. Blooms as large as her fist gazed up at the stars, sparkling with dew, their soft, sweet scent lingering in the cool evening air. A fountain sat in the middle of the lawn, the comforting sounds of its gentle splashing dampening the noise of the party outside, the water glittering as it fell in drops over the stone features of Aphrodite and her nymphs.

With the thrill of their dance followed so quickly by the exhilaration of escape, Esperanza couldn't remember the last time she had felt such a rush. Only this morning she had been preparing to present herself to Don Lorenzo and his charming, handsome son, desperate to prove that she could be the elegant lady everybody wanted her to be.

Yet now that the opportunity had arisen, she realized she didn't want to be that lady at all. Instead of finishing the evening as the sophisticated lover of the handsome Don Raúl, she was lying breathless in the grass with a street boy whose name she didn't even know. She glanced over at the boy beside her and saw that he was smiling in the bright moonlight, watching her with an expression of fascination that suddenly made her very aware of the state of her hair and clothing.

"Are you all right, *señorita*?"

"*Sí*." She sat up and ran her fingers through her hair self-consciously, avoiding his gaze. "I'm all right, considering that I've just been forced to dance against my will, rolled under a stage, dragged through a field and then thrown over a wall by a complete madman."

"Ah *sí*, but at least you didn't have to dance with Don Raúl," the musician grinned back at her. "How fortunate for you that there was a *real* gentleman present to rescue you from the fancy one with the title, eh?"

Esperanza tried to put on a haughty look, although she couldn't hide the amusement in her eyes.

"I did not need rescuing, thank you. I had the situation under control."

He raised his eyebrows at her, and she felt her cheeks flush.

"Really? That wasn't how it looked from where I was standing. You didn't seem very thrilled by Don Raúl's attention *at all*."

"I was just being ladylike," she sniffed. "It would have been inappropriate for me to have danced with a gentleman before we were a little better acquainted. I did not want people to think that I was being forward, or come across too keen."

"And yet, you danced with me." He flashed her a mischievous smile. "We've not even been properly introduced. But you turned down the great Don Raúl and danced with me instead. Does that mean you're 'keen' on me, *señorita*?"

"No! I- I-" Blood rushed to her cheeks again, and she cursed them silently, hoping that he couldn't see them glowing in the moonlight. His eyes were sparkling, a self-satisfied grin plastered across his face. She cleared her throat and tried to force her own features into a nonchalant expression.

"I was in a desperate situation, *señor*, as well you know. Any lady with half an ounce of self-respect would've turned down a dance with Don Raúl in that drunken, leery state. Yet somehow, I'm still regretting choosing you now, with this smug attitude of yours." She pushed him and he fell back on the grass, laughing.

"So, you admit you weren't enjoying Don Raúl's attention, then?" he giggled.

"*Sí*, all right." She gave up her façade, laughing with him. "*Dios*, he was awful, wasn't he? I would never have agreed to come here if I'd known."

"I'm very glad you did." His voice was gentle, and Esperanza could feel him looking at her again. She turned away, trying to hide her smile.

"I suppose I owe you my thanks, *señor*. You did rescue me from a very uncomfortable situation, and I am grateful to you." She nudged him. "Even if I am starting to suspect that you only did it to get one over on Don Raúl."

THE MUSICIAN'S PROMISE

"It was a true honour, *señorita*. I very much enjoyed dancing with you. And no, not just because it annoyed Don Raúl. Although I will admit, that was a bonus." She swatted playfully at his head. He dodged, laughing.

"Well, I hope you have plans for how you're going to rescue me from all of the other people we've annoyed this evening," she scolded, raising an eyebrow. "My mother, for a start. She had high hopes for tonight, she's going to be furious when she finds out that I chose to dance with you over Don Raúl, and I'll warn you now, she's much scarier than any Don."

"Sí, mi *hermano* is not going to be impressed either," the boy sighed, wincing. "He put a lot of effort into this *baile*. He got us both new clothes and everything. And now I've left him to entertain the guests all by himself. Trust me, if your mother wants to kill me, I'm afraid she'll have to join the queue."

Esperanza shifted guiltily.

"I bet you're regretting the first moment you set eyes on me, *señor*. I'm sorry to have caused you so much trouble."

"Not for a minute, *señorita*. It was one of the best moments of my life."

"Then you must've had a pretty rotten life so far." She felt her conscience give an unpleasant twinge. "I owe you thanks for helping my brother the other day. And an apology too, for my behaviour."

The boy shot her a strange, uncertain look.

"That wasn't the first time we met, *señorita*. You don't recognize me, do you?"

His voice was heavy with disappointment. Now it was Esperanza's turn to be confused, and she gave him an apologetic shrug. The boy sighed and stared down at the grass.

"When I was around eight years old, I ran away from the orphanage where I grew up. On my very first day living on the streets, I got on the wrong side of some bigger boys from the town and they chased me with sticks. They were kicking me and throwing stones, calling me 'street dog'." His voice caught. The tips of his ears were burning as he avoided her gaze, and Esperanza felt a lump in her throat. Something stirred in the back of her memory, and she suddenly knew where his story was going.

"You appeared out of nowhere," he told her, his voice hushed. "I looked up, and you were just there, standing in between them and me. You were so angry, shouting at them and calling them cowards. You hit one of the boys on the nose and made it bleed, and they all ran away. Tripping over each other like frightened dogs." He chuckled at the memory, closing his eyes.

"You asked me if I was an angel." Esperanza closed her eyes too, remembering the scene as though it were still happening right in front of her. The frightened little boy huddled against the wall, trying to protect his head with his hands, his skinny arms and legs too long for his dirty clothes, his hair uncombed and overgrown. More than anything, she remembered his big chestnut eyes blinking up at her with wonder through the tears, looking at her as though she had just been beamed straight down from Heaven. Nobody had ever looked at her like that before, or since for that matter. Those same eyes were staring at her now, not through tears this time, but still burning with emotion. "I remember. You really thought I was an angel."

"It was your eyes," he nodded. "I'd never seen anyone with blue eyes before. I thought you had to be an angel."

Esperanza laughed. "Yes, I remember. Nobody had ever called me an angel before. Most of the other children were frightened of my eyes, they thought I was a witch and kept away from me. How do you think I managed to scare all of those bigger boys away? They were all terrified I would turn them into toads."

"You were the most beautiful person I had ever seen," the boy confessed. "You helped me up, brushed me down, and told me I would be all right. And I knew then that I would be. You turned my life around, and I never even knew your name." He looked up at her with childlike wonder, the same awestruck expression in his eyes even after twelve years.

How could she have not recognized him? Those eyes had haunted her. She still remembered how she had screamed when her mother had dragged her away that day. She remembered her stubborn insistence that he was her friend, and how she had continued asking around after him for weeks, terrified of the possibility that he had not survived alone on the cruel streets of Santa Sofia.

"What happened to you?" she asked softly. "After that day when we met as children?"

He shrugged.

"I survived, I suppose. I was scared that I would be sent back to the orphanage if they found me around Santa Sofia, so I hitched a ride to Santa Juanita and found a group of street kids who let me tag along with them. That's where I met Diego."

"Diego?"

"My *hermano*. The other guitarist who was playing with me tonight. We're not really brothers, it's a street kid thing. We don't have any other family, so we all sort of adopt each other. Diego had a guitar. One day he heard me singing and must've seen some potential there, because he taught me to play and we started making money playing and singing together on the streets. Over time we got good, and now we tour around the towns and villages, playing in the plazas and for *fiestas* and *bailes*. Where there are Dons, there are always *bailes*. Don Lorenzo seems to be a particular fan of ours, he invites us to perform at every party he hosts. That's how I know your friend Don Raúl so well. Believe me, tonight isn't the first time he's gotten drunk at a party and made a total *verga* of himself."

Esperanza burst out laughing at his choice of language, and he put his hand over his mouth apologetically.

"I'm sorry, *señorita*. I shouldn't have spoken like that in front of a lady."

"Nonsense. I couldn't have put it better myself. So, do you often have to rescue damsels in distress from Don Raúl, then?" She tried to keep her voice impassive, telling herself that she didn't care, but she nonetheless felt a little burn of jealousy somewhere deep in her chest.

"*Sí*." He rolled his eyes. "He's like that every time. Drinks too much, can't keep control of himself. Usually, he just picks fights with people or makes inappropriate remarks to the ladies, but he has surpassed himself once or twice. One time he relieved himself in the fountain, and three ladies fainted. Another time, Diego had to bandage up his hand after he punched a statue because he didn't like the way it was looking at him."

Esperanza couldn't help but laugh. So much for the portrait of the refined, chivalrous gentleman that her mother had painted of him. It sounded as though she'd had a very lucky escape from being the object of Don Raúl's affections.

"Sometimes, he decides to get on the stage and join us for a song." The boy grimaced at the memory. "You try singing and playing the guitar while some huge drunken oaf is hanging around your neck, howling like a dog in pain. It's not easy, *señorita*."

"Don't be cruel," Esperanza scolded him, but she couldn't hide the laughter in her voice.

"I'm being generous. He's awful. That man can't sing at the best of times, but after a few drinks..." The boy threw back his head and howled tunelessly. *"¡Ay! Zandunga, Zandunga mamá por Dios..."*

"Shh, *idiota!* Someone will hear you!" She flung herself at him and clapped a hand over his mouth. They fell back on the grass together, giggling like children. He took her hand from his mouth with a grin and held it for a moment, stroking her fingers with his own, and she tried to ignore the little sparks of excitement shooting up her arm.

"So... you didn't answer my question. Do you often rescue ladies from Raúl, or am I an exception?"

"Actually, dealing with Don Drunkard is more Diego's territory than mine," he grinned. "Diego knows him better than I do; Raúl takes it better from him when someone needs to intervene. Even his servants are scared of him. But tonight was different. I couldn't stand back and watch. Not when it was you. The look on your face, Angel. I couldn't bear it."

He had stopped laughing now, his eyes large and shining.

"You still call me Angel?" she smiled. "I can't believe it's you, after all this time. I'm surprised you even recognized me after twelve years."

"Of course I recognized you." He reached out and took her hand, entwining his fingers with hers, and she felt her breath catch in her chest. "One look at those blue eyes and I knew it had to be you, protecting your brother in the plaza just as you protected me all those years ago. You're still the most beautiful person I've ever seen."

Esperanza felt heat rushing to her cheeks again. She had been told by men before that she was beautiful, but never like this. Never so sincerely. He turned her wrist over and saw the marks that Don Raúl's fierce grip had left on her, and his smile faded as quickly as it had appeared.

"He hurt you, Angel?" He stroked the marks on her arm, sending pleasant shivers up her spine. His fingertips were rough and callused from years of playing the guitar, but they still felt soothing against her skin.

"Esperanza," she told him, her voice almost a whisper. "My name is Esperanza."

He studied her face for a moment, as though trying to memorise every feature.

"Esperanza. *Hope*. A perfect name for an angel," he smiled. "My name is Arturo, but everyone calls me Artie."

"Artie." *Courage*. It suited him well. "Well, Artie, I am glad to have met you properly at last."

"The pleasure is all mine... *Esperanza*." He raised her hand to his lips and kissed it, and for a moment, Esperanza felt as though her heart was about to burst from her chest.

Their peace was shattered by raised voices echoing across the garden from the *hacienda*. They glanced at each other nervously, and it occurred to Esperanza that her parents must have noticed her absence.

"Come on, *señorita*," Artie sighed. "I think I'd better return you to your family before we give your mother any more reasons to want me dead."

He helped Esperanza to her feet, and she smoothed her hair and clothing, conscious of the horrors her mother's mind might jump to if she saw grass stuck all over the back of her dress. She was likely in enough trouble already tonight.

Checking that the coast was clear, Artie helped her back over the wall, and together they snuck back across the lawn towards the *hacienda*, taking care not to be spotted as they approached the courtyard. Esperanza held her breath as they hid in the shadow of an archway, listening to the sounds of voices laughing and the heels of shoes clacking against the cobblestones.

"It will look better if we go back in through different entrances," Artie whispered. "But first, let's make sure that Don Raúl isn't around. I'm not sure that he'll fall for the same trick twice in one night, no matter how drunk he is."

Artie was still holding on to her hand, his fingers entwined with hers, but Esperanza couldn't bring herself to let go just yet. She peered around the archway, searching the crowd for Don Raúl's bright red and gold waistcoat, but he was nowhere to be seen. Her shoulders relaxed with relief.

"Ahem," coughed an angry voice from behind them.

Esperanza jumped and dropped Artie's hand like a guilty child. It wasn't Don Raúl, but Artie's brother Diego, and he looked less than impressed.

"Hermano, thank goodness!" Artie smiled at him with relief. "We thought you were-"

"*Where in the hell have you been, Arturo?*" Diego hissed. "One minute you're there playing beside me, and the next, you've jumped off the stage and vanished into the night with the woman that Don Raúl is supposed to be dancing with, leaving *me* to pick up the pieces. Have you forgotten how important this *baile* was to me?"

Artie grinned apologetically.

"I know, Diego, I'm sorry. But I had to do it. This is the girl, the angel I told you about. Twelve years, *hermano*, and I've finally found her."

"I don't care if she's Santa Maria herself, beamed down from Heaven to save the soul of every street child in Mexico. You will get your sorry backside back onto that stage in the next *twelve seconds* and play another song, or so help me God, I will send you to visit the rest of the angels myself!" He grabbed Artie by the shoulder and tried to drag him towards the stage.

"Wait!" Artie begged, wriggling free. "When will I see you again, *señorita*?"

"I... I don't know."

"*Por favor*." His eyes were pleading. "I need to know that I'm going to see you again. Soon."

"Sooner than twelve years this time, *sí*." It was a promise. No matter what her mother or anyone else thought, she would make sure that this wasn't the last time she saw those chestnut eyes. "I'll find a way, *señor*. You have my word."

Artie nodded. He bowed and kissed her hand, and after flashing her one last smile, reluctantly allowed Diego to steer him back into the courtyard.

Esperanza stood alone and unsure. Reassured that she still couldn't see any sign of Don Raúl, she snuck around the side of the courtyard and through an archway, blending into the crowd on the dancefloor in the hope that nobody would notice her. Artie had rejoined Diego on the stage, and both were re-tuning their guitars, ready to play another song.

She spotted her father leaning against a nearby pillar, a glass in his hand and a worried frown on his face. His shoulders relaxed with relief when he saw her.

"*Mija*! Where have you been? I've been looking everywhere for you."

"I'm sorry, *papá*."

"I heard what happened with Don Raúl, the drunken fool. Are you all right?" Juan peered into her face, concerned.

"*Sí*, I'm fine. One of the *músicos* diffused the situation." She glanced up at Artie on the stage in front of them, and the corners of his mouth twitched. He could hear every word.

"The one who was dancing with you earlier? In that case, I owe the man a drink." He raised his glass to Artie, who smiled and nodded back in friendly acknowledgement. *This is a good start*, Esperanza thought. "But what about you, *mija*?

Where did you vanish off to? Tell me you haven't spent the whole evening hiding by yourself?"

"I'm fine, *papá*, really. After what happened, I just thought it might be a good idea to lie low for a little while."

Esperanza heard Diego snort from the stage.

"*Sí*, we can all see she's been lying somewhere," he muttered, eyeing up the grass stains on her dress. Esperanza heard a strange twanging sound from Diego's guitar as Artie kicked him, and she thanked God for making her father slightly hard of hearing.

Juan looked as though he was going to say more, but he was stopped by the approach of Don Lorenzo, who was meandering through the crowd towards them. His expression was not cold like Raúl's but softer and more welcoming, and full of kind concern.

"*Señorita* Esperanza." He bowed and kissed her hand. "I am so glad to see you. I would like to take this opportunity to offer my sincere apologies for my son's behaviour tonight. He has retired to his room as he is not feeling quite himself at the moment, but please be assured that I will express my displeasure to him tomorrow when he is a little more rested."

Sí, and a little more sober, thought Esperanza, but she decided it would be best not to say it out loud.

"I must say though, *señorita*, you are a most talented dancer," Don Lorenzo continued with a smile. "It was a pleasure watching you tonight. I know my son is already regretting that his poor conduct this evening denied him the chance to dance with you. It is most certainly his loss."

Esperanza bowed her head.

"You are too kind, *señor*. I hope that Don Raúl is feeling better soon."

It was a lie. She really hoped that the nasty, jumped-up little thug woke up with the headache from hell tomorrow morning, but she also knew that she couldn't say so out loud in front of Don Lorenzo. Besides, she couldn't blame the old man for his son's behaviour; Don Lorenzo had done nothing wrong. At least one of the Dons knew how to speak to a lady. It was just a shame that it wasn't the one that her parents had wanted her to marry.

"Esperanza!"

She tried not to wince as her mother's voice rang across the courtyard. Louisa did not sound happy, and Esperanza braced herself for the impact of her mother's sharp tongue. She only prayed that the bulk of it waited until Artie was out of earshot. Experience told her that her mother would not be impressed by her rejecting the son of a Don to dance with a street musician, even if the Don in question didn't blame her for it.

Louisa strode across the courtyard, wearing an expression not unlike the sort of look an agitated bull gave to a matador just before he charged. Esperanza said a silent prayer. However, as Louisa neared them, she spotted Don Lorenzo and slowed her steps, contorting her face into a forced smile. Angry as she was, she would not lower herself into making a public spectacle, especially in front of such an important man.

"Don Lorenzo." Louisa simpered. She was positively grovelling, almost kneeling as she curtseyed to him. "What a wonderful evening. Thank you so much for inviting us."

Lies, thought Esperanza. It turned her stomach to watch.

"Not at all, señora," Don Lorenzo bowed. "I was just apologising to your charming daughter for my son's behaviour tonight. It is his deep regret that his lack of manners prevented him from having the privilege of dancing with her. He was most disappointed to have made such a poor first impression, and I know he would be honoured by the chance to make up for it when he is feeling better."

Louisa's jaw dropped with surprise. Esperanza felt as though her stomach had done the same.

"Perhaps, *señorita*," Don Lorenzo continued, turning to Esperanza, "you and your family would like to join us for an evening meal here on… let's say, the twenty-second of the month? As my honoured guests, and Raúl's, of course?"

Esperanza heard another strange twang from one of the guitars on the stage, but this time she had a strong suspicion that it was Artie's. She opened her mouth to reply, but her mother cut in first.

"We would be delighted, *señor*." Her voice was breathless with excitement. Esperanza didn't need to look at Louisa's face to know that she was beaming from ear to ear, performing another one of her ridiculous deep curtsies. Esperanza fought to make her grimace look more like a smile, with little success.

"Excellent. Until the twenty-second, then." Don Lorenzo gave a curt bow and left to re-join his friends around the table.

Louisa squealed with delight.

"Did you hear that, *mija*? Don Raúl has taken a liking to you!" She clapped her hands together and laughed, oblivious to Esperanza's disgust. "Oh, you clever girl! All evening I've been angry with you for dancing with some worthless *músico* instead of Don Raúl, and the whole time it was just your plan to make him notice you. Oh, well *done*, *mija*. I may have a Don for a son-in-law yet!"

She danced away, grinning like a fool, and Esperanza turned to her father with a grimace of despair. She had thought that tonight's events would've put paid to the idea of her marrying Don Raúl. Now it seemed they had only spurred the notion on. Worse still, her mother had just described Artie as 'some worthless *músico*', and she was certain that he had heard.

"*Papá*. Don't make me go through with this," she begged. "You know what Don Raúl was like tonight. You wouldn't make me marry a man like that, would you?"

"*Mija*, this is the first time you've met the man. Don't worry yourself about marriage yet," he reassured her. "But for my sake, please just humour your mother on this one. Give Don Raúl a chance. If his father is right and he just had a bad evening, such a match has the potential to do a lot of good for this family."

He sighed, seeing Esperanza's scowl.

"I'm only asking you to spend a little time with him, *mija*. You never know, he might surprise you. Now, I think I've had enough excitement for one night. I'll ask Rafael to bring the carriage."

He left her simmering with quiet anger. She closed her eyes and took a few deep breaths, trying to calm herself. Artie and Diego started playing one of her grandmother's favorite love songs, *Golondrina Viajera*, and Artie was singing again. His voice washed over her like ocean waves.

"*Nadie sabe viajera que tu ausencia he llorado,
Con la dulce esperanza de que habrás de tornar...*"

(Nobody knows how in your absence I have cried, with the sweet hope of your coming back.)

How very fitting after tonight's revelations. His eyes were closed, his fingers dancing over the frets of his guitar as he sang, and she would have given anything at that moment for him to have been the Don instead of Raúl. She took a deep breath and joined him in singing the last few lines of the song.

"Yo te habré de esperar... Yo te habré de esperar..."

I will wait for you.

He looked up and met her gaze, a warm, beaming smile spreading across his face, his eyes alight. As she followed her father from the courtyard to where the carriage was waiting, she took one final look back at the figure on the stage. *I will wait for you,* she thought again, and Artie smiled as though he understood.

CHAPTER FIVE

Despite her best efforts, it was weeks before Esperanza managed to leave the farm again. The day after the *baile*, her mother had sprained her ankle tripping over a rogue chicken in the courtyard. What a chicken had been doing in the courtyard in the first place was anyone's guess, but Esperanza suspected her brothers had something to do with it. They had both been suspiciously charming and well-behaved ever since, attending to Louisa's every whim while she recovered with her foot propped up on cushions.

Esperanza had hoped for a little time to go into town and fetch the groceries or visit Catalina, but she hadn't been given a moment to breathe. Her father had been assigned the task of collecting groceries while she had been trapped indoors looking after the household. It had been most frustrating. Catalina was the only person she could trust to keep her secrets, and she hoped that talking might help her to sort out her scrambled thoughts and feelings about the *baile*.

Images from that fateful evening still whirled in her head every night as she tried to sleep. In her opinion, the night had gone as badly as it could've done in terms of any future with Don Raúl. Yet twice over the last few weeks, Juan had come home to tell her that Don Lorenzo had wanted to discuss formalising a courtship. Of course, Juan could hardly turn him down, although he was reluctant to confirm any arrangements until Raúl had at least been given the opportunity to make amends for his behaviour at their first meeting.

Esperanza was very grateful for this delay, although her mother did not share her views. Louisa had never been a patient woman, and she was keen to get arrangements formalised as quickly as possible for fear that Don Raúl may get bored with waiting and become distracted by some other *señorita*.

If she was honest, Esperanza would've been delighted if Don Raúl *had* turned his attentions to someone else. She had done as her parents asked. She had met him, and once had been enough. Each night she lay alone, trying to picture herself as Don Raúl's wife. What might it be like, being held by him? Kissed by him? She tried to imagine it, but every time she did, those cold, black eyes morphed into the warm gaze of the street musician.

She hadn't yet worked out how she was going to see Artie again. Being forced to stay on the farm for these past few weeks had not helped. Nothing she cooked had been good enough to meet Louisa's standards, nothing she cleaned quite spotless enough. Thanks to the recent storms, she hadn't even been able to leave the house to do the laundry, and she was starting to wonder how much longer she could take the strain before she and Louisa were forced to kill each other.

Yesterday, however, she had been finally given a reprieve. A note had arrived for Louisa from her sister, and whatever it said had broken Louisa's foul mood. Esperanza had found her hobbling around in the kitchen, making cakes for Tía Victoria and muttering to herself with excitement. Esperanza had been given strict orders to deliver them at exactly eleven o'clock. She knew that there must be an ulterior motive; Tía Victoria was an excellent cook in her own right, and was more than capable of making her own cakes. However, she was so desperate to get away from the farm for a day that she didn't dare question it.

Now, though, Esperanza was getting suspicious. Louisa had insisted that she was to wear some of her nicest clothes and even jewellery, which she never usually wore except on special occasions. She helped her to weave ribbons in her hair, and when Esperanza went to put on her boots, she realized someone had polished them. The boys had been forced into clean shirts and smart little neckties. Even Juan had not escaped Louisa's scrutiny, and she made him change his clothes twice before they passed her inspection. For all of her excitement at seeing Catalina, Esperanza suspected that she might have more to tell her friend before the morning was out.

Louisa had been insistent that she had to deliver the cakes to Tía Victoria before doing anything else, which Esperanza didn't mind. The cakes were just another thing to weigh her down, and Victoria's tailors' shop was only a few doors down from Catalina's house- it would be no inconvenience for her to drop them in on the way.

Tía Victoria was the best tailor in all of Santa Sofia. She had learned the trade from her husband Stefano, and she had continued running the shop by herself ever since his passing. With no children of her own, *Tía* Victoria doted on Esperanza and her brothers. She was a quiet, serious little woman, unlike her sister, Louisa, in every way except for her love of gossip. Esperanza wondered she had written to Louisa to have caused such excitement this time, and her worst fears were answered as the shop came into view and she saw a beautiful black stallion tied up outside, his red and gold livery emblazoned with Don Lorenzo's coat of arms.

Of course this was why her mother had insisted that she had to be there, at this exact time. She would have wagered everything that she owned on Don Raúl being the owner of that horse. She considered hiding in Catalina's house until she could be sure that he had gone, but it was too late; *Tía* Victoria's little round spectacles were glinting at her through the lace curtains, and she knew that she would never get away with escaping.

Bracing herself, Esperanza pushed open the door. Just as expected, Don Raúl was standing inside, his arms spread like a crucifix while *Tía* Victoria took measurements. The gleam in her aunt's eye told Esperanza that she was not in the least bit surprised to see her, although she did a very theatrical job of pretending otherwise.

"*Mija!*" she cried, her arms outstretched. *Tía* Victoria was not often one to express her affection physically, but today she threw her arms around Esperanza and kissed her as though it were the most natural thing in the world.

"Don Raúl, I believe you've already met my niece, Esperanza?"

The expression on Raúl's face when he turned and saw Esperanza reassured her that their surprise was mutual. He looked stunned for a moment; a little embarrassed, even. Then he bowed low.

"*Señorita*. What an unexpected pleasure to see you again."

"I could say the same to you, *señor*."

But it wouldn't be true, she finished in her head. She returned Don Raúl's bow with a polite curtsey, refusing to meet his eye. There was a long, awkward silence.

"I... I just wanted to apologise for my behaviour at the *baile*. I'm afraid that I allowed myself to get a little carried away." He cleared his throat. "Alcohol can make fools of even the best of men, and I'm deeply sorry for any offence that I may have caused you."

"I appreciate your apology, Don Raúl." Esperanza couldn't quite bring herself to say that she accepted. If what Artie had told her was anything to go by, then the behaviour that he was apologising for was far from a rare occurrence. Still, he was acting like a gentleman now, at least.

"You are a most accomplished dancer, *señorita*," he told her as she raised her eyes to look at him. "It has been my deepest regret that my poor behaviour forced you to dance with that clumsy *músico*. The whole experience must have been most humiliating for you."

"Actually, the *músico* was a perfect gentleman," she retorted. *Unlike you*, she wanted to add. "I very much enjoyed dancing with him."

Something flickered in Don Raúl's face, and Esperanza immediately wished that she hadn't said anything. She couldn't tell whether it was jealousy or just anger at the memory of her rejecting him to dance with Artie, but the flash of emotion barely lasted a second before he regained his composure.

"Well, be that as it may, I hope you will allow me to rectify my mistake soon. If you found dancing with a common *músico* so enjoyable, then I can guarantee you the thrill of your life when you dance with a gentleman who has received the proper instruction," he assured her, puffing out his chest. She did not answer him, but she felt her cheeks flush hot with anger at his snobbery. "I believe we are to have a meal together on the twenty-second?"

"Your father invited myself and my parents to share *cena* at his *hacienda* on the twenty-second, *sí*."

"I am looking forward to it, *señorita*. Perhaps we can share a dance then." He reached out and placed his hand on her chin, tipping her head back so that she had no choice but to look at him. "My goodness. You really do have the most beautiful eyes."

She took a nervous step back and he lowered his hand, making no attempt to hold on to her as he had at the *baile*. He was smiling at her now, although those black eyes were still as cold as ever.

"I came to give my *Tía* Victoria these," she said, desperate to change the subject. She pulled the parcel of cakes from her basket, handing them to Victoria, who was still smiling at her with twinkling eyes. "Now, if you'll excuse me, I have to meet my friend Catalina. She will be waiting for me."

She curtsied politely and reached for the door. Don Raúl caught her hand and bowed to kiss it.

"It was a pleasure to see you again, *señorita*," he told her. "I look forward to seeing you on the twenty-second for *cena*. And, of course, for that dance."

She nodded to him and stepped through the doorway, fighting the urge to slam it behind her, then darted past the horse and hammered on the familiar door on the corner of the plaza. It swung open, and Esperanza almost flattened her friend in her desperation to get in. Catalina gave a puzzled laugh, sticking her head out of the doorway and glancing up and down the street with interest.

"For the love of *Dios*, Catalina, shut the door!" Esperanza panted, almost throwing her basket onto the table and collapsing into a chair.

"I was just looking for the pack of coyotes that seem to be chasing you," Catalina replied, raising an eyebrow as she closed the door.

"It's not coyotes. It's Don Raúl."

"Oh? Your handsome nobleman suitor? What about him?"

"He's in my *tía's* shop."

"Ooh, let me see!" Catalina's eyes went wide with excitement, and she sprung to the window, peering through the half-open shutters in an attempt to spy into *Tía* Victoria's shop. Esperanza almost tackled her to the ground.

"Esperanza! What on Earth has gotten into you?" Catalina laughed. "Is your best friend not allowed to see your new suitor? Are you that possessive of him already?"

Esperanza groaned, collapsing back into the chair. She began to explain everything that had happened at the *baile*, and Catalina listened with great interest, making all the appropriate noises as Esperanza knew she would.

"So, wait, wait, wait," Catalina interrupted after a few minutes, raising a hand to stop her. "You're telling me that the man was drunk at his father's party, publicly humiliated you and then manhandled you in front of everyone... and your parents are *still* considering him as a suitor for you?"

"*Sí*, you've got the measure of it. It looks as though I'm going to be made to let him court me anyway, although I can't imagine my father forcing me to *marry* someone so vile against my will."

"I wouldn't put it past your mother, though," Catalina mused. "You're sure this *cena* you've been invited to isn't actually a surprise wedding ceremony, *mi compa*?"

Esperanza choked on her tea at the thought, and Catalina laughed again.

"I'm teasing you, Esperanza. Still, it's a shame. I quite fancied myself as the best friend of the new Doña Esperanza Alvarez. I was hoping to hear that you'd fallen madly in love with him and were planning on marrying and making little Dons as soon as possible, so that Francisco Junior could have a playmate around his own age."

Esperanza froze, not quite believing that she had heard correctly. Catalina rested her hand on her belly and grinned.

"Catalina... you mean, you're...?"

Catalina nodded, and Esperanza let out a squeal of delight. She knew how much her friend wanted this. She and her husband Francisco had suffered heartbreak several times over since their marriage three years ago, and Catalina had almost given up hope of ever having a child.

"Don't tell anyone yet," Catalina warned. "I don't want anyone to know, just in case it doesn't work out again. But Francisco tells me we're past the most dangerous phase. I've got a good feeling about this one." She stroked her belly with a loving smile, and Esperanza took her hand across the table.

"I'm so happy for you," she gushed. "If there's anything you need, anything I can do to help you, you only ever need to ask."

"Ay, I wish you'd been here a week or two ago," Catalina laughed. "The sickness... Francisco tells me it's normal and a healthy sign, but I don't remember Santa Maria vomiting her guts up over the Angel Gabriel every day of *her* pregnancy."

"No, I don't remember that chapter of the Bible either," agreed Esperanza, wrinkling her nose. "At least that's one advantage of being married to the local doctor. You can always be sure that he's seen worse."

"Sí, and the disadvantage is that I have to do his laundry afterwards," Catalina groaned.

The two of them chattered for some time about Catalina's impending arrival, comparing baby names and trying to imagine whether it would be a boy or a girl. Catalina made more hibiscus tea, and they sat together for some time, laughing and chattering.

"It's such a shame that Don Raúl has made such a poor impression on you," Catalina mused. "With his looks, I'm sure he could provide you with some very handsome babies, at least from what I've heard."

"Sí, but from what I've heard, good luck to the woman who ends up bearing them." Esperanza shook her head, thinking about what Artie had told her, and couldn't help grinning.

Catalina watched her for a moment, her brow furrowed, and eyes narrowed with suspicion. Esperanza tried to feign an innocent expression, but her friend knew her too well to be fooled.

"There's something you haven't told me, isn't there?" she said, narrowing her eyes with suspicion. "I don't remember you mentioning how this party ended. You said that Don Raúl tried to force you to dance with him... but you refused, and then what?"

Esperanza took a deep breath. "Then I got rescued. By a boy."

"Now it's all coming out," said Catalina, leaning forward. "Tell me about this boy."

She explained how Artie had danced with her, and how he had managed to smuggle her away. She described how they had lain on the grass together under the stars. How Artie had revealed that he was the same street boy she had befriended as a child, and how he had held her hand and kissed it, becoming so lost in the memory that her voice trailed off into silence.

Catalina sat staring at her with wonder, her cup of tea raised halfway to her lips, forgotten.

"Oh, Esperanza," she said in a hushed voice. "It seems that Don Raúl has more than one dark horse to worry about in his life, hmm?"

"Oh, don't be silly," Esperanza laughed, her cheeks growing hot. "He's just a friend from the past. We got on well the other night, but we could never be anything more than that. My parents would never consent to me being courted by a street boy." She sighed. "I know, I got carried away at the *baile*. I should never have gone with him into the garden or let him hold my hand."

"But you did, and now you can't stop thinking about him," Catalina finished. Esperanza nodded.

They sat in silence for a few minutes. Esperanza knew that she was being a fool, but that didn't make it any easier to stop. Not for the first time, she found herself wishing that Artie had been the Don and Raúl the poor street boy instead. It would have made everything so much simpler.

"Stop me if I am speaking out of turn," said Catalina, "but do you think that just maybe there's a possibility that your feelings for this boy are part of the reason you're so reluctant to give Don Raúl a chance?"

"You speak as though I have a choice," Esperanza reminded her. "My parents are making arrangements with Don Lorenzo already. They've arranged a meal at his *hacienda*, so I suppose we'll see what happens after that." She sighed, feeling a knot of dread tightening in her stomach at the thought.

"Ay, nothing knocks the romance out of a relationship like official courtship procedures," groaned Catalina. "That's the best thing about being married, not having to go through all that again."

"It's all right for you," Esperanza retorted. "You love Francisco."

"Sí, but don't forget it wasn't always like that. I barely knew Francisco when our parents first made the arrangements. By the time we got married, I had grown to like and respect him. I didn't learn to love him until a while later."

"Do you think I'll learn to love Don Raúl, if I give it time?"

"I don't know, *mi compa*." Catalina sighed and squeezed Esperanza's arm. "I don't know if he's a good man like Francisco is. But I do know that you will never be able to love Don Raúl if you've already given your heart to this street boy. You need to be careful. I don't want to see you get hurt."

"I know." Esperanza pressed her hands to her head, trying to stop her thoughts from swimming. "I know I'm an *idiota*. It's just the way that Artie looks at me, Catalina. Nobody has ever looked at me like that before. And his voice…"

"His name is Artie?" said Catalina suddenly. "As in, short for Arturo? And he's a street musician?"

"Sí…?"

"He doesn't have a brother? Daniel, or something?"

"Diego."

A slow smile spread across Catalina's face. She took Esperanza by the hand and led her through to the sitting room, where she opened the window and pointed out across the plaza at the *kiosca*. Esperanza could see that there were two musicians playing on the stage today, both holding guitars, and Esperanza knew who they were the moment she heard the singer's voice through the window.

"El tiempo pasa y no te puedo olvidar
Te traigo en mi pensamiento constante, mi amor…"

Triste Recuerdos. Esperanza closed her eyes, drinking in the lyrics. *Time passes, and I can't forget you…* Artie's voice rang across the plaza, as beautiful as the first time she had heard it. Listening to him made her feel as though she was breathing fresh air for the first time in weeks.

"They turned up in the plaza a few weeks ago," Catalina told her in a hushed voice. "Not long before I last saw you. They've been playing here almost every day since. I felt sorry for them out there in the storm last week though, I had Francisco take them out some tea. He said that the baby was turning my head soft, but he won't deny me anything at the moment." She laughed. "Is that him then? The one who's singing?"

"Sí," Esperanza breathed. "That's him."

She watched him as he played, feeling a strange fluttering in her stomach. She was pleased to see that he looked as though he had been taking much better care of himself. His face was clean, and his thick, floppy hair looked soft as though it had been combed. His clothes were ragged, but he had tried to smarten himself up with a red necktie which hung in a loose bow almost halfway down his chest. He kept his eyes closed as he played, lost in the song's emotion, and Esperanza found it easy to imagine what it would be like if he was singing those words for her. She stared at him in awe, a strange feeling of lightness dancing in her chest, almost afraid to look away in case it had all been in her imagination.

"Go on," Catalina ordered, nodding towards Artie. "Speak to him. I'm sure he's been waiting for you."

"I... I haven't thought of what to say." Esperanza felt as though her brain had evaporated, her legs turned to jelly.

"Hello would be a good start."

"I don't want to interrupt his music. I'll go later... when he's finished."

"You'll go now," Catalina commanded, taking Esperanza by the arm and marching her to the door. "You can either go over and say hello to him by yourself, or you can go over there with me, and I will tell him all about how you want to marry him and have twenty of his babies. Now go. Good luck, *mi compa*."

CHAPTER SIX

Before Esperanza knew what was happening, Catalina had thrust her basket back into her hand, pushed her out of the door and closed it behind her with a click. Don Raúl's horse was still outside *Tía* Victoria's shop, scraping his hooves against the paving stones and snorting angrily at anyone who passed too close. He rolled his eyes at her as she passed, but Esperanza didn't care. Her chest was tight with excitement. She took a deep breath and stepped into the square, aware of her friend's beady eyes already watching her again through the window. What was she going to say to him? All this time she had been imagining what it would be like to see him again, and yet not once had she considered what she would do when it happened.

Esperanza distracted herself for a moment at a fruit stall, buying herself time to think. She wanted to go over and say something intelligent and charming, but the only things she could think of were a rather pathetic 'hello' or Catalina's suggestion of 'I want to marry you and have twenty of your babies', which would be most inappropriate.

Before she had worked out what to do, however, she realized her feet had already carried her over to the *kiosca*. She felt so breathless that she wondered if she had accidentally run there without realizing, but it was too late to turn back now. Diego noticed her and gave a roll of his eyes to show that he was not best pleased by her appearance. However, Artie still had his eyes closed, lost in the lyrics of the song.

"Dime que cosa me hiciste que no te puedo olvidar..."

Esperanza suddenly knew how to attract his attention. She took a deep breath and began to sing in harmony with him, just loud enough for him to hear.

"Si vieras, Yo como te recuerdo
En mis locos develos le pido a dios que vuelvas..."

Artie's eyes snapped open, and he beamed at Esperanza as they sang the last few lines of the song together, his eyes fixed on hers as though afraid that she would vanish if he dared to look away. As soon as the sound of the final chord had faded across the plaza, he lifted his guitar strap over his head and almost threw the instrument at Diego, falling to his knees before the railings at the front of the stage so that his head was almost level with hers.

"You came," he breathed, his chestnut eyes sparkling. "I hoped you would. I came out here every day since the *baile*, just in case."

"*Sí*, and it nearly killed the both of us," Diego grumbled. Artie ignored him.

"My *mamá* has been unwell," Esperanza explained. "I would've come sooner, but I couldn't get away."

"You missed me too, then?" Artie winked.

"I never said that," she teased back, trying to hide her smile. "I liked that song you just played, though."

"I liked that you joined in," he grinned, his eyes twinkling. "Come on, admit it. You missed me too. Did you come here today just to find me?"

"No," she said defensively, feeling her voice go tight. "I was at the fruit stall buying some apples for my *mamá*, that's all. I heard your voice and thought I'd come and say hello. It was pure coincidence."

"No, it wasn't. You came looking for me." He puffed out his chest, beaming.

"And what makes you so sure of that?"

"Esperanza," he laughed, "your father owns one of the largest farms in the state. Most of the fruit on that stall probably came from your family's farm. You've got more apples than you know what to do with right outside your front door. Do you really expect me to believe that your *mamá* sent you all the way down to the *pueblo* to buy back your own fruit?" He grinned at her, and she found herself without an answer.

"*Sí*, all right," she conceded, her cheeks hot again. "I'll admit, I did come here hoping that I might find you, although I wish I hadn't now. I was going to offer you an apple, but I've changed my mind seeing as you're teasing me."

He laughed again.

"How can I resist teasing you when it makes you squirm so prettily? Come on, I'm sorry. I'm very glad that you came to find me. I was starting to worry that I had dreamed that night at the *baile*."

"You did dream it," grunted Diego from behind him. "Every damn night since. I should know, I'm the poor fool who has to listen to you talk in your sleep."

Artie rolled his eyes and leaned closer to the railings to whisper to her. She leaned in, too, feeling his soft breath warm on her cheek.

"Ignore him, *señorita*. He's just jealous." Artie reached through the railings to brush her hair behind her ear, making her quiver.

"Jealous of what?" she whispered.

"He's jealous because you offered the apple to me and not him." Esperanza burst out laughing and stepped back, swatting his hand away from her face. He laughed too, and Diego tutted and rolled his eyes.

"Would you like an apple, Diego?" she asked, grinning. "As your brother pointed out, I have plenty already."

"Thank you, Isabella," Diego grunted.

"Esperanza," Artie corrected him.

"Whatever." Diego shrugged. "We can eat the whole basket of apples if you want, but after we've done this last song. I need to trouble my brother to come and do his job for another five minutes before he goes running off on another of his little unscheduled breaks. We have to play music if we're going to make enough money to eat."

"I think that was what the *señorita* had in mind for you to do with the apple, but *sí*, point taken," Artie sighed. He turned back to Esperanza, a pleading look in his eyes. "I need to play one last song before I can take a break, or I'm worried Diego will shove that apple somewhere I'd rather he didn't. Will you wait for me?"

"Sí, all right," she shrugged. She wasn't going to complain about hearing him sing again. She shifted her basket from one arm to the other, wishing that she had not gotten so carried away with buying the fruit. Artie was right; she had more fruit growing on the trees back home than she knew what to do with. Her mother was going to think she had completely lost her senses when she came home with more.

"You can put your basket on the steps if it's getting heavy," Artie told her, picking up his guitar and tuning it carefully, his tongue sticking out with concentration. "I don't mind carrying it for you if you want to go for a walk after this. But first, let's see how fast I can play *Pajarillo Barranqueño*, shall we? One last song, Diego. You asked for this."

"Arturo, behave yourself," groaned Diego, trying to re-tune his own guitar before Artie's impatience got the better of him. "You're not a child. Play it properly."

Esperanza left her basket at the top of the steps and rushed back around to the front of the *kiosca*, giggling like a child. Whatever Artie was about to do, she had a feeling that she would not want to miss it.

"You're as young as you feel. Catch me if you can, *amigo!*" Artie cried, and with a loud *grito*, launched into the liveliest version of *Pajarillo Barranqueño* that Esperanza had ever heard. Diego's eyes widened in panic, and he almost dropped his guitar trying to keep up as Artie showed off, dancing as he played.

People were starting to pay attention, and before long, a small crowd had gathered, clapping along and dancing. Esperanza couldn't resist joining in, and this seemed to spur Artie on even more. There was a brief instrumental break in the music, and he gave another loud *grito* and plunged into the next verse with even more speed and enthusiasm than before. Diego's face was almost purple with exertion trying to keep up, but he didn't have enough breath to complain. The final verse of the song was approaching, and judging by the wicked look on Artie's face, he was about to push the music even faster.

"Don't you dare, Arturo..." gasped Diego, but Artie just flashed him one of his impish grins, taking a deep breath ready to sing again.

The song ground to a halt, interrupted by a sudden cacophony of noise coming from one of the side streets leading to the plaza, and the crowd scattered in panic. Esperanza could hear people screaming and the high, frightened whinny of a horse, and before she could process what was happening, Don Raúl's large black stallion burst riderless into the plaza, sending people flying left and right like skittles. He reared up, eyes rolling and mouth foaming, and struck out with his forelegs. The fruit stall where Esperanza had just bought the apples collapsed with a shriek of wood, sending splinters and fruit everywhere. People scrambled over each other to take cover, seeking shelter in nearby shops, side streets, and anywhere else they could.

The horse reared again, flailing out with his powerful hooves and snorting with terror. A few brave men approached him, trying to catch hold of his reins, and for a moment, Esperanza thought that two of them had succeeded. But the horse screamed in fury, effortlessly lifting both men into the air and throwing them onto the cobbles some feet away, where they lay groaning with pain.

Esperanza looked around for Don Raúl, who must surely have known by now that his horse was missing. There was no sign of him, nor anyone else who was foolish enough to try catching the stallion. She looked back towards Catalina's house, wondering whether she could make it to the door, but it was too risky. The stallion stood between her and the little road off the plaza; she couldn't get to the house on the corner without the risk of having her skull split apart.

"Esperanza!" Artie cried, reaching down over the railings of the *kiosca*. "Quick, take my hand…"

She reached up, but she was not tall enough to catch his outstretched hand over the top of the railings. She tried to get a foothold on the wall of the *kiosca*, but the stone was too smooth and her boot kept slipping. Her only hope of reaching him was to get to the steps around the side where she had left her basket, and she ran.

The slamming of a shop door behind him spooked the stallion again, and he leapt over the carnage of the fruit stall and galloped out of control towards the *kiosca*. The suddenness of Esperanza's appearance caused him to rear up again, screaming with rage. He kicked out, missing her face by inches, and in her panic, she caught her foot on one of the cobbles and fell. The horse snorted furiously, his nostrils flared and his ears pressed flat to his skull. One of his hooves smashed into the step beside her head, crushing the wood to matchsticks. Esperanza cried out in terror, bracing herself for the next impact.

It was at that moment Artie appeared above her.

He leapt like a cat from the *kiosca* railings, straight onto the back of the raging stallion. The beast screamed and bucked, his ears still flat against his head, but somehow Artie held tight. He lay flush against the saddle, his bare feet wrapped around the animal's sides and his fingers entwined in its flowing mane. His body was pressed against the horse's neck, and Esperanza realized after a moment that he was singing in the beast's ear, a gentle, soothing melody that seemed to hypnotize her as effectively as it did the horse. The animal calmed and grew quiet, his muscles relaxing and the fury leaving his eyes.

Once the danger had passed, Artie lowered himself back to the ground, still singing to keep the horse entranced. He reached out towards Esperanza's basket, which was still balanced at the top of the steps, and pulled out an apple. The animal sniffed at it, interested, and then took it from his outstretched hand with a deep grunt of appreciation, coating Artie's palm in a mixture of juice and slobber. Artie laughed and wiped his sticky hand on his trousers, then turned to help Esperanza to her feet. She accepted gratefully.

"Are you all right, *señorita*?" he asked. His eyes were bright and shining, staring straight into hers with an expression of concern that made her head feel lighter than air. She nodded speechlessly, trying to stop her knees from trembling.

She didn't have long to think on it, however. A roar from the other side of the plaza told her that Don Raúl had arrived, and he was not pleased about his horse's escape. She dropped Artie's hand.

For a moment, Esperanza hoped as Raúl stormed across the plaza towards them that he might show some gratitude to the man who had retrieved his stallion. However, to her horror, instead of thanking Artie for his heroism Don Raúl drew back his hand and delivered a sharp backhand across the boy's cheekbone. Artie fell to the ground. The horse reared up again in panic, his eyes rolling, but Raúl caught him by the reins before he had the chance to bolt. Esperanza froze in shock, and a few spectators stopped to see what was going on, whispering behind their hands and staring at Artie.

"Thief!" Raúl thundered, thrusting a judgemental finger at Artie. "I saw you take that apple from the *señorita's* basket!"

"*Sí*, to stop your horse from killing her!" Artie shouted back, his hand covering his face where Don Raúl had hit him.

Esperanza could see reddened skin through his fingers where a bruise was already beginning to swell.

"Silence!" Raúl drew his sword and pointed it at Artie's chest. The boy's eyes widened in fear, and Diego sprung from the *kiosca*, his hands raised in surrender.

"Please, Don Raúl, put the weapon away," he begged. "There is no need for violence. Whatever my brother has done-"

"Your brother has stolen from the *señorita*," seethed Raúl, his eyes narrowed. "I watched him take an apple from her basket, he doesn't even deny it. Someone, go to the *presidio* and fetch the soldiers. Tell them that Don Raúl has caught a thieving street dog and wants to see him suitably punished."

"No!" Esperanza cried, finding her voice at last. "Don Raúl, please. He's not a thief. I told him he could have that apple."

"You don't have to lie to protect this worthless fool, *señorita*," Raúl snarled, his eyes still locked on Artie's. "No doubt he was planning to use my horse to escape once he'd robbed you."

"Don Raúl," implored Diego. "You know my brother is not a thief. If anything, he deserves your thanks, both for catching your horse and for rescuing Señorita Dominguez from a nasty fate."

"Ay, and not for the first time, either," Artie muttered bitterly. Don Raúl clenched his jaw and took a step towards him, placing the sharp point of his blade against the bare triangle of skin just beneath Artie's collarbone. Artie's eyes widened as he felt the cold steel on his chest, and he shuffled himself backward away from Don Raúl until his back bumped against the steps of the *kiosca* and he could go no further. Esperanza could see that he was trembling, his breath turned to ragged gasps. Don Raúl seemed to take pleasure in his fear, closing in on him like a cat with a cornered mouse.

Esperanza could take it no more. She stepped between Artie and Don Raúl's blade, locking eyes with the older man and fixing him with a defiant glare.

"Don Raúl, are you really going to harm the man who just saved me from being trampled by *your* horse, and have him thrown into jail over a piece of fruit?" Her voice was authoritative, her sharp tone usually reserved for when her younger brothers were misbehaving and needed to be pulled back into line. "You are doing him a great injustice for his good deed, *señor*, and you insult me by calling me a liar for correcting *your* mistake."

Don Raúl stared at her. It was apparent that he was unaccustomed to anyone standing up to him, let alone young ladies he was trying to court. The gathering crowd were staring and muttering behind their hands, and Esperanza felt emboldened by how many of them were now glaring at Don Raúl. It was not uncommon to witness a soldier teaching some insolent street dog a lesson in manners, and whether the dog in question deserved it or not, people rarely cared. A gentleman standing in the middle of the plaza pointing a sword at a lady, though, was a very different matter. Don Raúl's eyes flickered from the crowd to Esperanza and back again, beads of nervous sweat forming on his forehead as the outraged murmuring grew louder around him.

"This has all been a big misunderstanding, *señor*," Diego assured him, trying to diffuse the situation. "It is valiant of you to protect the *señorita* from a thief, but she is right. No crime has been committed here."

Don Raúl swallowed hard. After a long moment, he sheathed his blade and Esperanza felt herself release the breath she had been holding.

"Forgive me, *señorita*," he said gruffly, bowing to her. "I never meant to offend you. I'm afraid that when I thought you were being wronged, I reacted on instinct. I am a passionate man, you see." He bent and kissed her hand, trying to force his lips into a charming smile, but there was still a deep bitterness in his eyes.

I see, all right, thought Esperanza. I see that you're a violent, evil-tempered thug who needs locking up before you kill someone.

"Thank you for trying to defend me, señor," she said with strained courtesy, "even though on this occasion it was completely unnecessary."

Diego pulled Artie to his feet, brushing the dirt from his back. He was trembling, although whether it was through fear or anger, Esperanza wasn't sure.

"It seems I owe you my thanks, *músico*," Don Raúl told Artie, unable to hide the hostility in his eyes despite his smile. Artie refused to meet his gaze, staring at the cobbles with one hand still pressed to his face where Don Raúl had hit him. Esperanza noted that although Don Raúl offered his thanks, he had not extended any sort of apology. She had a feeling that even if he had, he would not have meant it, and Artie would not have accepted anyway.

Don Raúl turned his back on Artie, nodding towards the black stallion with an air of self-important pride.

"He's a magnificent beast, isn't he? He is a purebred Andalusian, recently arrived from the Iberian Peninsula. A gift from my father. They're very strong, lots of stamina, which is exactly what will be needed over the next few days. I'm going to visit my father's gold mines up in the mountains." He was bragging, glancing at Esperanza to check that she looked impressed. "Well, *my* gold mines now, I suppose. Father has put me in charge of managing them. I'm certain the lazy *cabróns* up there aren't pulling their weight, and I intend to resolve the issue."

He looked to her again in anticipation of a reaction, but she refused to give him the satisfaction. If he thought that flaunting his father's wealth was going to make her forget how he had just threatened an innocent man at sword point, then he was very much mistaken.

"I'm afraid I'll be gone at least a week, perhaps more, however, I will ensure that I am back in plenty of time for our meal on the twenty-second. Hopefully, it will give me the chance to get to know you a little better, *señorita*. I may even bring you a little gift from the mines as a token of our new friendship and my high regard for you."

He gave her a meaningful smile and took her hand again, and Esperanza's stomach lurched. She knew that the moment gifts were exchanged, it would signal the start of an official courtship. She wasn't ready for such a formal commitment, especially from a man who so far had failed to demonstrate a single earthly reason why she should court him aside from his outrageous wealth.

Artie seemed to pick up on his meaning too, and his expression darkened. Diego put his hand on his brother's shoulder and whispered something to him, but Artie shrugged him off with a scowl.

"Thank you, Don Raúl, but no gift will be necessary." Esperanza withdrew her hand and curtseyed again. She was not prepared to discuss this with him now and certainly not in front of Artie. "For now, *señor*, my only wish is for your safe return."

"*Sí*, try not to get eaten by any mountain lions while you're out there, won't you?" Artie muttered. Esperanza cursed him silently. Why did he seem so intent on getting himself killed today?

Don Raúl turned to him, his eyes narrowed.

"What was that?" he growled.

"Just a warning, *señor*," Artie repeated. He was not smiling, and his eyes were cold. "There are wild cats in the mountains. They can be terribly fierce if you make the mistake of forcing your presence in their territory when it is *not wanted*."

"Mountain cats do not frighten me," Raúl sneered, "any more than street dogs do."

"Perhaps not, *señor*. But either will bite if you mistreat them."

The two men were staring each other down now, each refusing to break eye contact. Esperanza feared for a moment that Raúl was going to draw his blade again, but instead, he sneered, looking up and down at Artie's grubby shirt and ragged trousers with contempt.

"I will pretend I didn't hear that, for the *señorita*'s sake," Raúl snarled in a low voice. "Remember, *niño*. You may have done a good deed here today, but it doesn't change who or what you are. You were born a nameless street dog and you will die a nameless street dog, as worthless as the dust you walk on. Even your own mother knew that. *Señorita* Esperanza's kind heart does her credit, but don't make the mistake of thinking you're worthy of anything more than her pity."

He stepped back, and Esperanza saw pain and humiliation in Artie's eyes. Don Raúl's words had touched a nerve. She wanted to take his hand and tell him that it wasn't true, that he was worth ten of Raúl, but she didn't dare while the Don was still standing there with his sword on his hip.

"There you are, *mija!* We were wondering where you'd got to!" Juan strolled across the plaza towards them, oblivious to the splintered carnage all around him, and greeted Don Raúl with a bow. They exchanged pleasantries, during which time Diego pulled Artie away and back onto the stage. He picked up his guitar and resumed playing, glancing every now and then at Esperanza with a miserable expression of pain and longing. She smiled back at him, but it made little difference.

"I must go now *Señor* Dominguez, *señorita*," Raúl told them at last, "but I look forward to our *cena* together when I return. Until then, I wish you good health." He kissed Esperanza's hand one last time, bowed again to her father and swung himself up onto his horse. Esperanza watched as he rode away across the plaza, giving one final look of smug contempt over his shoulder at Artie.

Juan looked from Artie to Don Raúl and back again, his eyes widening as he noticed the destruction all around him.

"Did I miss something?" he asked, his brow furrowed in confusion.

Esperanza explained what had happened, omitting how she and Artie had been planning on sneaking away together after his final song. Her father might not have approved of that part.

"I recognize that boy," Juan realized. "He was the *músico* who diffused that unfortunate situation at the *baile*, wasn't he? And now he's saved you from getting crushed by a rogue horse? He seems like a good man to have around in a crisis."

"*Sí*," Esperanza agreed, hoping that he hadn't noticed her ears reddening.

"Hmm." Juan was watching Artie closely, his eyes narrowed. "*Mija*, go and find your brothers. I'll meet you by the cart."

She obeyed, leaving her father with Artie and Diego and headed towards the sweet shop at the other end of the plaza. Sure enough, her *hermanos* were munching on chocolate and chattering to a few other boys they knew from school, and Esperanza had to give them the meanest look she could muster before they conceded defeat and agreed to come with her.

Juan was already back at the cart by the time Esperanza got there. He and Rafael seated themselves at the front, and

Esperanza helped Miguel and Felipe into the back before climbing up herself, bracing herself for the inevitable nausea of travel. She tried to distract herself by thinking about the list of chores facing her when she got home, but her thoughts kept coming back to Artie.

The more she thought about it, the less she believed that Raúl's aggression towards Artie had anything to do with fruit. Could it be that he had seen Artie take her hand and suspected that there was something between them? Perhaps he had seen the way he looked at her, or even how *she* had looked at *him*, and it had made him jealous.

Even so, threatening him with a sword was inexcusable, and Esperanza found herself getting angry all over again. She wished she had not been so polite to Don Raúl now, especially as she could picture the pain and humiliation in Artie's eyes when he had mocked him. She should have said something, stood up to him in some way, at least so Artie knew she did not share Raúl's snobbish views. But it was too late now.

"Rafael, I meant to tell you." She heard Juan say from the front of the cart. "I've got a new farmhand starting on Monday. He's coming to help Ricardo with the horses, just three days a week. Can I rely on you to give him the tour? I've got a meeting with Don Lorenzo on Monday morning, so I won't be around."

"Not another recommendation from Jorge, I hope?" groaned Rafael.

"No, this one's already proven that he can handle a horse," Juan reassured him. "He caught and subdued a rogue Andalusian stallion in the plaza today. Esperanza saw it for herself, didn't you, *mija*?"

Esperanza sat up abruptly, making her brothers jump.

"Artie... Artie's coming to work on the farm?" she said, a little more eagerly than she meant to.

"Sí," Juan replied, turning to look at her with a raised eyebrow. "That's not a problem, is it?"

"No, not at all," she retorted, trying to feign a look of disinterest. "I'm just surprised he agreed to it, with all that time he spends playing in the plaza."

"The boy needs the money, I think," Juan admitted with a sigh. "Victoria mentioned those *músicos* when I saw her the other day. The poor kid and his brother sat out there every day last week, playing against the storm. Hardly a soul passed them all week. They can't have earned a single penny."

"Ay, you're too soft-hearted, *señor*," Rafael laughed. "But sí, it must be tough. Those boys probably haven't eaten in a while, with the weather being as it has. No wonder the kid jumped at the chance to earn a proper day's wage. Well, I hope he's as good as you say."

"I'm sure he will be. I have a good feeling about him," Juan promised.

You're not the only one, thought Esperanza.

CHAPTER SEVEN

Artie was nervous, but he smiled at the old man, determined not to show it. He had done odd jobs around farms before when he needed a bit of extra money, so this was nothing new to him.

"Do you have any other questions?"

"No, *señor*. I think you've covered everything."

Rafael was friendly enough, and he had been working for the Dominguez family for around thirty years, by his own estimation. That was always a good sign.

Artie was pleased to hear that *Señor* Dominguez treated his workers well, which was a relief considering his connections to Don Lorenzo and his family. Rafael told Artie about how Juan often brought them food while they were working and how they were always welcome to take fruit from his trees without even needing to ask. Their pay was more than fair, they were welcome to take *siestas* in the heat of the afternoon as long as they made up their hours elsewhere in the day, and Juan was never difficult about allowing them time off work if they were ill or their families needed them at home. If anything, it could be argued that Juan had a bit of a soft touch when it came to his workers, but Artie would have rather had it that way around than the alternative.

He had even been given work clothes to change into so that he didn't spoil his own clothing. It wasn't as though he had much to spoil, but he was still grateful. This way, Diego wouldn't be angry with him for looking scruffy when they performed, and in the evenings he could head straight from the farm to the plaza without having to go home and change first. The work trousers and baggy *guayabera* he had been given would be too big for him, he knew, but it didn't matter. Most of his own clothes were too big for him anyway; he was used to it.

"I'll take you down to the stables and introduce you to Ricardo," Rafael told Artie, "and then I'll let you get changed and start work."

"Ricardo being the current stable boy?" Artie asked nervously. He wasn't sure how this Ricardo would take it, having someone new turning up to tell him how to do his job.

"Sí," Rafael confirmed. "Don't look so worried. Ricardo will be delighted to have someone show him the ropes. To be honest, I think he knew from the moment he set foot on this farm that he was in well over his head. He's scared of the horses, *Dios* help him." Rafael chuckled.

He pushed open the door to the stables and gestured for Artie to go inside. It was warm and smelled of hay and horses, and several inquisitive equine heads poked out from their stalls as he entered. There was an odd sound coming from a stall at the far end, but aside from that, it was just as a stable should be.

A young man stepped out from the stall nearest to them, pitchfork in hand. He looked a couple of years younger than Artie, although he was around the same height with a more muscular build. He smiled with relief when he saw Artie.

"Ricardo, this is Arturo," Rafael told the young man. "He's here to teach you a bit of horsemanship."

"Thank you, *señor*," Ricardo nodded, reaching out to shake Artie's hand with a relieved smile. "I need all the help I can get, I'm afraid. I'm so desperate not to lose this job, but I know I'm no good at it. I'm surprised that *Señor* Dominguez hasn't fired me already, to be honest, but I promise I'll do my best to learn from you."

"Call me Artie. And don't worry, I'm sure you'll pick it all up soon enough." Artie was moved by the man's sincerity and only hoped that he could live up to the reputation he appeared to have already gained among the other farmhands.

"Ay, Ricardo is a hard worker," agreed Rafael, squinting towards the stall at the end. "Unfortunately, the same cannot be said about everyone who works here. Ricardo, is that who I think it is? Again?"

Artie could still hear the strange sound coming from the end stall and realized that it sounded an awful lot like a man snoring. Rafael didn't wait for Ricardo to answer but crept over to the stall and peered over the door. There was a huge man sound asleep in the hay, his head tipped back, drool running down his cheek and an empty bottle of tequila in his hand. His long hair was matted with dirt, his teeth blackened from chewing tobacco, and specks of black and grey hair peppered his cheeks. He looked around fifty, and life did not appear to have been kind to him. Artie wondered for a second if he was an escaped convict, although the lack of panic in both Ricardo and Rafael's eyes told him that this was probably not the case.

Rafael dipped his hand into the nearest water bucket, scooped up a fist full of water and flicked it into the face of the sleeping man. He had to repeat the action several times before the man began to stir like a bear coming out of hibernation, grumbling with annoyance at being woken.

"*Buenos días*, Roberto," said Rafael in a tone that told Artie he was less than impressed. "As much as I hate to interrupt your beauty sleep, I think it's time you got to work, don't you?"

The man's cold, black eyes finally focussed on Rafael, and he hiccupped. He pulled himself to his feet, grumbling and scratching himself, and Artie couldn't help but compare him to a painting he had once seen of a bullfight in Madrid. Roberto looked nothing like the matador, but he bore an alarming resemblance to the bull.

"Just a little *siesta, señor*. No harm in that," he grumbled. "Leave me in peace."

"The other men take a *little siesta*, Roberto, when they've worked themselves into exhaustion with hard labour all morning and the sun is too hot to continue. Then they get up and get back to work to make up their hours and earn their keep." Rafael regarded him with disgust. "You arrive at work drunk, sleep all morning, wake up for just long enough to drink a bit more tequila, and then go back to sleep. That's not a *little siesta*, that's taking advantage, and I'm not having it. I catch you doing it again, and I'll be docking your pay."

Roberto's eyes narrowed, and he dragged himself to his full height, towering over them all.

"You thought you'd snitch on me to the old man, did you?" he snarled at Ricardo, who cowered under his gaze. "I thought I made myself clear, *niño*. I don't like snitches."

"He did no such thing," Artie spoke up before he could stop himself. "Rafael was showing me around the stables, and we heard you snoring."

Roberto pulled himself up to his full height, glowering at Artie.

"You. Haven't I seen you before in the plaza? You're that street boy, the *músico*."

"This is Arturo," Rafael answered for him. "He's going to be giving Ricardo a bit of training in horsemanship and helping out on the farm for a few days a week."

Roberto took a step towards Artie, who had to fight not to gag at the stink of alcohol, vomit and worse. He laughed, propelling the odour towards them, and Artie was afraid for a moment that he might pass out.

"Lord knows the boy needs all the help he can get," Roberto sneered. "Boy's useless and weak, can barely tie his own laces. This one doesn't look much better, with those skinny little arms. Juan must have a soft spot for weaklings."

"At least I'm sober and conscious," retorted Artie hotly, "which is a better start to the working day than some of us have managed."

Roberto grinned, flashing a gold tooth. His eyes were narrowed, and Artie shuddered, suddenly aware that he had made a grave error.

"So, this one's got a bit of spirit," Roberto laughed, but there was no humour in his tone. "You want to watch who you're talking to, boy, or you're going to get on the wrong side of the wrong people. We wouldn't want anyone getting hurt." He cracked his knuckles, and Artie felt his knees buckling.

"That's enough, Roberto," warned Rafael. "You're needed in the barn. Get going."

For a few seconds, nobody moved. Artie held Roberto's gaze with bated breath, determined not to show weakness by backing down. Roberto was trying to intimidate him, he knew, and he couldn't afford to show any signs that it was working or else the older man would always see him as a target. Finally, Roberto turned away, although Artie suspected it was only because Rafael was watching.

"I'll see you later, *músico*," Roberto grinned, his voice low and threatening. He let himself out of the stall, ignoring Rafael and Ricardo, and staggered off towards the fields, still weaving slightly as he walked.

"You stood up to Roberto," said Ricardo, staring at Artie in wonder. "I've never seen anyone brave enough to do that."

"You need to be very careful there, lad," Rafael warned him. "Roberto is a nasty piece of work. He's not long been out of prison for violent robbery. He only got released because he somehow managed to frighten the victim into swearing that he wasn't the culprit, although everyone knows he did it. He's a dangerous man to get on the wrong side of. You'd better watch your back after speaking to him like that."

"So he turns up to work drunk, sleeps on the job, bullies the other farmhands, and now you're telling me he's a violent criminal," Artie said incredulously. "Why on Earth does *Señor* Dominguez employ a man like that?"

"Juan and Roberto were friends when they were young," Rafael told him, rolling his eyes. "He's felt like he owed him a debt ever since. Juan hasn't always been rich, see. His father and I used to work together on some Don's land. Then Juan got lucky, some wealthy distant relative in Spain died and left him everything in his will, including this farm. Roberto went the other way, got in with the wrong crowd. Turned to drink, started pickpocketing to fund his habit, it escalated into violent robbery and before anyone could help him get back onto the straight and narrow, it was too late, and he was in prison. Juan offered him a job to help get him back on his feet, but you can see for yourself how that's working out. He's been here six months now, and all we've had is trouble. Drunk all the time, forces the other lads to cover his workload while he sleeps it off, and gets nasty with his fists if anyone crosses him."

"Have you said any of this to *Señor* Dominguez?" Artie asked, but Rafael shrugged and sighed.

"*Sí*, for all the difference it makes. He still has this ridiculous notion that he owes Roberto a debt, and he won't hear a word against him. Still thinks that he can change if he's given enough chances. Roberto will never go back to being the friend he knew as a child, but..." Rafael shook his head. "We all know he's in denial, but if he won't listen, there's not much we can do."

Artie nodded. It was a difficult situation. He couldn't imagine how he would react if he and Diego were ever in such a position, but he knew he wouldn't be quick to give up on his friend either. He could hardly judge Juan for that.

Rafael left the two young men to their work, and Artie soon found himself enjoying his new job. He got on well with Ricardo, which was a good start. The other farmhands were welcoming enough towards him too, and he was very glad of the food that *Señor* Dominguez provided for them all in the barn at *comida* time. There was a large variety of fruit, homemade bread, beans, rice and tortillas. It was simple, but it was by far the best meal that Artie had tasted in years, and he couldn't help but wonder whether *Señorita* Esperanza had any hand in making it. Somehow, just the thought made it taste even better.

CHAPTER EIGHT

"You make sure that you scrub them properly this time. Your father is trying to present himself as a gentleman, he can't go wandering around with tomato stains all over his shirts." Louisa's voice was shrill through the kitchen window, and Esperanza was grateful that her mother couldn't see her rolling her eyes.

"Sí, mamá."

Esperanza was frustrated. It had been Artie's first day working on the farm, and she had hoped that she would have at least seen him from a distance a few times. She had hoped to intercept him in the field when he brought the horses in later that afternoon, but by the time she had finished sweeping the courtyard, both Artie and the horses were gone. It was most disappointing.

The recent foul weather had caused a backlog of chores, and laundry was no exception. Esperanza grumbled as she lifted the heavy basket onto her back, taking half a loaf of bread and a small towel on her way out. She had a feeling from the weight of it that this particular basket of laundry would take her a while, and she had no intention of going hungry while she did it.

At least she could have some peace at last, down in her favorite spot by the river. She always did the laundry in a little secret clearing that she had found back when she was a child. It was quiet and beautiful, a patch of soft grass on a gentle slope leading down to the river, surrounded by low-hanging trees and bushes whose leaves created a thick curtain of privacy around the whole clearing. A huge oak tree stood in the middle, its branches giving much-welcome shade on hot days or shelter from the rain whenever she was unlucky enough to get caught out in it. The view was spectacular, too, with the river flowing by and the silhouettes of the mountains standing tall on the horizon. It was especially beautiful in the evenings when the sparkling stars reflected in the water, and if the moon was full then it bathed the whole clearing in a soft, silvery glow. Sometimes Esperanza came here when she needed to think or spend some time away from her family, even when she didn't have any laundry to do.

She headed away from the house, down the hill towards the barn. It was unusually hot, even for the beginning of July, and Esperanza could feel her shoulders sweating beneath the heavy basket. She pushed through the foliage, cursing under her breath as it caught on the basket, and sighed with relief as she finally reached the edge of her favorite spot.

However, today she had a strange sense that she was not alone. There was a gentle splashing sound coming from over by the river, and she realized with horror that someone was there. She darted back into the foliage, frightened. Nobody else had ever known that this spot existed, as far as she was aware. How dare someone encroach on her private space?

She squinted through the leaves at the source of the splashing and saw a man crouched down in the shallow part of the river. He was shirtless, his smooth, wet back glistening in the sun as he bent over in the water, and Esperanza realized he was trying to wash what looked like a dirty white *guayabera*. He had no soap or brush and instead was rubbing the fabric with little stones in an attempt to scour the dirt from it. He wasn't having much luck in Esperanza's eyes, but the man must have been satisfied because he stood and wrung out the excess water before turning to hang the shirt on the branch of a tree to dry. She caught sight of his face and realized that it was Artie.

He stood on the grass in his bare feet and stretched, and Esperanza wondered how she could have ever failed to realize that it was him. His long, skinny arms, dark floppy hair and handsome cheekbones were instantly familiar to her, and although she knew she shouldn't, she cast a curious glance at his bare torso. His skin was so smooth and soft-looking. It stretched painfully over his protruding ribs, and Esperanza couldn't help thinking again that he looked underfed. His ragged trousers sat low on his slender hips, held up by a piece of rope which he had wrapped several times around the waist and knotted beneath his navel. His boots and battered straw hat lay beside the big oak tree, and Esperanza could see that he had already washed and hung his work trousers on one of the branches. Had she been there a few minutes earlier, she realized, he may not have been wearing anything at all.

Artie walked over to the tree and picked up his guitar, which had been leaning against the trunk. He sat down, rested his back against the tree and started playing, his eyes closed in concentration. A gentle smile came to his lips, and he began to hum along with the guitar, a beautiful melody that Esperanza didn't recognize. She leaned forward, straining her ears to listen.

A twig cracked under her foot, and Artie stopped. His eyes snapped open and he looked around, suddenly wary. He leaned his guitar back against the tree and picked up a large stick from the ground, brandishing it in her direction.

"Who- who's there?" he asked, and Esperanza saw fear in his chestnut eyes. There was no point in trying to slip away now.

She stepped out into the clearing, and Artie's expression immediately softened. He lowered the stick with a sigh of relief and gave her a broad smile.

"Señorita," he bowed. "I'm sorry, you startled me."

"What did you think I was? A mountain lion?" she asked, raising a cool eyebrow. He grinned.

"You can never be too careful. Did you come looking for me this time, or were you just lucky?" His eyes sparkled with hope, and Esperanza had to fight the urge to smile back.

"Neither. It's Monday, and Monday is laundry day," she told him in what she hoped sounded like a haughty voice, gesturing to the basket. "I'm afraid you've stolen my secret washing spot, *señor*."

"Maybe we can share it?" he winked. "I won't tell anyone if you don't."

"It looks like you've already done yours," she said, eyeing up the *guayabera* and work trousers which were hanging over the tree branch and then raising an eyebrow at his bare chest. His ears darkened with embarrassment as he excused himself, pulling a dry shirt from his bag. Esperanza turned away to allow him a little privacy, blushing a little herself and trying to hide her smile. She busied herself with the laundry, setting out her soap and brushes beside the river, ready to begin.

Artie followed her, pushing his damp hair out of his eyes, his baggy shirt hanging from his waistband.

"May I... may I help you with that, *señorita*?" he asked, eyeing up the large basket of laundry that she had dumped by the water's edge.

"Are you any good at laundry?" She eyed up his grubby *guayabera*, which was dripping from the branch he had hung it on. "Actually... never mind."

"*Sí, sí!* I can help you!" he bounded over to the basket with the enthusiasm of a puppy. "Just show me what to do!"

Esperanza looked at him warily. It occurred to her that although she and Artie had met a few times now, she really didn't know him all that well. Her family would be mortified at the idea of her being here alone with him, especially in such a secluded place. But he had offered to help her with her chores. And surely if he had any unsavoury intentions towards her, he could have acted on them on the night of Don Lorenzo's *baile* when they had been alone together in that garden. There was something in his eyes that told her she could trust him, and she chose to push her mother's voice aside and let her instincts lead the way.

"Like this," she told him, demonstrating. The water was refreshing, and she took her shoes off so that she could bathe her feet in the river while she worked. He watched her intently, his face contorted in deep concentration, and once she was happy that he understood what to do, she passed him a shirt from the pile.

Artie took a brush and some soap and started to scrub, the river splashing against the rocks and soaking his own shirt. It stuck to his chest, the pale fabric translucent from the water, and Esperanza noticed again how she could see the outline of his ribcage rising and falling as he breathed. It had only been a few days since their last meeting in the plaza, and now that he was closer, she could see a dark bruise beneath his eye from where Don Raúl had hit him. She felt a surge of guilt, remembering how she had just stood there and said nothing while Don Raúl had mocked him. Had their roles been reversed, she knew that he would never have just stood by and watched while someone humiliated her.

"What the… oh…" Artie's ears suddenly burned bright pink. Esperanza looked down to see that he was holding a pair of her undergarments. They must have gotten tangled with the shirt that she had handed him, and now he was holding them between his index finger and thumb, staring at the lace trim with embarrassed fascination. She gave a mortified yelp and threw herself on top of him, snatching the offending item from his hands. Artie burst out laughing, and she glared at him, her face burning with shame.

For a few minutes they continued scrubbing in silence, Esperanza still too horrified to look at him. No man had ever seen or touched her undergarments before. It was far too intimate, and she felt almost violated. A horrible fear crept through her that he might think she had passed them to him deliberately, perhaps to embarrass him. She glanced up. He didn't look annoyed, more amused. His eyes were lowered to his work, and now and again, he shook his head and gave a quiet laugh.

He must have sensed that she was watching him because he glanced up and caught her eye, grinning mischievously at her. A giggle escaped his lips before he could stop himself.

"Oh, stop it," Esperanza scolded him, splashing water at him with her hands. He squealed and laughed, then splashed her back.

She shrieked indignantly and splashed him harder, sending a spray of cold water into his face, which soaked his hair and dripped down his neck into his collar. She tried to press her advantage and splash him again, but Artie sprung forwards and caught her wrists, laughing. With one hand, he drew her against his chest, still holding tight to her wrists, while the other hand grabbed the soaking shirt that she had been cleaning and held it aloft, moving it towards her as though to allow the water from it to pour over her head.

"No, no, no!" she squealed. "I concede, I concede!"

He paused for a moment, a mock-thoughtful expression on his face. Water was dripping from his hair onto her face and chest, his shirt sticking to his skin like a translucent veil. Finally, he lowered the soaking fabric and released her hands, grinning at her as he bowed.

"Sí, all right. I accept your surrender. Although I still get the feeling you won." He shook himself like a dog, his hair sending water spraying at Esperanza and making her shriek with laughter again. Then he stepped out of the river and flopped out on the grass, enjoying the warmth of the sun on his wet skin. She followed him, and he smiled as she sat down beside him on the grass.

"So, Artie. It seems you and I are destined to be friends. You seem to be everywhere I go, you've rescued me twice when I've been in trouble, and now you've even seen my undergarments." She raised an eyebrow. "I think it's time I evened things out a little and learned a bit more about you."

"You want to see my undergarments? How very forward of you, *señorita*." He giggled, ducking as she flicked him with the towel as punishment for his impudence.

"You know what I mean. I don't even know your full name."

He looked away from her, embarrassed.

"I'm... I'm just Artie."

"Yes, but what about your family name?"

"I don't have a family name."

"You must do. Even orphans have family names."

"*Sí*, they do. But I'm... I'm not an orphan." He fiddled with the cuff of his damp sleeve, and Esperanza sensed he was summoning up the courage to tell her something important. "I... I was a foundling. Abandoned on the steps of the convent as a newborn. No note, no name, no clues as to who my parents were. Not that it matters." He feigned a cheery smile. "A noble name doth not a noble man make, or whatever it was Isiah said. That's what the nuns who ran the orphanage used to tell us, anyway. Miserable old bats, they were."

Esperanza laughed again.

"They had a point. I think Don Raúl is proof enough of that. You're more of a gentleman than he'll ever be, even with his fancy name." She gave him a warm smile, and he beamed back, clearly relieved that she didn't think less of him for his poor luck in early life. Her heart felt heavy, though. So that was what Raúl had meant when he had made that comment about Artie's mother. Artie seemed to read her mind.

"Don Raúl is wrong about me, you know," he promised. "I might've been born on the streets, but I won't die there. I am not even homeless anymore. I live with Diego in *el barrio bajo*."

He lives in the slums, Esperanza realized. It was better than the streets, but she still suspected her mother would not have approved.

"One day, when I'm a really successful *músico*, I'll move far away from where I am now, somewhere where nobody knows about my past. Diego wants us to travel the world." He picked up a stone and tossed it into the river with a flick of his wrist. It skimmed three times across the surface of the water before disappearing with a plop.

"Is that what you want?" she asked him. "To travel the world?"

"No." He looked up at her, a deep sadness in his beautiful chestnut eyes. "There has only ever been one thing I ever wanted, señorita. A family."

She swallowed hard. They were both silent for a moment, staring out across the river.

"Don't let Don Raúl get to you," she reassured him. "He is wrong about a lot of things, especially you. You're a very talented musician. I'm sure if anyone can make a success of it, you can."

"I write songs, too," he told her, his smile returning. "I've written one for you. Would you like to hear it?"

She nodded a little more eagerly than intended. She had never had anyone write a song for her. Sing for her, yes. She could remember with painful clarity that awful suitor who had taken it upon himself to torture her by wailing under her window… until she threw water over him to shut him up. But nobody had ever actually *written* a song for her.

She took a deep breath and prepared for what she knew was going to be unlike anything she's ever experienced before.

He stood and dried his hands again on the towel, then went over to the tree where his guitar was leaning, gesturing for her to come and sit with him as he tweaked the tuning pegs. She positioned herself on the grass beside him, and he cleared his throat and began to play. His fingers danced over the frets of the guitar, hypnotizing Esperanza as she watched. Then his eyes met hers, and he started to sing.

> *"My angel of hope, with your ocean blue eyes*
> *Sent down to Earth to save me*
> *Every minute I am with you*
> *Feels like Heaven to me*
>
> *All my life I dreamed you would return to me*
> *And now you are here, with your ocean blue eyes*
> *If this is all just a dream*
> *I hope that I will never wake up."*

Esperanza had to remind herself to keep breathing as he sang. That voice. She could have listened to it forever, so effortless and melodic, with such emotion that it seemed to speak to her soul. If that wealthy suitor who had attempted to serenade her from beneath her balcony had ever sung to her like that, she would have married him on the spot.

"That was beautiful," she breathed. Her heart was racing, and she realized that there were tears in her eyes.

"I'm glad you like it. I'm working on a third verse, but I'll have to play that one for you when it's finished." He pulled a little blue notebook and a pencil from the pocket of his bag and flicked through it, his brow furrowed in thought. It was full of his handwriting, lyrics to songs that he had written and ideas that he had scribbled down for future songs. "I've got the melody and the chords, but I'm still working on the lyrics."

"You can write!" Esperanza exclaimed. Such a skill was a luxury usually reserved for those wealthy enough to send their children to school. She certainly hadn't expected Artie to be literate.

"Sí. The nuns gave us lessons at the convent when I was little. I can read, too. I taught Diego, and then we started teaching other street children in Santa Juanita whenever we had time. We wanted to give them a bit of a chance in life, you know? To maybe get an honest job so that they didn't turn to a life of crime."

Esperanza's heart gave a little leap.

"You really are full of surprises, señor," she smiled. He grinned back, his eyes sparkling through those long, thick lashes, and she felt the butterflies spring up again in her stomach.

When the last of the laundry was done, Esperanza went to her basket and took out the bread. She ripped it in half and gave a chunk to Artie, and he accepted with a grateful nod, sitting down on the grass beside her to eat.

"I have enjoyed this, Esperanza," he told her. "Maybe I can help you with your laundry again next week? You know… if you need me to?"

"And what makes you think I need help?" she teased.

"I don't. But you shouldn't spend so much time in such an isolated place by yourself, señorita. Danger could be lurking anywhere." His eyes twinkled, a mischievous smile creeping across his lips.

"What kind of danger?"

"The wild kind."

"Don't start with all that rubbish about mountain lions again. Don Raúl wasn't stupid enough to believe it, and neither am I."

"Not lions." His eyes glittered. "Crocodiles."

Esperanza laughed.

"Nobody has seen a crocodile this far down the river in years."

"Oh, they have. It's just that nobody has lived to tell the tale."

His eyes flashed dangerously. He leaned closer to her, pointing out a large, mossy log that was bobbing out in the middle of the river, just visible above the water's surface.

"There he is, look. *El Cocodrilo Malvado*. He lies out there in the water, as still as he can," he whispered. "That way, he can fool his unsuspecting prey into thinking that he is just a log. Closer and closer he drifts to the bank of the river, ever closer to where his victim sits like an innocent lamb waiting for slaughter…"

His voice was so low that Esperanza had to lean her head close to his to hear every word, his lips almost brushing her ear, his breath tickling her neck and leaving a trail of goosebumps.

"See how his skin is rough and dark, like the bumps on the trunk of a tree… and then one bump *opens*… and you see a big… yellow… eye. And just as you realize what is about to happen… SNAP!"

Artie suddenly closed his arms around Esperanza's waist, and she screamed before she could stop herself. She fell in a giggling heap against his chest, embarrassed at her own girlish silliness. How could she have let him take her in so easily like that? There was just something so hypnotic about his voice, so exciting about his whole presence that she just couldn't resist. She pushed him away, laughing, and he leapt to his feet and grabbed the large stick that he had picked up earlier, wielding it at the river like a sword.

"Back, savage beast!" he cried, waving the stick at the oblivious log. "You come near my lady again, and I'll run you through!" He leaned back, panting as though he had just won a great battle, and grinned triumphantly at Esperanza.

"I don't think you'll be having any more trouble from him, señorita."

"I doubt I will. You really showed that log who was in charge."

"That's why you need me around," he boasted. "To protect you."

"The only thing I need protecting from is the madman standing in front of me."

"But you admit you need protecting! So, is that a yes?" He lowered himself to one knee and took her hand, gazing at her imploringly.

"You'll need protecting in a minute," she laughed, snatching her hand away. "I don't always do the laundry, you know. Sometimes my *mamá* does it if I'm busy. What would you do if she turned up instead of me?"

"I would climb up this tree and wait until you had finished being busy."

"But what about the crocodile, brave *señor*?" She did her best impression of a damsel in distress. "Surely you would protect my poor *mamá*?"

Artie took her hand again, his expression serious.

"*Señorita*, I have met your mother. Honestly, in the event of a battle, my sympathies would be with the crocodile."

Esperanza laughed and gave him a gentle push back onto the grass. He laughed too, and they both stared out across the river to the mountains on the horizon. The sun was beginning to set, painting the sky in shades of orange and pink, and the first dim stars glowed above. Esperanza couldn't remember the last time she had felt so contented. She glanced across at Artie, who was watching her with his head propped on one arm and a dreamy expression on his face.

"Will you come and see me in the *pueblo* again on Thursday?" he begged. "I'll be playing in the plaza in the morning, but afterwards, I could help you with your shopping if you like?"

"You still think I need help? Why, are there crocodiles in the plaza too?"

"I didn't say need. I said like." He looked at her with hopeful eyes. Esperanza realized that their hands were almost touching again, and suddenly she felt very hot.

"Maybe some help would be nice," she said in what she hoped was an offhand sort of tone. "The basket can get heavy. It would be useful to have someone to carry it, I suppose."

Artie's eyes lit up. Trying to hide her own smile, she stood and began fussing with the laundry, pulling the damp clothes down from the tree branches and putting them back into the basket. They had stopped dripping now, so she could carry them back to the house and hang them in the courtyard until they were completely dry. Artie stood to help her, careful to avert his eyes from any stray undergarments.

"Until Thursday then, *señorita*," he smiled as she put the last piece of laundry back in her basket. He took her hand and bowed to kiss it again, looking up at her through those warm chestnut eyes. She felt a tingle of excitement shoot up her arm and quickly removed her hand, trying again not to smile as she left him to gaze starry-eyed after her.

Something told her that Mondays and Thursdays were about to become her favorite days of the week.

CHAPTER NINE

"There. All finished." Diego secured the end of the bandage with a neat knot, tucking in the loose ends as gently as he could. "Does that feel better?"

"Sí. Gracias, hermano." Joaquin smiled through his grimace, flexing his fingers as though checking that his bandaged forearm was still working. "I'll try to be more careful next time."

"Ay, you'd better be," Diego warned him. "We're almost out of ointment. We won't have the money for another jar for at least a few more weeks yet, you can't afford any more burns."

"No," the boy agreed. "I'm lucky it was on my arm this time rather than my face. Can't afford to spoil my handsome looks before the wedding, Paloma might change her mind."

The young girl standing behind him laughed and put her arms around his neck, bending to kiss him on the cheek. Diego couldn't help smiling. Joaquin and Paloma had been together for as long as he had known them; they were childhood sweethearts. He knew as well as anyone that Joaquin could sprout horns and turn green, and Paloma would still love him just as much. Joaquin leaned back against her with a sigh of pain, but he was still smiling as he reached up with his good arm to entwine his fingers with hers.

"Do you want something for the pain?" Diego pulled out a half-empty bottle from his side-table and offered it to him.

"Pulque," Joaquin observed. "Sí, all right. It's a bit sour for my tastes, but I'll take anything to dull the senses a bit right now."

"That bad?" Diego grimaced. He took a glass from the table and poured.

"The pain? No, I can handle that. It's the images in my head that are harder to deal with." He shuddered, shaking his head although trying to dislodge something. "It was Gustavo who lit the dynamite, he lost his hand. I can still hear the screams before he fainted. It was awful."

Paloma squeezed his shoulder. His face was very pale, and Diego pushed the glass into his hand, encouraging him to drink before he passed out himself.

"I wish you didn't work in the mines," Paloma told him, tears gathering in her eyes as she stroked his cheek. "It's so dangerous. Every morning when you leave, I'm afraid that not all of you will come back to me."

Joaquin put his arms around her and pulled her onto his lap, hushing her with a kiss.

"As soon as I find another job, I'll take it, *mi vida*. But for now, we need the money. It's the only way."

Diego turned away for a moment to allow them a bit of privacy. Joaquin always tried to play down how dangerous his work was for Paloma's sake, but the truth of the matter was that the sooner he could find another job, the better. The same went for all of them. Alejandro, Eduardo, Marco… each of them had come home with nasty injuries at some point. It was why they had a pact. If one man couldn't work due to injury or illness, the others would pool what money they could to support him until he could work again. Either they all ate, or nobody did. That was how it was in their little community, and Diego wouldn't have had it any other way.

"Any word from Artie on his new job?" asked Joaquin, trying to change the subject. "Heard he persuaded Dominguez to employ him as a stable boy, the lucky *cabrón*."

"*Sí*, he started today." Diego rolled his eyes. "Although I'd hardly put it down to his persuasive skills, more his ability to attract trouble. The *idiota* got Dominguez' attention by almost killing himself in the middle of the plaza. He fought a rogue stallion and then got on the wrong side of Don Raúl's blade, all in one morning. It's like the boy's got a death wish at the moment."

"He annoyed Don Raúl *again*?" Paloma gasped, distracted from fussing over Joaquin. "What's turned him so reckless all of a sudden?"

"Love." Diego sighed, rolling his eyes again. "Dominguez' daughter just so happens to be this 'angel' he's been whining on about since the *baile*. When Artie saved her and proved to the whole town how good he was with horses… well, I suppose Dominguez knew he'd be missing a trick if he let him go."

Paloma beamed with delight, but Joaquin made a pained expression to mirror Diego's own.

"Oh, our little Artie, all grown up!" she cooed. "So when will we get to meet the lucky lady?"

"You won't, *mi vida*." Joaquin shook his head with a defeated sigh. "She's a rich girl, earmarked for Don Raúl. There's no chance that she'd go for a lad like Artie over him. I only hope he's got the sense not to let himself get hurt."

"Oh, I think it's far too late for that, *amigo*," Diego grumbled. "He's already lucky that Don Raúl hasn't had him thrown into a prison cell or even just cut out the middle-man and skewered him personally. I've warned him to stay away from that *señorita*, and now he's gone and taken a job at her family home. It's all going to end in tears, I'm telling you. Love affairs between the likes of us and the upper classes never end happily. It's not fair, but it's life. You can live by the rules or die by them as you so please, but they're still rules and they must be followed, no matter how much it hurts."

Diego took an aggressive swig from the bottle of pulque, wiping his mouth with the back of his hand. Joaquin and Paloma glanced at each other, and he glowered with irritation at their concerned expressions, turning away. He didn't want their pity. It had never helped before, and it wouldn't help now either.

"It's Artie I'm worried about," he told them, forcing his own heartache aside. "I don't know this girl well, but she doesn't seem to be putting him off. Quite the opposite, in fact. It won't do him any good."

"You think she's leading him along?" asked Paloma.

"Impossible to tell. If I had to guess, I'd say she genuinely likes him. I don't know if that makes it better or worse, but it doesn't matter either way. They can't be together, and they both know it." He shook his head. "I'll be the one picking up the pieces, you wait and see. I wish to God he'd never laid eyes on her."

"Well, I feel sorry for the girl if she does have feelings for Artie," said Paloma, putting her arms around Joaquin again. "How terrible, to be kept apart from the one you love. I wouldn't swap lives with her if she were the richest woman in all of Mexico. Money can't buy you the sort of happiness we've been blessed with."

"Perhaps not, but it can make you a hell of a lot more comfortable while you wallow in your misery," Diego grumbled. Both Joaquin and Paloma laughed, although he hadn't meant it as a joke.

Sudden, raucous laughter from outside told Diego that his other *hermanos* were on their way over, likely in search of a meal. He glanced over at the basket of wilted-looking vegetables on the table, trying to estimate whether he could salvage enough of them to cobble some sort of soup together. It wasn't as though he had much choice.

"I'll go out and get the fire lit," Joaquin offered, noticing Diego's glance towards their depleted food supplies.

"You'll do no such thing." Diego put a hand on his brother's shoulder, pushing him back into the chair. "You can't afford any more burns. One of these other lazy *cabróns* can do it, if they're sober enough. Ay, you three, what time do you call this?"

Alejandro, Eduardo and Marco came staggering through the doorway into the little hut, all roaring with laughter at something one of them had just said. They simmered down at the sight of Diego's withering glare, although all three of them continued to smirk and giggle like naughty schoolboys.

"Oh, Diego, you should've been there," Marco sniggered. "On our way home, we got a bit, ahem, *sidetracked* by a few fine ladies. One of them was quite taken with our Ed, wasn't she, boys? Until she realized he didn't have any money, 'course, and then she chucked him back in the gutter where he belonged."

"Ay, it wasn't because he had no money, *hermano*. It was because she caught sight of his ugly face." Both Alejandro and Marco roared with laughter, and Ed punched Alejandro on the arm.

"That's enough." Diego scowled at them. "I've already had to patch up one injury today, Alejandro, I'm not wasting any ointment on you if you earn yourself a black eye for winding up the other lads. As for you, Ed, have the sense to steer clear of the *putas*. I'm not wasting any of that good ointment on you either, and I'm certainly not rubbing it on *that* part of you if you pick up any little unwanted gifts, no matter how pretty the woman is." All three of the men roared with laughter again. "Now, Ed, you can go and get the fire lit. Alejandro and Marco, take those two buckets and go and fetch the water for the pot. Hurry up."

"It's your turn to cook tonight, is it, Diego?" asked Marco. "What are we having?"

"Vegetable Surprise," Diego grunted.

"Meaning?" Ed glanced over at the miserable looking vegetables that Paloma was trying to saw through.

"Meaning hot, stagnant water with three limp zucchini, two slightly mouldy cauliflowers and a cabbage that, frankly, the less said about the better."

"Aww, *hermano*, you spoiled the surprise," Alejandro pouted.

"Unless you have a nice fat chicken hidden under that filthy old shirt of yours, you'll eat it and be grateful," Diego snapped. "If you wanted some nicer food, then you should've bought some on your way home rather than stopping for pulque."

"Ay, I know," Alejandro confessed. "I'm sorry, Diego. But with the news we got today, me and the boys needed something to lift our spirits."

He stopped, interrupted by a silent, threatening shake of the head from Joaquin. He gestured over to Paloma, who was still chopping vegetables with her back turned, and then pressed a warning finger against his lips. Alejandro and Diego both nodded in understanding. Whatever Alejandro had been about to say, it could wait until Paloma was out of earshot.

Diego didn't blame his brothers for their tendency to drink when things got difficult. For one thing, pulque was a lot cheaper than food, and it certainly had the power to make a man forget about his hunger, or at least mind it less. All of them had known hunger, especially with the recent storms leaving them all unable to work. No work meant no pay, and no pay meant no food. Diego and Artie had tried to continue playing in the plaza, hopeful of earning a little extra money to keep them all going, but nobody had been brave enough to venture out to listen to them. The collective pot of money had begun to run dry even with their wages from Don Lorenzo's *baile*; feeding seven grown adults for two weeks had drained it quickly. Tonight, they would use up the very last of their rations. Diego would have to dip into their savings if they were to avoid starving, and that meant his dream moving a little further away from him yet again. Still, he couldn't begrudge his *hermanos* for that. They would have done the same for him.

The water was just about reaching a gentle bubble over the fire when Artie arrived home, breathless and panting from running.

"Ah, here it comes," teased Alejandro. "Where have you been, Romeo?"

"Keen for his *comida*, at least. He must've run all the way," Marco laughed, taking Artie's guitar from his back and stowing it under his bed out of harm's way. Artie nodded to him in gratitude, still too breathless to speak. He fell doubled-over against the wall, gasping for breath and clutching his chest.

"I'm less concerned about what he's running *to*, more worried about what he's running *from*." Diego caught his brother as he almost collapsed from exhaustion and dumped him onto his bed. "You haven't upset Don Raúl again, have you, *hermanito*?"

"Nah, he's just been chasing angels," Alejandro sniggered. "They're quick, I hear, especially the blue-eyed imaginary ones."

"No, I haven't. And she's not imaginary," Artie argued back, still trying to catch his breath. "Diego's met her too. I told you, she's real."

"Running from her father, then?" Marco suggested, and they all laughed again.

"Actually," Artie corrected him, "I was running from a pack of street dogs. They were after me for this." He lifted up his bag, which was stuffed full and looked heavy. "Although if you don't want any of it, I'm sure that Diego and I can finish it off. You hungry, *hermano*?"

Everyone stopped laughing and regarded Artie with hopeful interest. He opened the bag, revealing a bundle of fresh corn tortillas, a block of cheese, some rice, a large bag of beans, a whole selection of vegetables, and best of all, a bronze, freshly roasted chicken. The men froze in shock for a moment, staring at all the food as though afraid to believe it was real. Then Joaquin gave a loud whoop of joy, and Alejandro, Marco and Ed all piled on top of Artie on the bed, ruffling his hair and hugging him. Paloma laughed, taking the bag and spreading its contents out across the small wooden table to examine them. The chicken, in particular, smelled better than Diego could have imagined.

"Nice going, *hermanito*," Joaquin laughed. "Very nice going indeed. Diego, let's get all this cooked up. We're having a *fiesta* tonight!"

Once Paloma had helped him to cook up some of the rice and beans, Diego handed out bowls to the others and they all helped themselves to tortillas, filling them with whatever took their fancy. For the first time in far too long, there was plenty enough to go around. Diego felt a warm glow of satisfaction as he stretched back on his bed and closed his eyes, listening to the gentle chatter of the others around him.

He noticed that Artie hadn't eaten much. Instead, he sat with his back against the wall and played his guitar, humming to himself and jotting in his notebook with a dreamy smile on his face.

"New song?" Diego asked, and Artie nodded. The pencil was gripped between his teeth, his eyes closed in blissful concentration. The others, however, were getting a little mischievous. Whether it was due to the satisfaction of a proper meal or the pulque they had been drinking, Diego didn't know, but he could see them looking to Artie with raised eyebrows, mimicking his dreamy expression.

"Look at him," Marco sniggered, nudging Ed. "Lovesickness taken your appetite, Artie?"

"Nah, he's just thinking about another little chicken he'd rather be getting his teeth into," Alejandro joined in, wiggling his eyebrows.

"Actually, I ate earlier," Artie replied, not even bothering to open his eyes. "*Señor* Dominguez gave all of the farmhands *comida*, and then someone shared some bread with me this afternoon too."

The chatter died down as the others turned to listen in on the conversation. Diego didn't have to ask why they were so interested. He suspected that not one of them had ever been offered so much as a crumb of food while they worked in the mines.

Dominguez was renowned for treating his workers well; it was probably at least in part why his farm was so successful. He could afford to be choosy over who he employed, and those he chose tended to be hard-working and loyal, knowing that they were unlikely to find better pay or conditions elsewhere. It was rare that a job became available there, but Dominguez was always inundated with workers begging him for one anyway. Diego knew that every man in the room had at some point sought a job at the farm, himself included. It was pure luck that Artie happened to be in the right place at the right time in the plaza, and as much as Diego was concerned over his brother's heart, he would've been more concerned for his head if he had turned the offer down.

"Well, if you're not going to be eating that, I'll relieve you of it," said Ed hungrily, jumping up onto the bed beside Artie and snatching up his bowl. Artie cursed as the impact jolted him, his guitar strings twanging as the instrument almost slipped from his lap. Ed caught the notebook as it fell, food spilling down his chin as he sniggered at Artie's writing.

"*Every minute I am with you feels like Heaven to me,*" he read aloud in a mocking, sing-song voice. "*If this is all just a dream, I hope that I will never wake up.*"

Artie lunged at him, trying to snatch the notebook back, his ears pink with embarrassment as the other men roared with laughter. Ed held the little blue book out of his reach, and as Artie stretched to get to it, Ed darted an arm around his middle and pulled him into his lap like a child.

"Ooh, *señor!*" Ed lisped in what Diego supposed was meant to be an impression of a young maiden. "That's the nicest thing anyone's ever written about me! How could a girl possibly refuse?"

He pouted his lips as though to kiss him, and Artie pushed him off with some difficulty, falling straight into the arms of Marco. Artie struggled to get away, but Marco was much stronger. His grip was like that of a bear, and he picked Artie clean up off the floor and twirled him around in a dance, much to the amusement of the others.

"Take me to Heaven, *señor!*" he cried in the same high, girlish voice as his friend. The other men roared with laughter again, and Artie's ears turned even redder as he fought unsuccessfully to loosen Marco's grip.

"That's enough, now," Diego ordered. "Leave him alone."

He knew that Artie was well used to this kind of ribbing from the others, as they all were. It was all in jest, just as it always was, but he didn't want them to overstep the mark and upset the boy.

Marco dropped Artie obediently, still chuckling to himself. The boy picked himself up, glowering with anger and embarrassment, and snatched his notebook back from Ed, who put up no resistance this time.

"Wish I'd never taught you to read now, you ungrateful *cabrón*," Artie sulked, curling up on his bed against the wall and pulling his guitar back onto his lap.

"Ay, I'm sorry, *hermanito*," Ed apologised, still grinning as he ruffled his brother's hair. "You know we're only teasing. It's a rite of passage, being teased about your first love."

"If you say so," Artie grumbled, although Diego could already hear the anger simmering down in his voice. He knew it was all good-natured, even if they had touched a nerve, but he couldn't help feeling a bit sorry for his little brother. Artie was the youngest of them and the most sensitive. He could see the funny side of most things and usually took a bit of teasing as well as the rest of them, but it was clear from his face that he had not found this particular joke at all funny.

"Don't you pay them any mind, Arturo. They'll all be laughing on the other side of their faces when you and I are famous musicians in the big city," Diego promised. "Isn't that right, boys?"

"Don't think we're letting you leave us behind," protested Ed. "We'll be your backing singers! *Y aunque la vida me cuesta Llorona...*" He howled tunelessly, and the rest of the men joined in, putting their arms around each other and swaying in time to the terrible racket they were making. Even Artie had to laugh at this, and Ed put an affectionate arm around his shoulders, trying to get him to join in. Diego relaxed back on his bed, satisfied. All had been forgiven.

Alejandro reached up to offer Artie the bottle of pulque that they had been sharing around, but the boy shook his head.

"I'm not keen on pulque," he shrugged. "Too bitter for me."

"Ay," grinned Marco, unable to resist getting a final dig in. "He's got more expensive tastes now, *amigo*."

"Marco, I said leave it," Diego warned.

"He's got a point, though," Alejandro argued, turning to look at Artie. "You never mentioned how you managed to afford all this food, Arturo. You can't have bought all this. Did you... I mean, did you..."

"I didn't steal it, if that's what you're thinking." Artie bristled, offended at the suggestion.

"Then how?" Ed shifted closer to him. "Go on, Artie. Where did you get it? We won't tell."

"Nothing underhand, I told you. *Señor* Dominguez- oh, get *off me, Eduardo- Señor* Dominguez usually pays his farmhands weekly, but he told Rafael that I was to have today's wages upfront. Said I had to go and get myself a good meal. He told me he was worried that one of the horses farting might blow me over, I'm that skinny. I would've been offended, but the man was giving me money, so I didn't complain."

The other men suddenly went very quiet. Ed shuffled away from Artie, looking at him as though he had said something terribly offensive.

"What?" he said uncertainly, and Diego noticed him shrink back a little against the wall, his eyes darting from man to man around the room. The atmosphere was suddenly very uncomfortable, and Diego felt his throat go dry.

"You got all this with *one day's* money?"

"No, of course not," Artie corrected him. "Some of my wages are paid in food rather than money. That's where I got the vegetables and the beans today. I bought the rest from street vendors on my way home with the money, I thought it would be a nice treat for us all." His voice faltered, still unsure whether he had said something to offend them.

"How much is a day's pay at Dominguez', to get you all of this?" Joaquin asked. The other men were all glancing at each other, their expressions ranging from uncomfortable to furious.

"Well, the pay depends on the job," Artie confessed. "*Señor* Dominguez pays me as a skilled worker, because I've got a bit of experience and I'm training other people to do the job as well. I'm only doing three days per week, although sometimes I'll need to do other days or odd bits of overtime, but I'll get paid extra for that, so-"

"How much is Dominguez paying you, Arturo?" Marco snapped. "In money?"

There was a long silence. Everyone stared at Artie, who looked as though he wanted to scramble under his bed and stay there, but there was no escape.

"Eight pesos per month."

There was a sharp exhaling of breath from all around the group, and several of the men exchanged dark glances and shook their heads. Ed slid down off the bed and began pacing the floor, and Alejandro swore and took another swig from the bottle of pulque. Artie looked to Diego for support, but all he could do was shrug and pull a face to show that he didn't understand either.

"Vile, stinking *cabrón*," hissed Marco, snatching the pulque from Alejandro and taking a gulp of it himself.

"Hey," Paloma scolded. "I don't know what's rattled you today, boys, but I won't have you speaking to Artie like that, especially after he's spent his first wages on feeding us all. You take no notice, *hermanito*. I don't know what's got into them."

"I wasn't talking about Artie," Marco growled. "I was talking about that *cabrón* Don Raúl, gracing us with his presence at the mine today. Instead of the pay rise and improvement in conditions that we all petitioned for, he's going to do the opposite. And we're supposed to be grateful for it."

The other men grumbled angrily, and Diego felt his stomach give a little lurch. He knew how much the hope of a pay raise had meant to them all, Joaquin and Paloma especially with their wedding looming. He had been so sure that it was going to happen for them.

"No," Diego muttered. "That's not possible. I was told that the Dons were planning to give their miners a raise, to encourage more to come and work for them."

"Oh sí, they did," Alejandro laughed. "They've given the miners a raise. The so-called 'skilled' workers that they've imported from the United States, the foremen and the barreteros, operating the drills and the machinery, earning their *three pesos per day*. Three pesos! Us, though, we're Mexicans. We're not worth spit. We're just slaves, hauling the water, breaking the rocks, shovelling the ore. Crawling around in the dark underground, hauling two hundred pound sacks up those little log ladders. All the backbreaking stuff that those American *idiotas* don't want to do. And how much do we get paid for all that? Eighteen measly centavos a day!"

"Fifteen now," Marco corrected him with a snarl. "We're to sacrifice some of our pay to cover for this electric lighting they're bringing in. So now we're down to *fifteen* centavos a day, as if we can't afford to feed ourselves already."

Joaquin made a strange, strangled sound of frustration, and Marco clapped his hand over his mouth. Diego remembered that Joaquin had been trying to keep this information from Paloma, at least until he found a good time to tell her in private. He could see why now- she had been quiet and worried from the moment Marco had mentioned Don Raúl's visit, and at the news that the men's pay was being cut back she let out a little sound that was halfway between a gasp and a sob.

"They can't do that," she said in a tight voice. "Joaquin, please, they can't do that. What are we going to do?"

"We'll work it out, *mi vida*," he promised, pulling her onto his lap. "We'll work it out somehow."

Paloma burst into tears and buried her head in Joaquin's shoulder.

"We haven't quite got enough money for the marriage license yet," Joaquin explained, comforting Paloma as well as he could with his uninjured arm. "If it's not paid by the twenty-second, then..." he grimaced, and Diego knew what he was trying to say. The wedding would be off. They had waited for so long, and now it looked as though it would never happen.

Diego could feel Artie staring at him, and he turned away, trying to avoid his gaze. He knew what his brother was thinking. Their joint savings, every precious centavo they owned, was hidden in a tin beneath Diego's bed, ready for the day when they made their big break. Diego even had a chart working out an estimated date when they would have enough to do it. They had already had to chip into their fund once or twice for food, but there was still enough in there to cover the outstanding cost of Joaquin and Paloma's marriage license, and Diego knew Artie would never forgive him if he didn't offer it to them. It was the right thing to do, but knowing that it would put his own dream on hold for even longer stung like salt in a wound.

He finally met Artie's eye, and the boy shot a pointed look at the floorboard, then over at Joaquin, who was still holding a sobbing Paloma and stroking her hair, muttering words of comfort in her ear. Diego took a deep breath and nodded.

"Joaquin," he grunted. "Don't worry about the license. Artie and I can give you whatever you need to cover the shortfall. Consider it our wedding gift." The words stuck in his throat, but the relief on everyone else's faces made up for it.

"You're sure?" Paloma's eyes were pleading, a spark of hope returning to her.

"Of course," Artie promised her, and Diego smiled and nodded his assurance too. She squealed with relief, hugging each of them in turn, her cheeks wet with tears.

"I don't know how we can ever thank you," she gushed. "We'll pay you back when we can."

"Don't be silly," Diego hushed. "You don't need to worry about that. You just take care of each other, all right?"

"Sí," said Joaquin, putting his arm around her. "I think it's time we got some sleep, *mi vida*. It's another long day tomorrow."

He was wincing, and Diego suspected that his burned arm was hurting again. He took the bottle of pulque and handed it to him. If he couldn't do any more to heal the wound, at least he could give Joaquin something to dull the pain for tonight.

"That was good of you," Alejandro told him. "I know how much it means to you, *amigos*. Getting away from here, starting a new life with your music. We know you have to put your dreams on hold to help us all out, and it means a lot."

"Couldn't leave our *hermanos* to starve while we went off to get rich and famous," Artie grinned. "It would take the fun out of it."

"Still, you shouldn't have to give us your savings," Marco growled. "We're grown men in full-time work. It's humiliating, having to ask our *familia* to support us."

"You didn't ask, we offered," Artie reminded him.

"You shouldn't have needed to." Alejandro shook his head, picking up his bottle of pulque again. "It's disgusting, all that gold the Dons get from us, and it's still never enough. Now, apparently, we've got to use more dynamite in each blast to get the ore out faster. Our targets have increased, and we've got to meet them if any of us want to get paid. We're to use these new methods with all these toxic chemicals to leech the gold out of the ore, as if there weren't enough ways for us to die up there already. And all the time, for so little pay that we can barely afford to feed ourselves. It's wrong. Those mines belong to Mexico. To us. We should be the ones reaping the benefits."

"Sí, and the Dons know it," agreed Marco. "Why else would they be employing guards to search everyone as they leave? They want to make sure that nobody is leaving with any of that gold they're trying to keep for themselves."

"It's not just for that. It's to keep us in order, make sure we don't dare complain about our lot. By keeping us hungry, they make sure that we can't afford to strike." Ed ran his fingers through his hair. "Ay, if they'd not spent all that money employing guards and just used it to give us a pay raise instead, they wouldn't have needed the guards in the first place."

The men were silent for a long moment, all of them staring down at the floorboards. It was a hopeless situation. Diego had never had to work in a mine, but Artie had done it once. The memories still haunted him. He was always reluctant to talk about it, but Diego had often heard him cry out in his sleep as he relived his horrors, waking up in a cold sweat with tears on his cheeks.

"Someone needs to do something," Marco exploded. "Take a stand. We can't carry on like this."

"What are you suggesting?" Ed scoffed. "Another strike? You remember how the last one went?"

Diego did remember, and judging by Artie's involuntary shudder as he slid his hand inside his shirt to the scar on his side, he did too. Marco shook his head and leaned forward, lowering his voice to a gruff whisper.

"Don't know if you've heard." He glanced to the window to check that there was no movement outside. "But Madero is gaining support from his prison cell. The people are angry that Díaz rigged that election, and they're talking of revolution. If Díaz falls, the Dons fall with him. Social justice, at last, *amigos*. Fair pay. Fair conditions. Mexico for the Mexican people."

The other men were listening intently now, and Marco went on, his eyes burning with excitement.

"Alejandro, you could be a foreman of that mine, earning three pesos a day like the Americans. Ed, you'd never be turned down by a girl for being poor again, although I don't know if Madero could do anything to help your ugly face." The men laughed, and Marco turned to Artie, who was listening as though enchanted. "As for you, Arturo, you could be equal to the likes of Don Raúl. Never again would people sneer at you for being a foundling. You could even win the heart of that lovely *señorita* and take her as your wife."

Artie's eyes were shining, a look of breathless hope on his face. Diego, on the other hand, had heard his fill already.

"That's quite enough," he growled. "What do you think you're playing at, Marco, filling the lads' heads with all this rubbish? Do you even know what you're talking about?"

"*Sí, hermano.*" Marco's eyes twinkled with manic energy. "Revolution."

"Treason, you mean!" Diego hissed. "Do you have any idea what would happen to you, to *all* of us, if anyone heard you talking like this?"

"I'd rather die on my feet than live on my knees," Marco told him stubbornly, and Diego had to hold back from hitting him.

"You'll be dying at the end of a rope with that kind of idiotic talk," he snarled back. "You do as you please with your life, but don't you *dare* try to take everyone else down with you."

"Oh yes, because some great alternative we have in staying put!" Marco retorted, his voice rising. "Serving our whole lives as slaves to those who are rolling in money, as worthless as the dogs in the street. You think hanging is a threat to me? It would be sweet mercy compared to being trapped underground, dying slowly in agony." He shuddered in spite of himself and took another long, steadying gulp of pulque.

Something clicked in Diego's memory. Marco was terrified of small spaces. Diego had known this since they were children, but he had thought that he had been forced to get over it since starting work in the mines.

"So that's how you're planning to avoid suffocating underground?" he demanded. "You're going to get yourself hanged instead? Not the soundest plan you've ever had, *amigo*."

"I won't suffocate underground or hang," snapped Marco. "If it ever comes to it, I'll take things into my own hands before I let that happen."

Diego saw him pat his chest pocket with a shaking hand, as though reassuring himself that something was still there. His eyes narrowed. Now that he looked at it, there seemed to be a bulge in that pocket, a hint of something round and hard protruding through the thin fabric of his shirt.

"What's that you've got there, Marco?" Artie asked, noticing it too.

"Insurance." Marco reached into his pocket and held its contents up to the light. Diego had been right; it was a little bottle, filled with a clear liquid that glittered almost gold in the light of the oil lamp.

"Ay, I think I know what that is," whispered Alejandro, his eyes wide with horror. Ed was staring at Marco with a similar expression. "That's the chemical Don Raúl's had us using on the ore to get the metal out. What the hell are you doing with that, Marco?"

"Sodium cyanide," said Marco in a strange, trembling voice, staring at the little bottle as though hypnotized by it. "Just a drop of this could wipe out an entire army in less than five minutes, *amigos*. Quick and effective, so I'm told."

"Even you wouldn't be stupid enough to play with that stuff, Marco," Ed croaked. "If this is another one of your idiotic jokes, it's not funny."

"Don't believe me?" Marco gave a bitter laugh, bordering on hysterical now. He unstoppered the little bottle and held it out towards Ed. "Give that a sniff, *hermano*. Bitter almond. That's the smell of mercy. You ever heard the screams of a man dying an agonizing death, trapped in a collapsed mineshaft? I have. I swear to you, it will never be me."

Ed shuffled backward away from him until the back of his head bumped against the frame of Artie's bed. Sure enough, Diego could smell a waft of bitter almond even over the odour of sweaty men and roasted chicken that still lingered in the room. Marco certainly had not been joking about the bottle's contents, and he wore the expression of a man possessed.

"You will put the stopper back in that bottle and give it to me," Diego snarled, leaping from his bed and grabbing Marco by the scruff of the neck. "God, Marco, I could kill you myself. How stupid can you be? You're telling me that the Dons are employing guards to search people, and you think it's a good idea to steal their deadly chemicals and hide them in your pockets? You're mad."

He snatched the little bottle from Marco's hand. The glass was cold against his fingers, and Diego felt sick to think of what it contained. He turned and thrust it at Artie instead and felt the boy trembling as he took it.

"Hide this where nobody will ever find it," he instructed him, and Artie obliged. "As for you, Marco. Never, ever let me hear you talking like this again. You understand? Never. You ever get yourself trapped underground, know that your *hermanos* will march right up that mountain and dig you out, stone by stone if we must. There's enough in this world out to kill us already, without any of us doing deliberate injury to ourselves. I refuse to lose you. Any of you. Understand?"

He grasped Marco by the shoulders and shook him, forcing him to meet his gaze.

"I don't want to have to live on your charity," Marco said in a broken voice. "I don't want to break my back working all day every day and still not earn enough to live. I want to do a fair day's work for a fair day's pay. Is that so much to ask?"

"It shouldn't be, no," Diego agreed. "But we have to stick together if we're going to survive. Not go risking our necks with talk of revolution and carrying poison around in our pockets. We're no good to each other dead."

"Ay, you're right. I know. I'm sorry, *hermanos*. I'm sorry." His voice broke again, and he threw his arms around Diego's neck with a choked sob.

Diego wasn't sure what to do with this. He wasn't normally the sort of person to engage in physical affection, but on this occasion, he permitted it, reaching around to give Marco an awkward pat on the back. Truth be told, he felt a little shaky himself. Artie was the emotional, sensitive one of the group, and occasionally Ed when he had drunk too much. Not Marco, though. *Never* Marco.

Diego turned to Ed and Alejandro, who had both been watching with a mixture of horror and concern.

"You two, take him home and put him to bed. We'll forget that this little conversation ever happened, all right? Just keep an eye on him over the next few days and come straight to me if he says or does anything that concerns you. We need to look after each other, now more than ever." Diego helped the three of them to the door, where he checked that nobody was around before gesturing them back to their own hut across the street. "I'll see you tomorrow, boys. Get a good night's sleep."

He closed the door with a click, drew the bolt across and leaned back against it with an exhausted sigh. When he opened his eyes again, Artie was tidying up the bowls and bottles and storing them away in the sideboard, his face turned so that Diego could not see his expression. There was no sign of the little bottle, which Diego guessed Artie must have already hidden. Good. He didn't want to know where it was, or ever have to think about it again if he could help it.

The shabby little hut felt peaceful and empty now that everyone else was gone, and Diego took a moment to regain his bearings. He closed the splintered shutters on the window and tucked his boots underneath his rickety iron bed before pulling aside the floorboard and taking out his little tin of savings. His heart sinking with dread, he opened the little book that he used to keep his records and began to calculate, the numbers swimming around in his head until they made him feel dizzy. It was too late for this, and he was too tired, but he knew he wouldn't be able to sleep until he at least tried.

By the time he had finished, Artie had already undressed and was lying on his back on his bed at the other end of the room, wrapped in a ragged blanket. Diego could see that he was not asleep. His eyes stared up at the ceiling, as though lost in deep thought.

"You all right, *hermano*?" Diego asked softly.

"Mmm," Artie grunted, still staring upwards. Diego put out the oil lamp, and the two of them lay on their beds in the dark silence for a few minutes, neither able to sleep.

"Diego," said Artie at last. "Would you mind if I didn't play in the plaza on Thursday afternoon if I agree to play in the evening instead?"

"*Sí*, I suppose so." Diego knew that if he said no, Artie would likely do it anyway. Besides, the footfall in the plaza might be better in the evening. With the little money they earned playing on a Thursday afternoon at the best of times, it was worth giving the evening a try to see if takings were any better. "Why? What have you got to do on Thursday afternoon?"

"I'm going to help Esperanza with her shopping." Artie's voice was dreamy, and Diego couldn't help but groan.

"Wonderful. Why is it that all of my brothers seem so intent on dying young?"

"Is shopping with women really that dangerous?"

"It is when the woman in question is being lined up to marry Don Raúl, sí."

"I'm not afraid of Don Raúl," Artie assured him. "I'll be careful, though, if that's what you're worried about."

"I'm not worried about that," Diego grumbled. "I'm worried about having to kill you myself for keeping me awake all night bleating on about the Dominguez girl."

Diego heard Artie laugh in the darkness and couldn't help but smile. Normally he would have voiced stronger objections to his brother wanting to discuss a topic he so disapproved of, but tonight, it was better that he went to sleep dreaming of love rather than the horrors of the mines.

"She said that I'm her friend," Artie told him sleepily, and Diego could tell even in the dark that he was smiling.

"Well, I say that you're an idiot."

"Ay, you're probably right, Diego. You're probably right."

CHAPTER TEN

Esperanza never thought she would see the day when she enjoyed doing her mother's shopping, but as she weaved around the stalls in the plaza with Artie carrying her basket, the whole experience became a lot more fun. Artie could bring life into even the most mundane of things, and Esperanza laughed as he told her anecdotes about his and Diego's adventures, ignoring the people who pointed at them and whispered behind their hands.

"...they told us they wanted us to play after the speeches had been made," he explained as they perused a stall selling a rainbow of coloured ribbons, "but nobody warned us how many speeches there would be. Well, of course, speeches lead to toasts, and toasts involve wine. I was only a boy, I had never really had wine before. I had no idea how strong it was, and I was so nervous about performing that my throat had dried out, so I wasn't taking little sips. Someone kept refilling my glass between each toast. By the time Diego realized, it was too late. It was time to play, and I couldn't stand. I barely knew which way up to hold the guitar."

Esperanza laughed. His voice was so expressive, his words so animated, she could picture the scene as though she had been right there watching it.

"What did you do?" she asked, her eyes shining with amusement. "I bet Diego was furious with you!"

"Oh, he was," mused Artie. "Of course, I don't remember any of it, but Diego never tires of reminding me of what happened. He couldn't get me to balance on my stool without toppling over. In the end, he had to take his belt off and use it to tie himself to me, back-to-back, to keep me upright. I kept trying to get up and dance, and of course, that forced him to stand up too. I dragged him backward all around the stage with me. All while he was trying to play."

"Oh no!" Tears brimmed in Esperanza's eyes as she laughed harder. People were turning to look at her now, trying to work out what was so funny and eyeing up Artie with suspicion. "What about the wedding party? Were they really angry?"

"No, actually." Artie tipped his head on one side in thought, a mischievous smile on his face. "They thought it was hilarious. We earned a fortune in tips that night. I don't think they realized we were supposed to be a serious act."

"I can picture Diego's face!" Esperanza wiped her eyes, struggling to catch her breath. Just as she gained control over herself, she caught Artie's eye again and they both burst into fresh laughter.

"You... you have the most beautiful laugh, señorita," he told her, shaking his head as he wiped his eyes.

"I'm glad you like it. I've never laughed so much until I met you." She grinned at him, unable to hide her affection, and his eyes softened as he smiled back. The lady who owned the ribbon stall glared at them both, irritated that they were keeping her from her embroidery and silently threatening them to either buy something or leave her in peace.

"Esperanza?" came a sharp, familiar voice from behind them. They both turned to see *Tía* Victoria standing there, eyeing Artie up and down with great suspicion, her thick spectacles balanced delicately on her birdlike nose.

"*Tía* Victoria," Esperanza stammered in alarm. "I- I thought you would be in your shop today."

"I was. I just popped out to pick up some more ribbon. For your dress, actually, *mija*. The one your *mamá* has asked me to fix up for your evening with Don Raúl."

Esperanza's heart sank at the mention of Raúl's name, and she saw Artie lower his eyes to the ground in respect. *Tía* Victoria still had not taken her beady eyes off of him, and now she began to circle him, her lips pursed as she assessed him with an accusatory glare.

"And who might you be, young man?"

"My name is Arturo, *señora*," he replied, bowing.

"Are you not the *músico* I've seen playing in the square recently?" Her eyes narrowed, and she did not allow him time to reply. "What would a *músico* be doing wandering around the town with my niece, I might ask?"

"I have just started working for *Señor* Dominguez," he told her, bowing again. "I help out a few days per week when I'm not playing in the plaza."

Victoria's face brightened.

"Ah! So Juan has finally decided to employ a servant or two. About time, especially if you are associating with the aristocracy now." She regarded Esperanza with a proud smile. "It looks much better for you to have a servant with you to carry things and ward off any undesirable company. *Mija*, you can tell your father that I approve. Although he should have at least picked an ugly one so that he didn't risk making Don Raúl jealous. Still, a little jealousy can be a good thing sometimes. It can hurry a man along a bit with his intentions."

She winked at Esperanza, picking up a reel of soft gold ribbon and holding it up to the light.

"Look here, *mija*. Gold, to compliment your red dress. Your *mamá* thought that it would be a nice idea to dress you in the colours of Don Raúl's coat of arms. We thought it might make you look more as though you fit into his family, send him a hidden message, so to speak."

Esperanza forced her lips into a strangled smile and made a strange choking noise that she hoped sounded like an endorsement. It seemed to be good enough for *Tía* Victoria because she paid for the gold ribbon with a smile and headed back towards her shop.

As soon as she had gone, Esperanza turned on Artie with an angry snarl.

"Why did you tell my aunt that you were my *servant*?" she demanded. "Why would you say something like that?"

Artie shrugged.

"I didn't tell her any such thing," he reminded her. "I told her I work for your father, which is true. It was she who assumed that I was a servant. I just didn't correct her."

"No, you didn't." She was furious, although even she wasn't quite sure why. "Did you think that was the reason I came to meet you today? Because I wanted a servant? I wanted to spend time with you as my *friend*, Artie. If that's not why you're here, then I'd rather you go away. Like I told you the other day, I don't need your help, and I certainly don't need your *servitude*."

She tried to snatch her basket back, but he stopped her, putting a gentle hand on her arm.

"What do you think your mother would say about you being friends with me, Esperanza?" he asked, his eyes shining. "Or Don Raúl, for that matter? As much as I hate the thought of you with a man like him, I've got no right to stand in the way of your family's plans for you. The last thing I want to do is get you into trouble, and we both know that Don Raúl would not like the thought of us being friends."

"Well, I don't like the thought of *him*," she snapped. "We're even."

"That's just it, though. We're not even, are we? You're a lady, and I'm a street musician. If I'm going to spend time with you without people's tongues wagging, I can't just walk around with my arm in yours for everyone to see. Word would get back to your mother in minutes. But if you're seen with one of your father's servants, carrying your basket for you and helping you with your heavy shopping... well, that's different. It would be quite normal for a lady like you to have a servant to help her out, nobody would take any notice. If serving you is the only way that I can spend time with you, then it's a sacrifice I'll gladly make."

He looked so sincere that Esperanza felt her anger fading away almost as quickly as it had arrived. She sighed and put a gentle hand on his arm, checking that nobody was watching.

"All right. I understand. Don't look at me like that, I'm not angry at you. But I can't treat you like my servant, Artie. I just can't. I couldn't even pretend to think of you like that. I don't want anyone else to, either." There was sadness in his smile, and she felt her heart ache a little at the sight. "I agree with you that we need to behave appropriately. *As friends.* But if anyone else asks, that is what I will tell them you are to me. My friend. Not my servant, not now, not ever."

"All right," he agreed, nodding. "On your own head be it though, *señorita.*"

They continued their shopping trip in peace, and afterwards, Artie walked Esperanza back to the farm. They took the route along the river rather than the main road, which allowed Esperanza some time alone with him to listen to his stories and tell him some of her own. He laughed as she recounted all of the times that she had needed to take Miguel to see Doctor Francisco because of his obscure talent for getting strange objects stuck in his ears, and she found it just as amusing to hear about his past antics with the other street boys as they were growing up. The walk went by much faster than she would have liked, even though they had not been hurrying, and it felt like no time at all before they reached the gates to her father's farmland and had to say goodbye.

He met her by the river on Monday as promised, then in town on Thursday, then repeated the pattern the following week. Most of July passed in this fashion until one particularly hot Monday afternoon when Juan decided to allow the men to finish early.

Esperanza still had other chores to finish upstairs before she could take the laundry down to the river, so she wasn't surprised to see from her window that Artie had been persuaded to join in a game of *ulama* with the other men. This had become a regular after-work activity for the farmhands, and what Artie lacked in skill, he made up for in enthusiasm. She paused to watch him from her bedroom window, shaking her head in amusement at the familiar sight of him lunging for the ball and missing. He had improved since the first game she had watched, although he still had a long way to go before his skills were anywhere near those of the more seasoned players such as Jorge and Ricardo. Esperanza was pleased that Artie seemed to be fitting in so well with them. She just hoped that their friendship didn't leave him crippled, which she feared might be the case if his ball skills did not improve.

She busied herself with stripping her bed, shaking out the new sheets before throwing them across her mattress. A loud cheer from outside told her that someone had scored a point, and she smiled. Why men got so excited over sport she could never understand, but she could not help finding it quite endearing. She had never been able to stomach bullfighting or boxing, but a ball game she could learn to enjoy watching. Perhaps Artie might explain the rules to her later, assuming that he understood them himself.

She folded each corner of the sheet, tucking it neatly under the mattress, and stood back frowning at her handiwork. Something was not right, although she couldn't quite put her finger on what. The sheet was clean, the corners folded to perfection. All looked as it should.

It took her a moment to realize that the problem was not what she could see, but what she could hear. The cheering from outside was still going. Surely, though, even for the best of shots this was too long for anyone to be celebrating. The more she listened, the less it sounded like cheering; it was too angry.

She went to the window again. The farmhands were standing almost in a circle surrounding three men in the middle of the pitch; young Ricardo, who was doubled over on the ground, her father's old friend Roberto who was towering over the young man like an angry bull, and Artie, who stood between them. The men around the outside of the circle appeared to be shouting at Roberto, who seemed to find the whole thing most amusing. He and Artie were squared up to one another, both refusing to back down, and the sight made Esperanza feel as though her heart had stopped. It was like watching a twig picking a fight with a tree. What on Earth was he thinking?

After what felt like hours, Roberto finally caved to the pressure of the other men and backed off, waving his hands at Artie in casual surrender. Artie turned around and offered a hand to Ricardo, helping him to his feet and giving him a friendly pat on the shoulder to reassure him. The men retook their positions ready to restart the game, but Esperanza fixed her eyes on Roberto with a deep feeling of trepidation. She had known him for a long time, not well, but well enough to know that he would not allow any conflict to end in his own humiliation. This was not over.

The game restarted, and this time Esperanza did not take her eyes from the pitch. It was a lot more aggressive than the last few times she had seen them play, and although she knew that she did not understand the rules at the best of times, she suspected that in this particular match, it didn't matter. The rule book had been discarded long ago.

The ball flew from man to man, so fast that Esperanza struggled to keep track of it. She kept her eyes on Roberto, too afraid to blink. He was edging over to the side of the court where Artie stood, and although his face was turned away from him, Esperanza did not doubt that the direction he was moving in was far from coincidental. Artie was oblivious to his approach, almost hopping up and down on the spot in anticipation as the ball came over towards his part of the pitch, and Esperanza felt a desperate urge to fling open the window and shout a warning down to him.

The ball hurtled towards Artie, and Roberto seized his opportunity. Esperanza screamed as both men jumped at once, Roberto's huge hulking body colliding painfully with Artie's thin frame and sending the younger man sprawling on the ground some distance away, where he lay motionless in the dust. The other men were shouting again, most surrounding Roberto who was laughing. Ricardo and Jorge ran to Artie and rolled him over, blocking her view of his face, but she caught sight of a flash of scarlet on the ground beside him and knew that he was hurt.

Esperanza flew down the stairs and into the kitchen, almost knocking her father flat as she tried to get out of the front door.

"Mija? Hey!" He caught her by the shoulders. "Are you all right? I heard you scream."

"No, I am *not* all right," she snapped, tears of fury burning her eyes. She grabbed a couple of clean cloths and a bowl. If Artie was bleeding, then there was a good chance he would be needing them. "Your friend Roberto is a thug and a bully. I've just watched him hurt two of the younger men and *laugh* about it. I don't know why you let him get away with this sort of thing, *papá*. He needs to be thrown back in jail where he belongs."

"Calm down, *mija*. I'm sure there's a reasonable explanation." Juan was as cool as ever, and it only served to make Esperanza angrier. She pushed past him and stormed outside. Most of the men had already dispersed, grumbling with frustration, and Artie was nowhere to be seen. Roberto was still there, though, leaning against the fence with a twisted grin on his lopsided face and a small silver flask in his hand. He turned as Esperanza and Juan as they approached, and she could see gold glinting at her from between his blackened teeth.

"*Amigo,*" Juan smiled with an exasperated sigh, stepping out behind her. "My daughter thinks that she just saw you deliberately hurting two of the younger lads. Tell me, is there any truth in this?"

"*Sí,* of course," Roberto boasted. "We were playing *ulama.* You know what that can be like, *amigo.* It gets rough sometimes. The lads knew that when they agreed to play. Not my fault if they get in my way. It's all part of the game."

He took a swig from his flask, flashing Esperanza an unpleasant grin.

"There you are then, *mija,*" Juan shrugged. "You wanted an explanation, and Roberto has given one."

"But *papá-*"

"Enough, now. Go and get on with your chores. I'll hear no more about it." Juan nodded to his friend and walked off back towards the house without so much as a backward glance at her. Esperanza felt her cheeks burning with fury. Roberto raised his flask to her with a grin and staggered away towards the stables, where Esperanza betted he planned on taking a nap before crawling back to the hole he came from. She felt a sudden jolt of panic. Where was Artie? Had he headed back to the stables too, and was he about to be confronted by Roberto again, this time alone and with no witnesses to intervene?

"Ricardo," she called, spotting the young man sitting on the ground nearby looking a little worse for wear. "Where's Artie? Is he all right? Which way did he go?"

Ricardo pointed nervously down towards the river, and Esperanza felt her shoulders drop with relief. He had headed to their usual meeting spot, not back to the stables.

"He was bleeding a bit, *señorita,*" Ricardo mumbled. "Took a bit of a whack to the head, too, he was out cold there for a second. You're right about that thug Roberto, though. Be careful, or he'll have it in for you next."

"Good luck to him if he tries, Ricardo," she growled.

CHAPTER ELEVEN

Esperanza hurried down towards the river, trying not to attract too much attention as she snuck around the back of the barn and down the slope towards the bank of trees. Occasional spots of blood in the grass told her that Artie had indeed come this way, and she found herself almost running by the time she reached the clearing, bursting through the foliage with such force that she tripped on a protruding root and fell headlong into the grass.

Artie sat slumped against the large oak tree, holding his nose between his thumb and index finger. His shirt, which was still tied around his hips, was now soaked with crimson blood that dribbled down his chin and dripped onto his bare chest. She stumbled over to the tree and fell to her knees beside him, taking his free hand in hers. He looked up at her through thick, dark strands of hair and gave her hand a gentle squeeze.

"Ith arrite," he croaked, seeing the panic in her eyes. "By node ith beeding, dass all. I'be arrite, Epperantha."

He smiled weakly, and she narrowed her eyes, staring deep into his. His gaze was a little unfocussed, his speech slurred, although she reminded herself that it could just be because of his nose.

"Let me take a look," she ordered. "I want to make sure it's not broken."

He looked up at her again, and after a moment, nodded gingerly and removed his hand from his nose. It was still dripping with blood, but Esperanza was pleased to see that it was straight and unbroken.

"You'll be fine," she reassured him. "Let me just go and get you a wet cloth. The cold water will help to stop the bleeding."

She left him for a moment to fetch the bowl that she had brought with her, soaking a couple of cloth strips and bringing them back over to the tree with a fresh bowl of water. She instructed him to hold one of the cloths against his nose and squeeze to ease the bleeding, while she used another to wash the blood from his hands. He watched her with a dazed expression, allowing her to clean each of his fingers in turn before turning his hand over to run the cloth over his palm and wrist.

"You're trembling," she told him.

"I'be arrite," he told her through the bloody cloth, closing his fingers around hers again. He winced and released his nose, checking that the dripping had stopped before relaxing his arm. Now he could speak more clearly again, although his voice still sounded thick and faint. "It's only a bit of blood, I'll be fine in a minute. We were just playing a game. I ran into one of the other men."

"Sí, I know." She raised a disapproving eyebrow. "What did Roberto do that made you choose to pick a fight with him?"

Artie's guilty eyes met hers. He had obviously not been planning to tell her about his issues with Roberto, but as she had already seen enough with her own eyes to raise her suspicions, he knew that he would not be able to fool her into believing that all was fine.

"Roberto slept right through until *comida* today, and Rafael noticed him missing, so he came looking for him in the stables," Artie confessed. "He asked Ricardo how long Roberto had been in there, and Ricardo couldn't lie to him. The old man told Roberto he'd dock him half a day's pay for missing half a day's work. Roberto was livid, he told Ricardo he'd get revenge on him later. Poor lad spent the rest of the day petrified. That's why we both agreed to join in the game, in the hope that Roberto would have got bored and left for home by the time we'd finished."

"But Roberto didn't go home, he joined the game," Esperanza finished.

"Sí," Artie confirmed. "The game changed the minute he joined, it all became very aggressive. The next thing I knew, Ricardo was on the ground with Roberto's boot in his stomach. He wasn't even looking at the ball, just going for the kid."

"So you intervened?" Esperanza shook her head with a disapproving sigh. Secretly, though, she had to admit that she was impressed. She had known far bigger men than Artie back down to Roberto in the past, knowing how nasty he could be, but it seemed that what the boy lacked in physical stature he made up for in bravery. Or perhaps stupidity; it was hard to tell.

"How could I not intervene? I was the one who suggested that we should play in the first place. It was my fault we were even there. I couldn't very well just leave him there on the ground while Roberto kicked his head in, I had to do something."

"Those nuns certainly picked the right name for you," Esperanza mused. "*Courageous*. Although perhaps they should have picked one that meant *suicidal*, too. You know what you've let yourself in for, making an enemy of Roberto Hernandez?"

"I don't think today made much difference. Let's just say he disliked me already. I didn't have much to lose." There was a trace of bitterness in his voice, and he lowered his gaze to the ground, drawing his knees up towards his chest. Esperanza tilted his chin to make him look at her.

"Artie, are you telling me that this isn't the first time?"

His hesitation confirmed her suspicions. He tried to look away again, but she kept her eyes locked with his, her thumb stroking his cheek.

"Nothing you need to worry about," he reassured her. "It's mostly just hot air. Harmless words. It's not just me. Most of the other men get the same from him. I'd feel left out otherwise." He gave her a weak smile, which she did not return.

"That vile *cabrón*," she swore. "It's not harmless words, Artie. Look at you."

"I'm all right, Esperanza. It's just a bloody nose, I've had far worse. It's nothing, it doesn't even hurt. I'm just thankful they only had a leather ball to play with. Ricardo says that proper *ulama* is played with a hard rubber ball. Roberto could've given me far worse injuries with that."

"Hmm." She dipped her cloth in the water, wrung it out and began to clean the blood from his face. He gazed up at her and nuzzled his cheek into her palm, and she felt a tingle of affection shoot through her chest.

"Harmless words," she said again, brushing his bruised cheekbone tenderly with her thumb. "You be careful, Artie. There's no such thing as harmless words from that man. He's a filthy bully."

Artie laughed and flashed her a wicked grin.

"Well, you know what they say about bullies." His eyes sparkled with mischief. "They have to pick on others to make themselves feel big. It helps them to compensate for their small... um..." He faltered, reconsidering what he was about to say. "Actually, never mind."

His cheek grew warm against her hand, and he gave a small chuckle of amusement, closing his eyes and leaning back against the tree.

"To compensate for their lack of size in other more private areas?" Esperanza finished for him, raising her eyebrows. Artie's eyelids snapped back open, and he spluttered with surprised laughter at her crudeness.

"Esperanza! There was me thinking that you were a lady. For your information, I was going to say *brains*." He regarded her with mock horror, his own eyebrows raised in feigned disapproval.

"I knew exactly what you were going to say. And for *your* information, I am a lady, but I am not a nun." She winked. For all of her mother's efforts to teach her to behave properly, she had spent enough time around the farmhands to have learned a little from their sense of humour.

Artie stared at her for a second, then burst out laughing, causing a few fresh drops of blood to run down from his nose to his chin. Esperanza laughed too, glad that he did not seem to mind her inappropriateness. It was refreshing to say as she pleased, to be herself without worrying that she would be judged or scolded for it.

She reached up to wipe the fresh blood from his face, her fingers tender as they brushed over his lips. They parted at her touch. He stopped laughing and stared up at her, his eyes glowing. His breath was warm and ragged against her hand, and she felt his trembling fingers reach up to brush a stray lock of hair away from her face. His palm lingered on her cheekbone, and she suddenly felt as though she was falling into those big chestnut eyes.

"I- I should go and wash these cloths," she stammered, tearing her gaze away from his. He nodded and lowered his hand from her face, still looking at her with that expression of fascinated wonder.

She cleared her throat and stood up, distracting herself with the bloodied cloth. Her heart was pounding, and she willed herself to calm down, feeling strangely light and giddy as though it were she and not Artie who had taken a knock to the head.

She felt a thrill of satisfaction to see that their near-kiss had affected Artie as much as it had her. He took a few steadying breaths to calm himself, his hand pressed to his heart as though worried it was trying to escape from his chest. Then he stumbled over to the water's edge and squatted on a rock to splash his face with water. The loss of blood had affected his balance, however, and after a second, Esperanza heard a loud splash followed by a quiet curse. She turned to see him sitting waist-deep in the cold water, his skin soaked and his hair dripping down his face in thick, wet strands. She burst out laughing, unable to hold back despite his grumpy expression.

"That's one way to cool down," she giggled, wiping tears of laughter from her eyes as she offered him a hand. Artie had other ideas, though. His eyes narrowed, twinkling with mischief as she approached.

"Oh, so you think it's funny, do you, *señorita*?" he growled. "I'll show you how funny it is. C'mere."

She squealed with laughter and sprang back as he lunged for her, trying to pull her in after him, but his balance failed him again and he fell headfirst back into the water, spluttering and cursing. This was somehow even funnier than the first time he had fallen in, although this time she couldn't help feeling a little guilty for laughing as he sat in the shallow water shaking his wet hair from his eyes like a dog. She kicked off her shoes and rolled up her skirt before wading into the water to help him up, plopping him back down onto the rock where he sat and shivered.

"Here," she said to him, handing him the blanket she kept in the hollowed-out tree for them to sit on while they waited for the laundry to dry. "Wrap this around you, and give me your clothes. They could do with a wash anyway, seeing as you got blood all over them."

Artie accepted the blanket with a grateful nod, wrapping it around his waist like a skirt. She turned away to offer him some privacy as he reached underneath to untie his rope belt and peel the dripping fabric from his skin. When she turned back and held out her hand for him to pass the clothes to her, though, he faltered and stepped back.

"I can wash them myself, Esperanza," he said, shaking his head and holding the dripping fabric close to his chest. "You're a lady. You're not my wife. I can't ask you to do my laundry."

"You're not asking. I'm offering, as your friend." She stepped towards him and took the clothes, the firmness of her tone telling him that there was no point in resisting. "I may not be your wife, but if I am to end up married soon, I'll be damned if I'll do it for the likes of *him* and not you."

Artie did not argue. They were both silent for a few minutes, the unwelcome spectre of Don Raúl looming between them like a bad smell. Esperanza cursed herself for mentioning it, for reminding herself of the world that still existed outside of this clearing.

Artie watched her from his seat on the rock, his eyes cast down at the water. She could not bring herself to look at him but instead busied herself with scrubbing the bloodstains from his shirt.

"So... your meal with Don Raúl is still going ahead on Wednesday, then." Artie tried to keep his voice breezy, but the pain in his eyes gave him away.

"Sí," Esperanza snapped, a little more abruptly than she meant to. "And you can stop looking at me like that. You know I don't want to go, but the matter is already settled between my parents and Don Lorenzo. I don't have a choice."

He flinched as though she had slapped him. She knew she was being unreasonable by being angry at him; after all, she had been the one to mention Don Raúl. Still, what did he want her to say? That she would disobey her parents, refuse Don Raúl and marry him instead, as though that were an option?

She glared over at him, softening in spite of herself as she saw the desolation in his face. Taking her anger out on him felt like kicking a puppy; guilt crept over her, and she sighed. It wasn't really Artie she was angry with. It was the rest of the world.

"Artie," she said, at last, throwing the dripping trousers over the tree branch and turning back to sit on the rock beside him. "I'm sorry. I know that none of this is your fault. It wasn't fair of me to snap at you like that. I just want you to understand that it's not my fault either. I have no say in what happens next. All I know is that right here, right now, it's just you and me... and I'm happy. Let that be enough."

She reached out and squeezed his hand. He looked up into her eyes and gave her a gentle smile in return.

"I'm sorry I upset you," he breathed, drawing her hand up to his lips and kissing it. "We don't have to talk about it anymore. I think I might have something to cheer you up, though. Wait here."

He stood, still a little unsteady on his feet, and disappeared among the trees for a second. When he returned, she was surprised to see him holding a single red rose. Its velvety petals were a deep shade of crimson, just about on the cusp of opening into a large bloom, and she could smell its sweet scent even from where he was standing. She gasped.

"Happy birthday," he grinned. "For tomorrow."

She gaped at him.

"Thank you. How did you know?"

He shrugged.

"I made it my business to know. Here." He twirled the rose between his fingers and then reached out and tucked it into her hair, just behind her ear. "Beautiful, as always."

"Well, it's very sweet of you. Thank you."

She wrapped her arms around his chest in a gentle hug, careful to tilt her head so that she didn't crush the rose.

"It was my pleasure." He wrapped his own arms around her in return. She breathed in the soft, citrusy scent of his warm skin, suddenly aware of how little he was wearing. His heart was thumping fast against her cheek, his ribs rising and falling against hers, and she felt one of his hands stroking her hair as the other pulled her a little tighter against him. She gave a quiet giggle and unwillingly pulled away.

"What?" he asked, reluctant to let her go.

"I was just picturing my mother's face if she walked into this clearing right now and saw me in the arms of an almost-naked man wearing nothing but a floral skirt made from her favorite picnic blanket. I don't think she'd ever recover."

They both giggled, and Artie adjusted his makeshift skirt with an embarrassed grin.

"When is *your* birthday, Artie?" she asked, trying to distract herself from the odd tingling sensation that had taken hold of her body. She sat down on the grass, and he joined her, considering the question.

"I don't know," he said after a moment. "I've never had one. My parents left no note with me to say what the actual date was."

Esperanza cringed. She should have known that; he had told her before that there had been no note left with him at the convent. It was a stupid question to ask.

"I do have some idea, though," he told her, sensing her guilt and trying to ease it. "I was found on the nineteenth of April, in the year eighteen ninety. The nuns said that I was very young, no more than a few days old."

"Perhaps you could adopt the nineteenth of April as your birthday, then," Esperanza suggested, but Artie shook his head.

"The day I was abandoned? No, it's much too sad. I don't want to celebrate that date." He shuddered, and she cringed again. Of course he wouldn't want to celebrate the day he was abandoned. What was she thinking?

"When would you have it, then?" she asked him.

"The seventeenth of June." His response was instant, as though he had already spent a long time considering the topic. "It's the day I met you for the very first time when we were children. If I had to pick a birthday, I'd pick that one hands down."

She laughed at his earnestness. Of course he would pick that day; she should have guessed. His clothes were dry now, and she passed them to him, shaking her head with a smile of affection.

"Do you think I'm an *idiota*?" he asked, his chestnut eyes sparkling up at her.

"*Sí*," she teased him. "I do. But here's a belated birthday present anyway." She brushed his hair from his face, reached across and planted a loving kiss on his cheek. She felt the heat rising in his face before she had even moved her lips away, and when she stood back, she saw that he had closed his eyes and was wearing a breathless smile. She laughed again and gave him a gentle push back onto the grass.

"Go and put your clothes on, you fool," she giggled, and he obeyed.

Once fully dressed again, Artie helped Esperanza to collect her things and they sat together to re-tie their shoes before heading back up to the farm.

"Same arrangement next week, *señorita*?" he asked her, his voice brimming with hope. "If I promise not to bleed next time and try to keep my clothes on?"

"Unfortunately not."

"No? All right, well I can take my clothes off if you insist."

"You know that's not what I meant." She swung playfully at his head, laughing as he ducked away, grinning. "You can take your clothes off next week if you want to, but I won't be here to wash them for you. I'm busy this Thursday, too. I've got rehearsals for a dance performance I've got coming up. Then next Thursday, I'll be helping the other women to make *papel picado* for the Festival of Santa Sofia."

"So I won't see you for another *two weeks*?" Artie looked crestfallen. "I'm not sure I can survive that long."

"You'll see me next Saturday if you're going to be at the festival," she reminded him. "That's what I'm rehearsing for, I'll be dancing in the plaza with a few of the other girls."

"Sí, I'll be there," he promised. "Diego and I will be playing in the music competition. Will you stay to watch, after you've finished dancing? I could do with the moral support, to be honest. Diego has been making plans for what he wants to do with the prize money already. Talk about pressure." He grimaced.

"Of course." She put a reassuring hand on his shoulder. "I'll be there. And then, just two days later, it will be Monday again, and we can spend all evening down here to make up for the time we've missed."

"You admit you'll miss me, then?" he asked, his eyes twinkling with hope.

"No," she shrugged back with a teasing grin. "We'll just have an awful lot of laundry to catch up on, that's all."

CHAPTER TWELVE

Artie had not expected to see Esperanza again that week, given that she did not come down to the barn to set out the food for the men's *comida* on Tuesday. As it was her birthday, the family were all up at the house sharing a special meal, and Artie lacked any inclination to go up to the barn knowing that she would not be there.

Instead, he and Ricardo sat together in the stable's peaceful silence, sharing some of the fruit that they had picked from the trees on their way down. Juan had far more fruit growing on the farm than he could ever sell at the market, so it was no loss for him to allow the men to take some for themselves and their families. For all of Diego's griping about how they didn't have as much time for their music anymore, he couldn't pretend that the extra food wasn't welcome.

Artie felt bad for Diego. Since the fateful day of his brothers' pay cut, funds had been tight. Artie's salary was good but not good enough to support himself, his six brothers and Paloma. Diego had been forced to get himself a job at Don Lorenzo's *hacienda*, of all places. He never spoke about it, and Artie never asked. He suspected that the Dons probably didn't provide their workers with proper breaks, let alone food, and he didn't want to rub salt into the wound by reminding his brother of how good he had it working for Dominguez.

At least they both worked the same three days each week, so they could still play in the plaza together on their days off, but Artie knew his brother was waiting for the day when they could leave Santa Sofia behind and start on their path to stardom. Diego talked of little else, especially after a long day working for the Dons, and Artie found his own heart breaking a little more every time he thought about it.

He was so lost in thought that he almost forgot that Ricardo was there until the boy suddenly gripped his arm. There was a soft snuffling sound coming from one of the empty stalls at the end of the stable, accompanied by the soft shuffle of straw as something moved. The sounds were too human to be one of the farm cats, and Artie knew exactly what Ricardo was thinking.

Roberto.

The two men hardly dared to breathe. The snuffling sound came again, and Ricardo's grip on Artie's arm tightened. Together they crept towards the stable, bracing themselves to either fight or run if the necessity arose. The sound was coming from a mound of hay in the corner, which seemed to be quivering and making small whimpering noises. Artie crept into the stall and gave the little haystack a tentative nudge with his boot. It gave a gasp, and a pair of large, brown eyes peeked out at him from within.

"...Miguel?" Artie whispered, and the haystack quivered again. "Hey, *chamaco*. Are you all right? What are you doing in here?"

He bent down and brushed the hay aside, revealing the little boy cowering beneath. Miguel's eyes were red from crying, and he drew back towards the wall in fear when Artie pulled away his hiding place.

"Is it just you?" he asked in a choked whimper.

"Me and Ricardo. Just us," Artie reassured him. To his surprise, the little boy scrambled forward and threw his arms around his waist in a tight hug. Artie froze, unsure what to do. Miguel was different from the street children; he had parents to take care of him, a loving home. Still, a crying child was a crying child, and Artie's paternal instincts took over. He gathered up the sobbing boy and pulled him onto his lap, making calming noises to soothe him.

"What's all this about, *chamaco*?" he asked, rubbing the little boy's back as Miguel sobbed into his shirt. "Are you hurt?"

"N-no," Miguel hiccupped. "But I will be next time."

"Next time? Are you in some sort of trouble?" Artie pulled back and peered into Miguel's eyes with concern. "Trouble with your parents?"

Miguel shook his head, still clinging to the front of Artie's shirt.

"One of your school friends, then? Another boy?" Artie pressed him, but Miguel shook his head again. "Talk to me, Miguel. I want to help you. Whatever this is about, we can sort it out."

The little boy's face crumpled and he buried his face in Artie's chest again.

"Please don't ask me," he quivered, his voice thick and muffled. "He said I wasn't allowed to tell."

He let out a little wail, a fresh wave of sobs wracking his little body.

"All right." Artie hugged the child close, making soothing sounds again until the sobs subsided and his small frame began to relax. "*Chamaco*, you're always welcome down here with us. But aren't you supposed to be up at the house for your sister's birthday meal today?"

"No. We're not having *comida* until later when *Tía* Victoria gets here. I'm starving." Miguel pouted, and his stomach gave a timely grumble.

"Are you, now? Well, I might just have something that could help with that… if you stay… very… still…" Artie reached behind the little boy's ear, and with a flourish of his wrist, pulled out a little boiled sweet in a yellow wrapper. It was a simple trick that he had learned years ago, and it never failed to delight the children. Miguel squealed with joy, forgetting about his distress for a moment, and popped the sweet into his mouth.

"Thank you," he said, grinning. "I like the lemon ones, they're my favorite."

"I know. I remember, from that first day we met in the plaza and you choked on one." Artie winked. "I seem to remember that you left me a bag of them because you knew I was hungry. Well, I've been meaning to repay the favor."

He pulled two small bags from his pocket and handed them to Miguel, whose eyes went wide with excitement.

"This one I'll give you on the condition that you promise to share it with your brother." He pressed the brown paper bag into Miguel's hand. "And this one is for your sister. For her only, you understand? I don't want you to open it or show it to anyone else. Can I trust you to do that for me, *amigo*?"

"*Sí*," Miguel nodded. "You can trust me... *amigo*."

"Wonderful." Artie pressed the second little parcel into the boy's hands, this time a neatly-wrapped handkerchief containing a little hand-drawn birthday card and a collection of sweets which he knew to be Esperanza's favorites. He had been carrying them around all day in the hope that he would somehow find a way to give them to her, and now that Miguel had appeared, this seemed to be his only chance.

Miguel slid down from Artie's lap, grinning through a mouthful of sugar.

"Promise me something else, *chamaco*." Artie took him by the shoulders and peered into his eyes. "Whatever was wrong today- whoever it was who frightened you- I don't mind if you won't tell me, as long as you tell *someone*. These things... they're always better off not being kept a secret."

Miguel nodded again.

"Good lad. Now, go and give those sweets to your sister."

"My sister." Miguel paused, looking up at Artie with an innocent smile. "I'm glad that you and Esperanza are friends now."

"You... you are?" Artie asked, suddenly tense. "Who told you we were friends?"

"I just guessed," Miguel shrugged. "She likes you, you know."

"What makes you think that?" Artie pretended to be very interested in a bridle hanging beside one of the stable doors. He could feel Ricardo watching him.

"She had a big fight with *papá* over you last night," Miguel told him. "I didn't hear much of what they were saying, but she was really mad. She called *papá* a coward and said that he could learn from how brave you are. She told him that he should be ashamed for letting someone hurt you." He paused, suddenly worried. "*Did* someone hurt you? Are you all right?"

"I'm fine, *chamaco*. Don't you worry about me," Artie ruffled his hair. "Tell me more about Esperanza. Did she say anything else about me?"

"*Sí.*" Miguel grinned. "*Mamá* said that she shouldn't be friends with you, and Esperanza said she'd be friends with whoever she pleased. She did a lot of shouting about how *mamá* and *papá* might have the right to choose her husband, but they had no right to a say on her *amigos*. *Mamá* wasn't happy, but Esperanza threatened to mess things up with this fancy Don of hers tomorrow night if she banned her from being friends with you. So Esperanza won. *Papá* said that he was more than happy for you and her to be friends, as long as she didn't get 'carried away' and ruin things with that rich man they want her to marry." He looked up at Artie with round, excited eyes. "Well? Are you going to?"

"Going to what?" Artie was struggling to process Miguel's words. *Husband. That rich man they want her to marry.* It was all happening too quickly, far too quickly. His heart felt as though it had turned to lead.

"Are you going to carry her away?" Miguel asked, bubbling with excitement. "I'm sure she wouldn't mind. I don't think she's very fond of the man they want her to marry, she'd probably quite like it if you carried her away instead. I'll warn you, though, she's heavier than she looks. Me and Felipe can hardly pick her up between us."

Ricardo laughed at this, and Miguel frowned, oblivious to what was so funny.

"Go on, now, *chamaco*," Artie told him, trying to hide the wobble in his voice. "Go on back to the house before your *mamá* comes looking for you."

The boy obeyed, and Artie returned to his work, his mind whirring. Ricardo kept glancing at him with a strange mixture of amusement and pity in his eyes, a sad little smile hinting on his lips.

"All right. What is it?" Artie huffed, giving in.

"You're in love with *Señorita* Esperanza," Ricardo replied. He was not asking. "Does she feel the same way about you?"

"I don't know," Artie snapped, his voice cracking. "So what if she does? It won't make any difference. She's promised to Don Raúl, it seems, whether she likes it or not." He pulled at the bridle, catching his finger in one of the buckles and swearing at it under his breath. Ricardo put a hand on his shoulder.

"I know, *amigo*. It's a cruel world. I just want you to know your secret is safe with me," he promised. "I won't say a word."

Artie nodded in thanks, and the two young men continued with their work in silence. Artie tried to distract himself as much as possible for the rest of the afternoon. He washed and tended to old Dahlia's sore leg while he got Ricardo to practice dismantling and reassembling bridles. He did his best to keep a low profile again the following day, too, staying out of the way of the other farmhands so that he could wallow in his misery without having to make conversation with anyone. Ricardo's pitying glances did not help his mood.

Artie knew that he was being ridiculous. He had known all along that this day would come, that Esperanza's parents would start to push things along with Don Raúl. All he could hope for now was that neither family would try to rush things; the moment the courtship became official, the countdown to the wedding would begin, and then he would lose Esperanza forever. She had never even been his to lose, and yet the thought of being kept away from her made him feel as though someone had kicked him hard in the chest. Diego had warned him more times than he could remember that getting close to Esperanza would only lead to heartache, but he had not listened. Now he was paying the price, and he had only himself to blame for it.

Just as he and Ricardo were bringing the horses in from the fields and settling them down in their clean stalls for the evening, their peace was shattered by Rafael's appearance. Artie was not surprised to see him; he had just been to collect Victoria from her shop, so it was natural that he would bring the horse and cart back down to the stables afterwards. What was unusual was his mood. He mumbled and swore to himself as he stormed into the stables and threw his long driving whip onto the ground.

"Afraid I'm going to have to ask you both to work overtime tonight, boys," he growled. "Señora Dominguez has just announced to me that the cart *'just simply will not do'* for tonight." He put on a false, high voice, imitating Louisa. Artie sincerely hoped that neither she nor Juan could hear him. "I'm to prepare the blasted carriage instead. Honestly, she's had all week to tell me this, and she announces it *now*. They've got to leave in an hour!"

Artie couldn't think of anything he wished to do less than help the family to get to Don Lorenzo's *hacienda*, but he couldn't very well refuse. He had no choice but to grit his teeth and go along with it.

"Don't worry, Rafael. We'll clean up the carriage while you prepare the horses. Just say what you want."

"You'll have to do both jobs between you, I'm afraid," Rafael growled, his scowl betraying his irritation. "I've been told I've got to clean *myself* up. They don't want some scruffy old farmhand driving their carriage. *What would Don Raúl think?*" He imitated Louisa again, then kicked over a pail of water in annoyance. "I'm to go and get washed up and put on some fancy clothes of Juan's. I told him if he wanted a bloody footman, then he should've employed one. I'll do it this once, but in future, he can forget it. Not that Juan has been given much say in it either, mind. Still, all this silly fancy dress for the sake of impressing some stuck-up Don. It's ridiculous." He shook his head, still muttering to himself as he headed up towards the house. Artie's heart sank.

Ricardo went out through the back of the stable to clean up the carriage, leaving Artie to make sure that the horses were looking their best. He picked out a pair of handsome black mares of similar sizes, tying them up outside so that he could wash them without making too much mess in the stable. Then he bathed the animals with clean water before polishing their hooves, combing through the knots in their manes and tails and finally giving their fur a good, vigorous brush. The horses were delighted at his attention, snorting with appreciation as they tore at the nets of hay he had provided.

Artie could not resist glancing up at the house as he worked, wondering what Esperanza was doing inside. Once or twice he thought he heard raised voices, most often Louisa's, although occasionally either Miguel's or Felipe's too. Never Esperanza's, though.

By six-fifteen, the carriage and horses were gleaming and ready to go, and together Ricardo and Artie led them up towards the house. Artie felt as though he was walking to his own execution, and Ricardo must have sensed it because he kept glancing at him with doe-eyed sympathy.

"*Amigo*, if you don't want to be here, I could always-" he started, but it was too late. Rafael was already waiting for them by the house, looking grumpy and uncomfortable in a stiff jacket and smart silk necktie.

"Nice job, boys," he grunted. "Even the *señora* will be pleased with that."

Right on cue, Louisa burst from the house wearing a puffy dress of emerald green silk. She did a quick inspective lap of the carriage, nodded in approval, and then shouted for Esperanza and Juan to hurry up.

Juan appeared next, pulling uncomfortably at his smart clothes and flanked by Miguel and Felipe, who were both whining that they had not been invited to the fancy meal too. Victoria tried to pacify them, promising to read them stories and play their favorite games, but Miguel was having none of it. He swung from his father's arm, firing questions at him about why he had to go, why they couldn't come too, and why Juan had to wear such silly clothes if he wasn't the one who was supposed to be marrying the fancy rich man. Juan looked as though he would have appreciated an answer to the last question, too, although he was not brave enough to voice it considering the mood his wife was in.

Esperanza appeared, at last, framed in the doorway of the house, and Artie's heart dropped at the sight of her. She looked resplendent in a beautiful Spanish-style gown of crimson silk, the tight bodice embroidered with gold thread and embellished with tiny golden beads which sparkled in the light of the setting sun. Her ample skirt swirled around her like water as she moved, glittering golden patterns dancing along its hem. The low neckline sat off the shoulder, leaving the glowing skin of her collarbone bare except for a dainty gold cross that hung around her neck on a delicate chain. Her long, dark hair had been curled and pinned up away from her face to show off her graceful neck and secured at the back with an ornate gold clasp. She looked every inch a queen, and for a long moment, Artie lost all notion of who and where he was.

Esperanza looked down at the ground through her long, dark eyelashes, her face pale and worried, one hand fiddling with the ornate lace adorning her sleeve. A sharp reprimand from her mother forced her to stand straight, and her ocean blue eyes suddenly looked up to meet Artie's with an expression that made his knees buckle. He wanted to tell her how beautiful she was, but the words stuck in his throat and all he could do was stare.

"Well?" snapped Louisa, making both Artie and Esperanza jump. "Are you just going to stand there gawping, niño, or were you planning on opening the carriage door at some point?"

"Sí, of course, señora," Artie apologised. He bowed to Esperanza and twisted the handle of the door, offering a hand to help her up. Louisa had become preoccupied with reprimanding Juan for a mark she had noticed on his waistcoat, and Artie took advantage of the brief distraction to squeeze Esperanza's hand and look up into her frightened eyes.

"You look beautiful," he whispered. She smiled back at him and squeezed his fingers in reply. Whether it was nervousness or just plain lack of desire to see Don Raúl, he wasn't sure, but he could see a painful sadness in her eyes that made his heart hurt. He felt an overwhelming urge to snatch her up in his arms and run back to their favorite spot by the river, to hide away with her in a place where nobody would ever find them. Now, though, she had to go and spend an evening with the preening *idiota* she was apparently to marry, and there was nothing Artie could do but stand back and watch.

He helped Louisa up into the seat opposite her daughter as Juan climbed up into the front of the carriage beside a freshly groomed Rafael. The old man's face was stony, and he looked highly uncomfortable in his borrowed clothes. Artie would have found the sight quite amusing had he not been so fixated on Esperanza. He could say no more to her now that her mother had joined her in the carriage, but he gave her the most reassuring smile he could muster as he closed the door, feeling a knot of guilt twisting in his stomach. He may as well have been closing the door on her prison cell.

The carriage pulled away, and Artie caught one last glimpse of Esperanza's pleading eyes from the window as it lurched off towards the road. He stood with Ricardo, Victoria, and the children, feeling as though his heart had been ripped out and was being dragged along behind it.

"You wait and see," Victoria told the children, her chest puffed out with pride. "Your sister will be wed before the year is out. No man will be able to resist her, looking as beautiful as that. Even Don Raúl."

That's what I'm afraid of, Artie thought sullenly, watching after the carriage as it disappeared over the hill. *That's what I'm afraid of more than anything.*

CHAPTER THIRTEEN

Esperanza was silent for most of the journey to Don Lorenzo's *hacienda*, her stomach churning with nerves. Seeing Artie just before she left had not helped, and she had wanted to cry as she watched him fade away into the distance, standing there with that tragic, betrayed expression in his eyes. *He always knew that this was the way it must be,* she told herself firmly. *And so did I.*

The evening began without event, much to Esperanza's relief. Don Lorenzo and Juan did most of the talking in the time before the meal was served, Esperanza doing her best to listen as Don Lorenzo educated them in the ways of the Spanish court.

"The last time we were over there, it was for the royal wedding, of course," he told them, as though such a thing was an everyday occurrence for him. "His Majesty insisted we attend as his guests of honour. As a wedding gift, we had a special piece of jewellery commissioned for his English bride with gold from our mines. Do you remember, Raúl?"

He gave his son a pointed look, and Esperanza started, having almost forgotten that Don Raúl was there. He had been very quiet so far, agreeing with his father when prompted but otherwise just languishing in his chair in the corner, sipping on his wine every now and then. *He must have been warned to drink slowly, after what happened last time,* Esperanza mused.

Don Raúl cleared his throat and sat up. This appeared to be a cue for something, and Esperanza tensed, looking from one man to the other.

"Sí, Father, I do remember," Don Raúl said with a forced smile. "It was a sapphire pendant set in gold, with a matching gold chain." He pulled a small, ornate box from the pocket inside his jacket. "Very much like this one."

He opened the box, and Esperanza gasped. Inside lay a beautiful sapphire pendant, just as Don Raúl had described. He bent to one knee and offered it to her, and she would have scrambled backward out of the window had the high back of the armchair not prevented her from doing so.

"For you, *señorita*," he told her, looking up at her with smouldering eyes. "I had one made for you, just the same."

Esperanza stared at him.

"I- I can't accept, *señor*. It's too much."

"Nonsense," Don Lorenzo laughed. "It is the custom here for the start of an official courtship to be marked with gifts, is it not?"

"An official courtship?" she echoed, feeling faint. She put her hand on the arm of the chair to steady herself.

"I think what my daughter means to say," Juan cut in, "is that she thought perhaps Don Raúl may honour her with some chocolate or flowers when the time came to begin an official courtship." He shot a nervous glance at Esperanza. "I don't think that any of us were expecting anything as generous as this... especially so soon."

"Nonsense," Don Lorenzo laughed again. "My son knows what he wants. Why wait? Such a refined and beautiful lady needs a refined and beautiful gift as a token of his high regard for her. Go on, Raúl, help her put it on."

Esperanza felt as though she had no choice but to sit still and allow Don Raúl to lean forward and secure the chain around her neck, fumbling slightly with the clasp as he did. She caught a whiff of some sort of expensive perfume on his sleeves and closed her eyes, fighting the urge to push him away.

Only a few days ago, a semi-clothed Artie had hugged her against his bare chest, and she had not minded having a man so close to her at all then. *Perhaps that's the way to get through this*, she told herself as Don Raúl's fingers brushed her neck. *Perhaps when he gets too close, when he touches me, I just need to pretend that it's Artie and then I won't mind so much.*

It would not be easy, though, especially with that overwhelming, woody perfume smell choking her. Artie's skin smelled fresh and vibrant, like a cocktail of limes and oranges. Artie's fingers were long and gentle, while Don Raúl's were thick and coarse. The two were nothing alike.

After what felt like far too long, the ordeal was over, and when she opened her eyes she found that everyone else in the room was looking at her with admiration. She smiled weakly back at them, allowing Don Raúl to take her hand and kiss it.

"Our only request is that you do not wear it in front of the Queen," Don Lorenzo winked. "She might get jealous when she sees how beautiful it looks on you."

The two men laughed, and Esperanza forced herself to join in.

"I hardly think it likely that I will ever meet her, but if I ever do, I will bear that in mind," she assured him.

"On the contrary, my dear. I'd say it's quite likely." Don Lorenzo leaned back in his chair with a languid smile, glancing around to check that everyone looked suitably impressed. "We were intending on taking a trip over there, perhaps this time next year, to visit our Spanish estates. The Queen is around your age, I'm sure she would be delighted to meet you. The marriage must be going well. She's had four children in the same number of years of marriage so far, although I regret her youngest is now with the angels."

He crossed himself with a sigh.

"A terrible tragedy, to be sure. Still, I'm told the Queen is recovering well, and with their record so far I'm sure it won't be long before the King is blessed with another child."

"Sí, although with *his* record so far, there are no guarantees that the Queen will be its mother," said Don Raúl with a dry laugh. His father gave him a thunderous look, and Raúl hurriedly changed the subject. "Perhaps the next time we visit court, I will have a child of my own to present to His Majesty. Just think of that, señorita, to have one's own children playing with those of the Royal Family." His eyes sparkled at Esperanza, and she tried again to suppress a shudder.

The smell of cooked food drifted in from the dining room, and Don Lorenzo gestured for them all to follow him to where a large candlelit table had been prepared. So much for a light *cena*; there were enough bowls of elegant-looking tapas laid out here to feed all of her father's farmhands and still have enough left over for a second meal.

Esperanza had eaten very little that day, her appetite wrecked by nerves, and now at the sight of so much delicious-smelling food, she suddenly felt very hungry. She sat beside Don Raúl and allowed him to serve her from the dishes on the table. There was a spicy chorizo dish in tomato sauce, grilled shrimp, potatoes with herbs, corn, grilled *arrachera*, onions and *chiles toreados*, plus several other dishes that Esperanza didn't recognize. Whatever they were, they were tasty if a little too spicy for her liking.

Don Raúl poured her a glass of wine, and after a nod of permission from her father, she took a careful sip. It was strong and fruity, and she made a firm mental note not to drink it too quickly. She was suddenly reminded of Artie's story about the wedding, only realizing too late that Don Raúl was watching her.

"Is something amusing you, *señorita*?" he asked her, raising one eyebrow with a smile. "Or dare I suggest that you are enjoying yourself?"

"I- I was just thinking about my brother Miguel," Esperanza lied, thinking it best that she didn't mention Artie. "When he was very little, maybe two or three, he had this strange fascination for putting things in his ears. One time, he took a little bit of corn just like this and put it so deep in his ear that we had to take him to Doctor Francisco. It threw his balance right off, he was staggering around like a tiny little drunk man."

Esperanza giggled to herself. Artie had found this story hilarious, but the humour of the situation seemed completely lost on Don Raúl, and he stared at her as though she were speaking a different language.

"This is... funny?" he asked, raising an eyebrow.

"I... I suppose you had to be there," she sighed, her laughter fading. "Or at least know my brother to understand."

"I look forward to meeting him, señorita," Don Raúl told her. "I imagine it makes a girl a better mother when she's had experience with younger siblings." His cold, dark eyes regarded her over the rim of his wine glass, and she suddenly felt very hot.

"Do you have any siblings?" she asked him, desperate to steer the conversation away from the thought of having children with him. She already knew the answer, but at least asking the question bought her time to think of a different topic.

"Unfortunately not," he told her, leaning a little closer and lowering his voice so that his father could not hear. "I did once, but my younger brother was lost to a fever when he was four, and then both my mother and my infant sister passed away in childbed when I was nine."

"Oh," Esperanza muttered. She had already known that Don Lorenzo was a widower and that Don Raúl was an only child, but she had not been aware that the two things were connected. Otherwise, she would never have been so cruel as to raise the subject. "I'm very sorry to hear that, Don Raúl. You must miss them terribly."

He lowered his eyes, ending the conversation with a stiff nod of acknowledgement, and Esperanza made a silent note not to mention it again. Instead, he picked up the wine bottle, turning to offer her a refill.

"Would you care for some more of this excellent Rioja, señorita? It's from my father's own vineyards in Castilla. It's a particular favorite of mine."

She accepted against her better judgement, and he poured them both another glass.

Once everyone at the table had eaten far more than they should, Don Lorenzo suggested they retire to the courtyard to enjoy the night air. Esperanza stood, her head reeling a little from the wine, but Don Lorenzo stopped her before she could follow.

"Raúl," he said, taking his son by the arm, "why don't you take the *señorita* and show her the grounds? The roses are in full bloom at the moment. I think she would rather enjoy them."

Esperanza glanced up at her parents. Louisa looked delighted, and Juan gave her a permissive nod, an uncomfortable smile fixed on his face. It had never been part of the deal that she would be left alone with Don Raúl tonight, but without her parents' support, Esperanza had no good excuse to argue.

Gritting her teeth, she took Don Raúl's arm and allowed him to lead her out into the moonlight and across the lawn. The fireflies were bright, flitting about among the hedgerows and flowerbeds like little fairies.

"Where are you taking me, Don Raúl?" she asked, already fearing that she knew the answer. He smiled down at her.

"The walled garden, to see the roses, of course." He took a small key from his chest pocket and bent down to unfasten the padlock on the gate.

Esperanza swallowed hard.

"I'm… I'm not sure that it would be proper for me to be alone with a man in such a private place, *señor*," she told him, lowering her eyes. "My parents would not approve."

"Nonsense. They would be delighted, your mother especially." He was no longer smiling. "Now come on, *señorita*, don't be silly. We're officially courting now, and we need to get used to each other's company. It's hardly as though this is the first time you've been alone with a man. In fact, it's not even the first time you've been alone with a man *in this garden*, is it?"

He raised an eyebrow, waiting for her reaction. She felt her stomach drop.

He knows.

At least that would explain why he had been so hostile towards Artie in the plaza, even if it didn't excuse it. Somehow, he had found out about what happened between them that evening, and he was not happy. She met his gaze and he fixed her with an icy smile, gesturing again for her to lead the way through the gate. She had no choice but to obey.

The garden was exactly as she remembered it, with the roses shining in the moonlight against the stone walls. There was the fountain, with Aphrodite sitting above, surrounded by her fat little stone cherubs. And there, right in the middle, was the grassy bank where she had lain beside Artie on the night of the *baile*. The only difference tonight was the clouds, which blocked out the starlight and cast the whole garden in gloomy, ominous darkness.

Don Raúl perched himself on the edge of the fountain, trailing a hand in the cool water. For a long moment, neither of them spoke, although Don Raúl never took his eyes from Esperanza. It was as though he was trying to read her mind, and she wished that he would stop.

"So," he said at last, making her jump. "Alone at last, señorita. Perhaps now I can ask you a few questions, find out a little more about the mysterious girl with the blue eyes who escaped me at my father's *baile*."

"That's why you brought me down here, is it?" she asked, raising an eyebrow. "This is an interrogation?"

She braced herself, half expecting Don Raúl to begin asking her questions about the nature of her relationship with Artie, but he just gave her an unreadable smile and shook his head.

"Nothing like that. I just thought that if I'm to marry you as my father wishes, I should at least try to get to know you a little. Find out as much as I can about what sort of woman I'm dealing with before we're bound together for life."

"Oh." Esperanza relaxed slightly. She supposed it was a fair enough suggestion, although she still couldn't help feeling as though she were on trial. "Well, if that's the case, then perhaps you would be happy to answer a few questions for me in return."

"Very well. Ladies first."

She cleared her throat and thought for a second. She had a lot of questions in mind but did not want to come across as accusatory by charging straight in with the biggest ones. Instead, she opted to begin with something that she knew could not cause offence.

"I hear you're a big supporter of the arts," she said, trying to start with something positive. "Your father gifted the *kiosca* to the town, didn't he? It was a wonderful idea. They're having a music competition down there next Saturday."

"I know," he confirmed. "I'm the judge."

"Oh." She struggled to hide her disappointment at this news. If Don Raúl was going to be judging the contest alone, then Artie could kiss goodbye to his chances of winning, no matter how well he played.

"My father will be judging it jointly with me," he added, and she breathed a sigh of relief. Perhaps all was not lost in that case. "Can I assume you will be watching too, *señorita*? I know how fond you are of music." He was still smiling, but Esperanza noticed a hint of coldness in his tone. "Or should I say, musicians?"

If there was any doubt in her mind that Don Raúl knew about her friendship with Artie, it was crushed now. She tried to maintain a haughty expression, hoping that she could disguise her unease. As she had told her parents, she was proud to be Artie's friend, and she would not apologise for it.

"Sí, I am friends with a musician," she told him. "A very good one at that. But no, as it happens, I'm not going to the festival just to watch the music competition. I will be there, as I am every year, as a dancer."

"Ah!" he cried, brightening. "I hoped that you would be, especially as I didn't get to see you dance properly at the *baile*. I love dancing as much as I enjoy music. I'm partial to all forms of art, really. *Ars longa, vita brevis*. Hippocrates." He glanced at Esperanza's blank expression. "It means: life is short, but art lasts forever."

She nodded in approval. At least that was one thing they could find neutral ground on.

"Is that why your father thinks we would be a good match?" she asked, trying to steer the conversation away from Artie. "Because he knows that we have a few things in common, with our shared interest in the arts?"

"My father is interested in continuing the family line, nothing more," Raúl laughed. "I'm thirty-two now, and my father is in his seventies with no interest in remarrying. I'm his only hope of ensuring the survival of his family tree. He's keen to marry me off as soon as possible in the hope that I will provide him with enough grandchildren to secure his bloodline."

"And you?" she asked him. "Is that what you want?"

He shrugged.

"If I must marry, it may as well be to a beautiful and talented woman. You're young, you're healthy, and those magnificent blue eyes of yours make you a rare jewel indeed. Any man would be lucky to possess such a wife."

She drew in a breath as calmly as she could, smarting at his choice of the word 'possess'. Perhaps it was just a slip of the tongue on his part, but she resented the implication that she was just another bauble to be owned. If all he was interested in was beauty, youth and rarity, then perhaps he ought to buy a horse instead.

"Is that all you want in a wife?" she asked him, keeping her voice steady. "Beauty?"

He shrugged again.

"Does there need to be anything else?"

Esperanza took another deep breath and closed her eyes. Seeing as they were speaking frankly for once, she saw no reason why she could not be upfront with him. If this was the man her parents wanted her to marry, then she intended to find out what was really going on behind those dark, cold eyes.

"Do you think you could ever love me, Don Raúl?" she asked him, turning to look him in the eye. He started slightly at her boldness as though surprised that she had inquired about such a strange thing.

"I told you, I think you're beautiful," he shrugged.

"That's not what I asked."

He blinked at her as though he had never really thought about it.

"Love is an overrated commodity, *señorita*," he told her. "And not a good reason to marry someone. It is like fire. It burns powerfully, and sometimes it seems like nothing can put it out. But then one day the rains come, and it's gone. You look back and all you can see is the devastation in its wake." He shook his head, staring down at his reflection in the fountain.

"Is that your experience?" she asked, softening a little at the pain in his eyes. "Did you once love a woman, and she broke your heart?"

He smiled.

"No, *señorita*. No woman has ever had the honour of winning my heart. In fact, many would tell you I don't have one." He chuckled, shaking his head. "No, I'm talking about my father. He loved my mother like that. It caused him nothing but agony in the end." He looked up at the fountain above him, studying the faces of the stone figures with a strange melancholy. "He had this fountain made for her, you know, after she died. The statue is Aphrodite, but the face is my mother, Reyana. The Goddess of Love. You see the little cherub beside her, Eros? Well, that's my brother Emilio, the one who died of fever, and the baby in Aphrodite's arms... well, you get the idea."

Esperanza nodded, suddenly feeling a chill to see all of those cold stone faces watching her. It was such a romantic idea and yet so tragic. No wonder Don Lorenzo kept the gates to this garden locked.

"I'm so sorry to hear of your losses," she told him. "Is that why you don't want to fall in love? In case you get hurt like your father did?"

"I never said that," he corrected her. "I said that I don't want to *marry* for love. Marriage is a business arrangement as far as I am concerned, *señorita*, better all round when emotions stay out of it. It would be a nice bonus to end up loving the one I marry and to know her love in return, but it's not important to me and it's certainly not a prerequisite." He looked up at her with a wearied smile. "Does that horrify you?"

"No," she mused. "I appreciate your honesty, and I understand your reasons, even if I don't agree." He returned with a brief nod, accepting her view. She tried changing tactic. "All right, so you say that love is not important to you. Then what is?"

He thought for a moment, rubbing his beard.

"Honour," he told her eventually. "Pride. Respect. I'm a simple man to understand, señorita. I told you once that I am a passionate sort, and it's true. I've got my faults, just like everyone else. I'm not a bad man, but if anyone ever insults me or makes a fool of me, I'm not one to forgive easily. I reward my friends well and punish my enemies harshly."

"And what about your wife? How can she expect to be treated?"

"That would depend on whether she decides to make a friend or an enemy of me."

He looked up at her, and she found it impossible in the dim light to read whether he was being serious. The glint in those cold eyes sent a chill through her either way.

"I've been introduced to a lot of beautiful young ladies in the past, but you're the first who has not willingly thrown themselves at me. In fact, you've rejected my every advance so far." He looked her up and down as though trying to work her out. "You don't seem interested in my power, my wealth or my gifts. It makes me wonder what it is you *do* want."

"A good man," she replied, refusing to cower beneath his icy stare. "All of the power, wealth and generosity in the world does not guarantee that a man is kind. That's the only asset I'm interested in."

He shook his head, laughing.

"You surely don't see the world so simplistically, señorita. You must know that people are not split into good and evil, black and white. We are all shades of grey, every one of us. What you see as darkness, another would see as light. But if it's kindness you want, I can do that. Treat me well, and I will do the same for you."

"And what does that mean, treat you well?" she asked, turning to face him. "What do you want from me?"

He tilted his head on one side, regarding her with amusement.

"I want to *win* you. A victory is not sweet unless you've had to fight for it. All my life, I've been used to getting exactly what I want, señorita, but it's so boring when it's just given to me on a plate all the time. You, though, you're different. I think you might just be the challenge I've been waiting for."

"Hardly," she retorted, folding her arms and turning away to stare into the fountain. "I've not been given any say whatsoever in this courtship. I didn't even know that we were beginning official proceedings tonight. Your father has declared that he wants me as his daughter-in-law, and my parents have readily offered me up. Whether you 'win' me or not, you still get the prize either way. Some challenge."

"I agree," he nodded. "So let's make the game a little more interesting, shall we?"

She looked up at him, her eyes narrowed with caution. His face was unreadable in the dim light. Only his eyes gleamed brightly enough to be seen, watching her like a mountain cat.

"What did you have in mind?"

"How about this? We will allow our parents to continue to play matchmaker for us. We will jump through all of their hoops like good children, comply with all of their little courtship rituals. But you and I will be playing our own game, which will end with me winning the ultimate prize. You."

"You want to win my heart, you mean?"

"Your heart? Well, that would be the nice way of doing it, I suppose," he mused, smiling. "But your heart is not important to me. It's your hand I'm after. I will try the nice way first, as it seems so important to you, but should it fail, I have other methods of persuasion at my disposal."

He reached out to catch her chin, tipping it upwards so that she was forced to look at him. His lips were smiling, but his eyes were ice cold.

"You... you would take me by force?" she breathed, steeling herself to fight. Don Raúl rolled his eyes and laughed at her, releasing her chin and languishing back against the fountain as though such an idea bored him.

"Good grief, child, calm down. I'm not suggesting for a moment that I would rape you if that's what you're thinking. Don't be so vulgar. No, I am a gentleman. I have no need to raise a hand to you. I have far better ways of getting what I want."

He dipped his hand into the water, allowing the droplets to spill through his fingers.

"I told you before, señorita. I am a simple man to understand; I like to win. Before my father's *baile*, I would have considered marrying you out of duty alone and thought little more of it. But then you humiliated me, not once but three times, and all in full view of the public eye. You refused to sit and talk with me, you refused to dance with me, and then you made me look like an *idiota* in the plaza with your little *músico* friend. Oh, don't worry- I'm not angry," he assured her, smiling at her nervous expression. "If anything, I'm impressed. No woman has ever bested me before, let alone three times in as many meetings. You caught my attention. As I said, I enjoy a challenge. But now, simply possessing you is no longer enough for me. I need you to submit to me of your own accord, to make up for the humiliation you made me suffer."

"Right," she croaked, fighting to keep her face from betraying how unnerved she felt. *This man is unhinged.* "And that will make you feel better about the whole thing, will it?"

"Oh, sí. Nothing gets a man's blood pumping quite like the thrill of the chase, señorita," he told her. She could see the gleam of teeth as he smiled. "I don't want my father to ask on my behalf or your parents to accept me on yours. I want to hear it from *you*. When the time comes, I will ask you to marry me with my own lips. And you will say '*sí, Don Raúl*' in that sweet little voice of yours, and I will hear it with my own ears. I will settle for nothing less."

"And what if I don't want to?" she squared up to him now, so angered by his vanity that she felt her fear melting away. He laughed airily, as though she were a wilful child.

"Oh, believe me, you will want to. It's amazing what people want to do when they realize that the alternative is something they want even less." He stood too now, towering over her. His tone was not threatening but jovial, as though he were offering her a cup of tea. "I promise you this, señorita; by the time this year is out, if I ask you to sit with me, you will sit. If I ask you to dance, you will dance. And when I ask you to marry me, you will say yes."

He grinned down at her furious expression and chuckled, reaching out to brush her hair from her face. She flinched away, scowling, and he laughed again.

"Come now, señorita. It's not all that bad. I will be a good husband to you, as long as you are a good wife to me. You will live like a queen, the envy of every woman in Mexico. Assuming, of course, that you choose to make a friend of me rather than an enemy. I will be your husband, but how happy an arrangement that is for you will be down to your own decisions." He regarded her with an amicable smile, which she did not return. "As it happens, so far, I like you. I hope that in time, you will come to like me, too. You never know, I might win your heart yet, but for now, your obedience is enough for me."

He stretched as though awaking from a *siesta*, then offered her his arm. She did not accept, but he didn't seem to mind, strolling towards the garden gate as though to leave.

"Don Raúl," she called after him. "What if I never agree to it? Marrying you?"

He gave another airy laugh, waving a dismissive hand over his shoulder.

"Oh, you will, *señorita*. One way or another, you will."

CHAPTER FOURTEEN

Women, Juan decided, were impossible to understand and even more difficult to please.

It had been several days since that successful evening at Don Lorenzo's *hacienda*, or so he had thought at the time. Don Lorenzo seemed happy, his son seemed happy, and Juan himself was pleased with how the evening had turned out overall. Even his stubborn daughter had behaved herself with a little persuasion. It had been progress, in Juan's eyes. How naïve he had been.

Juan had not heard the conversation that took place inside the carriage during that journey home, but upon their arrival at the farmhouse Esperanza had flounced straight up the stairs to her room without so much as a word to either of her parents. Apparently, she was furious that she had been forced to commence an official courtship without warning. Juan had tried to tell her that he had not realized that it would all happen so soon either, but she had not been inclined to listen.

He found it very difficult to understand why his daughter was so angry. She knew they had been consulting with Don Lorenzo, and although Raúl's gift had been far more substantial than any of them had been expecting, he failed to see how this could be a bad thing. Surely any young maiden should be flattered that such a man held her in high esteem.

Juan shook his head, taking a wad of tobacco from the pouch on his belt and pushing it into his mouth. Louisa's irritated voice drifted across the field from an open upstairs window, chiding one of the boys for something. She had been furious with him as well, blaming him over Esperanza's stubborn lack of gratitude for their matchmaking efforts.

"You're far too soft on her," Louisa had snarled at him upon their arrival home that night. "If you hadn't always indulged her when she behaved so badly towards her previous suitors, she might not be so quick to behave in such a cold and ungrateful manner towards Don Raúl now."

"She was perfectly polite," Juan had argued back. "She did everything we asked of her. She talked with him, she sat with him during the meal and allowed him to serve her. She even allowed him to put that ridiculous jewel around her neck and show her around the gardens without an escort, which was more than we made her agree to."

"Sí, and all with a face like the wrong end of a dog while she did so," Louisa fumed. "Listen to yourself, Juan. You should not be making *agreements* with her. She is our daughter; it is her duty to obey us and trust our judgement on what is best for her. And what's best for her is Don Raúl. You cannot deny that, and if you do not come down hard on her soon, she might lose this opportunity. Don Raúl is the answer to all our prayers. He's perfect for her, even if she can't see it yet."

Juan rubbed his forehead. Something was niggling at him, something he couldn't quite put his finger on. Don Raúl was perfect, with all of his courtly manners and charm, his handsome figure and, of course, his position as the only living heir to Don Lorenzo's fortune. Don Raúl was a man that any girl in her right mind would marry in a heartbeat, given the chance.

So why hadn't they?

This was the question that Juan couldn't get out of his mind. Judging by the longing looks that Don Raúl had received from the fine ladies at his father's *baile*, Juan thought it highly unlikely that he had tried to court every one of them at some point and been rejected. The only other theory was that *Raúl* had been the one doing the rejecting, which also seemed implausible, yet it was the only possible explanation he could think of.

Then the next natural question was why, *why* would such a man be so interested in the daughter of a common farmer? True, Juan was very wealthy as farmers went, but he still had nothing compared to the rich *caballeros* of the Spanish court. As for blood and titles, he had none; he had acquired his fortune through luck, not ancestry.

As beautiful as Esperanza was, Juan refused to believe this was the only reason for Don Raúl's interest in his daughter. No, Don *Lorenzo's* interest, he reminded himself. Raúl had not even met Esperanza until after his father had already expressed a desire to add her to his family tree. There must be something she possessed which had singled her out in the Dons' eyes, something which none of the other girls could match, but what that attribute was Juan just could not fathom out.

"What does it matter *why*, as long as he wants to marry her?" Louisa had argued in response to his concerns. "Whatever his reasons, they do not alter the benefits to the whole family should Esperanza go through with this. You are her father, you know what this connection could mean for us. Make her stop this childish behaviour and step up to the duty she owes to her family before it's too late."

What this connection could mean for us.

He knew what Louisa had meant, but Juan's mind could not help springing to more cynical matters. He had heard his farmhands whispering in the barn and men muttering in the shadows of the taverna. There was an energetic restlessness in the air, a quiet, burning fury that seemed to grow stronger by the day.

Although he would never dare to admit it out loud, Juan held strong sympathies with these men. He had been poor too, once, although never as poor as they were. He felt more at ease with them than he ever had among Don Lorenzo's snobbish friends. But then, Juan paid his workers generously, fed them well and spent time getting to know them. Unlike Don Lorenzo's men, they had no cause to hate their employer.

Juan was proud that Esperanza understood the importance of empathy too. It had paid off for her already with the new boy, Arturo. Had she not shown him the kindness of offering him those apples, then he might not have performed that stunt to save her from the stallion in the plaza, and then Juan would not have gained one of the best horse whisperers he had ever had the fortune to employ on his farm.

Come to think of it, he wasn't sure that she and the boy even liked each other. Esperanza had reacted strangely when he first mentioned Arturo's employment on the farm, and Arturo himself had seemed less than thrilled at the prospect of helping her into the carriage the other day. Even so, Esperanza had fought for the *right* to be friends with him, and Juan was proud of her for doing so. Perhaps it was just her way of hanging on to some sort of control over her life, given the current circumstances. Perhaps, though, she understood as he did that respect was earned, not given. Especially in these turbulent times, when common workers could so quickly become dangerous enemies.

As it stood at the moment, though, Juan felt in far more danger from the women in his life than he had ever been from his workers. On one side, he had his feisty daughter spitting bullets at him for taking too active a part in arranging her unwanted marriage. On the other side was his angry wife, showering him with venom for not taking *enough* part in arranging that same marriage. Juan felt like a man held at sword point on the edge of a high cliff. Whichever side he chose, he was doomed, and the only choice he really had was over his preferred method of execution.

He sighed again, still trying to work out the best course of action. Assuming that the whispers of revolution never came to anything, as he reassured himself, they most likely would not. The benefits to the whole family of his daughter's marriage to Don Raúl would far outweigh the drawbacks. This was truest of all for Esperanza herself, although it was clear that she could not see it yet. Perhaps it was a lack of confidence in her own potential, or maybe Louisa was right, and it really was just pure stubbornness mixed with a flagrant disregard for authority. *Can't imagine which side of the family she gets that from,* Juan thought with a grimace, but still he resolved to confront Esperanza before the whole situation got any further out of hand.

Juan found his daughter under the shade of the fruit trees, practicing her dancing, and he leaned against a nearby trunk to watch her. He had never been much of a dancer himself, but he had fond memories of his mother dancing at festivals and the like, swishing her skirts and stamping her feet with the sunlight blazing in her hair. Esperanza was so like her. Her looks, her personality, and more than anything, her fiery spirit reminded him so strongly of the great Rosita Dominguez that it made his heart ache.

Not for the first time, Juan wondered what his mother would have made of Don Raúl. He was certain of one thing; she would have gone *loco* at the very suggestion of forcing her beloved granddaughter to marry anyone against her will. Juan would have some serious grovelling to do before the family *ofrenda* at the next *Día de los Muertos*, that was for sure, but for now, he resolved to focus on repairing his relationships with his living relatives. He could worry about the dead later.

"*Mija*, may I speak with you for a moment, please?" he asked.

"Why?" her voice was abrupt, and she still refused to look at him as she continued to twirl. "Have you come to tell me you've sold my soul to your rich friends, as well as my body?"

"Nobody has *sold* you, Esperanza. Body or soul." He was exasperated already, and the conversation had barely begun. He hoped that Don Raúl knew what he was letting himself in for, picking such a feisty bride. "Are you going to sit down and speak to me, if you're so keen to be informed of the decisions that are being made about your future?"

"Oh, so decisions have already been made, have they?" she looked at him at last, her eyes cold. He sat down on the ground and patted the grass beside him, inviting her to sit.

"Sí, they have," he confirmed. "Decisions with only your best interests at heart, I promise. But it hurts me to see you so unhappy, mija. I'm trying to understand. Why are you so hostile towards the idea of marrying Don Raúl?"

"He's a drunken thug who threatened my friend with a sword," she snapped. "So I'm not keen on the idea of being pawned off to him as part of your cosy business arrangement with his father, no."

"Esperanza, it's not like that. Come on." Juan sighed. "Don Raúl did not create a good first impression on you, but every man I know has drunk too much at a party at some point in his life. As for the incident in the square, it was a simple misunderstanding. I'm delighted at the thought of my daughter marrying a man who tries to defend her from harm."

Esperanza snorted with disgust.

"As for you thinking I'm somehow selling you off as part of a business arrangement, I want to set the record straight now. I had no intention of dragging you into my business relationship with Don Lorenzo, but he and his son have taken a shine to you, and I can't say I blame them for that. I will not deny that a bond of marriage to the Alvarez family would provide a lot of business advantages, but the reason I have consented to this courtship is because I genuinely believe that it is the best choice for you. Don Raúl can give you everything a girl could want."

"Everything except love." She turned to look at him, her blue eyes boring into his soul. "Did you think of that, papá? That perhaps I might not be willing to give up my chance of happiness for the sake of a few shiny jewels and silk dresses?"

Juan shook his head at her, smiling. Sometimes it was easy to forget just how young she was, still caught up in the childish fairytales he used to read to her at night before she went to sleep.

"Oh, sweet girl," he smiled, reaching out to take her hand. "That's not how it works in the real world. I barely knew your mother when we got married, and then we had to spend quite a long while getting to know each other and becoming friends. Any real affection didn't come until much later."

Esperanza was silent for a long moment, her brow furrowed in thought.

"How did you feel, *papá*?" she asked at last. "When your parents told you that you were going to marry some girl you barely knew?" Her tone was almost accusatory, as though willing him to admit that the whole idea was as awful as she pictured it to be.

"Honestly? I was grateful," he confessed. "I was horrifically shy around women, and I would never have managed to impress a woman like your mother if all I'd had to depend upon were my conversational skills. Of course, it helped that I'd come into money. Her parents would never have accepted me before I inherited the farm."

Esperanza smiled then. It was only slight, but it was a start.

"I can't imagine *mamá* marrying a poor man, no. But then, I can't picture *Abuelita* agreeing to marry off her only son to a woman he barely knew, either."

"Neither of them really got a say in it. Our fathers made the arrangements. As for me, I was only too happy to agree, especially after I saw how beautiful your mother was."

She sighed, rolling her eyes at him.

"You men. Is that all you care about? How beautiful a woman is?" She shook her head, infuriated. "Don Raúl said something similar when I asked him why he wanted to marry me."

"Does it offend you that he finds you beautiful?"

"No, of course not. What offends me is..." she faltered for a moment, fiddling with her hair as she searched for the words to explain. "Papá, he said some very strange things to me when we were alone in that garden. He told me that he wouldn't accept your promise that I would marry him, he needed to hear me agree to it with my own lips. He wanted to *win* me."

"Really?" Juan was unable to hide the surprise in his voice. Perhaps Don Raúl was more modern than he had thought. Or maybe he had just worked out that the way to Esperanza's heart was to allow her to think that she was in charge. She was her mother's daughter, after all. "Well, *mija*, I'd have thought that you would've been delighted with that. You've been saying all along that you wanted to be given more control over your own destiny. Perhaps Don Raúl has worked this out about you, and he's giving you what he knows you want."

"No, *papá*. It wasn't like that." She shook her head. "The way he said it... it was almost like he was threatening me."

Juan sighed. For all his difficulties with understanding women, he could see the fear in Esperanza's eyes and thought that for once, he knew what was going on in that pretty head of hers.

"You know what I think, *mija*? I think you're frightened," he told her with ill-placed confidence. "Being told you're to marry someone you don't know, it's only natural that your reaction is to rebel, to push back against it. You've always resented being told what to do, whether it's a big thing like this or a little thing like being allowed to be friends with the farmhands. It's your way of trying to regain control of your life because you're uncomfortable with decisions being made on your behalf. I understand, and I respect you for it."

The look she gave him told him that she did not agree with this theory at all, serving only to cement his belief that he was right. In fact, he would be happy to bet that if she had been left to her own devices all along, Esperanza would have likely chosen to marry Don Raúl of her own accord. Perhaps Raúl had it right, and the best way to handle Esperanza was to make her feel as though she was in charge. He was a clever man; Juan had to give him that.

"If you respect that I want to be in control of my own life, does that mean you would allow me to make my own choice over who I marry, *papá*?" she asked him, blinking those beautiful blue eyes. "If I were to fall in love with someone, would you let me choose him over Don Raúl? Even if he wasn't rich and didn't have a fancy title?"

Juan stared at her, a sudden horrific possibility dawning on him. *Is she trying to tell me that she has some sort of lover?*

"Esperanza," he said firmly, looking his daughter straight in the eye. He could feel the tiny hairs standing up on the back of his neck. "I'm going to ask you a question now, and you need to tell me the truth. Are you trying to tell me that there's a man... I mean, do you... I mean, have you..." he cleared his throat, trying to untangle his words. "Have you engaged in any sort of, well... *physical relations* that might harm your marriage prospects?" The look of horror and outrage on his daughter's face told him that he had failed in his effort to be tactful.

"*Dios mío, papá*," she snapped at him, mortified at the question. "How could you even ask such a thing? What do you take me for, some kind of *puta*?"

Juan sighed with relief, feeling his shoulders relax. Although he had offended her, her disgust at his suggestion told him that he had nothing to fear. Of course her honour was still intact; as if any man had ever stood a chance of getting near her anyway, if her past record with suitors was anything to go by.

"Forgive me, *mija*, I had to be sure. I would never seriously suspect you of such a thing." Juan tried to laugh it off, but he was too embarrassed to look his daughter in the eye and she knew it. "Going back to your question. You were asking hypothetically, of course, but the answer is no. I would not allow you to marry a poor man, no matter how much you loved him."

"And what if I didn't care what you thought?" Her eyes were defiant, her lower lip curved into a scowl. He had seen the look many times, on the face of her grandmother in those rare moments when someone dared to say no to her.

"You know the law, Esperanza," he told her with a stern glare. "Young men and women must both have the consent of their parents in order to marry, you'd never find a priest to perform the ceremony without it. I can't imagine you being happy living in sin and poverty, exiled from your family and with no dowry to support you." He raised his eyebrows, and Esperanza turned away from him in anger. Even she had no argument against him this time.

Juan shook his head and sighed. He should've been angry with her for the disrespectful way that she was speaking to him, he knew. Still, it was bad enough that he had fallen out with her over Don Raúl and then offended her further by questioning her honour. He was not about to make matters worse by pursuing an argument with her about a hypothetical man who did not even exist.

"You've never known what it's like to be poor, Esperanza, but I do," he told her, placing a gentle hand on her shoulder. "I remember it, back when I was a young man, before I got the farm. I remember what it feels like to go to bed with no food in your belly. I know what it's like to be sick and unable to afford medicine. I will not allow any daughter of mine to live like that or raise my grandchildren in those sorts of circumstances. Not when I can give you the best."

"Has it ever crossed your mind that the best you could give me is my freedom?" she pleaded. Those beautiful blue eyes were filling with tears again, but he had to stay firm.

"It's not your choice to make, *mija*," he reminded her. "Your *mamá* and I have a duty to secure your future, and we have done so. You will marry Don Raúl. We have given his father our consent, and there is no backing out of it now. I will compromise with you, though. If Don Raúl is happy to wait until you say yes to him, then so will I. You will only marry when you agree to, and not before."

"You promise?"

"I promise."

They sat together for a long moment, neither speaking. Esperanza fiddled with a loose thread on her skirt, avoiding his gaze. She looked truly miserable, Juan thought, but at least she no longer seemed angry with him. One day, she would understand that he was only doing what was best for her. That day might be a long way off yet, but one day she would thank him for this.

"I understand your reasons, *papá*," she told him, her voice cracking, "but I still believe that you have made the wrong choice. I will never be happy with Raúl. We have nothing in common."

"You can't know that yet," Juan assured her. "The best thing you can do for yourself is to at least try to start the marriage on the right foot. He's tried to show an interest in your dancing. Perhaps it's time you started trying some of the things that interest him. You never know you might surprise yourself." He thought for a moment, his mind replaying conversations he'd had with Don Lorenzo, trying to pull out something of relevance. "He likes hunting, although I can't see blood sports appealing to you. Horse riding, though, I think you might like. Maybe I can ask that boy Arturo to teach you, he knows a thing or two about horses."

To Juan's surprise, Esperanza did not seem to find any argument with this suggestion. If anything, she appeared to show a spark of enthusiasm for the idea- her damp eyes lit up, and she nodded. Riding it was, then. They were getting somewhere at last.

"Excellent. Good girl. I know it will please Don Raúl to see you making an effort for him. And then you've got the festival on Saturday when he will get to see you dancing. Perhaps you could even smile this time, eh?" She had been practicing that dance almost religiously, and he couldn't help hoping that it was because she knew Don Raúl would be watching her perform it at the festival. Now, having seen her enthusiasm at learning to ride, he wondered if perhaps she could learn to like the Don after all.

"Come now, *mija*. It's almost four o'clock. Rafael said that he would take you to your dance rehearsal in the cart, Ricardo could do with practicing his driving skills anyway. I'll go and let Rafael know you're ready if you go down to the stables to tell Ricardo to get the cart prepared."

"*Sí, papá.*"

She wiped her eyes with her sleeve and hurried off towards the stables, her hair rippling in the sun behind her.

My little girl, he thought, feeling a pang of sadness in his chest. *You'll thank me for this one day. I hope.*

CHAPTER FIFTEEN

Esperanza watched from the upstairs window as the mariachi band tuned up their instruments in the *kiosca*, their handsome matching *charro* suits gleaming white in the sun. The day of the festival had finally arrived, and it was customary for last year's music competition winners to open the festival by accompanying a display of traditional dancing from a select number of talented local girls. Esperanza and Catalina were both among the honoured few, and Esperanza had come down to the *pueblo* early today so that she and Catalina could get ready together.

The weather was glorious, in contrast to the previous few days when the heavy rain had prevented anyone from putting up decorations. This had worked in Esperanza's favor, as it now meant that her mother and aunt were both busy helping to make the plaza look beautiful rather than fussing over the dancers. Francisco was occupied with helping to set up stalls of street food and alcohol around the edges of the plaza, so the girls were at liberty to chatter and gossip as they pleased.

"I had a talk with your little *músico* yesterday," Catalina grinned, gesturing for Esperanza to turn around so that she could help her fasten her skirt. "I've seen him a few times over the last few days, staring at the place where this street meets the plaza, wilting like a daisy every time some young woman comes out from here or your aunt's shop and it isn't you."

"Oh, stop it," Esperanza tutted, rolling her eyes.

"I'm serious. I had to go out and talk to him by the end of the day yesterday, I felt that sorry for him sitting there in the rain with nobody listening to him play."

"No, you didn't. I'm not falling for your teasing, so don't waste your breath." Esperanza allowed her friend to push her onto the stool in front of her dressing table, doing her best to sit still as Catalina took out a hairbrush and began to tackle the knots in her hair.

"I'm not teasing you, Esperanza."

She glanced up at Catalina's expression in the mirror, and to her surprise, saw that she was telling the truth.

"I wanted to find out a bit more about this mysterious street musician, to make sure that he really was as wonderful as you seemed to think. I introduced myself to him and told him we were both looking forward to seeing him play today. He was very keen to talk to me when I mentioned your name."

She shook her head and sighed, a little smile playing on her lips.

"He was so happy when I told him I knew who he was. I said that you were always talking about him, and his little face lit up. It was very sweet. I can see why you find him so endearing, *mi compa*. I have to admit, I couldn't help falling a little bit in love with him myself by the end of the conversation." She winked.

Catalina finished brushing Esperanza's hair, leaving it to hang in soft, dark ripples down her back as she took the basket of fresh roses from the bed. The smell of their perfume hung heavy and intoxicating in the warm air, and Esperanza could not help but think of the rose Artie had given her the last time they were alone together. She would support him with pride today, whether everyone else liked it or not.

Catalina wove the roses into the braid she had made in Esperanza's hair, where they sat in a beautiful floral crown. Esperanza stared at herself in the mirror, admiring her friend's handiwork. She had never managed to get her own hair to behave itself, but somehow Catalina had worked some sort of witchcraft to persuade the flowers to stay in place.

"I can't promise I can make yours look as good as you've made mine, but sit down and I'll give it a go," she offered, and the women swapped places, Esperanza taking up the hairbrush.

Catalina's hair wasn't as thick as Esperanza's, so it did not take nearly as long to comb through and braid to match her own. Every dancer had been allocated a different coloured silk skirt to wear, and Esperanza's was a bright cobalt blue to match her eyes while Catalina's was a vivid crimson. Their white blouses were embroidered with flowers around the neckline and sleeves, and a rainbow of brightly coloured ribbons had been sewn all around the hems of their skirts. As they required free movement to dance, the girls were not required to wear corsets, which was a great relief to Catalina with her swelling abdomen.

"You're not going to be able to keep this baby a secret for much longer," Esperanza warned as she helped her friend to adjust her skirt.

"This?" Catalina rubbed her belly with a loving grin. "Oh, that's not the baby. It's all the cake I've been eating. I'm starving all the time at the moment. Francisco says it's lucky we live near to the bakery, or otherwise, he's afraid I might wake up hungry from my *siesta* and eat him instead."

"Baby likes cake, then?" Esperanza laughed. "I can't imagine who he takes after."

Whoever had been responsible for decorating the plaza had done a marvellous job. *Papel picado* zig-zagged up and down every side street and adorned every stall that Esperanza could see, each ornate flag unique. Large, vibrant paper flowers and fans hung from every tree like giant fruits, washing the whole plaza in a rainbow of colour. The *kiosca* was most resplendent of all, covered in a mixture of paper decorations and fresh flowers, the scent of which Esperanza could smell before she even entered the plaza.

The dancers processed into the middle of the square, where they got into place ready for the performance. The waiting crowd whooped and cheered in encouragement, many of them already holding mugs of beer, pulque and tequila that they had purchased from the surrounding stalls. Delicious smells emanated from other stalls selling *carnitas* and filled tortillas, and children danced around stands adorned with hand-carved wooden toys. The festival was a celebration, and the people here were very much ready to celebrate.

The dancers' first task was to curtsey to the judges, although it took Esperanza a few moments to spot where they were. Don Raúl sat with his father, overlooking the plaza from the balcony of the town hall opposite the *kiosca*. Both men were smiling, glasses in their hands, and Esperanza hoped that the presence of Don Lorenzo might deter his son from drinking too heavily on this occasion. Raúl spotted her among the troupe of dancers and gave her a cordial wave, which she returned with a polite smile and a curtsey. If the Dons were going to be judging the music contest, she wanted to ensure that Raúl remained in the best mood possible for Artie's sake.

The mariachi band struck up a few chords, and Esperanza and the other girls picked up their skirts ready to dance. She spread her arms so that the fabric formed a wide arc, twirling it so that the ribbons danced in the sunlight. Her heels clicked against the cobbles as she turned, her petticoats swirling around her. The dancers proceeded around the plaza in perfect synchronisation, weaving around each other in a twirling rainbow of silk and ribbon.

Esperanza tried to focus on the dance, but she couldn't help glancing out at the cheering faces in the crowd. There was her mother, smiling and clapping along with *Tía* Victoria beside her. Her brothers, laughing and trying to copy the dancers, twirling around until they stumbled from dizziness. Her father was there too, standing over with Pedro and some of his other friends from the taverna, all of them swaying and waving their beer mugs to the music with broad smiles on their faces. Doctor Francisco stood with his brother-in-law Carlos, and there were the farmhands, some with their arms around their wives or holding small children aloft on their shoulders. The only face Esperanza couldn't see was the one she was most keen to find.

Catalina must have noticed her eyes searching the crowd because she caught Esperanza's attention as they twirled and gave a subtle nod towards the *kiosca*. Esperanza followed her gaze and was relieved to spot Artie standing on the steps towards the back, leaning against one of the pillars and watching her with a faraway look in his eyes. He looked tired, and she felt a slight twinge of worry at seeing how he was resting his head against the pillar, almost as though he did not have the strength to hold himself up. She noticed how he kept glancing up at Don Raúl in his privileged spot on the balcony and couldn't help wondering if he was a little bit afraid of him. She wouldn't have blamed him after what had happened the last time they met.

The dance finished to rapturous cheering from the crowd. The dancers turned to curtsey to the two Dons on the balcony, who stood to show their appreciation for the performance. Don Raúl was still smiling, and when Esperanza caught his eye, he raised his glass to her. She looked away, pretending not to see.

There was a short break before the music contest was to begin, and Esperanza took the opportunity to slip through the crowd and around the back of the *kiosca*. She spotted Artie sitting alone on the cobbles in the shade of one of the houses, leaning against the wall with his head tilted back. His eyes were closed, but he wasn't asleep. He seemed to be taking deep breaths, in through his nose and out through his mouth, as though trying to calm himself. Checking that nobody was watching, she snuck over and knelt beside him.

"Artie? Are you all right?" She placed a gentle hand on his arm, and he jumped, his eyes flickering up to meet hers.

"Esperanza." He gave her a wide smile and placed his hand on top of hers, his eyes lighting up at the sight of her. "You danced beautifully, as always."

"You didn't answer my question." He looked away, but she refused to back down, keeping her eyes fixed on his until he met her gaze again. "What's wrong? You look as though you haven't slept in days. Is something bothering you? Are you unwell?"

She raised her hand to his forehead, her brow creased with worry, and was relieved to find no sign of a fever. He smiled even more at her concern for him, his eyes shining at her touch.

"He's not ill," said a sharp voice behind her. Diego bent down next to her, holding out a mug of water for Artie. "He's just got this silly notion into his head that he shouldn't perform in the competition. He's worried that he will let me down."

"What?" Esperanza let out a giggle of surprise. "Don't tell me that you've got stage fright? You, of all people?"

"Of course I haven't." He turned back to Diego with a frown. "I've already told you. I'm not worried about performing. I'm worried that with Don Raúl as the judge you don't stand a chance of winning if you perform with me. You know the man hates me, but he doesn't have a problem with you. There's a lot of money at stake here, *hermano*, money that would keep a roof over our heads and food in our bellies. You should go on by yourself, at least give yourself a chance."

"And I've told *you*, we perform together or not at all," Diego said curtly. "I can't do this without you, Arturo. Now stop this nonsense. We're going to be on soon, and I won't have you moping around on the stage like a wet rag. We can win this. Pull yourself together and get on with the job."

Artie sighed and ran his hands through his soft, thick hair, causing it to stick up even more than usual. So this was what he was worried about; Don Raúl bearing a grudge against him and denying his brother a fair chance of winning the competition.

"You try talking to him," Diego ordered Esperanza, scowling. "He listens better to you than he does to me these days." He stood and walked off in the direction of the *kiosca*, shaking his head in frustration. Artie gave an exasperated sigh, covering his face with his hands.

"Hey," she said softly, positioning herself to sit against the wall next to him. "Come on. You always say that music isn't about winning competitions, it's about communicating with people. Making people happy. You're an expert at that. Who cares what Don Raúl thinks?"

Artie gave a hopeless shrug.

"Normally, I'd agree with you. But we've got a lot riding on today. It's not so much me, it's Diego. He's got plans for that money."

"If you're worried that Don Raúl isn't going to give you a fair chance, then appeal to Don Lorenzo instead," Esperanza persisted. "Play to the crowd. Make them go wild for you, get them dancing like you did on that day when Don Raúl's horse escaped. Perform so well that he has no *choice* but to name you the winners."

Artie shot her a weak smile.

"These other acts are good, *señorita*."

"Then be better," she insisted. "I know you can. You've got the best voice in all of Santa Sofia, all of Mexico I'll bet. You play that guitar as though you were born with it. You can do this, I know you can. I believe in you."

She reached out and took his hand, threading her fingers through his, pulling it down into the gap between them so that nobody else could see. His eyes shone at her touch, and he looked up at her with longing.

"I've missed you, Esperanza," he whispered, squeezing her hand. "I wish everybody shared your high opinion of me."

"Don't do it for everybody," she whispered back. "Do it for me. Just for me. As far as I'm concerned, you've won already."

He beamed at her, the light returned to his eyes.

"All right. Just for you." He glanced around to check that nobody was watching, then raised her hand to his lips and kissed it. "If Diego insists that I must perform with him, then I will do it for you, and yours is the only opinion that will matter to me."

He pulled himself to his feet, helping her up beside him.

"Now, how do I look?" He puffed out his chest and struck an attempt at a dashing pose. He was dressed in the same smart outfit that he had been wearing the night of Don Lorenzo's *baile*, with his handsome royal blue waistcoat and red belt and necktie. He had even polished his boots. Somehow, though, he still looked scruffy. His floppy hair was sticking up from the number of times he had run his hands through it, and the top few buttons of his oversized shirt were unfastened, exposing the soft skin beneath. His baggy sleeves were rolled up as always, but one was above the elbow and the other halfway down his forearm. Esperanza laughed and pulled a comb from her skirt pocket.

"I can tell you're nervous, you've been running your hands through your hair. You look like a porcupine. Come here." He grinned at her as she ran the comb through the thick strands, smoothing it down and brushing it out of his eyes. It was so soft, she wanted to run her fingers through it herself.

She looked down, trying to distract herself from how his eyes were sparkling at her, and noticed that his necktie was tucked inside the collar of his shirt. Her hands drifted down his jawline towards his collarbone to fix it, but as her fingers brushed over his neck he gave a strangled gasp and crumpled like a child, shivering and clamping his hands over the skin that she had just touched. She stared at him as he dropped to his knees before her, panting, his eyes squeezed shut.

"Artie," she said with wonder, a slow grin spreading across her face. "Are you... ticklish?"

"N- no," he lied, hunching his shoulders and pulling his collar up around his neck. "I'm just a little sensitive around... argh, no! Esperanza, please! No, no, no..."

He squealed as she reached out towards him, scrambling back against the wall with his hands raised to protect himself.

"Come here, you fool," she laughed. "I'm trying to help you up."

She reached out to him again, and he whimpered, clutching his collar and looking up at her with distrustful eyes. She laughed again; he was worse than her brothers.

"What on Earth are you two doing over here?" hissed Diego's voice behind her. "Do you want to attract the attention of the whole plaza?"

"I didn't mean to!" Esperanza protested. "I was only trying to fix his necktie, I didn't know I'd found his weak spot."

"I think you already know far too much about my brother's *weak spots* for your own good." Diego reached down and hauled Artie to his feet, brushing the dirt from his waistcoat. Artie was still breathless and quivering, his ears pink. "So, are we doing this then or not?"

"Sí," he panted, avoiding Esperanza's gaze. "We're doing it."

"Which song are you going to play?" she asked, fighting the urge to help him brush himself down. Those uneven sleeves were still bothering her, her fingers itching to reach out to him and fix them. "*Pajarillo?*"

Diego looked at her as though she had gone mad.

"No. It's so difficult, there's so much potential for it to go wrong. We can't take a risk like that in this sort of competition. The whole town is watching."

"That's why you have to play it," Esperanza insisted. "The whole town has heard all of your everyday songs. They smile, they walk by. Look at what happened last time you played *Pajarillo*. You set the whole *pueblo* alight. I want to see you win this contest. You need to hit them with your best shot."

Artie hesitated for a moment, then nodded.

"*Sí, Pajarillo*. Esperanza's right, we've got to take a risk, Diego."

"Oh, fine," Diego conceded. "On your head, be it. Go on, then. Go and fetch your guitar. We're on after this next lot, you'd better make sure you're all tuned up and ready to go."

Artie gave them both a nervous grin and moved as though to walk away, but Esperanza stopped him with a hand on his shoulder.

"Wait," she said, pulling a rose from her hair. She reached up and tucked it into the chest pocket of his waistcoat. "For luck."

He beamed at her and placed his hand over hers, holding it for a moment against his heart, then bowed to her before drifting back towards the *kiosca* with a faraway smile.

Esperanza felt a pang in her chest as he walked away, suddenly nervous on his behalf. She hoped that her advice would prove sound. If nerves got the better of them and this performance ended up a disaster, then both of the brothers would be completely justified in blaming her for choosing such a difficult song. Still, she had seen Artie play it before. She knew how brilliant he could be. If anyone could pull it off, he could.

"I hope you meant what you just said, *señorita*," Diego muttered. She could sense that he was nervous too.

"Of course," Esperanza assured him, trying to sound more confident than she felt. "*Pajarillo* is your best chance with this crowd. I wouldn't have said so otherwise."

"I didn't mean about the song. I meant about you wanting us to win."

Esperanza turned to him, confused.

"Of course I want you to win. Why would you ever think otherwise?"

Diego edged a little nearer to her, glancing around to check that nobody else was listening.

"You know why this contest is so important to us, don't you?" he asked her quietly, still watching Artie out of the corner of his eye. "That sort of prize money, that's our ticket out of here. We can go travelling like we always planned, take our music all over Mexico. Maybe even go north up into California. We can start again, somewhere where nobody will ever know that we were once just a pair of street orphans. We can live a respectable life."

Esperanza's heart suddenly felt very heavy. It wasn't as though Artie hadn't told her; he had explained his plans that very first time when they had sat together by the river and he had helped her with the laundry. Why should his intentions have changed? He deserved the chance to start anew, away from the prejudices of the stuck-up people in this town who were too full of their own importance to see beyond his ragged clothes and lack of breeding. Maybe he would even find some nice girl and get married. He could have the family he had always longed for. What right did she have to hold him back from that?

"I know," she nodded, trying to hide the tightness in her voice. "He told me all about it."

"Good," Diego grunted, still not meeting her eye. "I just wanted to make sure that you were clear on the matter, señorita. I'm sure you're aware my brother harbours quite a fondness for you. A fondness that can never come to anything, especially with your connections to Don Raúl."

He cleared his throat, glancing up towards the balcony where the Dons sat watching the competition unfolding, and Esperanza noted a strange, sad expression on his face. She felt a little rush of warmth for him, recognizing how much Artie's happiness meant to him. Diego had never been a great fan of hers, she knew, but she couldn't blame him for that. It clearly pained him to see his brother getting so close to her, knowing that he was only setting himself up for an inevitable fall.

"I am led to believe that official courtship discussions have taken place, and gifts exchanged? Don Raúl is now your official suitor and intends to become your husband?" Diego's voice sounded even gruffer than before.

"Sí." Esperanza looked at the ground and swallowed hard, trying not to allow herself to get emotional. "Believe me, Diego, I wish it were not so."

"You and me both," said Diego, his voice catching a little. "But the world is what it is, and we must sometimes accept that life is not fair. Do us all a favor, though, and don't tell Arturo today. Let him have this moment to enjoy himself without having all that heartache to contend with as well. It's been bad enough these last few days since he saw you all dressed up for Don Raúl the other night. I think it finally made him realize what I've been trying to tell him all along; that you and he are worlds apart, and there's nothing he can do to change it. It's been killing him."

Esperanza nodded. So that was why Artie looked so tired and why he had been watching the balcony with such a strange expression on his face. She glanced over at him standing by the *kiosca*, tuning his guitar and practicing complicated finger patterns up and down the fretboard with his tongue sticking out in concentration, and felt a lump forming in her throat.

"If you're going to watch this suicide mission of a song that you've set us both on, then I suggest you go around to the front and get yourself a spot, *señorita*," Diego told her, putting a gentle hand on her shoulder. "We're on next."

CHAPTER SIXTEEN

Esperanza took herself around the side of the *kiosca* to where Catalina and her brothers were waiting. She had to fight to steady her breathing, willing herself not to cry. *Today is about him,* she reminded herself firmly. *If he's leaving, then he's leaving, but right now he's here and he needs you.*

"There you are!" cried Catalina with a smile. "I'm told that your *músico* is on next, I was worried you were going to miss him."

Oh, I'm certainly going to miss him, Esperanza agreed. She felt tears springing to her eyes and fought hard to hold them back.

"Hey, are you all right?" Catalina's smile faded, and she looked at Esperanza with concern. They had known each other too long for Esperanza to be able to hide her feelings from her.

"Fine," Esperanza lied, putting her arms around her brothers. She manoeuvred them all close to the front, right into the centre where she knew Artie would be able to see her. "I'm just a little anxious for them, that's all. I know how much this contest means to them both. I hope their nerves don't get the better of them."

"We're about to find out," Catalina told her, nodding towards the stage. Diego ascended the steps, followed by Artie, and Esperanza forced her own feelings to the back of her mind. This was Artie's moment, not hers, and she had a duty to him as a friend if nothing else.

He looked so serious, his brows furrowed in concentration as he muttered to himself, but at the sight of Esperanza, his face broke into a nervous grin. She grinned back, giving him a nod of encouragement, and he took a few deep, calming breaths as he prepared himself to sing. He still looked tense, and he kept glancing up at Don Raúl on the balcony. *Stop it*, Esperanza wanted to tell him. *Looking at him won't do you any good. Look at me. Sing it for me.*

Artie glanced back down at her, his eyes full of fear, and Esperanza knew she had to do something. Fixing him with her most encouraging smile, she raised her hand and blew a subtle kiss in his direction. The impact was exactly as she had hoped. He froze for a moment, the breath catching in his chest as his face split into a beaming smile, his ears tinging pink. His chest swelled with pride as he raised his hand high in the air, letting out an ear-splitting *grito* that echoed all around the plaza. People stopped mid-conversation to look at him, and an eerie hush swept across the square as everyone turned towards the *kiosca*.

Then, with an energy that sent tremors through the whole plaza, Artie launched into an even more joyous and thrilling performance of *Pajarillo* than the last time she had heard it. His voice was bright and lively, his fingers dancing over the frets of his guitar as he sang.

"*Pajarillo, pajarillo, pajarillo barranqueño, Que bonitos ojos tienes, lástima que tengan dueño!*"

Diego was keeping up with him this time, his face a little ruddy with exertion but a smile on his lips. He nodded at Esperanza, and she grinned back at him, relieved that her advice had paid off. This was the Artie she knew, doing what he did best. He was the best *músico* in all of Mexico, she was sure of it, and now she just had to hope that the rest of the crowd agreed with her.

Artie was dancing too now, throwing in the odd little spin or jump here and there and performing little tricks with his guitar. The crowd watched him with interest, smiling and nodding, some clapping along to the music. *Come on*, thought Esperanza. *Put your drinks down and dance.* She looked around hopefully, but the people were too hot from the sun, too sleepy from drink to stir themselves as they had done the last time. If they were going to wake up and dance, then someone would need to encourage them.

Esperanza took a deep breath and picked up her skirts, fanning them out around her so that the sunlight caught all of the colours of the shining ribbons sewn around her hem. She began to dance, swirling the fabric around herself, her heels clicking on the cobbles. Catalina picked up on what she was doing and joined her, copying her footwork and mirroring the movement of her skirts. The two of them spun and twirled, and the crowd began to stir, cheering them on as Artie and Diego played.

Esperanza beckoned for her brothers to join in, which they did, squealing with laughter and swishing their arms as though they had skirts too, puffing out their chests like matadors and stomping their feet on the cobbles. Their little friends from the crowd came over to join them, and before Esperanza knew it, she was surrounded by children, dancing and laughing along with the music, cheering whenever Artie performed a trick with his guitar. He beamed down at her, holding her gaze as he sang the lyrics which made her heart swell.

"*Abre mi pecho y verás lo mucho que yo te quiero...*"

Open my chest and you will see how much I love you. He gave her a bold wink before spinning away across the stage, and Catalina had to take Esperanza's hand to remind her to keep dancing.

More and more people started to join in. Girls were pulling their menfolk to their feet, begging them for a dance. Couples who had already drunk a little too much beer were stumbling over each other, laughing as they fell into each other's arms. Esperanza even spotted her parents joining in, Juan pulling Louisa out of the crowd to dance despite her laughing protests.

A small group of young women stood to one side of the *kiosca*, nudging each other as they eyed Artie up with interest and batted their eyelashes. Esperanza glared at them, and Catalina laughed.

"Artie isn't the only one with competition today," she winked. "You'd better watch your step, *mi amiga*."

"They had better watch theirs, otherwise I will have to go over there and strangle the lot of them with their own hair ribbons," Esperanza scowled, making Catalina laugh again.

Artie changed up a key for one final verse, giving it one last boost of energy. Diego was dancing around the stage now as well, the veins standing out from his sweat-covered forehead in concentration. Esperanza and Catalina gave a final burst of effort, too, whirling and spinning around each other like tropical birds with their brightly coloured skirts flying. The song drew to a close, and both women knelt breathlessly in their finishing positions as Artie let out one final loud *grito* from the stage.

The crowd went wild, whooping and cheering, crying out for more. Artie and Diego bowed, huge grins of pride on their faces. Esperanza could not resist glancing up at the balcony and was surprised to see both Dons standing and whistling with the rest of the crowd, nodding to each other in approval. Diego smiled up at them, reveling in their applause, but Artie only had eyes for Esperanza. He locked gazes with her, and she blew him another subtle kiss while the crowd around her screamed and cheered.

"Go on," Catalina whispered, her eyes shining. "Don't do anything I wouldn't do." She winked, and Esperanza hurried off through the crowd to the steps at the back of the *kiosca*.

To her dismay, she found that the girls who had been making eyes at Artie while he was singing had also had the same idea. They had congregated on the steps of the *kiosca*, blocking the way down so that Artie could not miss them as he came off stage. She glowered at them, but they ignored her, too busy adjusting their hair and skirts to pay her any notice. She had no choice but to stand back and wait her turn.

Artie appeared at the top of the steps, and all of the girls began to chatter at him at once, congratulating him on his performance and simpering compliments at him. He looked baffled for a moment, looking from one to another with a confused frown, stepping back as one of them tried to touch his arm. Then he saw Esperanza, and his grin returned. For a moment she thought that he was going to push his way through the girls on the steps, but he seemed to think better of it, and instead slung his guitar onto his back and vaulted over the railings.

He landed like a cat on the cobbles, sprang towards Esperanza and swept her up in his arms, spinning her around until she laughed. She wrapped her arms around his neck, grinning smugly over his shoulder at the girls on the steps. They glared back, looking distinctly sour as they dispersed, grumbling. She knew that she should be more careful of being seen, but in the heat of the moment, she couldn't have cared less if President Díaz himself had been watching her.

"I'm so proud of you," she whispered, nuzzling her head against Artie's neck. He squeezed her tighter, unable to find the words to reply. She could feel that he was trembling from the adrenaline, yet his arms were as strong and comforting as always.

"If you're quite finished," Diego grumbled, rolling his eyes as he followed Artie down the steps. Esperanza could see even he was smiling through his gruff exterior. "I'd advise you to put her down, *hermano*, before you attract trouble."

Artie complied, reluctantly letting Esperanza go. His eyes were full of breathless emotion. Diego's clapped him on the shoulder so hard that his knees almost gave way, no longer able to hold back his pride.

"You did well, *hermano*," he congratulated him, ruffling his hair. "And look, it seems we've got a fan club approaching."

Not those girls again, Esperanza thought, gritting her teeth and bracing herself to tell them where to go. To her relief, though, it wasn't them- this group consisted of young men, one with his arm around a smiling girl.

"*Mi familia!*" cried Diego, embracing the nearest two in a tight hug. "We're so glad you made it!"

"Wouldn't have missed it for the world," smiled a handsome man who couldn't have been much older than Esperanza. "Arturo, *mi amigo*, you did us all proud today."

These people must be his street family, Esperanza realized. She smiled nervously at them, recognizing that to Artie, this was the equivalent of introducing her to his parents.

"You must be Esperanza," smiled the young man, taking her hand and bowing. "We've heard a lot about you, *señorita*. I'm Joaquin, and this is my wife, Paloma."

"Your wife," grinned Artie. "How does it feel saying that at last, *amigo*? Are you used to it yet?"

"I don't think I'll ever get used to it. I'm the luckiest man in the world." Joaquin bent down to give the pretty girl beside him a loving kiss on the cheek. "First time we've left the hut since the wedding, isn't it, *mi amor*?"

The other men laughed, and the young woman chided her new husband, looking away with shy embarrassment. He put his arms around her, kissing her again.

"Congratulations," Esperanza smiled, and the young woman beamed back, nuzzling her cheek against her husband's chest. They looked so happy. Esperanza watched them with wistful longing, wondering what it must be like to be married to someone you felt like that for. To have the freedom to be with the person you loved. She glanced at Artie, who gazed back at her with an expression that made her heart skip.

"We have heard great things about you, *señorita*," said Paloma, giving Esperanza a shy smile. "Your dancing was wonderful."

Esperanza nodded in thanks, returning her smile. She found herself liking this girl far more than any of the snobby, high-born women she had met at Don Lorenzo's *baile*.

The group chatted for a while, Artie continually glancing at Esperanza. He seemed delighted that she was getting along so well with his street family, and she was relieved to find herself fitting in. They were far more pleasant to be around than Don Raúl's snobbish friends, and she soon found herself chatting and laughing with them as though she had known them for years.

After what felt like hours, a boy came running over to tell them that the contest was over and that all of the competitors were to be summoned back to the *kiosca*. Artie looked so pale that Esperanza thought he might faint. He sensed her watching him and edged a little closer to her.

"Will you watch the judging?" he asked.

"Of course." She gave his arm a gentle squeeze. "As long as you promise to stay conscious for it. You look as though you're about to keel over."

He gave her a weak smile, touched by her concern.

"I'm just tired, señorita. Don't you worry about me."

She led him around to the front of the stage, where they stood with Diego and the rest of the nervous-looking competitors. Catalina joined them, along with Miguel and Felipe, who were both buzzing with excitement. Esperanza stood back, allowing Diego to take his place beside Artie. Today's events were about them, she reminded herself. Not her.

Don Raúl and his father came down from their balcony and proceeded onto the stage, smiling and waving cordially at the crowd. Esperanza noticed that both Joaquin and Paloma were wearing stony expressions, as were the rest of Artie's street family.

"Joaquin and a few of the other boys work up in one of Don Lorenzo's gold mines," Paloma explained, catching sight of her puzzled expression. "The Dons are not kind employers."

Esperanza nodded in understanding. She hadn't realized that some of Artie's friends worked for Don Raúl, but if he didn't treat his workers well then it at least explained some of the animosity Artie felt towards them. She couldn't ask Paloma to explain any further, but she made a mental note to ask Artie about it at some point.

Don Lorenzo held up his hand, and the crowd fell quiet. The moment had arrived.

"Señoras y señores," he began, smiling down at everyone. "It has been my great pleasure to judge the great array of talent that has been demonstrated here in Santa Sofia today..."

As his father addressed the plaza, Esperanza noticed Don Raúl scanning the faces below. She tried to hide behind Diego, but Don Raúl must have seen her because as soon as he looked in their direction his face broke into a warm smile and he and stood a little straighter, puffing out his chest. To her surprise, his eyes were sparkling with life for once.

"I think he's warming to you," Catalina whispered to her.

"More likely it's the drink," she whispered back.

"Perhaps he's got wind?" Catalina suggested, and Esperanza snorted with laughter. Diego turned and gave them both a withering look.

"...So on to the winners!" Don Lorenzo continued, and Esperanza forced herself to pay attention again. "The winner of the annual *Competencia Musical de Santa Sofia*, and the grand prize of two hundred gold pesos, is..."

Esperanza crossed her fingers. Artie's eyes were closed, and although she couldn't see Diego's face, she could tell that he was holding his breath.

"*Dos Hermanos!*"

The crowd went wild again. Esperanza had to jump backward as Diego leapt in the air with a loud *grito* of triumph. Artie reeled with shock, and both Esperanza and Joaquin lunged to catch his arms, afraid that he was going to fall. Diego grabbed his brother's hand and held it aloft in triumph, laughing as his street family cheered and clapped the pair of them on the back.

This meant as much to them as it did to him, she knew. Diego and Artie represented all of them; they were living proof that two orphaned boys from the streets could do just as well as those wealthy men who had expensive instruments and had been tutored in the arts since they could walk. Finally, this could be their chance to move away and make successes of themselves, just as they had always dreamed, no longer ragged street orphans but respected professional musicians.

Esperanza cheered and clapped with the crowd, trying to ignore the stabbing pain in her heart. Diego pushed his way towards the steps, dragging a dazed Artie behind him. The sound of whistling and cheering was almost deafening as the two young men were pulled up onto the stage to shake hands with the Dons, and Esperanza took a moment to turn away and try to gather herself together. She felt Catalina put an arm around her and realized that there were tears streaming down her face.

"Oh, *mi compa*, what's the matter?" Catalina cooed, pulling her into a hug. Esperanza couldn't reply, breaking down in her friend's arms with a sob that nobody else could hear over the noise of the crowd.

The people were chanting for Artie and Diego, demanding to hear them play again. They relented with very little persuasion, and after a moment, Esperanza heard them launch into their own lively rendition of *La Llorona*. The crowd cheered, singing along at the tops of their voices, and Catalina steered Esperanza around to the back of the *kiosca* and sat her down on a bench in the shade of a tree. She perched beside her and pulled a handkerchief from the pocket in her skirt.

"Talk to me, *mi compa*," she begged. "I haven't seen you cry in years. What's going on? Surely you're happy that they won?"

"I'm delighted," Esperanza replied honestly, smiling through her tears. "They deserved to win. I'm so proud of them. It's just... look, I know it's selfish of me, but... they're going to use that prize money to leave Santa Sofia and start a new life. And I'll be left here, married to a man I don't love, and I might never see Artie again." The words caught in her throat, choking her. "I'm just going to miss him so much."

She broke down. Catalina wrapped her arms around her and rocked her like a child, and the two of them sat together without speaking, listening to the crowd's celebrations and the beautiful sound of Artie's voice echoing around the plaza.

"*El que no sabe de amores, Llorona, no sabe lo que es martirio...*"

He who doesn't know about love, weeping woman, doesn't know what agony is. How true those lyrics were, and how cruel. They were both trapped; Artie by poverty, and she by social expectation. Her cage was ornate and gilded, while his was simple and plain, but they were both cages all the same. The least she could do was allow him to take the escape route he had been granted without making him suffer the guilt of knowing the pain it would cause her to be left behind.

Esperanza could hear the song drawing to a close and tried hard to pull herself together. Catalina helped, dabbing her face with the handkerchief and trying not to smudge her makeup. At last she stood back, and Esperanza forced a watery smile.

"There." Catalina smoothed her hair back into place. "Your eyes are a little red, but that will soon pass. Otherwise, nobody would ever know you'd gotten yourself so upset."

"Thank you," Esperanza sniffed. "I'm sorry. I don't know what came over me."

"I think I do," Catalina replied, giving her hand a sympathetic squeeze.

"Esperanza?" Artie was coming down the steps of the *kiosca* wearing a huge grin, and after a moment, he spotted her over on the bench. She stood, and he half-ran towards her, sweeping her into a fierce hug. "We won. We won, and all because of you."

"Hardly," she laughed, choking a little on the lump in her throat. "You're the one with all the talent. All I did was remind you that you had it."

He put her down and stroked her hair back from her face, his grin fading as he saw the redness in her eyes.

"You're crying," he said, brushing her tears away with his thumb. "What's the matter?"

"Happy tears," she lied, forcing a smile. "I'm just so pleased for you and Diego. I know how much this contest meant to you both."

He smiled lovingly back, and emotion overcame her. Before she could stop herself, she stepped back into his arms and buried her face in the soft fabric of his shirt to hide the tears that were once again spilling from her eyes. She pressed her cheek against his chest, desperate to feel the strong, comforting thumping of his heartbeat. It was the only way she could reassure herself that he was still real, still here with her, if only for now. He wrapped his arms around her, stroking the exposed skin on the back of her neck with his thumb and drawing in the beautiful scent of the flowers in her hair.

"This is the best day of my life," he whispered into her hair, his eyes closed. He held her against his chest with a blissful sigh, his heart pounding hard against her cheek, and she reciprocated by wrapping her arms even tighter around him. She didn't care who might be watching. She never wanted to let him go.

"*Esperanza!*"

Oh no. Not now. Esperanza and Artie sprung apart as Louisa stormed across the courtyard towards them. She did not look happy. Esperanza prayed that she had not been watching them for long, but she knew deep down that it was already too late. She looked to Catalina in panic, her mind blank.

Fortunately, Catalina's brain worked fast. She sprang forward and threw her own arms around Artie's neck, much to his bewilderment.

"Play along with it," she hissed in his ear. "For Esperanza's sake."

He complied, trying to disguise his own baffled expression as he patted her awkwardly on the back.

"Congratulations again, *señor*," Catalina cried, loudly enough for Louisa to hear. "It was a well-deserved win. We are so very happy for you."

Esperanza caught on immediately to what her friend was doing. By making it look as though everyone was just excited and congratulating Artie on his success, it would seem like Esperanza had been simply joining in with the celebration rather than stealing a romantic moment with him. It was worth a try, at least.

Louisa reached them and grabbed Esperanza by the arm, her eyes narrowed with suspicion.

"Señora Louisa!" Catalina greeted her with theatrical enthusiasm, releasing Artie and holding her arms out to hug Louisa instead. "Did you see? Arturo and his brother won the music contest! You and Juan must be so proud to have a celebrity working on the farm!"

"Sí, something like that," Louisa said, looking with narrowed eyes from Esperanza to Artie and back again. She didn't seem sure how to proceed, keen not to make an unnecessary public scene. Something wasn't right with this picture, she could tell, but she couldn't quite put her finger on what.

"We were just congratulating Artie on his success, mamá," Esperanza reassured her, playing along with Catalina's charade. "Didn't the boys do well?"

"Sí, they did. Very well done, Arturo. Please pass on our congratulations to your brother, too."

Esperanza breathed a sigh of relief. The deception had worked, and Louisa's suspicion had dissipated. Almost.

"Your eyes are red, Esperanza," Louisa said with surprise, turning her daughter to look at her. "Have you been crying?"

Esperanza faltered, but once again, Catalina sprung to the rescue.

"My fault I fear, señora," she confessed. "Although I'm pleased to say that they're happy tears. I've just told Esperanza the news that I'm expecting a baby in the New Year."

Louisa let out a squeal of joy, throwing arms around Catalina's shoulders. Catalina cringed, and Esperanza felt a pang of guilt. She knew that her friend had not wanted to tell people just yet, but now that Louisa knew the news would be halfway to Europe before they even got back to the farm.

You owe me one, Catalina mouthed over Louisa's shoulder. Esperanza pulled a face and mimed a silent 'thank-you' back to her. She would have to make her friend a lot of cakes to compensate for this. Artie was smiling blankly at them all, trying to pretend that he had some idea of what was going on.

"Well, at least that explains why there's so much celebration going on over here," laughed Louisa, wiping tears of joy from her own eyes. "Santa Sofia seems to have blessed us all in one way or another. Still..." she turned to Esperanza. "I would appreciate it if you could resist getting too over-enthusiastic with your celebrations in future, *mija*. I would not want Don Raúl to see his future wife hugging another man. People will soon find out that you are courting now, it would not do to cause him any embarrassment by setting tongues wagging. You never know, Catalina, if all goes to plan then your little one will have a playmate on the way before the year is out."

She gave a high laugh, not seeming to notice that nobody else joined in. Catalina gave a quiet groan, which she tried and failed to turn into a sound of interest. Esperanza heard Artie exhale quietly behind her as the news hit him like an arrow to the heart. She couldn't bring herself to look at him. Instead, she lowered her gaze to the ground and tried to control the spinning in her head. She felt as though she might faint.

"You look very pale, *mija*," Louisa observed, taking her hand. "I think perhaps it's time we called it a day. Come on, let's go and find your father and your brothers. I fear that Rafael might have had a little too much to drink to drive the cart home, but perhaps that young lad Ricardo might oblige for a few extra *centavos*."

"Sí, mamá," Esperanza croaked. She hugged Catalina goodbye, fighting back her tears again.

"Thank you," she whispered in her friend's ear, her voice wobbling.

"It will be all right, mi compa," Catalina promised her. "I'll look after him. Don't worry."

She turned to Artie, too choked with emotion to speak. He looked pale and shaken, staring at the ground with a look of silent pain. She wanted to reach out to him, to throw her arms around him again and hold him until the rest of the world disappeared, but there was nothing she could do with her mother standing beside her.

"Congratulations again on your win, Arturo," she mumbled, her voice cracking. He did not even seem to hear her but continued to stare at the ground with a look of utter desolation.

Catalina gave her a reassuring nod, and with an aching heart, Esperanza allowed her mother to lead her back across the plaza. The crowd were still singing and drinking, dancing as though they had no cares in all the world. Diego was still on the stage, sharing a traitorous toast with the Dons to celebrate his win. It seemed that every girl Esperanza could see was in the loving arms of a young man, smiling and laughing as they kissed in shop doorways, sharing the blissful happiness that she could never know.

By the time Esperanza looked back, Catalina had directed Artie to a bench and was sitting with a motherly arm around him. He looked as broken as Esperanza felt, his body stooped over and his head in his hands. Had Louisa not been gripping her arm so tightly, Esperanza would have run back to him, take his hand and continue running until they reached the ends of the Earth.

CHAPTER SEVENTEEN

When Artie didn't arrive at work on Monday, Esperanza's worst suspicions were confirmed. She had even waited down by the river on Monday afternoon in their secret spot, just in case, but he never came. When he failed to show for work again on Tuesday, she knew that something must be badly wrong.

"Rafael," she called, stopping the old man as he passed the stables. "I'm looking for Arturo. Do you know where he is?"

"Good morning, *señorita*," Rafael greeted her, surprised. "You're up very early. I've only just got in myself."

"I couldn't sleep." She chose not to mention that she had already been up and dressed for several hours, sitting in the stables in anticipation of Artie's arrival.

"Fair enough. Well, you won't find Arturo around today. He sent a message yesterday morning to say that he had not been feeling himself since the music competition and asking whether he could swap his days this week to give himself time to recover." The old man stretched, the bones of his shoulders creaking. "I'd have suspected him of drinking too much after his win, but he went home just after the judging without touching a drop. Must've already been feeling a bit rough."

Esperanza suspected that she knew exactly how Artie had been feeling, and she felt even worse for hearing it.

"Rafael," she said again, making up her mind. "When my parents wake up, could you tell them I've headed down to the *pueblo*?"

"Of course. I'm heading back down there myself shortly with the cart; I've got a few deliveries to make to the plaza. You can come with me if you like. I know you're not fond of the cart, but it'll be quicker than walking if you're in a rush."

"Perfect, thank you, Rafael. I'll write *mamá* a note, in that case, and meet you outside the barn in a few minutes."

As the cart rattled towards town, Esperanza used her time to work out a plan for what she was going to do once she got there. It occurred to her that she didn't know where Artie lived. Perhaps if she asked around, someone might be able to point her in the right direction- everyone knew who he was now, at least, since his success at the festival. She just hoped that he would still want to see her.

"That's odd," Rafael grunted as the cart approached the outskirts of the *pueblo*, snapping Esperanza out of her reverie. "What's going on here?"

Instead of the usual gentle morning bustle of people around the taverna, the air was alight with panicked shouting. Esperanza and Rafael glanced at each other, and he slowed the horse to a walk, the wheels of the cart clacking against the rough cobbles.

The shouts and wails of misery erupted into terrified chaos as they neared the busy square, with people running in all directions, wailing and crying, some hugging each other while others jostled and pushed in their hurry towards the plaza. Esperanza clung to Rafael's arm in fear, and the old man patted her hand, his eyes wide with worry.

"Don't you worry, *señorita*. I won't leave your side," he promised.

The horse stopped just beside the doorway of *Tía* Victoria's shop, its way blocked by a large and noisy crowd outside Catalina's house. Esperanza drew back in horror at the sight of them. Most of them were men, although some were accompanied by wailing women, and all were suffering from horrific injuries of some sort or other. Many were bleeding, others burned, some holding out limbs at odd angles and moaning with pain.

"Catalina!" Esperanza called. The door was open, the crowd seeming to extend into Catalina's house. With a thrill of fear, Esperanza leapt down from the cart and pushed her way through, ignoring Rafael's protests. She had to almost climb over some of the waiting men to get through the doorway, and by the time she got inside the house, she realized that she had blood all over her skirt. It was definitely not her own.

"Esperanza!" Catalina's voice called out from a stool beside the kitchen table, where she was busy patching up a man who was wailing with agony, his shirt hanging off his shoulders in rags. "Thank God you're here. Quick, grab a stool. You have to help me."

"What the hell happened?" Esperanza dragged a stool over to sit across the table from her friend. She pulled the nearest man into the chair facing her, foraging among the medical equipment on the table for ointment and bandages so that she could dress a nasty burn on his arm.

"There's been an accident up at one of the mines," Catalina said grimly, threading up a needle that she had been soaking in alcohol to stitch her patient's bleeding shoulder wound. "It happened last night. Francisco went straight there with a cart full of medical supplies, but it turns out that it was much worse than he thought. He sent back the cart full of injured men so that he could concentrate on the ones who needed immediate treatment. They're loading it up with more supplies to take it back up there again."

"It was an explosion," said the man, his voice weak from pain. "One of the big tunnels caved in. There's a lot of men trapped down there still. We were the lucky ones with the minor injuries." He whimpered as Catalina began to stitch his wound, biting down hard on the empty sleeve of his shirt to stop himself from screaming.

"What do you need me to do?" Esperanza asked, taking a spare apron and tying it around her waist. She had gained some medical knowledge while watching Catalina patch up Miguel and Felipe after their occasional bumps and scrapes, but she had never seen anything like this before. It was going to be a very sharp learning curve.

"I'll send the more minor injuries over to you. Any cuts, grazes, minor burns and suchlike you can handle, and I'll deal with things like dislocated joints and missing digits. You might have to stitch a few wounds, but don't worry, I'll talk you through it."

Catalina grunted with frustration at the man in front of her, who was struggling to keep still.

"These stitches will take much longer if you keep squirming," she snapped. "Now keep still, or I'll have to knock you out. And I'll warn you, I won't do it the nice way. I'm saving the chloroform for patients with worse injuries than yours."

"Sí. Sorry, señora," he whimpered, eyeing up the frying pan that was suspended from the ceiling above the table. "I'll be brave."

Esperanza set to her task, clenching her teeth to stop her hands from trembling. She was accustomed to dealing with burns from her own clumsy experience in the kitchen, but she had never experienced any like these before. One of the pale, sweating men who was placed in front of her was burned so severely that his shirt sleeve seemed to have melted into the skin on his arm. Esperanza tried to peel the fabric back to take a look and only just sprung out of the way in time as he vomited and passed out on the floor with a resounding thud.

"He's gone into shock," Catalina cried, abandoning her own patient to roll the man onto his side. "Someone, bring me some water. Quickly! Good grief, what was Francisco thinking sending this man here? He should be in the hospital with injuries like this."

"With all due respect, señora, you didn't see the state of the men Doctor Francisco was sending to the hospital," said her abandoned patient, blood dripping down his face from a painful-looking gash in his head. "They made our wounds look like paper cuts."

A few of the frightened girls who had been accompanying their menfolk were drafted into helping out. Catalina would not let them treat any of the patients, trusting only herself and Esperanza to do anything technical, but the younger girls were set to work with cleaning up any errant bodily fluids, boiling pots of water on the stove and fetching more medical supplies from the store inside the town hall. They flitted about like terrified moths, crying and whimpering with fear at the carnage around them, but Esperanza managed to block out their whining. At least she would be able to concentrate on helping the men who needed her this way, without having to concern herself with menial tasks like mopping up blood and sterilising things.

"Señorita Esperanza!" Rafael appeared breathless and pale in the doorway, pushing his way through the injured men to get to her. He was trembling, his forehead covered with beads of sweat. "Have you heard what's happened? My nephew, Daniel- he works in that mine. He's only fourteen, señorita."

"Oh God, no," she gasped. "Have you asked around to see if anyone has heard anything?"

"There's a list on the church door," said her current patient, wincing as he rotated his wrist. "Someone's been making a list of the dead they've brought down so far, and they've been updating it as they- ouch!"

He yelped with pain as Esperanza kicked him in the shin.

"I've looked already," Rafael told her, his voice trembling. "Daniel's name isn't on there. He's my sister's boy, señorita. He's the nearest I've ever had to a child of my own. I don't know what I'd do if- if he-"

He broke off, unable to continue.

"If he's not on the list of the dead, then he might not have been found yet," said the irritating patient again, clearly thinking that he was being helpful. "There were quite a few bodies still trapped underground when we left, they might still-"

"Shut up," Esperanza snarled. "Keep your wrist still while I speak to this man, and then when I'm finished, I'll give you a compress to ease the blood flow from your broken nose."

"But my nose isn't broken," the man protested.

"Not yet. Open your mouth again, and it will be."

He took the hint and fell silent.

Esperanza stood and took Rafael by the arm.

"Listen carefully, *amigo*," she told him, trying to keep her voice calm. "I want you to take the cart and load it with medical supplies. Francisco has given a list to the town hall of what he still needs, there's still plenty in the store. Then you're to take that cart up to the mine and follow Francisco's instructions from there. Go and find your nephew, take him home, and when he's feeling up to it in a few days' time, bring him up to the farm, all right? I will talk to my father. Daniel can work for us from now on. He never needs to set foot in a mine again."

"Thank you, *señorita*." Rafael's eyes filled with tears. "I will not forget this."

He left in a hurry, and Esperanza took a moment to say a silent prayer for Daniel as she unwound a bandage for her irritating patient. Her father never took workers under the age of sixteen, but Rafael was like one of the family. It was the least they could do for him after his years of loyal service.

As long as the boy is still alive, said a nasty voice in her head. She had been so busy thinking about the injured, it hadn't crossed her mind that there might also be a heavy death toll. A nasty image appeared in her thoughts of what it must be like for the men who were trapped down there in the dark, surrounded by the remains of friends who had been blown apart by the blast or crushed by falling rocks. She suddenly felt very sick.

"Are you going to finish patching me up or what?" said the irritating patient, interrupting Esperanza's horrifying daydream.

"You're done," she snapped back, tugging the knot in his bandage tighter until he squeaked. "Now get out before I give you a real injury to complain about." She booted him off the stool and he hobbled away, clutching his sprained wrist and muttering to himself.

After several hours of stitching and bandaging, Esperanza finally felt as though they were getting control of the situation. There were only about a dozen patients left now, mostly men with minor injuries who had allowed others with more serious wounds to go in front of them in the queue.

"Artie was right about you," Catalina told her, holding her patient's hand as she disinfected a nasty graze with alcohol. He yelped at the stinging sensation, and she ignored him. "You are an angel. I don't know what I'd have done without you today."

"Hardly," said Esperanza. "I came here today to tend to the sick, but I wasn't expecting this."

"The sick?" Catalina looked up at her. "Who's sick?"

"Artie." She finished tending to the man in front of her, who thanked her and moved aside to make room for the next patient. "He hasn't turned up for work this week. I intended to come down here and find him if I could."

"You should've got here earlier." Catalina shot her a dark look across the table. "He wasn't hard to find this morning."

Esperanza looked up, startled.

"He was here this morning?" she asked, fearing from Catalina's expression that she would not like the answer. "Was he hurt?"

"Oh, no." Catalina raised her eyebrows. "When I say he was here, I don't mean *here* as such. I mean out there, in the plaza. I wouldn't have noticed, what with all the patients I already had lined up at my door, but he was making quite a scene. It was impossible to miss."

"Making a scene? Artie?" Esperanza couldn't imagine it. Artie was so gentle, so patient. He wasn't one to shout or swear, let alone cause a ruckus in the middle of the plaza. "What on Earth happened? Was he drunk?"

"No, I don't think so," Catalina sighed, shaking her head. "He wasn't slurring or anything, his words were loud and clear. Which may prove to be very unfortunate for him if what he said gets back to Don Raúl or his father."

"The Dons? What have they got to do with it?" Esperanza froze, a feeling of foreboding creeping over her. Catalina was more serious than she had ever seen her before, and there was fear in her eyes.

"The mine where the accident happened," Catalina said quietly, nodding out of the window at the chaos outside. "It was one of Don Lorenzo's gold mines, which it seems Raúl was in charge of. I don't know exactly what happened, but some of the things your Artie was saying…" she shuddered. "This is serious, Esperanza. If it gets back to the Dons, he could be arrested for treason. And you know the penalty for treason."

Esperanza did know the penalty for treason. She had never seen a man publicly executed before, but she had heard that it made for very unpleasant viewing. The thought of having to watch Artie stand blindfolded and alone before a firing squad or atop the gallows made her blood run cold.

"What did he say?" she whispered.

"Nothing I can repeat in present company." Catalina glanced around at the other men who were still waiting to be treated. "Just trust me, it was enough to get him into a lot of trouble. I thought his brother was going to have to knock him out to get him to shut up."

Esperanza felt numb. She prayed to every saint she could think of that he had not caused any further trouble since his departure from the plaza. Whatever was wrong, he was clearly hurting, and she couldn't bear the thought of him hiding himself away to suffer alone.

"I have to find him."

"Too right you have to find him," Catalina agreed. "If I'd known he wasn't at the farm yesterday, I'd have written to you myself to demand that you come and talk to him. He was in pieces after you left the festival. I don't think he'd care if Don Raúl did have him arrested for treason. He's lost all hope now he knows your courtship is official."

Esperanza's heart plunged.

"What hope was there to lose? Artie has known all along that my parents were planning a match for Don Raúl and me." She swallowed hard, fighting back tears. "Believe me, if I had the choice, I'd marry Artie in a heartbeat. You know how much I care for him."

"I know, *mi compa*. But go easy on the boy. He likes you so much more than you realize, and after twelve years of searching for you, the thought of losing you again so soon is breaking his heart."

Esperanza was silent, the lump in her throat too tight to allow words out. She wiped the blood from the forehead of the man in front of her, dabbing at it with an alcohol-soaked cloth to disinfect the gash above his temple. The man was very quiet, his eyes wide and staring.

"I think you might be a little concussed," she told him gently, trying to force Artie from her mind until she had finished dealing with these last few patients. "Do you have anyone to take care of you when you get home, just to keep an eye on you and make sure you're all right?"

The man shook his head.

"I- I did have my brother," he told her in a choked voice. "But he's... he's still down there in the tunnel. I don't know if he's... I mean, if he managed to..." He faltered and stopped, the words catching in his throat. "I'd rather stay in the plaza for now if it's all the same, señorita. Just to keep an eye on that list."

He looked out of the window towards the church door, and Esperanza knew what he was trying to say. She nodded, still trying to hold back her own tears. It struck her for the first time that perhaps this was why Artie had behaved so strangely in the plaza that morning. Perhaps he had seen a name on that list that he recognized, and it had tipped him over the edge.

"Oh, you've got to be joking..." Catalina hissed, letting out a string of curses. Esperanza looked up, following her friend's horrified gaze out of the window into the plaza. Another cart had arrived, and by the groans and screams of pain she could hear coming from the direction of the square, she could tell that it was full of more injured men.

"Brace yourself, *mi compa*," Catalina grumbled through gritted teeth. "Artie's going to have to wait a bit longer."

The injuries of the men in this new cohort made the last lot look like children who had been scrapping in the playground. This time, there were broken limbs to contend with, a man who had lost his entire foot, and some men who were so severely burned that they could not bear to be touched. One man had lost an eye and wouldn't stop screaming, blood pouring from the empty socket, and Esperanza had to excuse herself for a moment to sneak out into the garden and be sick. She had no time for self-pity, though. Every wound was severe enough to require stitching now, and there was blood everywhere, soaking right through her apron and leaving deep crimson stains on her blouse and skirt. She didn't have time to be squeamish.

"Why has Francisco sent these men here rather than the hospital?" Catalina demanded. "They need to be seen by proper doctors, stitched up by proper surgeons."

"Hospital's full," croaked her patient, who had gone so grey that Esperanza thought he was going to pass out from blood loss. "We went there first, and they sent us away. It was either here or we'd have had to go all the way to the next town, and well, I don't think all of us would have made it, to be honest."

"Plenty of us didn't," added a man behind him. "We're the ones they managed to dig out alive after being trapped down there all night. We're the lucky ones."

He gulped, and his friend on the stool burst into tears. Esperanza looked away in horror. She couldn't afford to let herself think about it, or she would not be in a fit state to help the men who could still be saved. She had to focus on each moment as it happened for now and reserve her tears for later.

The next man Esperanza saw had a deep gash in his leg and was bleeding heavily. His face was coated with so much dust that all she could see was the whites of his eyes, which were wide with shock. He was muttering to himself incomprehensibly, rocking back and forth on the stool, and Esperanza had to lift his chin to get him to look at her.

"So dark," he babbled. "So dark, and so much blood. Those screams, they won't stop. They're still down there. Somebody get them out, they're still down there."

"Señor," she told him. "I'm going to have to clean and stitch that leg of yours, you understand? It's not going to be nice, but I want you to stay as still as possible for me. I can give you something to bite down on if you want."

His eyes slipped into focus, and he looked at her with astonishment.

"Your eyes," he gasped. "I know you. You're the angel. *Dios Mío*, am I dead? You're the angel."

She smiled, remembering the first time that someone had mistaken her for an angel. That sweet little street boy with the chestnut eyes burned in her memory, and she felt a little stronger.

"Don't worry, *señor*. You're alive, and you're going to stay that way if I have anything to do with it. Now, keep very still for me, all right?"

She reached down so that she could raise his leg up onto her stool for better access to the wound, but he grasped her by the shoulders, staring at her as though he could not believe his eyes.

"I know you," he said again. "You were there, at the festival. Artie's angel."

She stared at him, forgetting about his leg for a moment.

"You know Artie?" she demanded, squinting at his face through the grime. "Who are you? What else do you know about me?"

It was too late. The man fainted, and Esperanza had to brace herself as his full weight came crashing down in her arms. *At least I know he'll keep still while I'm stitching him this way*, she thought grimly, lowering him to the floor and kneeling beside him with her needle in her hand.

It was nearing three o'clock by the time all of the patients had been dealt with. As the last one closed the door, Catalina burst into tears and collapsed into a chair.

"We did a good job today, *mi compa*," Esperanza told her, stroking her hair in an attempt to comfort her. "Some of those men, they wouldn't have lived if not for you."

"*Sí*, I know, I know," she sobbed. "It's just been a very, very long day. Thank you so much, Esperanza." She wiped her eyes with her sleeve, grimacing as she noticed how filthy it was. She looked to Esperanza, then back to herself, then back again. "Good grief, look at the pair of us. You can't go out looking for Artie like that. He'll think that an evil spirit has risen from the grave and come after him. Quickly, clean yourself up in the water trough outside and then go upstairs and change."

Esperanza obeyed, picking out a simple white blouse and blue skirt from Catalina's wardrobe. She brought her own blood-soaked clothes back downstairs to put in her basket, but Catalina took them from her with a shake of her head.

"I'll deal with this. I'll have to wash mine anyway, I might as well do yours at the same time. You need to get yourself after that reckless man of yours. You've still got one life left to save today, *mi amiga*."

She tossed her a large, thick blanket and pointed towards the door.

"What's this for?" Esperanza asked.

"It looks like it's going to rain. You need something to protect you, and that's the best I've got at the moment. Now, when I saw Artie leave the plaza this morning, he went down the side road to the left of the church. I don't know where he was headed, though, so you might have to use your intuition. Get going. And Esperanza…"

Esperanza turned back to look at her friend, tucking the blanket under her arm.

"Find him, for God's sake. Before it's too late."

CHAPTER EIGHTEEN

The plaza was eerily quiet considering how many people were there. Women sat beneath the trees, weeping and comforting each other. The only children she could see were not playing but clinging close to their mothers' skirts, and many of them were wailing. Several people were standing around a new notice which had been nailed to the church door, and Esperanza could tell from the occasional cries of anguish from those gathered around it that it was an updated list of the names of those who had been killed. She felt her stomach turn.

She looked over towards the *kiosca*, where Artie had been playing only a few days earlier. The stage was empty now.

Esperanza walked around towards the steps at the back, searching the crowd for someone she recognized. To her relief, she spotted Diego sitting alone on the steps with his head in his hands. She thought for a moment that he was crying, but when he looked up his eyes were dry. He certainly wasn't looking good, however; his face was pale and his eyes bloodshot, and his clothes looked as though he hadn't changed them in days.

"Diego?" She approached him with caution, very aware of how fragile he looked.

"Esmerelda." He turned away from her, trying to avoid a conversation, but she persevered.

"It's Esperanza. You know it's Esperanza."

"Whatever." He avoided her gaze, a stony expression on his face. She could tell that he was not in the mood to talk and decided to cut straight to the point.

"I'm looking for Artie. I hear he caused a bit of a scene in the plaza this morning."

Diego glowered, standing up from the steps and advancing on her with such a threatening snarl that she recoiled in shock.

"What have you heard? Who told you?" he growled, his eyes narrowed.

"A concerned eye-witness, who is only interested in Artie's wellbeing." She would not let him intimidate her. "I don't know what he said, but I was told that I should find him and talk some sense into him before he got himself into trouble."

"Talk some sense into him, indeed." Diego gave a bitter laugh. "Since you came back into his life, any sense he had went out of the window. I barely know him anymore. I can't see how you talking to him more is going to help to restore his senses, *señorita*, when you're the reason he's been behaving like a lunatic in the first place."

"I only want to help him," Esperanza protested. "I'm worried about him too, Diego. I don't want him to get into trouble any more than you do."

"Then leave him alone. Forget about everything you've heard, and keep your nose out," Diego snapped. "Actually, here's an even better thought. Forget about Artie completely and let him move on with his life before you get him killed."

"Not before I've spoken to him." She refused to back down. If Artie told her himself that he didn't want to see her anymore, that he wanted her to forget about him, then she would do her best to obey. But she had no intention of taking orders from his angry, jealous brother, no matter how noble his intentions might be. "Where is he, Diego? Is he safe?"

"God knows. I sent him down to the river to cool off, before he got himself arrested," Diego spat. "He's behaving like a complete *idiota*. Picking fights he can't win, shooting his mouth off in the middle of the plaza. He will be swinging from the gallows before the week is out if he carries on with this reckless sort of behaviour."

The thought put a chill up Esperanza's spine. Catalina had not exaggerated, then. That didn't sound like Artie at all.

"If he's behaving recklessly, then that's all the more reason why I need to find him and work out what is going on. Now, *where is he*, Diego?" she asked him again through gritted teeth. She was losing patience now, and the longer she spent arguing with Diego, the longer Artie was suffering alone, potentially getting himself into more trouble. "I need to see him. Whatever he's said, whatever he's done, I swear I won't tell a soul. I just need to know that he's all right. Please."

"Trust me, *señorita*, you'll be the last person he wants to see today. He's upset. He knew people who were working up there in those mines, people who won't be coming back down. Someone like you would never be able to understand. He's not in a fit state to speak to anyone at the moment. Leave him be."

Esperanza's patience snapped. *Someone like me, indeed,* she thought. *How dare he.*

"I think, actually, that it's you who will never understand," she snarled. "If Artie is hurting, then he needs me, and I will damn well be there for him no matter what you or anyone else says. I appreciate that you care about him, Diego, but don't you dare make the mistake of thinking that you are the only one."

She turned on her heel and stormed off across the plaza. Diego called after her, but she had no intention of stopping. He had already wasted enough of her time.

Esperanza cursed under her breath as she stormed through the backstreets of Santa Sofia, heading towards the river. Even the beggars didn't try to stop her today, sensing as she passed that she would have trampled them underfoot if they dared to get in her way. She knew from what Catalina had told her that Artie couldn't have headed back towards the slums, so he had to be somewhere between the plaza and the farm. *I sent him down to the river to cool off,* Diego had told her. Of course, there was no guarantee that he had listened, but she had to start somewhere and the river was the best clue she had.

The first spots of rain started to fall as she headed out of town and down towards the copse of trees where her grandmother's old house still stood. The cottage had been empty since the great *Señora* Rosita Dominguez had passed away, the garden becoming tangled and overgrown. Louisa had been pressing her husband to sell it for a long time now, but Juan had never had the heart.

Esperanza felt a sharp pang of sadness as she looked across at the empty front window, knowing that her *abuelita* would never stand in that kitchen again swearing at another batch of failed, rock-hard cakes. The mournful silence as she walked towards the house reminded Esperanza of how she always used to be able to hear her grandmother singing at the top of her voice, sometimes from right across the field.

Her *abuelita* would have loved Artie, she knew. Rosita was a passionate woman, wild-spirited like Esperanza. She would have understood what her granddaughter saw in Artie and would have likely done everything that she could to help them be together, bullying even Louisa into submission if needs be. Now, though, she was gone. Esperanza would have to fight her battles alone.

There was no sign of Artie near the cottage, so Esperanza proceeded to walk in the direction of the farm, following the river downstream. The rain was falling more heavily now, soaking through her hair and blouse. She increased her speed, heading for the shelter of the trees. Aside from the sound of the rain, all was so quiet that it was almost hard to believe that she had been surrounded by chaos such a short while ago. The tranquil, natural beauty of the riverside showed no traces of the tragedy happening in the mountains just a few miles away; lizards zig-zagged across her path as she walked, and black-spotted toads croaked from the rocks at the water's edge.

She could see fish jumping out of the river up ahead, creating large splashes with their bodies as they hit the water. This was not an unusual sight in itself, but something about their uncharacteristic lack of grace piqued her attention and she stood to watch for a moment. It did not take her long to realize why they looked strange- they were not fish at all, but stones, which someone was throwing from the riverbank just the other side of the trees. She had a strong suspicion that she knew who it was.

Esperanza pushed through the foliage, squinting through the rain at the figure standing in the shallow water and launching stones into the middle of the river. Rain was dripping from his hair, and his shirt was soaked through, the translucent fabric sticking to his body. He turned and saw her, but to her surprise, turned away again, scrubbing at his face with his wet sleeve. He picked up another large stone and threw it as hard as he could into the water with a grunt.

She walked towards him, a feeling of dread rising in her chest. Pain and anger were radiating from him, and Esperanza began to doubt herself as she drew nearer to him. Perhaps Diego had been right, and he really didn't want to see her. It hadn't crossed her mind before, but she had never seen Artie lose his temper. What was it that he had been shouting in the plaza that had frightened both Catalina and Diego so badly? She started to wonder if they had been right to fear. Part of her wanted to turn back and run, but she couldn't just leave him hurting like this. This was Artie. Her Artie. Whatever he was going through, she knew he needed her, now more than ever.

"Artie."

"Esperanza." He kept his head turned from her, trying to hide the pain in his eyes. "What are you doing here?"

"I heard about the accident in the mine. Diego told me that you lost friends. I am so sorry."

He gave a hollow laugh.

"You heard it was an accident, did you? What happened yesterday was no accident, señorita, and I didn't lose friends, they were taken from me by the Dons, just like everything else." His voice was thick with emotion, simmering with fury. She could see that his fists were clenched and felt her confidence waver even more, fear prickling up her spine like tiny needles. "They were murdered, those men. Murdered by your precious future husband and father-in-law."

"If you're referring to Don Raúl and his father, then I can assure you that they were nowhere near the mines yesterday." She tried to keep her voice steady, but she bristled at the accusation that Don Raúl was in any way precious to her.

"They didn't need to be there, they're still guilty as hell," Artie snarled. "Don Raúl signed their death warrants on his last little trip to the mountains. Said they weren't getting his gold out quickly enough for him. He ordered them to lay more dynamite for each blast, to speed things up. It was a disaster waiting to happen, but would he listen? The tunnels collapsed. God knows how many innocent lives snuffed out, just like that. And that's not taking into account the ones who are still down there, trapped underground. Injured. Dying. Being slowly crushed under the rocks, suffocating down there in the dark, drowning in the mud. You think your Don friends are going to dirty their pretty white gloves digging them out or waste their precious gold rescuing them?"

Esperanza's mouth suddenly felt very dry. So this was why Artie was hurting so badly. She didn't want to imagine it, the pain, the terror that those men must be suffering. She willed herself to believe that Don Raúl would not just abandon them to their fate, that he couldn't be so cold as to just leave innocent men to die, although an unpleasant voice in the back of her head told her that Artie was right.

"I'm sure that they will do everything they can," she told him in what she hoped was a reassuring tone, regretting the words as soon as they left her lips.

"Oh, you're sure, are you?" He turned to her and stood in the shallow water, his eyes wild with emotion. His face was wet with tears, and she could see that he was shaking. "Stop fooling yourself, Esperanza. Those men down there don't matter, they're just another commodity. Their lives, their families, none of it matters. Just as long as the Dons get their gold."

He took another stone and threw it as hard as he could into the river. It landed with a loud splash, startling the water birds and sending them squawking into the air in a frenzied flurry of wings. Then he sank to his knees in the shallow water with a strangled sob.

"All those innocent lives shattered," he croaked, letting the tears fall. "And that's just the ones we know about. The ones who have names to record, loved ones to mourn them. It's not even counting the ones like me. No family, no one to miss them, just forgotten. Worthless, nameless street dogs."

His voice broke.

"You're not worthless. You mean the whole world to me. Please, Artie, you're breaking my heart." Tears were rolling down her own cheeks now. She longed to reach out to him, but she was too afraid. She didn't know this man kneeling in the shallow water before her, broken and helpless. This wasn't the bubbly, charming Artie she had grown so fond of. This was raw and real, a beautiful soul falling to pieces right in front of her. She wanted to fix it all for him, to tell him that it would all be all right, but it would've been a lie and they both knew it. There was no fixing this.

"You'll be in good company if your heart is breaking, señorita," he told her, closing his eyes. "There are plenty more broken hearts in this town today and all of the other towns where those men lived. They weren't all like me. Many were husbands, fathers, sons. People who were loved."

He gave a quiet sob and turned away from her again to scrub his face with his sleeve.

"The things I've seen in those mines, Esperanza. Not just the injuries, the burns, the lost limbs, but the ones who get sick, too. The ones who die slow, agonizing deaths as they cough up their lungs from all the dust or get poisoned from the chemicals. If they're lucky, they get taken back down the mountain to die in the arms of the ones they love. The worst are the ones who never make it that far. The ones who fall and live, but can't climb back up again. You can't imagine the screams when men are dying alone and afraid down there in the dark. That sound, Esperanza. It's the sound of hell. There's nothing worse, except for the silence that follows. It never leaves you."

He closed his eyes and lowered his head, tortured by the memories that haunted him.

"Artie, please, stop. I can't bear it. Come back to me. Please, come back to me." Esperanza was openly sobbing now. She had always known that the world was cruel, but before today, she had never been forced to think about it on this level. She wished that there was a way that she could go back to the blissful oblivion of ignorance, to forget all that she had heard and seen, but it was too late. She could picture the faces of all of those men he was mourning for, their wives, their children. She could see their suffering, as raw and as real as though they had been standing right there in front of her.

Each agonizing breath wracked Artie's chest now, his hands gripping handfuls of his thick hair as though he was trying to rip the images from his head. It was unbearable to watch.

"Artie, please," she begged again. "You're frightening me."

"Good. You should be frightened." He turned to her, his eyes wild and dangerous. "This is the man you're marrying,

Esperanza. This is what he does to people. The least you can do is go into it with your eyes open. You and your family, all you see are the flashy clothes and *baile cenas*, the huge estates and the sparkly jewellery. Did you ever stop to think about where he gets it all from? It's paid for in blood, *señorita*. The blood of innocent men like Joaquin."

Esperanza's body went numb.

"Joaquin? Joaquin is dead?"

The words jarred horribly in the air. Artie's face crumpled and his head dropped onto his chest, his shoulders heaving as he sobbed. He let out a low, quiet moan like a wounded animal and covered his face with his hands, his body doubling over in the water.

Esperanza flew to his side, throwing herself to her knees beside him in the shallow river and wrapping him in her arms. His body collapsed in her embrace, and she held him tight against her chest until she could feel every shuddering movement of his ribs against hers. They sobbed together, letting the rain soak through their clothes, clinging to one another in the shallow water.

CHAPTER NINETEEN

The two of them knelt together in the water for a long time, their tears mingling with the rain. Those words kept ringing in Esperanza's head, echoing around her mind until she felt sick. *Joaquin is dead.*

"He was twenty-three," Artie told her in a broken voice. "*Twenty-three years old, Esperanza.*"

"Does Paloma know?" Esperanza pictured the shy, smiling girl she had met at the festival, her face shining with adoration at her new husband, and felt her heart break a little more at the memory.

"She was told late last night, just after I was. Ed found him, he brought back his wedding ring. We still haven't seen

Alejandro or Marco. Diego went over to break the news, I was too much of a coward." He shuddered. "I could hear her screaming from the other end of the street. I never knew a human being could make a noise like that."

His whole body was shaking, soaked from the rain.

"Come on." Esperanza stood and pulled Artie from the water, leading him towards the shelter of an elephant tree. He followed her as placidly as a child, his eyes glazed, and she sat him down among the protruding roots. She knelt on the ground beside him, wrapping Catalina's blanket around them both for warmth, and cradled his head against her collarbone.

"Poor Paloma," she whispered, stroking back the thick wet strands of hair from Artie's face. He let out a quiet whimper of exhaustion and closed his eyes, relaxing into her arms. "So recently married, too."

She remembered how happy Paloma had looked as her new husband held her, the way the two of them had looked at each other, their eyes so full of love and excitement for the future. Now all of that had been taken away, all of that happiness gone in a blast of fire and smoke. Esperanza couldn't bear to imagine what she must be going through.

"It's worse than that," Artie told her in a hollow voice. "She's with child."

"Paloma is pregnant?" Esperanza sat up, confused. "How does she know already? They've barely been married a week!"

"Don't be so naïve, señorita." Artie looked up at her with a tragic smile. "They weren't going to waste their lives pining for each other while they saved up the money for the marriage license. She told him the news on their wedding day. He had his entire life ahead of him, and now that little unborn baby is all that's left. A little baby who will never get to meet his papá." She felt his chest shudder as another angry sob caught in his throat. "Just another life ruined by the Dons and their greed, the vile *cabróns*. They'll get what's coming to them."

"Artie." Esperanza tried to soothe him, rubbing a gentle hand up and down his trembling spine. "You've got to stop this kind of talk. You'll get yourself into trouble."

He shrugged her off, a bitter fire in his eyes.

"I'm not afraid of Don Raúl," he snapped. "Revolution is coming, Esperanza. People are beginning to take a stand. They're starting to fight back against tyrants like the Dons. Raúl's days are numbered, and when his time comes, I will be right there at the front to avenge Joaquin and the others with my own hands."

"Artie!" Esperanza gasped, horrified. No wonder Diego had wanted him out of the plaza if these were the sorts of things he had been saying. She grabbed him by the shoulders and stared into his eyes, which were hard and cold. She had never seen him look at her like this before, and it chilled her to the bone. "Stop it. You've got to stop this. Now. Please."

"Why? Why are you and Diego still defending him after all he's done? You don't think he deserves to answer for it?" Artie's voice was icy, his every muscle tense, and she was surprised to find her own body bristling with anger in response.

"I'm not defending him!" Esperanza almost shouted at him. She wanted to shake him, to wake him up from this nightmare. "I don't give a damn what happens to him. I hope he burns in hell for what he did. I care about *you*, Artie. I care about what will happen to you if anyone hears you talking like this. Don't make me live to see the day when I am forced to watch Don Raúl hang you for treason."

"And what would it matter if he did?" he snarled, tears springing to his eyes again. "What have I got left to live for?

He's taken everything from me. My friends. My dignity. The woman I love."

Esperanza froze. She stared back at him, her eyes wide with shock, her anger forgotten as his words sunk in.

"At least if Don Raúl has me hanged, I won't have to watch as he takes you from me and destroys you piece by piece." His voice trembled with emotion, his anger dissipating as despair set in. "I don't care if he knows how much I hate him. Let him take me. I'm a condemned man already. Hanging will be a sweet mercy, compared to a lifetime of watching the love of my life bound to a man like that."

He turned away, leaving Esperanza's head whirling.

"The love of your life?" she croaked.

"You. It's always been you." He looked up at her, his voice still thick with emotion. "I have loved you from the second I set eyes on you, Esperanza. And yes, I know I never had a hope, but I can't help it. How am I ever going to bear watching you marry *him*, knowing that I'll never be allowed to see you again? Lying awake every night, wondering what misery he's putting you through, knowing there's nothing I can do but love you from a distance? And all while that heartless monster gets to kiss you, and touch you, and... and father your children." He swallowed hard, the words paining him. "My God, Esperanza, if he ever hurts you, if he ever raises a single finger against you..."

He broke off, unable to continue. She felt her own heart crumble, and hot tears spilled down her cheeks once more.

"Artie... Oh, *mi corazón*..."

She knelt up and wrapped her arms around him, burying her face in his neck. He clung to her, the heat of his skin warming her even through the damp fabric of their clothes, and she could feel the fast, reassuring throb of his heartbeat pounding against her own chest.

"Tell me you haven't agreed to be his wife, Esperanza. Please, God, tell me it's not too late," he begged, his trembling voice muffled in her hair.

"Artie, listen to me." She pulled away to look into his eyes. "I've agreed to nothing. It's true that Don Raúl is now officially courting me, but I promise you, it was neither my choice nor my wish. My parents can give him my hand, but he will never have my heart. That…" She took a deep breath to steady herself, reaching up to tenderly brush the tears from his cheeks. "That belongs to you, and only you. Now and forever."

Artie stared at her for a second, too choked to speak. Then he made a sound that was halfway between a sob of joy and a cry of pain, threw his arms around her and pulled her tight against his chest. He was trembling with emotion, each ragged breath making his whole body shudder, and Esperanza nuzzled against him, laughing and crying all at once as he buried his face in her hair. She had always dreamed of what it might be like, falling in love with someone who felt the same way about her, hearing those three sacred words from his lips. She had never imagined that the moment would come just as she was forced to face a lifetime as the wife of his sworn enemy. It was too cruel.

"Why didn't you tell me?" he asked, pulling away for a moment to look down at her with big, wistful eyes. "When your mother said that was all official now, that you'll be married before the year is out, I didn't know what to think. It's all moving so fast."

"I'm sorry," she told him, stroking his cheek. "I just didn't want to ruin such an important day for you. Not when you were so happy."

"Is that the real reason you were crying in the plaza the other day, after the music contest?" He leaned into her palm, turning his head to kiss her wrist, and she felt a tremor of excitement shoot up her arm. She hadn't planned on telling him the truth about how she had felt on the day of the festival. Still, after how he had just poured his heart out to her, the least she could do was offer him a little honesty in return.

"I was delighted that you won the contest. You deserved it. It's just that when I found out it meant you and Diego leaving Santa Sofia... well, I realized I was going to really miss you." She felt a lump in her throat and brushed her thumb over his cheekbone. He grinned, his chestnut eyes shining with affection.

"I knew you would admit that you missed me eventually," he teased, and she couldn't help but laugh. He took both of her hands in his. "That's the real reason you were upset? Because you thought I was going to leave you?"

She nodded, a little embarrassed to admit it. Artie's eyes were sparkling, and he placed one of her hands over his heart, pressing it down so that she could feel the quickening beat beneath her fingers. She felt her own heart matching its pace.

"Oh, *mi amor*." He reached up to stroke her hair, his face glowing with affection. "That might have been the plan once, *sí*. But that was before I found you. I could never bear to leave you now. Besides, there's no reason why I can't still be a professional *músico* in Santa Sofia. With any luck, Diego and I will get a lot more work in this town now that everyone knows who we are. I could still make a respectable gentleman of myself yet."

He winked down at her, and her heart gave a little leap. Maybe he was right. If he became successful, perhaps it wasn't completely unreasonable to dream that one day her parents might approve of him as a potential match for her, as long as she managed to keep Don Raúl at bay for long enough. If Artie wasn't leaving, then they had time, and where there was time, there was also hope.

However, if he really had changed his plans, then it still left questions unanswered.

"The prize money," she reminded him. "You told me you had intentions for it if you won."

"Sí, I did." He sighed, his smile fading. "I was going to buy a new guitar. There was a really nice one I saw in the music shop, dark wood with gold markings. It's got the most beautiful tone, steel strings and everything. With that and some nice smart clothes of my own, I thought I might finally have looked like a professional *músico*. But never mind, it's not to be." He shrugged, feigning a cheerful expression. "I might still have enough saved up for a reasonable second-hand guitar if I catch the shop owner in a good mood."

"Hold on," said Esperanza, her eyes narrowing. "What about the prize money? Are you telling me that the Dons have broken their word and refused to give it to you?"

"No, they've given it to us." He gave a sad, bitter laugh. "Diego can do as he pleases with his share, but I'm not keeping a penny of mine. Not with the knowledge of where it came from, the blood that Don Raúl spilled to get those gold coins. Every time I looked at that guitar, I would always see Joaquin's reflection looking back at me. It would feel like betraying him every time I played a note. No, if I'm going to make it as a professional musician, then I will do it without Don Raúl's help."

"What will you do with the money, then?" she asked. "Give it back to him?"

"No. I'm giving it to Paloma, for her child. Lord knows they'll need all the help they can get, and they certainly won't see any from the Dons."

Esperanza nodded in understanding. Artie lay back against the tree trunk with an exhausted sigh, opening his arms to invite her in. She readily accepted, cuddling against his chest as he pulled the blanket back around them both, cocooning them in warmth.

"You're a good man, Arturo," she told him, nuzzling against his collarbone.

"Sí, I know."

They were silent for a long while, watching as the rain slowly started to ease off. The sun was coming out again, making the wet grass sparkle, and Artie began to tell Esperanza stories of his adventures with Joaquin, how they had grown up together on the streets and the silly tricks they used to play on each other. Esperanza had no idea that it was possible to feel so sad and so happy all at once as they lay entwined in the grass, laughing and crying together at Artie's memories of his brother.

A dove was cooing somewhere in the tree above them, calling to his mate across the river. Esperanza could feel the soothing rise and fall of Artie's ribs beneath her head, his breathing calm and even at last, the thumping of his heartbeat soft in her ear. She kissed his chest, and he let out a sound of blissful contentment.

"*Dios Mío*," he said weakly. "At least Joaquin died knowing what this felt like. He knew how it felt to be in the arms of the woman he loved." He kissed her hair, and she cuddled against him, breathing in the soft citrusy scent of his skin. "I'm glad you came to find me, Esperanza. I never wanted you to see me in that state, but I don't know what I'd have done if you hadn't."

"You frightened me today," she confessed, her fingers tracing around the pocket over his heart. "I've never seen you like that before."

"The way I spoke to you was unforgivable. I'm so sorry, mi amor." He lifted her fingers to his lips before placing them back over his heart. "I never meant to scare you. It's just that it haunts me. Sometimes in my dreams at night, I see them all again, I hear the screaming." He shuddered, closing his eyes.

"What do you see, Artie?" she stroked his chest, soothing him. "What happened to you? I want to understand."

He swallowed hard, hesitating for a moment.

"Do you remember the strikes four years ago, up in the mines over in Cananea?" he began. She nodded. "Well, I was there. I was only sixteen, and I took a job in the mine for a few days a week. The mine owner was some *cabrón* called Greene from the United States, a good friend of the Dons. That's when I saw what it was really like; the misery, the injuries, the deaths. One day, we decided that we'd had enough and went on strike. Of course, President Díaz and Don Lorenzo didn't take kindly to us rising up against their rich American friend. They were worried that it might set a bad precedent, so they decided to stamp on it before the dissent spread to their own mines. Do you remember what they did, *señorita*?"

Esperanza did remember, but she was too afraid to say it aloud. She had known about the strikes and the president's response to them, but she had completely forgotten that Don Lorenzo had also been involved. The realization made her feel sick.

"Between them, Díaz and Lorenzo sent in three hundred armed soldiers," Artie told her. "It was horrific. Twenty-three innocent men were shot dead and even more wounded. I was right there, I saw it all. My friend Bernardo died in my arms, a bullet through his chest. I never knew a man's body could contain so much blood. I thought I was drowning in it. Sometimes in my nightmares, I can still smell it, still taste it."

His breathing was catching in his chest now, his voice starting to wobble again. Esperanza took his hand, stroking his arm to soothe him.

"I should've run, but I couldn't just leave him there. He was my *hermano*. One of the soldiers caught me. I tried to fight him off, and he wounded me with his bayonet."

He pulled up his loose shirt to show her a puckered scar in his left side, just below his ribcage. Esperanza swore under her breath, unable to believe that she had never noticed it before. He was lucky that it hadn't punctured a lung.

"He arrested me, blindfolded me and dragged me behind his horse all the way back down the mountain. I was thrown into the prison along with fifty or so other men and left there to die. I was a child."

Esperanza's stomach churned with horror. To think, the worst she had ever imagined Artie going through was the occasional spell of hunger and loneliness, the discomfort of sleeping on the street under the stars. She had no idea that he had ever suffered mistreatment like this. She reached out and ran her fingers over the scar, and he closed his eyes, shivering at her touch.

"How did you escape?" she whispered.

"Diego rescued me," he told her, his voice trembling. "He was working for Don Lorenzo at the time as a gardener for one of his estates. When he heard I'd been arrested, he went straight to Don Raúl himself and pleaded for my life. I don't know how he did it, but somehow he persuaded him to sign the papers for my release. Both of us swore from that day that we would rather starve than ever go near a mine again."

"Is that why Diego is still on friendly terms with Don Raúl, in spite of everything?" she asked. "Because he feels that he owes him a debt for signing your release papers?"

"If it is, then he's an idiot. I reckon Diego's more afraid of him than anything else." Artie shook his head. "The men who survived are still there, in that cell. Their wives and children likely starved on the streets without them. All those lives destroyed, all for the Dons and their greed."

He closed his eyes again with a shudder, his hand sliding unconsciously back to the scar on his side. Esperanza felt an overwhelming need to hold him, to protect him from the pain of his past. She shifted beside him, cradling his head against her neck. One hand stroked his hair while the other slipped inside his shirt, her fingers tracing over the puckered skin of his scar. He shivered and exhaled quietly, melting at her touch.

"Does it hurt?" she whispered.

"No." He rested a trembling hand on top of hers, gazing up at her with sparkling eyes. "Please don't stop."

Esperanza obeyed, stroking his warm skin. He let out a blissful sigh, relaxing in her embrace, his eyes closed. She smiled down at him and kissed his hair, wishing that they could stay like this forever. There was nothing she wanted more than to lie here with him, to protect him from the horrors of the outside world. To save him from himself too, if she could.

"Artie," she breathed, her words tickling his neck and making him quiver. "You said that you love me."

"I do."

"Then I want you to promise me something, for my sake if not your own."

"Anything for you."

"I need you to promise me you're not going to go looking for trouble with Don Raúl." She pulled away from him a little, forcing him to look into her eyes. "I mean it, Artie. There are better ways to honour Joaquin and the others than getting yourself arrested again, or worse. They wouldn't have wanted you to throw your life away."

He didn't answer, and she took him by the shoulders, turning him to face her. The sparkle had vanished from his eyes at the mention of Don Raúl, and she felt the lump of emotion returning to her throat.

"Promise me, Artie. Please," she insisted, her voice cracking. "Not for his sake, for yours. I meant what I said. You mean the world to me. I couldn't bear to see you hanged or lined up before a firing squad. I would never survive it. I need you."

His expression softened at the sight of the tears welling in her eyes, and he pulled her to his chest.

"All right, *mi amor*, I promise," he breathed, stroking her hair. "I promise. I won't go looking for trouble with Don Raúl. You're right, it won't bring back what I've lost. But if he ever does anything to hurt you, Esperanza, if he ever so much as threatens you, I'll warn you now I will not be able to stand by and watch. I don't care if I hang for it."

It wasn't quite the solid reassurance that she was looking for, but Esperanza knew it was the best she was likely to get. She kissed his chest again, burying herself in the scent of his shirt, and felt him sigh with longing.

"*Mi amor*," he whispered, his voice soft and low in her ear. "I wish we could stay here forever. Just you and me. We would be so happy."

"Until my parents sent out a search party for me, and then we would both be very, very unhappy." She gave him a sad little smile. The sun was beginning to set over the trees behind them, and she knew she would soon be in serious trouble if she didn't start thinking about going home. She would already have a lot of explaining to do for her long absence today.

"Sí, I know. You're right." He sat up with a reluctant groan. "*Angel of my heart, if our love can only ever be a dream, then let me die before I wake.*"

"Are those song lyrics?" she asked. "I don't think I know that one."

"That's because I haven't finished writing it." He winked, grinning.

"It sounds sad." She brushed the grass from her skirts as he picked up her basket for her, placing the now dry blanket inside it. They would walk back to the farm along the riverside rather than taking the road. It was a longer route but far more beautiful, and she would be able to hold his hand as they walked with far less risk of being seen. They both needed it today.

"Perhaps it is a sad song. Perhaps not." He offered her his hand, his eyes shining as she entwined her fingers with his. "I don't know how it ends yet."

CHAPTER TWENTY

Much to her surprise, Esperanza's parents were not angry at all when she returned home that evening. News travelled fast in Santa Sofia, especially when coupled with a healthy dose of exaggeration, and any sign of a disaster sped it up even more than usual. By the time the news of Esperanza's activities reached her parents, it had been made to sound as though she had spent the day raising men from the dead.

If her parents were keen to shower her with undue credit, it was nothing compared to the farmhands' reaction. Esperanza almost dropped the bowls she had been carrying when she went down to the barn to deliver the workers' *comida*, only to be met with every man who worked there, whooping and cheering to show their appreciation for her. It seemed that every single one of them had a friend or relative who had been patched up to some degree by the 'angel with the blue eyes', and they were all very keen to express their gratitude by kissing her hands and showering her with freshly picked flowers.

One man, of course, was happier to see her than anyone else. Just as she was leaving to return to the farmhouse, he sneaked out behind her, grabbed her hand and pulled her behind the barn.

"Artie!" she cried, surprised. "What the hell do you think you're-"

Her words were muffled against his shoulder as he caught her in a tight hug, sweeping her off her feet as though she were no heavier than a rag doll. The flowers she had been holding scattered across the grass like confetti.

"Put me down," she objected, trying to wriggle out of his grasp. "Artie, what is the meaning of this? You nearly gave me a heart attack, grabbing me like that!"

He obeyed, lowering her to the ground and kneeling before her to kiss her hand. She stared down at him in bewilderment.

"My brothers," he choked. "Marco and Alejandro. You saved them, *mi amor*. Why did you not tell me yesterday when we were down by the river?"

"I didn't know," she confessed. "Are you sure it was me and not Catalina?"

"Certain," he promised her. "Marco remembered your blue eyes. He wanted me to thank you personally. You stitched up his leg, but he fainted before he could express his gratitude."

"Marco," repeated Esperanza, suddenly remembering the man who had referred to her as Artie's angel. "Of course. I remember now." She had not even recognized him through all the grime and blood on his face, and then the memory had been driven from her mind by all of the other wounded men she had to tend to.

"As for Alejandro," Artie went on, his eyes twinkling. "At first, he was a bit too overwhelmed with shock to recognize you as you patched up his head wound, but then he heard you say my name. You were talking to Catalina about me." He grinned at her, and she felt her chest tighten with panic as she tried to recall the conversation.

"I- I don't remember-"

"Fortunately, he did. He told me all about it. How much you care for me. How you would marry me if the choice were yours to make." Artie kissed her hands again, his eyes shining with affection. "To think, all that time, I was ranting at you about the mine workers' plight like you were some naïve little fool, with no idea that you'd spent your whole day stitching their wounds and helping to bind their broken limbs. I'm such an *idiota*."

"You weren't to know," she soothed him. "You were upset, it was understandable. I'm surprised you're even here today given the circumstances."

"I didn't plan to be, but when I found out what you did, I couldn't stay away." He stood, reaching out to brush her hair back from her face, his hand caressing her cheekbone. "Just knowing that you care for me, that you would choose me if you were free to do so- I'll cling on to that thought and be grateful for it."

"Mmm, well I'm glad to hear it." She smiled, nuzzling her cheek against his palm. "Especially as we're going to be enjoying a lot more time together in the near future. *Papá* thinks I should learn to ride to impress Don Raúl, and he suggested you as my instructor. If you're up for the challenge, that is."

Artie looked down at her as though he did not trust his own ears.

"You want me to teach you to ride," he said slowly, "so that you can impress Don Raúl?"

"No," she corrected him. "I want you to teach me because, unlike dancing, horseback riding is an activity I can do with Don Raúl without having to let him touch me. The fact that it will be a good excuse to spend a lot more time with you is a nice bonus, too."

Artie's face broke into a wide grin, and he slipped his arms around her waist and pulled her towards him.

"Well, when you put it that way," he whispered playfully, his breath tickling her skin, "how soon can we start?"

As it turned out, they could start even sooner than Esperanza had dared to hope. The following morning, Juan called Esperanza away from her chores to introduce her to a beautiful white gelding named Zafiro, whom he had just purchased from a horse breeder in a neighbouring town.

"I thought he might be good for you," Juan told her, examining the gelding with pride. "I mentioned to Don Lorenzo that you were interested in learning to ride, and he put me in touch with his best contact. I'm told that this handsome chap has a very sweet nature, very gentle and easy-going. Perfect for a young lady learning to ride."

"He's beautiful, *papá*. Thank you." Esperanza held out her hand for the horse to sniff, just as she had seen Artie do in the past. The soft, velvety nose waffled interestedly at her fingers, his ears perked with curiosity at the girl before him.

"Rafael has given him a quick glance over already, but I'll get Arturo to give him a thorough check and make sure we've got a suitable saddle and bridle."

"Rafael's back?" asked Esperanza, surprised. "How is he? Did he mention his nephew at all?"

"Sí. Fortunately, the boy is fine, if a little traumatised by the horrors he's witnessed over the last few days." Juan fixed her with a disapproving glare. "Rafael tells me that you promised him a job. You know that I have a rule of never hiring anyone under the age of sixteen, *mija*."

She lowered her gaze.

"Papá..." she pleaded. "I understand, it's just that considering how much Rafael has done for our family over the years, would it not be fitting to make an exception?"

Juan's expression broke into a smile, and he gave her a fond wink.

"It's moments like this that make me so proud to have you as a daughter, Esperanza. You can make an old fool like me remember that sometimes you need to break your own rules for the sake of doing the right thing."

Esperanza felt her shoulders relax.

"There's no shame in going back on your word if it's for the right reasons," she agreed.

"Good. In that case, I've no shame in telling you that I already said yes to Rafael. Daniel starts on Monday." He winked again, glad to see how pleased she was at the news. In truth, Esperanza suspected that her father would have likely offered the boy a job even without her intervention, especially after seeing Rafael's distress.

"I'm delighted to hear it, *papá*," she smiled, pressing her advantage. "Perhaps, in that case, I might still pray that you'll learn from this and go back on your word to Don Lorenzo."

"Don't push your luck, or I'll give you something to learn from," he growled.

It had been worth a try, at least.

Esperanza had attempted learning to ride once before as a child, but she'd had neither the interest nor the patience to pursue it further after the first few times she had fallen off. When she danced or sang, she only had her own body to worry about, with no other external personalities or opinions to get in the way. Horse riding, however, was a different game altogether. Trust was something that Esperanza had never been good at, and to begin with she found her body stiffening with resistance every time the animal moved.

"You need to relax your hips," Artie explained to her. He was leading the horse around the paddock on a rope so that she didn't have to worry about steering, but Esperanza still felt far from safe. "Feel the motion of the horse, and let your body go with it."

"That's easy for you to say," she snapped, clinging to the saddle for balance. "You're used to this. I don't feel even slightly relaxed."

"All right. Let's try a different method, then."

He unclipped the lead rope from the horse's bridle and tossed it from the paddock.

"What are you doing?" she cried, panicking. "You can't just leave me to-"

But he wasn't leaving her to do anything. Before she knew it, he had vaulted up onto the horse's back behind her and was reaching around to take the reins.

"Come on," he said, tickling her ear. "Let's go for a little walk, shall we? I promise, *mi amor*, I won't let you fall. You're safe with me."

It was much easier to relax with Artie's arms around her, his hips gently rocking back and forth behind hers with each movement of the horse. One of his hands was on her waist, steadying and reassuring her, the other holding on to the reins. She could feel his breath warm on her neck as he muttered words of encouragement, although whether they were aimed at herself or Zafiro, she neither knew nor cared.

After no time at all, she managed to relax into the horse's movements and forget her fear, to the point that she was heartily disappointed when Artie guided the horse back towards the stable and vaulted to the ground. Her legs almost gave way as she swung down beside him, and he had to catch her to prevent her from falling.

"Careful, there," he laughed, perching her on the edge of a hay bale. He tied Zafiro to the tethering post outside the stable door so that he could remove the saddle from the horse's sweat-drenched back. "I think that's enough for one day, don't you, Firo? Let's give the lady's legs a rest, give her a moment to remember how to use them. It's a strange feeling, the first time you sit on a horse."

He presented the gelding with a bucket of cool water and a net of fresh hay, and the animal responded with an appreciative snort.

"I'm fine," Esperanza lied. In truth, her legs felt like jelly, and she wasn't convinced that she would be able to walk back up to the farmhouse for at least a few more minutes yet. "I think I was getting the hang of that. I could have gone on for another half hour, at least."

"Speak for yourself, *mi amor*." Artie winked, keeping his voice low. "Five more minutes of being pressed up against you like that, and I'm afraid my heart might have given out. And I did promise that I wouldn't let you fall off."

He kept his promise. Esperanza had a riding lesson every day that week, and she learned quickly under his gentle instruction. After only a few days, she was confident enough to ride Zafiro solo around the outskirts of the farm at a gentle trot, with Artie riding beside her on her father's chestnut mare.

A week later, Esperanza headed down to the stables at the usual time to meet Artie, only to find that someone had beaten her to it. There was a certain amount of high-pitched giggling coming from inside, and as Esperanza pushed the door open, she was met with the sight of her two brothers pinning Artie to the ground with long sticks pointed at his chest.

"Surrender, pirate Blackbeard!" cried Miguel, waving his stick at Artie's chest as Felipe watched on, giggling. "Or I will cut off your head and feed it to the sharks!"

"Argh, the great Lieutenant Maynard!" Artie threw his hand to his forehead with a dramatic groan. "I will never surrender! Never!"

"Then *die*, you devil!" Miguel plunged the stick he was holding into the gap under Artie's arm, and the stable boy dutifully screamed and gasped until he finally lay still with his eyes closed and his hands crossed over his chest.

"What on Earth is going on in here?" Esperanza asked in mock-disapproval, her arms folded and eyebrow raised. All three of the boys jumped to attention like naughty schoolchildren, and Esperanza fought to keep a straight face. "Arturo, are you being a bad influence on my brothers?"

"No!" all three of them objected at once.

"Miguel was sad because someone hurt him at school today," Felipe explained, "so Artie was cheering him up by teaching him how to fight."

Miguel nudged his brother in the ribs, scowling.

"Is one of the boys at school being mean to you, *hermano*?" Esperanza asked him, concerned. It wasn't like Miguel to have problems with his friends; he was usually popular enough that bullies left him alone. It was probably just a falling out between boys rather than an ongoing problem, but still, it concerned her to think that anyone had hurt him. "Do you want to talk about it?"

Miguel shook his head again, tears gathering in his eyes, and Esperanza conceded. Miguel was the sort of child who did not respond well to being pressured. She would mention the issue to her father later and hope that he would be able to cajole it out of him, but for now, she would not risk embarrassing him in front of Felipe and Artie by making him cry.

"So, you're a fencing tutor as well as a riding instructor now, are you?" she asked, turning to Artie. "I had no idea you were skilled in so many fields, señor. Tell me, when was the last time you won a fight?"

"Never," he confessed, grinning. "I'm ashamed to say that I have never won a fight in my life, señorita."

"I'm not surprised. You fight like a girl." Felipe giggled, jabbing at Artie's ribs with his stick.

"Oh? Fight like a girl, do I?" Artie caught the stick and snatched it from Felipe's hands with a playful growl. "C'mere, you!"

He lunged for the boy and missed, and Felipe danced away giggling, which in turn made Miguel forget his sadness and giggle too. Esperanza knew this was exactly what Artie had been trying to achieve, and it was working. She couldn't resist joining in and stepped forward to snatch Felipe's stick from Artie, catching him by surprise.

"Tell me, then," she teased, prodding Artie's chest with the stick until he was backed right up against the door of the nearest stall. "What's wrong with fighting like a girl? Are you trying to say that girls are weak?"

"Girls aren't as strong as boys," Miguel declared, puffing out his little chest. "It's a fact."

"Oh really?" Esperanza raised an eyebrow. "I seem to remember defeating you two enough times throughout the years."

"That's only because you're a grown-up, and we're children," Miguel argued. "You couldn't beat a grown-up man. Bet you couldn't beat Artie."

"Ooh, I bet I could," Esperanza teased, tracing the stick down his shirt until it rested on the button just above Artie's navel.

"Yes, I bet she could too," said Artie, raising his hands in nervous surrender.

"Prove it," Miguel challenged her, and the two boys giggled with excitement. "Go on, Artie. The last one standing is the winner."

Artie's worried eyes darted to Esperanza's face as Felipe tossed one of the sticks over to him.

"I can't. It's wrong to hit girls."

"It's fine if they challenged you," Miguel insisted. "And even more so if they hit you first. Look out, Artie!"

He turned just in time to parry a blow from Esperanza's stick, only realizing too late that she had not been aiming to hit him, only distract him from her next move. With graceful skill acquired from years of practice with two younger brothers, she took advantage of his now unprotected chest and twirled into him, reaching up to assault the sensitive spot on his neck with her tickling fingers. He crumpled as she knew he would, tumbling backward into the hay with a squeal and dragging her down on top of him.

"That's cheating!" roared the boys in synchronised outrage as Esperanza cheered, giggling at Artie who was still spluttering in the hay beneath her.

"I think this means I win." She grinned, brushing his hair back out of his eyes with her fingers.

"Oh, really?" he panted back. "I believe the rules stated that the last one standing was the winner. We both fell together. I think that means it was a draw, señorita."

"Ah," she nodded. She still had him pinned to the hay beneath her, trapped at her mercy. "Well, you know what that means, don't you? *Tiebreaker!*"

Artie yelped with laughter as her hands shot back up to his neck, tickling the sensitive spots behind his ears. He squirmed and squealed beneath her, trying to defend himself. Finally, he managed to catch her arms and pin them, flipping her over so that she was now on her back in the hay with his body pressed on top of hers. Their faces were so close that their noses were almost touching, and she was suddenly acutely aware of how warm he felt against her.

"Gotcha," he grinned, his eyes sparkling.

"Artie's the winner!" cried Miguel. Esperanza jumped, remembering at once that her brothers were watching her. Artie hurriedly rolled away, pulling her to her feet beside him. Her whole body was tingling, and she had to lean against the stable door to steady herself. "Here, Artie, you need a prize!"

The little boy pulled a little paper-wrapped sweet from his pocket and held it out to the victor, who bowed.

"Thank you, *chamaco*," Artie smiled, "but this belongs to the lady, I fear. Had I dared to let go of her hands, she would have had me at her mercy again in a heartbeat. To tell the truth, she always does."

He winked and presented the sweet to Esperanza, who accepted it with a trembling hand.

"Now, boys, I'm afraid that Esperanza and I need to get on with our riding lesson. Will you be all right, Miguel, now that your brother is with you?"

Miguel nodded. The two boys headed back up towards the farmhouse as Artie distracted himself with fetching Zafiro's saddle. Esperanza was still trying to get her breath back, and she unwrapped the little sweet and popped it into her mouth, trying to focus her mind on the taste of the sugar to stop herself from thinking about the way her body was still tingling.

There was a small bucket in the corner which the stable boys used as a rubbish bin, and Esperanza went over to dispose of her sweet wrapper. She caught sight of a crumpled ball of paper on the floor, which somebody had evidently tried to throw out and missed the bucket. She would've transferred it to the bin without a further thought had she not caught sight of Artie's name scrawled across it in spidery handwriting.

"Artie!" She called, frowning as she unfolded it. "What's this?"

His head poked out from Zafiro's stall, trying to work out what she was looking at. His cheeks were still glowing from their fight, his hair sticking up at all angles.

"Looks like a bit of paper to me," he shrugged.

"Looks like a love note to *me*," she retorted, a little more snappily than she intended. The note was simple, clearly written by someone with a limited level of literacy judging by the spelling and misshapen letters. It was very obviously a woman, though, and one who appeared to have been very moved by Artie's performance at the festival. Esperanza felt her blood bubbling.

"Oh, that," said Artie, shrugging again. "Sí, someone gave that to Diego to pass onto me. I put it in my pocket and forgot about it until I got in today."

"Is this… *usual* for you?"

He seemed to sense her displeasure and came out of the stall, wiping his hands on his shirt.

"It's not the first," he confessed. "I seem to have attracted a bit of attention thanks to the competition, but I've not wasted much thought on it. Why? Does it bother you?" He tipped his head on one side, concerned by her expression.

"No," she lied. "You're free to do as you please. I don't care how many girls you've got writing you silly little notes. It's nothing to me."

She tried to turn her back to hide the tears that were gathering in her eyes, but he took her hand and pulled her to face him.

"Esperanza..." He raised her hand to his chest and pressed it against his heart. "That girl's note was in the bin, where it belonged. And I am here with you, where I belong. Make of that what you will." He winked and kissed her fingers, then turned back to continue his work, leaving her tingling again.

For the rest of the day, the existence of Artie's fan club bothered Esperanza more than she cared to admit, despite his reassurances. As she and her family sat down for *cena* that evening, she tried to put her worries aside and concentrate instead on listening to their stories about their day. It proved to be a difficult task, though, as they seemed far more interested in what she had been up to.

"Esperanza," Louisa frowned, her eyes narrowed in suspicion. "You seem to have straw in your hair."

"Oh, that must have been from earlier," Miguel chirruped. "Esperanza was rolling around in the hay with Artie."

Louisa spluttered on her glass of wine, sending it spraying across the table and soaking Felipe.

"Esperanza was doing what?" she gasped, her eyes bulging.

"Not like that." Esperanza grimaced at the innocence of his words. "I... I tripped over in the stables while we were getting Zafiro ready for my lesson and accidentally took Artie down as I fell. That was all it was. The boys were there, they'll tell you."

She glared at her brothers, and they had the good sense to nod in corroboration, not wanting to get Artie into any trouble.

"Good grief, Esperanza," Louisa fumed, still recovering herself. "You'll be the death of me if rumours like that start getting out. What would Don Raúl think if he heard-"

"How are your riding lessons going, *mija*?" Juan interrupted, changing the subject for fear that his wife was on the brink of one of her hysterical turns. "Has it been worthwhile, getting the boy to come up here on his days off and give you extra lessons?"

"Oh, *sí, papá*," Esperanza assured him. "I'm very much enjoying it." She corrected herself, trying to hide her enthusiasm as her mother's eyes flashed towards her again. "What I mean is, I've already learned so much."

"Excellent," Juan nodded. "Would you say you're getting quite confident now then, *mija*?"

"Oh, definitely. You were right to recommend Arturo as my instructor, *papá*. I'm feeling very confident thanks to him."

So please don't take him away from me, she begged silently.

"I'm delighted to hear it." Juan smiled across the table at her. "Perhaps you'd like to come for a ride with me tomorrow in that case, then, seeing as you're now so confident."

Esperanza faltered. She had walked straight into this one and cursed herself for it. Nothing she had said was a lie, but her confidence came from having Artie beside her, not from her own abilities. She wasn't sure how she would feel about going for a ride without him, but she was hardly in a position to refuse.

"Sí, all right," Esperanza agreed, giving her father the most convincing smile that she could manage. "Where are we going?"

"I have a business meeting with Don Lorenzo at his hacienda," Juan answered, avoiding her gaze. "He requested for you to come along, too. I thought we'd ride rather than bothering Rafael for the carriage just for a quick meeting. I'm sure that Don Raúl will be most impressed to hear of all you've learned, *mija*."

Oh, I'm sure he will be. Esperanza gritted her teeth, picturing the faces of those mineworkers that she and Catalina had tended to only a week earlier. *Let's see how impressed he is to hear the rest of what I've got to say to him, too.*

CHAPTER TWENTY-ONE

"I'm not comfortable with this, Esperanza." Artie frowned, checking Zafiro's girth strap for the hundredth time. "You've barely been learning for more than a week. Are you sure you're going to be all right?"

"I'll be fine," she reassured him, smiling down from the saddle. "My *papá* will be with me the whole time, and I won't be doing anything you haven't already taught me. You needn't worry about me, Artie."

She knew he would worry anyway, but in reassuring him, she found it easier to convince herself that she would be fine. Artie's concerned face peered up at her from beneath his battered straw hat, and as he checked her stirrups once more, she felt him give her ankle a comforting squeeze.

"You look after her, *amigo*," he whispered to Zafiro, scratching the horse's neck. "She means the world to me."

A shout from Juan told them he was ready, and with one last smile at Artie, Esperanza nudged her steed forwards. The two horses plodded side-by-side down the dusty track and away through the fields, short-cutting their way over to Don Lorenzo's *hacienda* in the distance. The August air was cool and fresh after the morning's rainstorm, the wet grass sparkling in the sunlight. Esperanza listened to her father's soothing voice as he schooled her in the differences between various breeds of horse, her hips relaxing into the gentle rhythm of her own steed. She had grown very fond of Zafiro, and she told Juan so, to his great joy. For the first time in far too long, father and daughter spent a very happy hour together in one another's company, and it was only when they passed through Don Lorenzo's gates and began the long walk down the straight drive leading to the *hacienda* that Esperanza started to feel her nerves setting back in.

"Please, *mija*," Juan begged, shooting her a warning glance. "Remember what we agreed. This meeting is about business, not the accident at the mine. I don't want you bringing it up."

"We didn't agree." The reasons for her current hostility towards the Dons resurfaced in her mind, and she gritted her teeth. "I said that I wouldn't raise the subject, but I made no promises about what would happen if *they* did."

Juan glared at his daughter, but the appearance of Don Lorenzo on the steps of the *hacienda* prevented him from saying anything more.

"Lovely to see you, my dear," beamed Don Lorenzo as a servant took Zafiro's reins from her. "I'm afraid that Raúl has not returned home yet from his morning walk, but he should be back at any moment. In the meantime, may I offer you a glass of cordial while you wait? You must be thirsty after your ride."

She accepted with cold politeness and followed Don Lorenzo through to the courtyard, where it appeared he been going through some paperwork.

"That's a beautiful horse you arrived on, señorita," he said. "Your father told me you have been learning to ride. I trust that you are enjoying it?"

"Very much thank you, señor," she returned with a polite curtsey. "I am pleased to say that the horse is as good-natured as he is handsome. Please thank your contact on my behalf for his recommendation."

"No trouble at all, señorita. Raúl was most impressed to hear that you have been learning. I know it means a lot to him, that you're making such an effort for his sake."

He shot her a knowing look, and she tried to twist her own grimace into a convincing smile with little success.

Juan and Lorenzo had been engaged in deep discussion for almost an hour before Don Raúl finally returned home. He stormed into the courtyard with a face as dark as thunder, although upon seeing Esperanza, he forced himself to feign a smile, bowing to her before crossing to the table to offer his apologies.

"Raúl." Don Lorenzo eyed him with cold displeasure. "I was expecting you over an hour ago. How do you think you will ever be ready to take over for me when the time comes if you are not here to attend meetings with our most important associates?"

"My apologies, Father," Raúl grunted. "I went into town to collect something, but the fool didn't have it ready yet."

"I'm sure it will be worth waiting for," said Lorenzo as he nodded at last for Raúl to sit. The explanation had clearly satisfied him, and he turned back to Esperanza with a smile. "It's only been a few weeks. Carlos is an artist, and you cannot rush art."

The servant returned, wheeling a tray laden with a selection of sweet cakes and snacks, which he laid out on the table alongside the wine that was already waiting.

"Did you say Carlos?" Esperanza repeated, her eyes narrowed. "As in, Carlos from the *pueblo*?"

"You know him?" Raúl grunted, pouring himself a glass of wine.

"Sí," she told him. "He's my friend Catalina's brother. And a jeweller."

Juan's face darkened and he glared at her, sensing exactly where the conversation was headed but powerless to stop it.

"You've got me, *señorita*." Raúl grinned, raising his glass to Esperanza with a wink. "I'm having something special made for you. Gold from my own mines, of course."

Juan let out a groan, and Esperanza felt her anger simmer to a boil. Don Lorenzo blinked at them both, looking from his son to Esperanza and back again with an expression of mystified bewilderment. She no longer cared that either of their fathers were listening or that they were guests in Don Lorenzo's home. She was ready for this.

"How can you brag about your gold mines," she said in a voice thick with incredulous fury, "after what happened there only a week ago?"

"Esperanza..." Juan warned.

"Last week's events were... well, most upsetting, *señorita*," Lorenzo admitted, taking a little cake from the offered tray and brushing the crumbs from his fingers. "A most unfortunate accident. Raúl and I have been inundated with paperwork, and it's going to set production back a month at least."

"I'm sure that must have been very hard for you both," Esperanza snapped. "But forgive me if I reserve my prayers for those men who have been injured, crippled or killed by that 'unfortunate accident'."

Juan put his head in his hands, muttering under his breath. Don Lorenzo stared at her for a moment, the little cake frozen halfway to his mouth. Then he cleared his throat, placed it down in front of him and regarded her with polite concern.

"I can see that you have been deeply moved by these tragic events, *señorita*. Your compassion does you justice. I beg your forgiveness for my tactless words. It has been a long time since we had a woman around the house to remind us to engage our hearts as well as our heads in such matters. Of course, our top priority at the moment is ensuring that this sort of thing never happens again. We are putting every effort into establishing the cause of the explosion, although at present we believe that one of the workers must have laid down a little too much dynamite, and the resulting blast was more than the walls of the tunnel could take."

"A tragic case of simple human error," agreed Don Raúl, watching her over the rim of his wine glass. "Some poor *idiota* got his calculations wrong. Drunk, I expect. Many of the workers are dreadful for that, you know. We've even had to install guards to keep a check on it."

"Those workers were not *drunk!*" she objected, outraged. How *dare* Don Raúl try to turn this back on the workers, to make out as though the accident had been their own fault. "They were following *your orders*, Don Raúl, from your last visit to the mines. You told them they had to use more dynamite to get the gold out faster or risk having their pay cut for not meeting their targets. They all told you it was too dangerous, but you forced them to do it anyway. Didn't you? *Didn't you?*"

There was a stunned silence around the table. Esperanza looked to Don Lorenzo, who was staring open-mouthed at his son with an expression of horror. For the first time, the idea crossed her mind that perhaps the old man had no idea about what had really been going on.

"Raúl?" he said shakily, breaking the silence. "Is there any truth in these accusations?"

"Of course not, Father. The *señorita* must be mistaken. She has been listening to vicious, idle gossip and nothing more." Raúl gave a harsh but unconvincing laugh and glared at Esperanza with ice-cold venom. "This is why ladies should stay out of business, *señorita*. They have a tendency to believe every rumour they hear and allow their emotions to rule their heads."

"It's better to be like that than to have no emotions at all and not care that your actions have destroyed hundreds of lives," she spat. "Have you even spared a moment to think about them? To consider their families?"

"No. Nor will I," he snapped, standing up to face her. "There's nothing to be gained from hanging on to the past, *señorita*. Life moves on, and so must we."

"The thing is, though, life doesn't always move on for everyone, does it?" she raged, angry tears springing to her eyes and her voice trembling with fury. She was on her feet now, too incensed to stay still. "Men lost their lives last week. Wives lost their husbands, children lost their fathers—all for the sake of that gold. And you sit here, bragging about your mines as though those people don't matter? Did you think I would be impressed?"

She leaned across the table, and he did the same, the two of them facing each other down.

"I'll tell you what you can do to impress me, *señor*. Don't bother using your filthy gold to make silly little baubles for me. Give it to some of those families whose lives you've destroyed. Pay some of those medical bills they're now crippled with or feed the hungry children you've deprived of their fathers. Explain to *them* how they're supposed to move on with their lives, and believe me, they will be happy to tell you exactly what they think of the *drunken idiota* who got his calculations wrong."

"Esperanza," thundered Juan, rising to his feet at last. "That's enough. I will speak to you outside. *Now.*"

Esperanza turned and flounced from the courtyard, refusing to acknowledge either of the Dons who stared open-mouthed after her. She didn't care if she had offended them. It was time that someone stood up to them and forced them to face the consequences of their actions, and she was proud to be the one to do it.

"What in hell's name do you think you're doing?" Juan hissed once they were out of earshot of the courtyard. He grabbed her arm and wheeled her about to face him, his teeth clenched with anger and embarrassment. "What would your mother have said if she had heard all that?"

"Funny," Esperanza snapped back. "I was just about to ask you the same question."

Something changed in Juan's face, and Esperanza knew she had crossed a line. He let go of her and stepped back, suddenly breathless, staring at her as though she had just slapped him. She could see that he was hurt, but she had meant what she said, and there was no taking it back now. Her *abuelita* would have been ashamed to see her own son sitting at a table with those men and calling them his friends, and he knew it as well as she did.

She turned from him in disgust and strode away towards the front of the house, resolving to wait there for him rather than spend a moment longer having to look at Don Raúl. The sound of retreating footsteps told her that Juan had chosen to return to the courtyard rather than following her, and after a moment, she heard the traitorous rumble of his voice again as he apologised to the Dons for her behaviour.

Esperanza had no desire to hear anymore. She flopped down onto the steps outside the *hacienda*, cursing under her breath. A year ago, she would have wagered everything she had on her father taking her side in this situation. Never had she been more disappointed to be proven wrong. She put her head in her hands, tears squeezing out from between her clamped eyelids.

A gentle hand on her arm shocked her back to the moment, and she wheeled to confront its owner. While the face that greeted her was familiar, however, it was one of the last that she expected to see.

"Diego?" she whispered, blinking up at him. He was wearing a gardeners' uniform, and his clothes and skin were smudged with dirt. "What are you doing here? Did... did you hear all of that?"

"I think the entire estate heard all that, *señorita*," said Diego, his face pale. "Are you mad? Speaking to Don Raúl that way?"

"Not mad. Just standing up for what's right." She looked up at him, hoping that he might be pleased with her for standing up for his brothers and their friends. However, his eyes told her that he was far from it, and he shook his head with a grim expression of fear and horror.

"Oh, Esperanza," he croaked. "You have no idea what you've done."

The sound of approaching footsteps echoed along the stone walkway behind her. Esperanza turned to see Don Raúl strolling towards the steps where she sat, smiling as though nothing had happened. When she turned back, Diego had vanished.

Raúl reached down to offer Esperanza his hand.

"Come, *señorita*," he told her with a fixed smile. "You've been learning to ride, I hear. So, let's go for a ride."

"You must be joking. I'm going nowhere alone with you."

"Yes, you are," he corrected her, beckoning the servants whom she realized were leading both Zafiro and his own black stallion across the lawn towards them. "I wish to speak to you. And believe me, you will much prefer it if neither of our fathers hear what I have to say. Now, if you please."

His hand was still outstretched, and she glared up at him. She was helpless to refuse, and he knew it. However, that did not mean that she was going to make it easy for him. Ignoring his offered hand, she stood and allowed the servant to help her onto Zafiro's back. Don Raúl laughed and heaved himself into the saddle of the big black stallion, which Esperanza noticed was trying hard to bite the servant who held him.

Don Raúl said a few gruff words to his horse and dug him in the sides with his heels, nudging him into a brisk walk. Esperanza was smug to see that while her own steed seemed to follow her thoughts as much as her actions, Raúl was having to fight considerably harder to get his fiery mount to behave.

"You remember Diablo?" Raúl yanked the misbehaving horse hard in the mouth with the reins, and the beast responded with a violent toss of his head.

"How could I forget? The name suits him. He's a dangerous lunatic."

Like his master, she wanted to add.

Don Raúl shook his head, smiling with cold amusement.

"No. He's just spirited. Just the way I like them best." His eyes glittered, and Esperanza was no longer sure that he was just talking about horses. "You see, señorita, I find when I'm dealing with a spirited creature, it's a waste of time arguing with them. The best thing I can do is to work out what makes them tick. Discover what they like, what they're afraid of, and use it to my advantage. Take Diablo, for example."

He gave the horse a hearty slap on the neck, and the beast flattened its ears and rolled its eyes, its mouth foaming.

"Say, for instance, that I want him to jump that wall over there," he continued. "He doesn't want to do it, and I can't lift him and throw him over. He's got to *choose* to do it. So how am I going to persuade him? I could lure him over by putting something on the other side that he wants. A basket of apples perhaps, or a nice mare he fancies the look of." He grinned at her, flashing a neat row of pearly white teeth. "Or, I could use a different method. I know he doesn't want to go over that wall, but given a choice between that or feeling my whip against his flanks, he'll choose the wall. You see? He's made his own choice, but I'm still the one in control."

Esperanza suddenly noticed the wooden riding crop that Don Raúl was holding tucked against his side. She did not like to think of how it might feel to be struck with something like that, and for one wild moment wondered if he planned to beat her into submission.

"And how are these training methods working out for you?" she asked, forcing her fear aside. "You didn't seem to be very 'in control' of your horse the last time I saw him in the plaza."

"Ah, well, I was still getting to know Diablo then," Raúl confessed, ruffling the stallion's thick mane. "I hadn't learned his weaknesses yet. It turns out he's terrified of loud, high noises. A couple of children were playing in the street near him that day, and that was enough to send him over the edge. You see, fear can be an excellent motivator, but it can also be dangerous. Push it too far, and the creature will become reckless and take silly risks. It's all about finding a balance."

They were entering the woodland now, following a pretty track that wove through the trees. For a few minutes they rode together in silence, accompanied only by the chirruping of birds high in the trees above them. Sunlight dappled the path through the leaves, which still dripped from the morning's rainstorm. The air was cool and crisp, and Esperanza knew that in any other company she would have found the walk very enjoyable.

"So, señor," she said at last. "I don't believe that you brought me all this way just to talk about training horses. What was so important that it couldn't be discussed in front of our fathers?"

Raúl slowed Diablo's walk so that he could turn in his saddle to face her.

"What I needed to say, señorita, was that I'm sorry."

She felt her jaw drop with surprise. She wasn't entirely sure what she had been expecting him to say, but this was not it.

"Let me tell you the real reason why I was late today. I went down to the *pueblo* to see Doctor Francisco this morning to discuss how much we owe him for all of the work that he has done over this last week. That's when I heard about what you had done, helping the doctor's wife to tend to the injured." He raised his eyes to hers, and Esperanza could see that for once, they were warm and shining. "I wanted to buy you a present, as a thank-you. And to apologise for what you had to go through. No lady should ever have to endure a sight like that."

Esperanza shifted in her saddle to face him. While the sentiment had perhaps been well-intended, she still thought it highly inappropriate given the circumstances.

"It's not me you owe your thanks to or your apologies," she told him. "It's true, isn't it? You told those men that they had to use more dynamite to blast the ore out more quickly."

"Sí, to my great regret. I am to blame for the deaths of those men and the injuries suffered by the others. I was trying so hard to impress my father, to reassure him that he was leaving his business in good hands. I thought that if I could increase the product yield, then it might prove to him that I can be the success he always wanted me to be." He shook his head. "Instead... well, you've seen for yourself."

"I have. Is that why you didn't want to talk to me at the hacienda? You didn't want to admit to your father that it was your order that caused the accident?"

"Partly, sí," he admitted. "But it's also partly because I don't think he could handle having to think about the human cost. Numbers, facts, financial loss- that sort of thing he can manage, señorita. But real, individual people? Their families, their children? It's more than his poor old heart can take. It's not that he doesn't know they exist. It's just that allowing himself to think about them, to grieve for them, will only hurt him. It won't bring them back."

For a moment, Esperanza almost felt sorry for the old man. The moment soon passed, though, as she remembered Artie's broken sobs as he knelt in that shallow water and the pain in his eyes as he described the horrors of Don Lorenzo's mines.

"It's true that your father can't bring them back," she agreed. "But knowing about them might move him to do something about the appalling conditions they are forced to work in. Oh, sí, señor. I know all about it, and I also know that it's become worse since you took over. I know that the real reason you employed those guards is that you are worried about your workers rising up against you again, and quite frankly, I wouldn't blame them if they did. You'd best start listening unless you want to be on the receiving end of a nasty revolt."

She regarded him with haughty disapproval, her eyebrows raised. Clearly, Raúl had not expected her to know so much; his expression betrayed his surprise and irritation. They rode in silence for a few minutes as he searched for something to say.

"I've agreed to put in new electrical lighting," he argued at last. "To make it safer down there."

"At their own expense," she retorted. "And they're of the belief that you did it so that you could force them to work longer hours, not through any concern for their safety. Hardly what I'd call an act of gallantry."

Don Raúl shrugged.

"What am I supposed to do, señorita? What choice do I have but to make sacrifices where I must and capitalize where I can? My father judges my worth by the amount of gold I can add to his bank account."

"And *I* judge a man's worth by how he treats others, señor. Make whatever sacrifices you must, but not at the expense of the innocent." She turned away from him and tried to press Zafiro forward past Diablo, but the larger stallion kept pace with ease.

"Esperanza," Raúl begged, "Please. I have made mistakes, I know. My father has taught me many things about business, about money and how to make as much of it as possible. But I still have so much to learn, things I can learn from you. From your compassion and your kindness." He reached over and took her hand. "We could do it together, Esperanza. My brains and your heart. We could fix all of my father's mistakes, make sure that nothing like this ever happens again. We can make things better for the mineworkers, for everyone. With you beside me as my wife, we could be unstoppable."

She withdrew her hand and stared hard into his face, trying to read his expression.

"You want me to agree to marry you."

"Sí."

"And you thought that playing on my wish to help the mine workers might work in your favor, is that it?"

His eyes flashed and his smile faltered, but he held her gaze.

"Tell me this then, *señor*, seeing as you are apparently the one with the brains in this partnership." She leaned towards him, lowering her voice. "If you went to see Carlos today to have a gift made for me, as thanks for helping to tend the wounded mine workers…"

"Sí, I did."

"…then how do you explain how your father already knew about it when you came in?" she finished.

Don Raúl had no answer to that. He just stared at her for a moment, then nodded and sat back upright in his saddle, smiling.

"You've got me, *señorita*."

"But you have not got me." Her voice was cold. "You think you can charm me with pretty jewellery and prettier lies, *señor*. But if you really understood me at all, then you would be trying to impress me with compassion, not gold."

"So that's the way it's going to be, is it?" he said, regarding her with a sad smile. "You wanted me to appeal to your heart, so I did. But you still say no to me."

"It would seem so. I'm sorry that this conversation has not proved fruitful for you, *señor*."

He gave a quiet, bitter laugh.

"Oh, but there you are wrong, *señorita*." She looked up to see that his face had split into an unpleasant grin, the ice returned to his eyes. "You've given me exactly what I brought you here for. Information. And believe me, you're nowhere near finished yet."

He lunged towards her and seized Zafiro's bridle, making the horse's eyes widen in fear. The animal tried to jerk his head away, but Don Raúl was too strong, his hold too tight.

"Let go of my horse, Don Raúl," said Esperanza, her voice tight with fear. She grabbed at his wrist, trying to twist it away, but he simply laughed and held on tighter.

"Not until you've told me what I want to hear. Question one. Who told you about my orders in the mines?"

"I can't remember," she lied, fighting to keep her voice steady. "Some of the men were talking about it in the doctor's house while I was stitching up their wounds. Now please, *señor*, release my horse."

"Lies," he snarled. "Those men know the penalty for inciting rebellion, stirring up trouble against my father and me. They wouldn't be so reckless as to make complaints about me to the woman I am courting. No, whoever told you must have known you. They knew that you would take their side over mine. So I'll ask you again. Who was it?"

"Don Raúl, please, you're frightening me. Let me go."

"Tell me! Now!"

Diablo snorted and pawed the ground, unnerved by the high, childlike fear in her voice. *He's terrified of loud, high noises*, she remembered suddenly. An idea sprung to her, reckless and possibly even suicidal, but she was desperate. It was the only way. She filled up her lungs and let out the loudest, highest shriek she could manage.

The effect on the stallion was instantaneous. His eyes rolled back in his head and he let out a scream even louder than hers, rearing up onto his powerful back legs and spinning about, lashing out with his flailing hooves. Don Raúl released Zafiro with a cry of frustration and lunged for the reins of his own steed. He fought to stay in the saddle as Diablo reared and plunged, foaming and screaming, and Esperanza seized her chance.

"Go, Firo! GO!" she bellowed, wheeling the gelding around to face away from the path, away from Don Raúl and the stallion he was fighting to control. Zafiro did not require any further encouragement. His haunches gave a powerful spring, and before she knew it, they were whistling through the forest at unimaginable speed, weaving between the trees and jumping over fallen logs.

Esperanza had already lost both stirrups and given up any hope of steering and instead lay flat against the saddle with both hands buried in Zafiro's mane. She clung to the horse with every muscle she possessed, praying that she could trust his instincts and agility to get them both as far away as possible from Don Raúl. At least they were at an advantage here; while Diablo was bigger, more powerful and would easily win a race on the flat, Zafiro's smaller size and nimble agility allowed him to weave around the trees and fit through gaps that would only slow the larger stallion. Hopefully, they could lose Don Raúl and get away across the fields before he could catch up with them.

The wind whipped through Esperanza's hair as Zafiro broke through the line of trees at the edge of the woodland and bolted towards the tall iron gates of Don Lorenzo's grounds. The gates were open, and the little horse had no trouble darting straight through them and away. She heard surprised shouts from the guards as they leaped out of Zafiro's path, his hooves spraying up clumps of gravel and dirt and leaving them spluttering and bewildered.

The horse ignored the stony dirt track, choosing instead to leap up the grassy bank and take a shortcut across the field. Esperanza clung on for dear life as the powerful muscles pumped beneath her, the hooves thundering and head bobbing as he bounded up the steep incline. As they reached the top, Esperanza dared to glance back for just long enough to see Diablo breaking free of the trees behind her. There was no sign of his rider, and the stallion seemed to be having a whale of a time charging around in the ornate flower displays leading up to the *hacienda*, leaving a trail of terrified gardeners scattered in his wake.

If Zafiro had begun to slow a little as he reached the top of the incline, then he certainly made up for it on the descent. Esperanza squeezed her eyes tight shut with fear and pressed her face against the strong white neck as the horse's hooves thundered across the rough terrain. She uttered a prayer to Saint Christopher, Saint Eligius and every other relevant figure she could think of, hoping against hope that the horse was at least heading back in the direction of the farm and she would not end up lost and wandering the wilderness for days when he finally ran out of energy. There were no signs of that happening any time in the near future, though, and for now, all that she could do was cling on and try to remember to keep breathing.

If you feel that you're going too fast, lean back and pull on the reins. Those had been Artie's words, and it had seemed so easy then, with the comfort of his warm body pressed up behind hers. Now, she couldn't even find the stirrups, and Zafiro had long since stopped listening to her. His ears were flat against his head, his teeth set against the bit, and he was charging full-tilt across the fields with his mane and tail flying behind him.

Squinting out through narrowed eyes, Esperanza realized that she recognized the landscape around her. There was the signpost directing travellers down to the *pueblo*. There was the boulder on the side of the road, which she sometimes sat on to rest on her way home from town. They were heading back towards the farm, she realized with a flood of relief. There in the distance was the fence with the heavy wooden gate leading through to the fields she had walked so many times to and from the house, marking the entrance to her father's land. It grew closer and closer with each pounding hoofbeat, the familiarity of it filling her with joy and relief that she could hardly contain. Just beyond, she knew she would soon see her home, and beside it the stables where Artie would be waiting.

"Good boy, Zafiro!" she cried. "Woah, now. We're home."

But the horse did not stop. Instead, he collected his pace for a second and eyed up the fence, bobbing his head up and down as though assessing the height. Then, before Esperanza had the chance to realize what he was going to do, he gave a final burst of speed and galloped straight towards the gate.

"Zafiro, no!" she cried, but it was too late. His back legs coiled beneath him like a spring, and he launched himself over the fence like a bullet from a gun.

Esperanza held her breath, squeezing her eyes shut tight and clinging to the horse's neck with all of her remaining strength. She felt the powerful body lunge forwards and up, and then there was a brief moment of complete weightlessness as the horse flew through the air with the grace of a swallow. Time seemed to stand still. Then, as though in slow motion, she was falling. She braced herself for the impact, waiting to feel her body collide with the horse beneath her, but it never came. Instead, she kept on falling, the white blur of Zafiro's tail shooting past the corner of her eye before she had time to process what was about to happen. The ground came up to meet her, and then the whole world vanished into blackness.

CHAPTER TWENTY-TWO

Esperanza became aware of three things as she blinked into consciousness. First, that she had a headache from hell. Second, that it was morning, which she gathered from the incessant shrieking of the birds in the tree outside her window, making her head pound even harder. And third, that she was not alone.

For one glorious moment, she wondered if perhaps the dream had been real after all. She rolled over gingerly, her eyes still adjusting to the bright sunlight streaming in through the window, trying to catch the scent of the citrusy warmth of Artie's skin from the soft sheets beside her. She was met instead with the faint smell of rosewater, which was odd. Come to think of it, Artie didn't snore either. Or wear ladies' nightdresses, at least as far as she knew.

"Catalina?"

Her bedfellow gave a sharp snort and a groan. It was indeed Catalina, and she looked just as tired as Esperanza felt as she opened a groggy eye and gave her friend an exhausted smile.

"Ah, good morning, Sunshine," she croaked. "How's the patient today?"

"I feel like I've been run over by a cart," Esperanza grumbled, holding her pounding head. Catalina passed her a mug of water from the bedside table, and Esperanza drank, feeling a rush of relief as the liquid soothed her parched throat.

"Maybe you were," Catalina shrugged. "We still don't really know what happened to you, only that you hit your head. I offered to stay over and keep an eye on you. Do you remember anything at all?"

Esperanza thought hard, trying to push past the throbbing in her skull. Bits of memories shimmered in her mind as though through a thick mist. She remembered Artie carrying her up to the house and how his beautiful chestnut eyes had been wet with tears as he held her. She remembered her father's eyes, tired and worried as he apologised to her over and over. She also remembered another pair of eyes, dark and cold, staring at her with venom across a large wooden table.

"Don Raúl," she said slowly. "I had an argument with him. He said something about jewellery, and I lost my temper."

"Ah, yes. That would make sense." Catalina nodded, reaching for the jug to pour Esperanza another mug of water. "I spoke to my brother yesterday morning. Don Raúl went to see him about something he's having made for you, and

Carlos told him that he refused to do any more on it until he's been paid upfront in full."

"That's very brave of Carlos," Esperanza mused. "Why did he do that? Because of what happened in the mine?"

"In a way, sí," Catalina sighed. "Most of the shops in town have agreed to do the same thing in solidarity with Francisco. After the accident, Francisco sent the Dons a letter about the cost of the medical care for all of those injured workers. Of course, most of those men haven't got a centavo to their names. Some of those who survived the blast will still go on to die; the hospital won't treat them further without payment. Don Raúl came down to see us yesterday morning to share his opinion that it's not his problem, that his workers knew that the work was dangerous when they agreed to do it and that he and his father will not be contributing a single centavo. Meaning that we've almost bankrupted ourselves with medical supplies that we'll never get reimbursed for, Francisco will never get paid for all that work he did, and as for the men who needed hospital treatment, *still* need hospital treatment..."

Her teeth clenched with anger, and for a moment, she looked as though she was about to cry.

"Honestly, Esperanza, until now, I've wondered whether you were being a bit hard on Don Raúl because you'd had your head turned by your handsome *músico*. Now, I'm convinced you were being too generous in your description. He's a vile, heartless *cabrón*, and I would rather die tomorrow than see my best friend married to such a man."

"You're in good company," Esperanza assured her, thinking about Artie's words the last time they had discussed the subject. "He's a dishonest rogue, too. He told me he'd been down in the *pueblo* to discuss how much he owed Francisco for his work. He never mentioned that he had refused to pay."

"No, I bet he didn't. It will be interesting to see if he changes his tune now that he knows you were involved." Catalina shook her head in frustration, busying herself with the clothes that she had draped over the chair beside Esperanza's bed. "I told your father about it, and he had the cheek to tell me I must've misunderstood. He didn't think that Don Lorenzo even knew about it. I warned him, if I heard him make one more excuse on the Dons' behalf, he'd be the next one with a head injury."

She began to dress herself, pulling her slip on over her head with such savagery that Esperanza thought she was going to tear it. Then she took the comb from Esperanza's dressing table and attacked the knots in her hair, grimacing in the mirror as Esperanza watched from the bed, her mind whirring. Something was stirring in her memory, angry words and a sickening, twisting feeling of fear that she could not quite place.

"I remember something," she muttered. "I was riding through trees with Don Raúl, and he was angry. He wanted names of those who had been speaking out against him."

Catalina froze, staring at Esperanza in the mirror, the hairbrush forgotten in her hand.

"Did you tell him?"

"Of course not." Esperanza bristled, offended that Catalina even had to ask. "You know what he would do to Artie if he thought he'd been trying to spread revolutionary ideas."

That sickly feeling was still bubbling in her stomach, though. She had been so confident about outsmarting Don Raúl by showing off just how much she knew that it had not crossed her mind that she had been playing right into his hands. If Don Raúl found out that the name of one of Artie's brothers was on that list of the dead, it would be all too easy for him to make the connection.

Catalina gave her a worried frown, her brow furrowed.

"*Mi compa*, when you said that he was angry..."

"He didn't hurt me," Esperanza reassured her. She knew where her friend's mind had been going. As much as she couldn't remember all of the details of what had happened, Esperanza was certain that if Raúl had struck her then it would've taken more than a fall to erase her memory of it. "He did frighten me, though. I remember that much."

"Hmm." Catalina's brow furrowed again with displeasure. "He told your father that your horses got spooked by a bird. One of Lorenzo's servants reported hearing you scream, and-"

"I did!" Esperanza cried suddenly, sitting bolt upright in bed as it all came flooding back to her. "I did scream, Catalina. But I didn't scream because the horse spooked- it was the other way around."

Catalina looked at her as though she had gone completely mad.

"Are you trying to tell me that you deliberately screamed to make the horses panic? Why on Earth would you do something so stupid?"

"Raúl grabbed Zafiro's bridle. I told him to let go, but he wouldn't, so I screamed to frighten his horse and force him to release me. Zafiro never spooked at all, I told him to run. I remember seeing the gates of the farm, and that must have been when I fell."

"*Dios mío.*" Catalina swore under her breath. "So it was Don Raúl who caused you to get hurt. He frightened you that badly that you would do something so stupid just to get away from him?"

"I suppose so." She thought back to something that Raúl had said to her about using fear as a tool to train horses. *Push it too far, and the creature will become reckless and take silly risks.* Perhaps horses and people weren't so different after all; both could either be saved or destroyed by their instincts when motivated by fear. "The next thing I knew, Artie was there. He carried me here and put me on the bed. My brothers were there too, and then my father came, and then you and Francisco…"

Francisco had given her some tablets then to ease the pain in her head. Some sort of opiate, she assumed, as everything had become a little hazy after that.

"Yes, that's right." Catalina gave a mischievous grin. "What do you remember after that, *mi compa*?"

"I remember Artie coming back," she said nervously. "He was keeping watch over me as I slept."

"No," Catalina corrected her. "That was me."

"No, I'm sure. He was lying beside me. He kept waking me up to look into my eyes." Esperanza remembered it vividly. She had tried to pull him close to her, but he just wanted to stare into her eyes, talking to her in soft words that she had not been able to understand.

"No. Really, it was me. I was checking you for a concussion."

"Oh." Esperanza blushed, remembering the finer details of the dream. "So… that bit when he…"

She trailed off, biting her lip. Catalina chuckled.

"Still me, I'm afraid. Although it would explain why you kept trying to put your hands all over me. It was like trying to sleep next to an octopus."

Esperanza covered her face in horror. She had heard that opiates could make people behave strangely, but she had never heard of anyone making a mistake such as this before while under their influence.

"Oh, Catalina, I'm so sorry!"

"Don't worry about it," Catalina grinned, winking. "I was quite flattered to tell the truth. With Francisco being away so much lately, it's the most attention I've had in weeks. Artie's a lucky man, I'm only sorry that the first time you kissed him it turned out to be me."

"Oh, God. Catalina, tell me I didn't-"

Catalina burst out laughing at the sight of her mortified expression.

"No, you didn't. I'm winding you up, *mi compa*. You should see your face!"

Esperanza took her pillow and swung it at Catalina's head, cursing and laughing with embarrassment.

"You're a cruel woman, Catalina Rivera," she chided. "Mocking the afflicted. And you the doctor's wife, too."

"Ay, I know. But my husband is so serious all the time. I'm afraid I have to take my fun at my friends' expense instead, *mi compa*," Catalina giggled. "I tell you what, though, that Arturo of yours is sweet. You know, he waited outside all night watching your balcony, just in case you took a turn for the worse? He made me promise to inform him immediately if anything happened to you. I don't know what he thought he could do to save you unless he was planning to break into the house, battle his way past your mother and give you the kiss of life. But it's sweet that he made the effort all the same. Take a look, he's probably still there."

Esperanza's heart fluttered. She swung her legs over the edge of the bed and stood up, steadying herself as her sore head whirled. Her left ankle was aching, too, although she had no idea why. She hobbled to the window, supporting her weight on the windowsill. Sure enough, Artie was there, sitting beneath a tree just as Catalina had said. His back was resting up against the trunk, his face pointed up towards her bedroom balcony. His hair was standing on end with the number of times that he had run his hands through it, and Esperanza strongly suspected that he had not slept a wink all night.

The sharp sound of heeled shoes on the stairs made both women turn around, and a moment later, Louisa burst into the room. *Señora* Dominguez never had been one to bother with formalities such as knocking, especially in her own home.

"Esperanza!" she cried, rushing to the window to fuss over her daughter. "*Mija*, what are you doing out of bed? You should be resting. Come on, sit yourself down, and I'll bring you girls some *almuerzo* and a mug of *atole*. Now, would you prefer some eggs or-"

"Actually, señora," interrupted Catalina, reading Esperanza's mind. "We were just discussing taking our *almuerzo* outside. Under the shade of the fruit trees, perhaps. I think that the fresh air will do her some good."

"Oh." Louisa blinked at her in surprise. "Well, who am I to argue with the doctor's wife? Very well then, Catalina. I tell you what- I'll put together a basket of food, and we can all eat together. You head on down there, and I'll meet you as soon as I've finished making the pastries."

"Perfect," Catalina smiled back.

A few minutes later, Esperanza limped down the stairs, clinging to Catalina's arm for support. Her ankle was still throbbing with pain, and she gritted her teeth as they passed through the kitchen, keen to avoid raising Louisa's suspicions. Fortunately, Louisa was too busy preparing the food to pay them much attention, and the two women managed to get out of the door and past the kitchen window before Esperanza had to lean on Catalina for support again.

"I don't even know how I hurt my ankle," she grimaced, wincing as she limped towards the fruit trees. "I would say maybe I twisted it on the stirrup as I fell, but I remember losing both stirrups before I even got out of Don Lorenzo's garden."

"I can answer that," Catalina grumbled. "It was last night. You tried to get out of bed, you were saying something about how we needed to dance. You got your foot tangled in the bedsheet and nearly knocked yourself out again."

Esperanza cringed.

"I'm so sorry, Catalina. Thank you for staying to take care of me. I am very grateful, you know."

"You should be. If I hadn't stayed with you last night, you'd have had your mother instead," Catalina pointed out. "And if she'd have seen the way you were behaving, she'd have gone down to the stables with her kitchen knife and gelded your beloved Artie on the spot."

Artie was already on his feet by the time Esperanza reached the fruit trees, almost dancing on the spot with anticipation at the sight of her. His eyes widened in alarm when he saw how she was limping, and he rushed over to help, lifting her into his arms like a child. She felt the pain in her ankle evaporate.

"You've got roughly five minutes until Louisa gets here." Catalina pushed Artie further into the grove where he would be out of sight of the kitchen window. "I'll keep a lookout. Make it quick, all right?"

She moved away to allow them a little space, leaning in the shadow of one of the far trees to keep an eye on the house. Esperanza looped her arms around Artie's neck, and he carried her to a quiet spot beneath the biggest tree, gently placing her down on the grass so that she could lean back against the tree trunk.

"You're all right," he croaked, sitting back so that he could take a good look at her. His eyes were red from exhaustion, and he stared at her as though afraid she might break if he dared to touch her. "I'm so sorry, *mi amor*."

"You're sorry?" she repeated, confused. "What on Earth are you sorry for?"

"I promised I'd never let you fall. I promised." He gave her hand a gentle squeeze. "My God, Esperanza. When I saw Zafiro appear over that hill without you... I thought bandits had attacked you or a wild animal or something. I had visions of having to follow a trail of your blood to find you." He swallowed hard, tears welling in his eyes. "Luckily, the ground was still soft from the rain, I could follow the hoofprints back to the gate, and there you were. I thought you'd broken your neck. You were just lying there on the ground. I wasn't sure that you were... I mean, I couldn't see any sign of movement. You were just lifeless. I never should've let it happen."

His voice cracked, and Esperanza reached out to pull him towards her. Why was it that the people who should be sorry for their actions never were, and yet the people who had nothing to apologise for always seemed to be feeling guilty for something?

"Come here, you fool. You've been up all night overthinking things, haven't you? None of this was your fault." She tried to put her arms around him, but he shrank away from her as though afraid to hurt her.

"Yes, it was. I taught you to ride. I should have taught you what to do if your horse bolted. I left you undefended."

He ran his hands through his hair, his eyes full of pain.

"Artie, please. Come here." She reached for him again. "For goodness' sake, you're not going to hurt me. I bumped my head, I didn't turn to porcelain. The only pain I feel now is seeing you like this."

Those few last words did the trick. His expression softened, and he reached towards her and wrapped his arms around her with a shuddering sigh. She relaxed against him, enjoying the warmth of his chest beneath her cheek and the comfort of his fingers in her hair.

"Please, *mi amor*," he whispered. "I have to know. What happened? Did Don Raúl do this to you?"

She hesitated. Lying to Artie felt wrong, but she had no choice. Since his reckless outburst after the mining accident, Esperanza could not pretend that she trusted him to control himself if he found out the truth.

"Don Raúl's horse spooked and went *loco*, just like he did in the plaza," she told him, careful to keep as close to the facts as possible. "It frightened me, and I took off with Zafiro. We got back as far as the farm and he tried to jump the gate before I could stop him. I fell, and that's when you found me."

There were no lies, but she still felt awful for withholding the truth from him. Still, it was better than seeing him arrested for killing Don Raúl. He pulled her close again, cradling her head against his chest.

"Oh, *mi amor*," he muttered, breathing in the scent of her hair. "I'm just so glad you're all right."

"You're not, though. Look at you, Artie. You're in no fit state to work today. You need to go home and get some sleep."

"Mmm, I suppose. Rafael said the same thing. I told him I'd work Friday this week to make up for it, but I couldn't bear to leave before I'd seen you for myself." He stifled a yawn and relaxed back against the tree, lacing his fingers through hers. "I wish I could stay here with you. I don't want to let you out of my sight after what happened yesterday."

"I know." Esperanza sighed. There was nothing she wanted to do more than to spend the day down in their favorite spot by the river, lying beside Artie in the grass while he slept off his long night's watch with his head cradled in her lap. "I wish it, too. But there's no way I'll escape my mother today. She'll be here in a minute, no doubt with enough food to satisfy half the *pueblo*. You'd best not let her see you."

"Ay, I know. Just give me a moment longer." He nuzzled her hair, his fingers entwined with hers. She caught sight of Catalina out of the corner of her eye, who mimed vomiting.

The thundering of approaching hooves made them all turn. It was a messenger, and Esperanza noticed with a twinge of dread that he was wearing Don Lorenzo's household colours. He halted his horse outside the house and knocked on the front door.

"Artie," whispered Catalina urgently. "You'd better go. *Señora* Louisa may well head straight down here once that man has delivered his message."

"All right." Artie stood, bending to kiss Esperanza's hand. "Until Friday then, *mi amor*. Take care of yourself. And if anything happens, if you need me for any reason, send for me immediately. Do you promise?"

"I promise," she agreed. She forced herself to release his hand, feeling a slight wrench in her chest as she did so. "Now go, before I get you into any more trouble."

He bowed to her and left, disappearing into the trees with one last wistful glance.

"Is he always like that?" asked Catalina, once she was certain that he had gone. "Worries a lot, blames himself for things, struggles with sleep?"

"*Sí*, occasionally," Esperanza shrugged. "He's had some past traumas that I know still haunt him. He was at the mines in Cananea when the soldiers put down the strikes a few years ago."

"Hmm." Catalina nodded, frowning. "That would explain a lot."

Before they could discuss it further, Esperanza spotted Louisa heading down towards them from the farmhouse. She was almost running, which was alarming enough in itself, but Esperanza was more concerned about the manic smile plastered across her mother's face.

"Esperanza!" she panted, almost throwing the basket of food onto the ground as she thrust a letter into Esperanza's hands. "You have a letter from Don Raúl, look! You've got a letter too, Catalina. We've all got one. Open it, *mija*, open it!"

Esperanza and Catalina exchanged glances. Their letters bore matching blood-red seals depicting the Alverez family crest, but the names inked on the front of each envelope had clearly been written by different hands.

"After you," Catalina nodded.

Esperanza tore the thick parchment from its envelope, wrinkling her nose as she realized it had been infused with the same woody perfume she had so often smelled on Don Raúl himself. Her mother was staring at her expectantly, waiting for her to read it aloud, and with a deep breath, she began.

"My dearest Esperanza. Do you remember what I said to you when we were discussing how to train horses? Well, it seems that I failed to heed my own advice. I do not blame the horse for what he did; I deserved what I got for losing control of the situation. I take full responsibility for what happened and apologise unreservedly. I assure you that such a mistake will not happen again. Wishing you a speedy recovery from your fall. Don Raúl."

Both Louisa and Catalina stared at her for a moment in silence. Louisa snatched the letter from her hands.

"Is that it?" she asked incredulously, turning it over to check that nothing had been written on the back. "*Dios mío*, I was expecting a letter professing his love and concern for you. This is more like an apology to his horse."

Except that the horse is me, Esperanza thought. She looked up at Catalina, who gave her a faint nod of understanding. To give Don Raúl his due, he had been clever. To anyone else, his words would appear exactly as Louisa had taken them. Even Esperanza herself would have read it the same way had she not recovered her memory of their conversation.

It was Catalina's turn next. She read the envelope with a suspicious scowl, examining the neat calligraphy.

"It's addressed to Francisco," she muttered. "But it does say urgent. So I suppose I'd best open it on his behalf, hadn't I?"

She tore the envelope open, making Louisa squirm with horror at the destruction of the elegant wax seal. Esperanza watched her eyes dart from left to right and back again, her lips moving soundlessly as she read. Her eyes grew wider and wider in surprise, and by the time she reached the end of the letter, she had to lean against the tree to support herself.

"It's from Don Lorenzo. He's had a change of heart and wants to pay us for all of his workers' medical care. Says it was all a misunderstanding."

"A misunderstanding my foot," Esperanza sneered. "But he's doing the right thing now, though, and I suppose we ought to be grateful for that."

"Save your gratitude for tomorrow night." Louisa was wearing a wide grin. She had been reading a letter of her own, and she brandished it at Esperanza like a trophy. "Don Lorenzo has invited us for *cena*, he says he wishes to apologise to you in person for all that has happened. Isn't that nice?"

Esperanza felt a flutter of panic in her chest.

"But *mamá*," she stammered. "Don Raúl-"

"Won't be there," Louisa finished. "He has a prior engagement, apparently. So you need not worry about him seeing you not looking your best, *mija*. You're lucky you got away with just a few little scuffs and bruises. It would've been awful if you'd suffered anything disfiguring. Especially with you having such a pretty face."

Priorities, mamá, thought Esperanza. Trust Louisa to be more concerned about her daughter looking pretty than suffering permanent brain damage. Still, she was too relieved to argue; Don Raúl would not be there tomorrow night. The accident had bought her time but not reprieve, and she knew she would not be able to escape the rest of his inquisition for long. Assuming, of course, that he did not find out about Artie's treason some other way.

The rest of Esperanza's day was spent leisurely, lying beneath the fruit trees with Catalina while Louisa fussed over them and brought them more food than they could ever eat, refusing to leave them alone until the boys came home from school to distract her. Miguel was still making a nuisance of himself, harassing Louisa and getting under her feet until she finally lost patience with him and sent him to bed early.

"I know he's struggling with the attention that Esperanza's been getting these last few weeks, but really, he's old enough to know better," Louisa huffed. "Now, where are those earrings I had a moment ago? God knows what I've done with them. Honestly, I think I'm going mad, thanks to that child being under my feet all the time. I keep putting things down and then can't remember where."

Esperanza chose not to point out that this was nothing new.

Miguel was still in a foul temper the following day when he came home from school, whining and clinging and even being rude to *Tía* Victoria in his desperation to persuade his parents not to go out that evening. To top it all, today, he had fallen over and skinned both of his knees on his way home from school and arrived back at the farmhouse bleeding and howling. Esperanza and Juan did their best to stay out of the way, hoping that the chaos might burn itself out in their absence.

By the time they were in the carriage on their way to Don Lorenzo's that evening, almost everything had returned to a surprising level of calm. In fact, the whole evening was pleasantly uneventful; Don Lorenzo was even more gracious towards Esperanza than usual, and the absence of Don Raúl meant that she could relax as she listened to the chatter around the table and daydreamed.

The evening was warm, so they took *cena* out in the courtyard, and Esperanza reminisced about the night of the *baile* when Artie had danced with her in that very same spot. She would have to suggest they danced together again sometime soon, perhaps when they were alone down by the river. It had been such a wonderful feeling. Perhaps next time she would suggest something a little slower. And maybe something that would not end in them both lying tangled together on the ground as it had last time, although she had a feeling that neither of them would mind so much if it did.

CHAPTER TWENTY-THREE

Artie sensed that something was wrong the moment he arrived at the farm, and it wasn't just that it should've been his day off. There was something urgent about Rafael's body language as he stood in the doorway of the house with Juan and an unusual level of noise coming from inside. Panic was in the air, and Artie felt fear rising in his own chest in response. Something had happened, he knew it. Something bad.

Esperanza.

His mind immediately started to race, and he found himself breaking into a run as he neared the house.

"Rafael?" he panted, the old man turning to him as he heard his approaching steps. "What is it? Is *Señorita* Esperanza all right?"

"It's not her, *niño*. It's the little boy, Miguel."

"Miguel?" Artie stopped in his tracks. "What's wrong with Miguel?"

"He's missing." The old man sighed and rubbed his forehead. "*Señor* Juan said he's been acting off recently, tearful and clingy, badly behaved for his aunt last night. Victoria put the boys to bed after *cena*, and that's the last time anyone saw him. Felipe woke Juan and Louisa this morning to say that his brother was gone, and his bed's not been slept in."

Artie felt his stomach drop. He knew that something had not been right with Miguel, but he had assumed that after Esperanza had mentioned it to Juan that it would have all been dealt with. True, the boy had been spending a lot of time in the stables over the last few weeks, but Artie had just put that down to the fact that he always had sweets. Now he thought about it, perhaps the poor child had been using it as somewhere to hide. Who or what from, though, he couldn't guess.

"Did he leave a note or anything?" he asked. "Any indication of where he was going or why?"

"None." Rafael ran his hand through his hair with a worried sigh. "Juan is setting out to look for him as soon as he's finished checking the house, and all of the farmhands' work for the morning is to be put on hold until the boy is found. My nephew Daniel is searching the barn. The ladies are just getting dressed and then they're going to come and help too." He turned to gaze out across the field, shooting a worried glance towards the river. "Hopefully the lad has had the sense to stay on the farm at least. If he's taken it upon himself to go off further afield... well, it doesn't bear thinking about."

Artie knew exactly what he meant. Bandits, wild animals, burst riverbanks... there were any number of dangers that could mean a swift and sticky end for a frightened little boy on his own in the middle of the night. He needed to be found, and soon, before any harm came to him. Assuming, of course, that it wasn't already too late.

"I'm going to check the stables," Artie told Rafael. "Just in case he's hiding down there."

"Good idea," Rafael agreed. "I'm off to look around where he usually plays. We'll check the farm first, and if there's still no sign of him, then we'll have to send down to the *pueblo* for more help. I'm sure that Don Lorenzo would be happy to offer some men to assist, but let's hope it doesn't come to that. I don't think Juan is keen to owe that man any favors if he can help it."

He and I both, thought Artie. *Especially if those favors would have to be repaid in some way by Esperanza.*

There was no sign of Miguel down in the stables, and the damp ground showed no trace of his little footprints. The hay in the empty end stall was as undisturbed as it had been when Ricardo had left it the evening before. Juan and Rafael had already begun to search around Miguel's usual haunts, and Artie could hear Louisa and Esperanza upstairs in the house calling for the little boy with growing desperation in their voices. He was sure that Esperanza was crying, and it made his heart ache to hear.

Felipe was waiting for him when he returned to the farmhouse, being comforted by a worried Rafael.

"...he was being really awkward, wanting to walk the long way home so that we didn't have to come past the gate," Felipe explained. "So I left him to walk home by himself. I thought he was just being funny about it 'cause that's where Esperanza got hurt. I told him that he was being stupid. I knew he was upset with me, but I didn't think that he... he would..."

"It's not your fault," Artie reassured him. "Miguel wouldn't tell anyone what was wrong, I tried too. This has been going on for months, *chamaco*. I promise, whatever you said to him, it wasn't the reason why he ran away."

Felipe nodded, his eyes full of tears.

"You have no idea where he might have gone, though?" Rafael asked, his brow furrowed. "He hasn't got any favorite new hide-and-seek spots or anywhere he likes to play that you haven't already told us about?"

"No," Felipe mumbled. "I know where he *didn't* want to go, but I don't know where he *did*. If he's not in the stables, then I've got no idea."

"All right," Rafael sighed. "We'll keep searching, then. You stick with me, lad. We've already lost one of the Dominguez boys, I'm not going to be responsible for losing the other one."

"I'm going to take one of the horses and head down towards the gate," Artie told him, making up his mind. "See if I can find any reason why Miguel was so scared to be down there. Then I'll go down to the track by the river, see if I can retrace his footsteps home from school yesterday. He might have some sort of hideout down there that we don't know about."

"It's worth a try," Rafael shrugged. "We'll just have to hope the river's not too high, and if it is, that the boy had the sense not to get too close to it. But in the dark..." he trailed off. Artie knew what he was thinking and gave a little shiver. If he dared to think about the possibility of finding Miguel washed up somewhere on the riverbed, then he might lose the confidence to go out looking for him at all. Still, there was a good chance that Esperanza's little brother was out there alone and frightened, cold and hungry from a night spent out in the rain. Artie knew that he had to try, at least.

Artie didn't even waste time to saddle up Zafiro in his hurry to start his search. He rode bareback down as far as the gate before stopping to search around for clues. There was the spot where he had found Esperanza, the grass glittering with morning dew as though nothing had ever happened. Something else was shining in the grass too, and he dismounted to get a closer look. To his surprise, it was an empty tequila bottle, discarded quite recently, judging by its cleanliness. Inside, he could see what looked like a few little bits of scrunched up paper. He tipped them out onto his hand, and upon closer examination, realized what they were. Sweet wrappers, and Miguel's favorites, no less. It was as though someone had drained the bottle, eaten the sweets and then poked the wrappers inside the bottle to dispose of them all at once. What Miguel would have been doing with a bottle of tequila, though, Artie had no idea.

Unless he wasn't the one eating the sweets, he realized. *Unless someone took them off him. The owner of that tequila bottle, for example.*

A glint of gold caught his eye, down in the grass right by the gate. He bent down to take a closer look, and to his surprise, found it to be an earring; a shining gold stud with a small emerald drop. Esperanza must have lost it when she fell. He put the earring in his chest pocket, making a mental note to return it to her when he saw her later. It was hardly likely to be her top priority right now. He swung himself back up onto Zafiro's back and nudged the horse's sides, resolving to head down towards the river to see if he could find any more signs that Miguel had been that way.

To Artie's frustration, any footprints he might've found in the soft ground by the river had already been washed away by the rain during the night. He trudged along the bank, resolving to at least follow the river as far as the *pueblo* before turning back. If he went far enough then he might run into one of his street friends, and they could put the word out to everyone to watch out for the missing child too. There were a lot of people living in the slum area of Santa Sofia, and news travelled fast via the street network. If Miguel had been seen anywhere around the town, then one of them would know about it. They would need all the help they could get if he wasn't found soon.

Eventually, Artie reached the little abandoned cottage by the river, which he knew had once belonged to Esperanza's grandmother. The garden was so overgrown that the windows were almost hidden from view, grass and vines tangling around the doorframe. It was a shame; the cottage looked as though it could have been a very charming home for someone, if only somebody had spent a little time maintaining it.

Artie dismounted for a moment, allowing Zafiro a few minutes to drink from the river before starting their journey back to the farm. There had been no sign of Miguel anywhere along the way, which Artie reminded himself was in some way a relief. There were no marks in the ground to indicate that anyone had slipped and fallen into the water, no dislodged stones or ripped up plants hinting that somebody had been trying to cling on to something before being swept away. As disappointing as it was that Artie had not managed to find him, nor had he found any reason to believe that the little boy had met with misfortune, and that was good news in itself.

Artie had been staring at the dirty cottage window for some time before he realized exactly what it was he had been looking at. The glass was crusted over with dust from years of neglect, and yet there it was, standing out clearly as the sunlight streaming through it: a child's handprint.

Artie glanced around, trying to see if anything else was out of the ordinary. Now that he thought about it, the grass seemed to be a little compacted down between the gate and the door, as though someone had attempted to enter the house through the door and then tried the window when they found it locked. The grass was also a little disturbed over by the tree, as though something had nested there.

"Miguel?" he called gently, pushing his way towards the nest. "Are you there? It's me. It's Artie."

There was a choked whimper from somewhere in the long grass, and Artie felt relief flooding through him. He had found Miguel, and from the sound of it, he was all right.

It didn't take Artie long to persuade Miguel out from his hiding place. He was hungry and frightened, but he seemed to have managed to escape the worst of the rain and was uninjured as far as Artie could tell. Artie knew that he should get the boy back home as soon as possible, not least because he knew how worried everyone was, but every time he tried to suggest it, Miguel just broke down again and threw his little arms around Artie's waist.

"Please," he begged, sobbing into Artie's shirt. "I can't go back. Nobody listens to me. It's not safe for me there. I can't tell you any more than that."

"All right," Artie soothed him. "If you can't tell me, perhaps I can guess. I found an empty bottle of tequila by the gate to the farm, filled with sweet wrappers. Your sweet wrappers, I'm guessing. Now, I doubt that you have a secret tequila habit at the age of six…"

"Nearly seven," Miguel protested.

"Nearly seven," Artie corrected himself. "So if it wasn't you, there's only one man I can think of who carries tequila with him. And I suspect that those *were* your sweets, and you either gave them to him... or he took them from you."

Miguel's trembling lip told Artie that his suspicions were correct.

"A big man, with hair that looks like it's never met a comb, a gold tooth and breath that could kill a donkey at twenty paces. Does that sound familiar to you, *chamaco*?"

The little boy nodded and gave a little sob, his face crumpling.

"You can't tell him you know, Artie. He'll kill me."

"Why, though?" Artie asked him, trying to piece it all together. That day when he had found Miguel crying in the stables, the little boy's recent behaviour, all of those mysterious injuries. Even a man like Roberto surely wouldn't hurt a little child just for the sake of a few boiled sweets. It didn't make sense.

Miguel pressed his head against Artie's chest, and something in his shirt pocket jabbed painfully against his skin. The realization hit him like a stone.

"Miguel... you wouldn't happen to know anything about this, would you?" He reached into his pocket and pulled out the little earring, holding it up to the light to show him. Miguel's eyes went wide.

"You found it!" he cried, reaching out as though to take it from him. Artie closed his hand around it.

"Down by the gate," he confirmed. "You'd best start explaining, *chamaco*. Trust me, when your mother finds out that you're the reason she's been losing all of her jewellery, it will be in your interest to have someone else on your side."

Miguel took a deep breath and began to explain, his voice trembling. The pieces began to fall into place at last. Roberto had started off by harassing Miguel in the fields when he was playing, demanding the odd sweet from him, and Miguel had been too frightened to refuse. Then it had progressed to pocket money. Finally, Roberto had seen Esperanza wearing a little gold chain on the day that she had confronted him over the *ulama* game. Driven presumably by revenge, he had cornered Miguel that afternoon as he played in the fields and ordered him to steal it for him. Miguel had refused, and Roberto had twisted his little arm until he cried. The following day, he had approached Miguel again, and this time the little boy had caved in and agreed to deliver the necklace to a hole in a tree trunk by the gate so that Roberto could collect it later. Since then, Roberto had demanded more and more, forcing Miguel to bring him jewellery belonging to both Esperanza and their mother and hurting him if he did not deliver what was asked. Miguel had become terrified of being left alone, fearful that Roberto would find and punish him.

"So these earrings," said Artie, trying to keep his voice steady. "You took them from your mother on Wednesday when she left them in the kitchen. But then you went to take them to Roberto yesterday and lost one along the way, presumably when you climbed over the gate. What did Roberto say when you turned up with only one half of the pair?"

"He was really cross," Miguel admitted in a wobbly voice. "He pushed me on the ground and said that it was worthless without the other one, and I had to bring him the missing one by first thing this morning or... or else." He swallowed hard, fighting back a fresh wave of tears. "But you've found it now. So I can give it to him, and it will all be fine."

Artie shook his head.

"Oh, I don't think so, *chamaco*," he said grimly. "We're going to see your father and get this whole thing sorted out. Now."

"No!" Miguel cried, grabbing Artie by the shoulders. "You can't, Artie. Please. He said he'd kill me if I told anyone."

"I'm sorry." Artie patted the little boy on the back in what he hoped was a reassuring way. "I have to, Miguel. Look at you. This has gone on too long already."

"He won't listen," Miguel warned. "That man is *papá's* friend. He'd never turn on him, not for anything."

"Well, I'll make him listen. I don't know how, but I have to. I promise you, Miguel, that man will never be allowed to hurt you again. Not if I have to shoot him myself, like the dog he is. Trust me."

Miguel stared hard at him for a long time, then gave a nervous nod.

"All right. I trust you."

Artie took a slow and careful ride back to the farm, holding the mane of the horse in one hand to steady himself and supporting Miguel's small form with his free arm. Once or twice, he was afraid that the boy was going to jump down from the horse and run, but Miguel stayed put, quivering and whimpering all the way. It was only when they re-entered the farm that he finally began to sob, turning to bury his face in Artie's shirt again.

Esperanza and Rafael both ran out towards the horse as it drew nearer to the farmhouse. Esperanza's eyes were red from crying, and the expression of love and relief on her face when she looked up at Artie almost knocked him clean off the horse. He managed to hold himself together for Miguel's sake, passing the little boy down into Esperanza's arms.

"Shh. It's all right now. Look, you're home. Here's your sister."

Esperanza took the little boy and held him tightly, tears of relief spilling down her cheeks. Artie's resolve cracked. He swung down from Zafiro's back and put his arms around them both, not caring who might be watching.

"You're home now, *chamaco*. It's going to be all right." He turned to Esperanza. "*Señorita*, I need to speak with your parents. Urgently."

"I'll find them. I think they went looking out towards the barn," Rafael told them. "I'll tell them we've found him, señorita, and send them to speak to you at the house."

Esperanza nodded. Artie lifted Miguel into his arms again, and together, they went up towards the house, Artie steeling himself for the confrontation that was to come. Juan would not want to hear it, he knew, but he needed to be told the truth. Forcing him to accept it would be another matter. At least with Esperanza by his side, though, Artie knew that he had an ally. Roberto was Juan's best friend, but Miguel was his son. Surely, there could be no contest.

CHAPTER TWENTY-FOUR

Esperanza led Artie through to the family room, where he tried to put Miguel down onto one of the soft sofas. Miguel was still whimpering, refusing to let go of Artie's shirt, but instead of arguing, Artie sat down on the sofa and allowed the little boy to stay on his lap, cuddling into his chest with little hiccupping sobs. Esperanza put her arms around them both, but before she had a chance to ask any questions, the loud clatter of voices from outside announced the arrival of the rest of the Dominguez family. Louisa burst into the room, followed by Felipe and Juan, and finally Victoria. Louisa's eyes were wild, her face pale, and she almost collapsed with relief when she saw Miguel curled up on Artie's lap, sobbing but unharmed.

Juan grabbed Artie's shoulder with a shaking hand.

"You found him," he said in a voice that trembled with emotion. "First Esperanza, and now Miguel. How can I ever thank you? Just name what you want..."

"I don't need a reward, *señor*," Artie told him. "But I do need to speak to you. Now, if we could. The *señora* too."

Juan and Louisa exchanged concerned glances.

"Miguel, I want you to go with *Tía* Victoria and Felipe," Louisa told her son, her voice still trembling. "They will help you get cleaned up, and then you can change out of those dirty clothes."

Miguel looked up at Artie, his eyes swimming with tears.

"Will you stay here until I come back?" he asked, sniffling. "You won't go away?"

"I promise. I won't go away until you say that you feel all right for me to do so. Nobody's going to hurt you now, *chamaco*."

Louisa looked alarmed, but if she objected to Artie's familiarity towards her son then she didn't say anything. Miguel hugged Artie around the neck and then lowered himself from his lap, taking his brother's hand and heading out of the room and up the stairs.

Everyone turned to Artie, waiting for some form of explanation.

"I found him hiding in the undergrowth at his late grandmother's house," Artie told them. "He couldn't get inside, so he spent the night curled up under the tree in her garden. I also found this."

Artie pulled the single, sparkling earring from his pocket, and there were gasps all around as they all realized that it was one of the pair that Louisa had spent so long searching for only the day before. He dropped it into her hand and she examined it, her brow furrowed with confusion.

"What are you saying?" she asked in a hushed voice. "Miguel... did he... did he take this?"

"Sí," Artie confirmed. "And several other pieces of your jewellery, too, señora. This has been going on for a little while, I'm afraid."

"But why? My son is not a thief!" Louisa began to get defensive, her eyes narrowing with anger, although she seemed unsure about who she should be directing it at.

"He wasn't doing it by choice, señora," Artie assured her. "It seems that someone has been forcing Miguel to steal jewellery from you, with the intention of selling it, I suspect. Miguel told me that there were consequences if he didn't comply. He ran away in the early hours of this morning because he lost one earring out of the pair, and he was frightened that his tormentor would punish him for it."

Esperanza let out a gasp of horror, and Artie had to hold back from reaching out to comfort her. He could understand her shock; the pieces all seemed to fit together at last, and the picture they formed was an ugly one. For weeks, she had been mentioning how forgetful her mother seemed to have become- an earring missing here, a gold chain there. Now it seemed that this had been going on right under the family's nose the whole time. That limp Miguel had developed when he claimed to have fallen while climbing a tree. The black eye after the playground fight with the boy whose name he mysteriously couldn't remember. Why he'd had no pocket money to buy sweets these last few weeks and kept begging Artie for his sugar fix instead. It all made sense at last.

"Who?" Esperanza croaked. "Who would do that to a little boy?"

"It has to be someone on the farm," said Artie, turning back to Juan with a frown. "Someone who isn't afraid to bully those who are smaller and weaker than him. Someone with a record for violence and petty crime. Perhaps someone who needs money, who has some sort of addiction to satisfy. A drinking addiction, for example. Can you think of anyone who matches that description?"

"No," said Juan firmly. "It couldn't be. He's my friend, he would never."

"With all due respect, señor," Artie argued, "Miguel knew exactly who it was. He's been too afraid to tell you, in case Roberto punished him for it. He was scared that you would believe Roberto over him."

"It can't be him, though. Miguel must have got it wrong. Roberto is my friend." Juan's voice faltered as reality began to set in.

"Really?" Artie raised an eyebrow. "Miguel was quite sure of the description. Tell me, señor, how many large, hairy, foul-smelling men do you have working here? Ones who happen to have one gold tooth and a weakness for tequila?"

"For goodness' sake," Louisa snapped. "I'll get to the bottom of this." She stormed from the room, and Artie heard her footsteps thundering up the stairs. She returned moments later, holding Miguel by the arm.

"Miguel," said Juan, bending down to the little boy's level. "*Mamá* and *papá* aren't cross. We know that someone made you take *mamá*'s jewellery, someone who hurt you if you didn't do what they said. Now, who was it?"

Miguel looked alarmed and glanced over at Artie and Esperanza for support.

"Just tell them what you told me, Miguel," Artie reassured him. "It's all right."

"Roberto," Miguel sniffed, trembling. "The big man with the gold tooth who says he is your friend."

"Roberto," confirmed Louisa, and Miguel's face crumpled. He burst into tears, throwing his arms around his father's neck. Juan looked stricken.

"Louisa," he said in an empty voice. "Go and ask Rafael to gather all of the farmhands outside the barn. We're sorting this out right now, once and for all. Miguel, you will stay here with *mamá* and *Tía* Victoria, where you'll be safe. Felipe and Esperanza, you'll stay here too."

"Don't think for a minute that I'm staying here while the man who has stolen my jewellery and hurt my son gets pulled to task." Louisa's face was almost purple with anger, her teeth set. "This is a family matter, and we will face him as a family."

"I agree," Esperanza fumed. "I'm coming too, *papá*."

Juan conceded with a nod, unable to find the strength to argue with them. Together they headed down towards the barn in silence, where the farmhands were gathering with perplexed expressions on their faces.

Artie had to fight to keep his breathing steady. He was trying not to think about what might happen next when Roberto found out that he was the one who had uncovered the truth. Frightening as the prospect was, the adrenaline pumping through his veins made him too angry to care. Come what may, bringing Roberto to justice was a decision Artie knew he would never regret. Not now that he knew how low the man was prepared to stoop for the sake of greed.

Roberto was, unsurprisingly, the last to arrive. He looked a sorry state as always, stinking of tequila, his long dark hair matted and dirty, his eyes bloodshot and unfocused. *Drunk already*, Artie thought, glaring at him with an expression of loathing.

"*Amigos*," Juan addressed them, as he always did. "I'm afraid that I've called you all here today on a very serious matter concerning my son Miguel."

Artie watched Roberto's face through narrowed eyes. Something flickered in his expression at the mention of Miguel's name, and he glanced from Juan to his wife and daughter and finally to Artie himself. The two men locked eyes, and Artie knew in an instant that Roberto was fully aware of who had exposed his secret.

"I have it on good information that one of you has betrayed my trust. Forcing my son to steal from his family and then trying to sell the stolen goods for money," Juan continued. There were gasps of horror from everyone around the barn, except for Roberto, whose small, yellowed eyes never left Artie's. "I am giving that man the opportunity to come forward now, confess what he has done and return what he has taken. Otherwise, I will be forced to involve the soldiers down at the *presidio*, which I'm sure nobody wants."

None of the men moved.

"Of course," Juan continued with a sigh, "I could always go down to the jewellers' shop in the *pueblo* and ask for a description of the man who has been trying to sell my wife's jewellery."

He turned and looked directly at Roberto. Now there could be no doubting that he knew the thief's identity, and Artie held his breath as the two men stared each other down. There was another long, tense silence, and then Roberto spoke.

"I think, *amigo*, that you are playing games with us. You already know who your man is." His voice was a deep growl, and to Artie's horror, there was laughter in his tone. He had expected him to at least feign remorse.

"I fear I do. I had just hoped that I was wrong." Juan's eyes were locked with those of his old friend, and the rest of the farmhands stepped back, the truth of the situation sinking in. "Where's the jewellery, Roberto?"

"I don't know what you're talking about," Roberto sneered. For the briefest of seconds, Artie saw his eyes flick over to the hooks by the barn door where the farmhands stored their bags for the day.

"You won't mind us checking your belongings, in that case?" Artie suggested. He went over to the hooks and took down Roberto's roughly woven sack, loosening the neck as he handed it to Juan to allow him access to the contents. Roberto made a small involuntary movement, but stayed where he was, a look of venom on his face.

"You do this, *amigo*, and there's no going back," he warned. "I will consider it an unforgivable act of disrespect."

Juan ignored him. He opened the bag and tipped the contents out onto the floor, and Artie helped him to go through the pockets of Roberto's spare clothes, his tobacco pouch and even an empty bottle of tequila that had been stowed in there. There was a little bit of money, a couple of handkerchiefs and even a small sewing kit, but no sign of any jewellery.

Roberto began to laugh, and Juan threw the bag on the floor in frustration. If Roberto had been responsible for stealing the jewellery, then it was already long gone. They had no proof that he had taken it in the first place.

"See? I told you. I don't know what jewellery you're talking about. You've got nothing on me."

"Wait." Artie held up his hand. He looked from Roberto to the bag, to the sewing kit, then back to Roberto again. His eyes narrowed as his brain whirred, trying to piece together everything in front of him. Roberto didn't strike him as the sort of man who liked to engage in embroidery in his spare time. Why keep a sewing kit in his bag? *Unless...*

"Rafael," he said, not taking his eyes off Roberto. "Could you lend me your penknife for a second?"

The old man obliged, and a fleeting look of panic crossed Roberto's face.

"No, stop-" he snarled, but it was too late. Artie picked up the bag and plunged the knife into it, separating the outer fabric from its hidden lining. The bag fell apart, and there was a clink as several items of jewellery fell to the floor. There was Esperanza's gold chain, a ring, several earrings and a pendant belonging to Louisa, and a large, dark sapphire on a chain. And there, among all of the shining gold and glittering jewels, lay the missing emerald earring.

CHAPTER TWENTY-FIVE

The barn was silent. Everyone stared at Roberto, waiting for a reaction, but his face seemed to be frozen in noiseless fury, his narrowed eyes fixed on Artie. Juan, on the other hand, was staring at the jewellery on the floor, his face a picture of betrayed anguish.

"Tell me. Was it worth it?" he asked quietly. "Throwing away your job, your friend, everything I've done for you, all for a few bottles of tequila?"

"You think this is about tequila?" There was no laughter in Roberto's voice now. "Everything you've done for me, indeed. You've only ever helped me because it made you feel superior. You think you're so much better than the rest of us.

Rubbing shoulders with the nobility, having your fancy meals with the Dons while the rest of us down here have to scrimp just to eat." He took a menacing step closer to Juan, looming over him, their eyes locked. "Their day is coming, *amigo*. When the Dons fall, so will you, and everything that is yours will finally belong to us. Madero wants to free the people, give them back the land that is rightfully theirs, by force if necessary. He's going to build an army, you know. An army of the people. They're coming for those like you and your fancy friends. You know what they say? *La tierra es para el que la trabaja*. The land is for those who work it. And so it will be, soon. You wait and see."

"Get off my premises," Juan ordered, his voice trembling with rage. "You're fired! Get out of Santa Sofia and never come back."

Roberto laughed, a bone-chilling bitterness in his eyes.

"I'll make you remember this, old friend."

"You're no friend of mine. You're just a vile *cabrón*, a thief and a bully who terrorises good people and hurts innocent little children. You're a pathetic drunk, and if you ever come near my family again, I will personally shoot you between the eyes like the dog you are. Now, *get out*."

Both men stood silent for a moment, staring each other down. Then Roberto lunged, grabbing Juan by the throat. Louisa and Esperanza both screamed, and Artie sprang forward, seizing the pitchfork he had already spotted leaning against a nearby haystack. He wedged it between the two men, pressing the sharp prongs against Roberto's throat. Roberto let go of Juan, who staggered backward, gasping, and moved back towards the wall of the barn with his hands up, the prongs of the pitchfork still pressed against his skin.

"You will leave now," Artie commanded. His heart was pounding with adrenaline, although to his surprise, he felt more angry than afraid. Roberto had tried to harm Esperanza's family, and nobody was allowed to get away with that. "You will go and never come back."

"You'll regret this, *niño*," Roberto snarled. "Choosing *their* side over the side of the people. I'll make sure of it."

"This has got nothing to do with the people or their revolution," Artie growled back. The anger was bubbling through his veins, and he had to hold himself back from skewering Roberto there and then. How *dare* he use the plight of men like Joaquin and his brothers as an excuse for his own moral corruption. "This isn't about them, it's about a bitter old drunk who hurts little children, and you're lucky that there are ladies present, or I'd have run you through already. Now, get out."

"*Señor* Dominguez!" cried little Daniel from the doorway. "Look, the soldiers are here! I can see them coming up the road!"

Panic flashed over Roberto's face, and while Artie was distracted glancing towards the barn door, he seized his chance. Artie felt the pitchfork twist as Roberto wrenched it from his grasp, and then before he knew what was happening, Roberto's large fist flew hard into his stomach, knocking the air out of him. He had less than a second to recover before the fist came again, this time striking just below his sternum. Artie collapsed, doubled over and gasping for breath on the floor of the barn, tears of pain rolling down his cheeks. Several of the other farmhands lunged for Roberto at once, but he was too quick and managed to bolt out of the door and away towards the trees before anyone could stop him.

Artie couldn't breathe. The world was spinning above him, making him feel terribly sick and faint as he struggled to cling to consciousness. He heard Esperanza cry out in fear, and she threw herself to the ground beside him, throwing her arms around him in a protective embrace. Her frightened, tearful eyes swam in and out of view as she cradled his head in his arms, stroking his cheek with her thumb. At last, his diaphragm kicked back into life and he took a shuddering gasp of air.

"I'm all right, *mi amor*," he croaked, clutching his stomach and wincing as she helped him into a sitting position. "I'm all right."

He glanced around. To his great relief, Louisa had her back to them, so busy fussing over a shaken Juan that she had somehow missed the interaction between himself and her daughter. The rest of the farmhands were gathered around the doorway trying to see the approaching soldiers, but Artie noticed that old Rafael's eyes were flicking between himself and Esperanza with a strange expression of interest, his eyebrows raised. Artie tried to ignore him, wincing as Esperanza helped him to his feet. He hoped the old man's hearing was such that he might think he had mistaken his choice of words.

"I don't see any soldiers," commented Ricardo, squinting at the road.

"That's because I lied," Daniel admitted. "There aren't any soldiers. But Roberto doesn't know that."

The other men laughed, and Ricardo gave the boy a friendly clap on the back.

"He'll be halfway to California by now," laughed Rafael. "Well done, boy. That's the last we'll be seeing of him."

The farmhands began to disperse, returning to their work now that the drama had passed. Artie took great care in gathering up the recovered jewellery in his handkerchief, tucking it away in the safety of his chest pocket, and together he and the Dominguez family headed back to the house.

Miguel's little face was peering at them through an upstairs window, and they had barely stepped into the family room when he burst in and almost bowled Artie over in a fierce hug.

"Hey," Artie laughed, ruffling his hair. "It's all right, *chamaco*. We're all fine. He's gone. Your *papá* told him never to set foot in this town again, and he ran away."

It was the abridged version of events, he knew, but he was also aware of how much it would mean to Juan to be seen as the hero of the day in his son's eyes. The little boy's trust in his father needed repairing, and this would be a good start. Esperanza smiled at him, touched by the gesture.

Miguel turned to Juan, admiration in his eyes.

"You did it, *papá*? You chased him off?"

"You don't have to worry about him anymore, *mijo*," Juan assured him. "I'm so sorry I didn't put a stop to it sooner. From now on, I want you to know that you can always talk to me if you're worried about anything. I'll always listen to you, I promise."

Miguel wrapped his arms around his father, a smile returned to his face at last. Artie backed out of the room, resolving to return to the stables and give the family a little space. They needed some time together now, and there was no place for him in this picture.

He was just about to leave the house when he remembered the jewellery still wrapped in his handkerchief. Artie reached inside his pocket and pulled it out, noticing how the metal had already left dirty black stains on the white fabric. It was filthy; he couldn't return it to Esperanza and Louisa like this. There was a washing up bowl and brush by the sink, and after a moment's hesitation, Artie decided to give the jewellery a quick clean. It couldn't hurt.

He scrubbed each piece in the soapy water, taking care not to tangle the delicate gold chains, and laid them all out on a small clean towel to dry. Finally, he came to the sapphire and paused, turning the sparkling jewel in his fingers. So, this was the gift that had commenced Esperanza's official courtship. He had never seen Esperanza wearing it, but he doubted that she had any other jewel fine enough to match the description. Artie suspected that if he had saved up every centavo he had ever owned, he could still never have afforded anything like this.

He ran his fingers over the smooth round stone with its gold setting and chain, and his mind drifted back to the metal's origins. He wondered whether anyone he knew had once extracted this gold from the depths of that haunted mine, whether any of his brothers had crawled with it through those claustrophobic tunnels or hauled it up the rickety log ladders. Perhaps Joaquin or one of the others who had been blown to pieces or crushed beneath the rubble. He caught sight of his own reflection in the jewel's smooth surface, and for a second, he could have sworn that he saw Joaquin staring back at him, betrayal in his eyes.

Artie steadied himself against the sink, trying to take deep, slow breaths. He could feel his knees trembling, and then suddenly, two familiar arms were snaking lovingly around his waist as a warm head pressed up against his back. He let out a sigh of relief, a burning affection flooding his chest as one of her hands crept up the fabric of his shirt to rest against his heart.

"Thank you," she whispered. His heart was pounding against her hand, her chest warm against his spine, and he felt the tension leave his muscles as his panic melted away.

"Anything for you, *mi amor*," he whispered back.

She turned him to face her, noticing for the first time what he was holding.

"Is this bothering you?" she asked, seeing the pain in his eyes.

He shrugged in what he hoped was an offhand sort of way, but she saw straight through him as she always did.

"I- I just wish I could afford to get you such nice presents, that's all." He chose not to mention Joaquin. It was bad enough that his grief was still so raw; he didn't need to upset Esperanza with it too.

She took the pendant from him and dumped it on the sideboard, then took both of his hands in her own.

"Artie," she reassured him, looking up into his eyes. "I haven't thought about that fancy necklace since the night Don Raúl gave it to me. I didn't even notice that it was missing. That rose you gave me, though- I keep it preserved by my bedside so that I can look at it every night as I go to sleep, and it's the first thing I see in the morning when I wake up. There are more ways of measuring value than looking at how much something cost."

"Sí, I know." He smiled at her, feeling his chest swell with pride. Don Raúl could spend as much money as he pleased, but he could not buy Esperanza's affections. Those were reserved for him alone.

"Come on," she grinned. "My father asked me to fetch you."

Artie gathered the jewellery carefully back into a handkerchief and followed her back through into the family room. His stomach churned with nerves, although he couldn't quite put his finger on why. Everyone was there, and they all turned to look at him as he came in. Suddenly flustered, he went over to Louisa and knelt before her, unsure of what else to do.

"Your jewellery, señora," he said, presenting the folded cloth to her. "I've given it all a good clean to make sure all of that vile *cabrón's* filthy fingerprints are gone. It's as good as new."

He held his breath as Louisa looked him up and down, a strange look on her face as though she was seeing him properly for the very first time. Then Artie felt a hand on his shoulder, raising him to his feet, and before he knew it, Juan was embracing him like a brother. The room erupted with sound; Miguel and Felipe were cheering, Louisa was babbling words of gratitude, and above it all, he could hear Esperanza's bright, happy laugh.

"What did I tell you, *mija*?" Victoria winked at Esperanza. "I knew that your father had chosen well when he employed this man as his servant!"

"Servant?" Juan released Artie and turned to face her, his frown a mixture of confusion and disapproval. Artie felt his stomach drop. If the truth came out now, then he could say goodbye to spending Thursdays with Esperanza in the *pueblo*. He crossed his fingers and said a silent prayer.

"This man is not my servant," Juan announced, clapping a proud hand on Artie's shoulder. "He's my friend. Today we will all have *comida* together in the barn, and then the men will be given the rest of the day off, as my apology for what they have had to put up with from Roberto these last few months. Arturo, you can take the whole week off, on full pay. You've more than earned it after today. Tonight, though, I would like you to join us for *cena*. As our guest of honour, and as part of our family."

Miguel and Felipe both cheered, and Esperanza beamed at Artie who was standing frozen to the spot in shock, a slow smile spreading across his face as Juan's words sunk in.

As part of our family.

It was more than he could have ever wished for. That evening, he sat around the table in the courtyard as Louisa served them all with fresh bread, beef, corn and a selection of delicious food Artie didn't even know the names for. He had seen and smelled such delicacies in the past, usually at fancy *baile cenas* and the like, but nobody had ever offered him so much as a crumb until now. Tonight, he was the guest of honour, seated at the table between Juan and Esperanza while she poured him wine and the boys filled the air with laughter and stories.

When all of the food had been laid out, Juan cleared his throat, and everyone around the table closed their eyes and bowed their heads.

They're going to say grace, Artie realized. He had never been one for religion- it was hard to believe in a benevolent God after witnessing such suffering as he had, but he nonetheless bowed his head with respect as Juan began the prayer. No sooner had he closed his eyes when he felt a hand slip into his beneath the table. Esperanza was smiling at him with affectionate longing, her eyes sparkling.

"I want to talk to you," she mouthed silently to him. "Later. Alone."

He grinned back at her and nodded, heat rising to his cheeks.

She withdrew her hand as the prayer finished, careful not to allow any of her family to see that they had been having a private moment of their own, and Artie took a second to steady his breathing as chatter resumed around the table.

For the whole evening, nobody allowed Artie to so much as lift a finger. Juan chatted and laughed with him as though they had known each other all their lives, while Louisa and Esperanza flitted between the table and the kitchen with plates and jugs of wine, beer and flavoured water. Artie had never felt more at home, especially with Esperanza beside him, brushing her hand against his whenever her parents were not looking and shooting him loving glances. *This is what it's like to be part of a real family,* he realized.

Once they had all eaten their fill, the *cena* became a *fiesta*. Artie fetched his guitar from the barn, and the boys danced in the courtyard, laughing and squealing with Esperanza while he played. Juan and Louisa joined in too, both a little tipsy from the alcohol as they spun around the cobbles, clinging to each other as they stumbled and laughed. Artie only had eyes for Esperanza, though, swishing her skirts and swinging Miguel around to the music, her eyes occasionally flashing with mischief at Artie.

She would make an excellent mother someday, Artie thought, not for the first time. The idea had crossed his mind before, but it had always given him a feeling of sadness and anger, conjuring up unwelcome images of Don Raúl. Now, though, whether it was the wine that clouded his head or just the wonderful family atmosphere in the courtyard, Artie dared to think about what it would be like if *he* were to become Esperanza's husband. He pictured her dancing in the square while he played his guitar, laughing and playing with children who had her beautiful blue eyes and his unruly black hair. How wonderful it would be to sing them lullabies as they went to sleep, to read them stories and hear them call him 'papá'. The thought brought a lump to his throat, and he had to stop singing for a moment to clear it.

"Getting tired, *amigo*?" Juan laughed, clapping a hand on his shoulder. "Ay, boys, it's past your bedtime. Come on, up the stairs. I'll come up and tell you a story. It's been far too long since I last took the time to do that, hasn't it?"

Louisa took the children up to get them ready for bed, and after a minute, Juan followed, leaving Artie and Esperanza alone in the courtyard. The moment her father's footsteps had disappeared up the stairs, Esperanza launched herself at Artie, pushing his guitar out of the way so that she could sit on his lap. Her warm body pressed against him, her face dangerously close to his, and Artie felt his heart give a leap of excitement.

"So," she giggled, a little tipsy herself. "How long do you think we've got before my mother realizes she's left us alone together?"

"With how much wine she's had tonight, I'd be surprised if she didn't pass out upstairs on one of the boys' beds and doesn't wake until morning." Artie grinned, wrapping his arms around her.

"How irresponsible of her, leaving me here alone with such a handsome man." Esperanza giggled again, running her fingers through his hair. "Anything could happen."

I wish, Artie thought, blushing as he tried to resist the images that flashed through his imagination. He reached out to stroke Esperanza's face, noticing that she was wearing the delicate gold chain he had returned to her earlier. He traced his fingers over it, trying to push the thoughts of the gold's origins to the back of his mind again. Don Raúl had ruined enough of the beautiful things in this world already. He would not ruin this moment too.

"It was my grandmother's," Esperanza told him, shivering with pleasure as he ran his fingers across her collarbone. "She gave it to me when I was a baby, as a Christening present. I've worn it a lot since she died. It means a lot to me, it helps me to feel close to her again."

"I'm glad I managed to get it back for you, in that case," Artie smiled, his heart heavy. "Sometime, I'd like to give you something that you can wear so that you can always feel close to me too."

So that you can remember me, when you're married and I'm not allowed to see you anymore, his mind added. He felt the lump returning to his throat and fought to suppress it, nuzzling against Esperanza's neck so that she couldn't see the tears gathering in his eyes. He cursed himself for the amount of wine he had drunk during the course of the evening. Wine always made him more emotional, and the last thing he wanted was to ruin the evening by upsetting Esperanza.

"I did have one idea, now you mention it," she told him, her voice soft and low in his ear. "I've been thinking about how nice it would be if you gave me a ring to wear. I could give you one to match as a symbol of our commitment to each other. At the front of a church, perhaps, in front of all of our friends and family. And a priest."

Artie froze. There was no mistaking her meaning, and he knew it wasn't the first time she had voiced a wish to marry him. He had never dared to discuss it with her, though, knowing that such a thing could never happen in reality. It was too cruel.

"Esperanza," he croaked, his voice shaking. "Please don't talk like that. Don't give me hope where there is none. I can't bear it."

"A week ago, I would've agreed with you." She pulled back from him, placing her hands on either side of his face so that she could look directly into his eyes. "But you didn't hear the conversation between myself and my father after we came back from Don Lorenzo's. He's starting to see the light, Artie. He saw Raúl's reaction when I accused him over what happened in the mines, and it's opened his eyes at last. He was disgusted with Don Raúl for letting me get hurt and for not even coming over in person the following day to see that I was all right. He's changing his mind, Artie, I know he is. It's not going to take too much more persuasion for him to break the whole thing off with Don Lorenzo, and I'll be free again."

Artie swallowed hard. He could hardly dare to believe what she was telling him. His hands were shaking, and she could feel it, laughing as she took them in her own and raised them to her lips.

"Even so, Esperanza, freedom from Don Raúl doesn't mean that you'll be free to marry as you choose," he reminded her, his heart pounding so hard that he thought it might jump right out of his chest. "Your mother would never allow you to marry someone like me. Please, don't tease me like this. My heart can't take it."

"Someone like you?" she repeated, kissing each of his fingers in turn. "You mean the hero who found her missing son, saved her husband's life, rescued her daughter from being killed by a stallion in front of the whole plaza, and is now the most beloved *músico* in Santa Sofia? I'm sure she can be talked around to the idea, given a little time."

"But Esperanza, none of that changes the fact that I'm a street boy. I've not even got a name to give you."

"We can easily fix that," she assured him, leaning forward to press her forehead against his as she slipped her arms around his neck again. "You'll just have to take mine, won't you?"

Artie's composure broke. Hot tears rolled down his cheeks, his trembling hands reaching up to stroke Esperanza's face. He needed to kiss her, to show her all the love he had been forced to hold back for so long, but she placed a gentle finger on his lips to block him.

"Not here," she whispered, her eyes sparkling. "Meet me on Monday in the plaza around midday. We'll go somewhere we can be alone, and I'll see if I can find some way to thank you personally for what you did today."

She leaned across and kissed the sensitive spot on his neck, just behind his ear, and Artie felt as though he might pass out with happiness. He held her tight against him, letting his tears soak into her hair.

"I love you, Esperanza," he whispered, and she kissed his neck again with a sigh.

The sound of footsteps on the staircase made them spring apart like naughty children, and Artie hurriedly pulled his guitar back onto his lap as he tried to compose himself. His heart was pounding so hard it hurt, each breath fast and shallow as though he had been running, but Juan didn't seem to notice as he stumbled back into the courtyard with a beaming smile on his face.

"Esperanza," he gushed, throwing his arms around his daughter with tears in his own eyes. *Another victim of the wine*, Artie thought. "How long has it been since I last danced with you? Far too long, I think. Will you play something for us, mijo?"

Mijo. Son. Artie looked around stupidly, realizing after a second that Juan was talking to him. His heart skipped. He knew it was only a term of affection, used all the time as an amicable way for an older man to address a younger one, but to Artie, it meant the world.

"Of... of course, señor," he beamed back. He struck up a few chords, and Juan twirled Esperanza in his arms until she laughed.

Son, Artie thought again. If what Esperanza had said tonight was true, and there was a chance that everything might work out for them after all, he realized he might find himself hearing that word a lot more in future. He could be Juan's son, Esperanza's husband, perhaps a father to his own children, too. It would take effort to make it happen, but he knew the fight would be worth it. He was prepared to do anything, risk everything, if it meant finally being able to call

Esperanza his own. After tonight, perhaps there was hope for him yet.

Arturo Dominguez, he thought to himself. Now, that's a name I could get used to.

A HERO'S HOPE

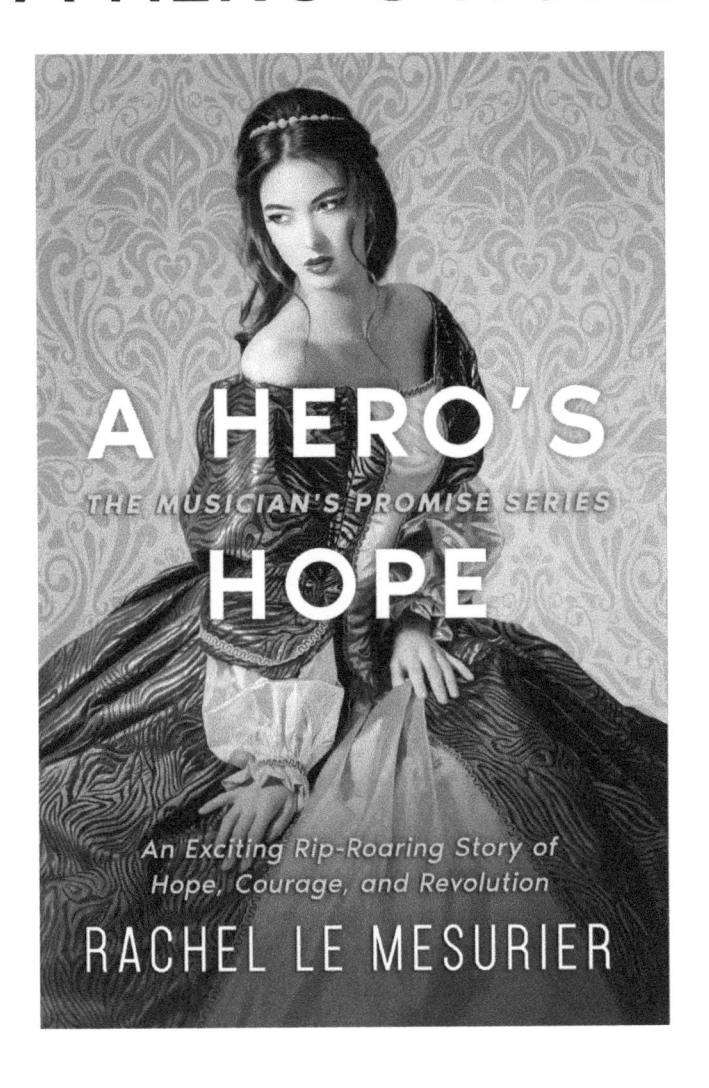

An Exciting Rip-Roaring Story of Hope, Courage, and Revolution

RACHEL LE MESURIER

— THE MUSICIAN'S PROMISE —
BOOK TWO

CHAPTER ONE

"Another drink, Pedro. And make it a strong one." Diego slammed the coins down on the counter, thrusting out his mug so that the barman could refill it. He had already had a bit too much, he knew, but the barman had better sense than to argue and topped up his mug with beer once more all the same. Today, Diego planned to drink himself into oblivion, and he defied anyone to try to stop him.

Why was Arturo such an *idiota*? Diego remembered a time when he and his brother had been inseparable. They wrote songs together, they performed together. They shared a dream. They were going to go away and become stars, to play and sing for the whole world.

And then *she* had come along. It was bad enough that Artie spent every spare moment trailing around after her, making a laughing stock of himself in front of the entire town. Diego had tried to warn him that no good could come of it. He had even tried to deter the girl herself, first asking nicely, then explaining, then ordering her to leave Artie alone. She had ignored him too.

Now, Diego was lucky if Artie even bothered to come home. On Monday, he had stayed overnight in the stables because the silly little *puta* had managed to fall off her horse and he wanted to keep watch over her. On Friday, he had rolled in at God knows what time, starry-eyed and gabbling some nonsense about her father considering him to be 'part of the family' because of some stupid jewellery he had found.

That was when the argument had started.

"I was their guest of honour tonight," Artie had said in a dreamy voice that made Diego want to smack him. "It was wonderful, Diego. They shared their food with me, we talked and laughed all evening. It was like being part of a real family."

"Oh, a *real* family, is it?" Diego had snapped, offended. "And I suppose raising you off the streets since you were eight years old means nothing to you now?"

Artie had laughed at first, not realizing that he was being serious.

"Don't be ridiculous, Diego. You're my *hermano*, and you always will be. But you know how much I've wanted this. For Esperanza's family to start to accept me. To finally feel like I belong there, with her."

"You belong *here*," Diego had growled. "With me, and your brothers, and your sister. We need you, Arturo."

"You've got my earnings." Artie's smile had begun to fade then. "Everything I have, I've shared with you. With all of you."

"That's not the point," Diego said through gritted teeth, fighting the urge to grab Artie and shake him. "It's not about money. It's about you being here for us. For God's sake, Artie, open your eyes. Paloma has lost the love of her life, she's in pieces. Marco has barely uttered two words since the mining accident, and he was a man on the edge even before that. God knows how long it'll be until he can work again. Ed and Alejandro take it in turns between looking after him and going back up to those mines to clear the rubble, digging out more bodies every day. They're still suffering from shock and injuries themselves, but they have no choice. I'm trying to work three days a week and hold everyone else together myself, while you're busy prattling about with horses and playing the hero for some fancy rich girl you can never actually be with, and *it's not fair*, Artie."

"What do you want me to do?" Artie snapped. "Give up my job at the farm? I have been paid overtime for every single one of Esperanza's riding lessons. We've lost Marco and Joaquin's salaries, and Ed and Alejandro are only able to work part-time. We need that money, Diego. You know we do."

"Money alone isn't enough." Diego ran a frustrated hand through his hair, trying to find the words to make his brother understand. "Artie, you're never *here* anymore. How many times have I sat there in that kiosca with my guitar, playing alone because you never bothered to show up? Ever since that girl came onto the scene, our music has dropped off your list of priorities, as have I."

"That's not true. I've been working overtime so that I could save up some money for a new guitar, one that carries the sound better in the plaza. I'm going out to buy it this weekend. And I've been writing more songs than ever."

"Ay, and a fat lot of good they've been, too," Diego spat. "Ridiculous whining love songs that we can't even play because the lyrics are so obviously about *her*. Don Raúl would have the flesh flogged from your bones before we'd finished the second verse."

"I can't help it," Artie shrugged. "I write whatever songs spring into my head. She's my inspiration."

She's a pain in the arse, more like, Diego thought darkly. Fine. If Artie insisted on writing songs about her, he could at least make the lyrics a bit more subtle. Stop mentioning ocean blue eyes and involving the phrase 'angel of hope' in every other verse, for instance. Or better still, find another girl to write about.

"You've attracted enough of a fan base since the competition," he reminded him, raising a coy eyebrow. "I'm sure you'd easily persuade one of those pretty little *perras* to give you some 'inspiration'. I've read some of their letters to you. A few of them are quite poetic. They'd be all right for song lyrics, with a little tweaking. I especially liked the one that mentioned the delightful shape of your-"

"Their attention is very flattering, *hermano*," Artie interrupted huffily, rolling his eyes. "But I love Esperanza. Don't try to tell me you don't remember what that feels like. You found the love of your life once and have never so much as looked at another woman since, in all these years. So don't you go preaching to me about how I should forget Esperanza and move on."

Artie gave him a meaningful look, making Diego flush with anger. The topic of his love life was off the table. It always had been, and always would be. Everyone knew that. Artie had been goading him on purpose, hoping that it would force him to back off and end the conversation, but Diego refused to be so easily manipulated. Had anyone else dared to raise the subject, Diego would have already shut their mouths for them.

"Don't you *dare* try to drag my heart into this," he hissed, his eyes flashing with fury. "Yes, for your information, I *do* remember what love feels like. I also remember what it felt like when I chose to sacrifice my own heart to protect the one

I loved. To accept that society would never allow us to be together and face reality before it got either one of us into the sort of trouble we couldn't get out of."

Artie wilted with guilt, realizing that he had overstepped a line, but Diego was already too angry to back down.

"I faced the same reality that *you* are going to have to deal with sooner or later," he snarled, trembling with rage. "I didn't want you to follow my example. I wanted you to learn from it. I don't want you to feel the same pain that I went through, the pain of having the one you love taken from you and being forced to watch while she marries another. I tried to spare you all of that, but you wouldn't listen. Your story is the same as mine, only one chapter behind."

"She... she cares for me," Artie said in a small, stubborn voice. "She wants to marry me. She's going to try to persuade her parents. She doesn't care about what everyone else thinks, she sees me as an equal."

"For God's sake, Artie, can you not hear yourself?" Diego rounded on him, snarling. "You're *not* her equal, and you never will be. You're a servant. You spend your days shovelling horse manure while she floats around in silk dresses and jewels, laughing at you. It doesn't matter how many times you come to her rescue or how many favors you do for her. Her family will *never* see you as equal. They will never let you marry their daughter. Not when they could marry her to someone like Don Raúl."

"Esperanza doesn't want to-"

"What Esperanza wants doesn't matter. She has a duty to her family," Diego told him bluntly. "As you do to yours."

Artie fixed him with a cold glare.

"I will try to do better to support you, Diego. But whether you like it or not, I have a duty to her too."

"You have a duty to her as a servant," Diego sneered. "Nothing more."

It was Artie's turn to get angry then, his temper finally cracking.

"You know, those are fine words coming from the man who works as a servant to the Dons," he spat. "The same Dons who murdered your brother and left your sister widowed. You spend your days crawling around licking their boots, and you tell me that I'm betraying my *hermanos*?"

Diego had heard enough. He flew at Artie in a fury, towering over him with his teeth bared.

"I will not take lessons from a stupid, naive little *pendejo* who puts some fancy *puta* before his brothers," he bellowed.

"And *I* will not take lessons from a boot-licking traitor who seems to care more about Don Raúl than the men he murdered," Artie shouted back, standing his ground.

Diego lost it. He lunged forwards and grabbed Artie by the front of his shirt, slamming him against the wall with such force that the whole hut shook. The sound must have alerted the others because before Diego could decide whether or not to punch Artie, the door flew open with a crash and Alejandro burst in, swiftly followed by Eduardo and Paloma.

"Diego, what the hell do you think you're doing?" Alejandro cried in horror, grabbing Diego's shoulders and tearing him away from Artie while Ed wedged himself in between them in case Artie had any bright ideas about fighting back. "You two were shouting loud enough to wake the–"

"Whole street," Ed interrupted, finishing for him with a stern sideways glance at his brother. Any mention of the dead had the tendency to set Paloma off, and that was the last thing they needed with Diego and Artie already at each other's throats.

"We... we were just having a stupid argument and it got out of hand, that's all," Artie assured them through gritted teeth.

"Ay, because my brother seems to have forgotten what we're supposed to be doing all this for," Diego retorted, still furious. "Our music. Our future. Our *hermanos*. He's too busy wasting his life away pining for that stupid rich *puta*."

"You will not talk about the love of my life like that."

"The love of your life, indeed! You know nothing about-"

"That's enough, the pair of you!" Paloma commanded. Diego had never seen her look so angry. "We heard every word of what you were arguing about. Now you can fight all you want about music, and duty, and love. Rip chunks out of each other for all I care. But don't you *dare* do it in my husband's name or mine. Is that clear?"

Diego and Artie had both backed down then, cowed by Paloma's fury.

"*Sí*, Paloma. *Lo siento*," they mumbled together. Diego had no real intention of letting Artie's comments go so easily, but they could wait until Paloma was out of earshot. She had already suffered enough over these last few weeks without having to listen to her brothers fighting.

"Seeing as you did drag our names into it, however, let me tell you this," she continued, turning to glare at Diego. "If Joaquin was still here, he would hate to hear you two falling out over something so stupid. I don't need babysitting, Diego. Artie is doing more than his duty by making sure that we are all provided for. Joaquin would've told him to spend every waking second with the woman he loved if he were still here. Make every second count. Hold her tight while you've still got the chance."

Nobody had an answer to that. Alejandro and Ed looked away, unable to find anything to say. Artie became tearful again at the thought of Joaquin, trying to avoid looking at Paloma for fear of losing control of himself. Diego felt his anger draining away. Of course, he did not agree with her, but there was nothing to be gained from arguing.

"Joaquin taught us all to make the most of the time we've got," he told them all. "That's why we need to focus on getting this music career off the ground. The sooner we get famous, the sooner we can live the life we want to."

He tried to change the subject, trying to inject a bit of positivity into the conversation, but everybody looked more serious than ever.

"As long as that's the life you *both* want," said Alejandro quietly, glancing sideways at Artie.

Diego suddenly felt uneasy. He tried to mask it with a smile, clapping Alejandro on the back.

"Of course it is, *amigo*. You wait. Give it a year, and Artie and I will be on a sold-out tour around Mexico, earning more money than we know what to do with. He'll have so many women chasing after him, he'll forget all about the Dominguez girl."

He had expected the others to laugh. Smile, even. But not one of them did. He found out later that they had already known what Artie was going to say, standing there shuffling his feet, taking deep breaths as he always did when finding it difficult to get the words out. And Diego had felt his heart break at that moment, his dream shattering before him. He had walked out of the hut that night and had not spoken to Artie since.

He had seen him, certainly. Artie had been playing in the plaza as usual, and Diego watched him from a distance. He was so talented, so full of life, reveling in the sound of that pointless new guitar of his. The minute he began to sing, the whole plaza lit up. Diego was a good musician, but he was nothing without his brilliant, vibrant younger brother. If Artie wouldn't join him, his dream of travelling the country as a successful musician was over. Dead. And all because of some silly little *puta*.

A silly little *puta* who, just an hour or so later, wandered right into the taverna. Diego thought he was hallucinating to begin with, pinching himself to check that his hazy eyes were not deceiving him. No, the pinch hurt, despite how much he had drunk. She was real, standing at the bar trying to ignore the stares of the men around her. Women were a rare sight in the taverna unless they were serving wenches or ladies of ill repute, although nobody would have mistaken her for either. Even the men who had never met her had heard of Juan Dominguez's daughter with the blue eyes.

The landlord saw her and stopped speaking to the group of young men at the bar, greeting her with a polite smile.

"Señorita Dominguez! What can I do for you this fine morning?"

"*Hola*, Pedro. I've just come to collect my father's invoice for the drink he had you send up for our little celebration on Friday night. He's gone to a farmers' market in Santa Juanita for the next few days, but I'll have Rafael bring you the money tomorrow on his behalf." She was trying to sound cool and professional, but Diego could see that she was uncomfortable in these surroundings. *Good*, he thought savagely.

"Of course, *señorita*. Let me just get it for you."

Pedro left her to stand at the bar, trying not to catch the eye of any of the men who were watching her. She did not notice Diego sitting in the shadows glaring at her.

"Oi, you!"

Diego sighed, gritting his teeth and bracing himself for a confrontation. It wasn't unusual for drunks in the taverna to pick fights with a man drinking by himself, just for sport. It was a bit early in the day to expect trouble, but Diego was ready, nonetheless. He stood up, flexing his fingers. He could do with hitting something anyway.

"Aren't you the guy who won the music contest? You and your brother?"

"Oh." Diego threw himself back down on his stool, picking up his mug of beer again. The man didn't want a fight after all, then. Shame. "Sí, that was us."

He had been so full of hope on the day they won that contest, so convinced that it was the start of a new life for them. And then *she* had ruined it, just like she had ruined everything else.

"So why aren't you in the plaza now, performing with him?" piped up another man in the group. "Saw your brother there. Best I've heard him play since the festival."

Diego glanced over at Esperanza. She was listening now, suddenly interested at the mention of Artie. Diego pretended that he hadn't noticed her and resisted the urge to grin. He couldn't undo the damage that she had done, he knew, but he could at least make her suffer a bit. He wouldn't even have to lie.

"Ah sí, amigo. I was planning on joining him this morning, but when I saw him there with the new love of his life, I just couldn't bring myself to interrupt." The other men laughed.

"Sí, he certainly looked happy," grinned one of the men, joining in. "*Tus Besos*, he was singing. You know, the one about kissing. *Tus besos se han quedado en mi cara mujer...*" he began to howl drunkenly, the other men in his group joining in with the song.

Diego glanced at Esperanza's face again. She was giving them her full attention, her whole body turned towards them so that she could hear every word they said. Her face was a mask of confusion, and Diego had to hold himself back from laughing. *She deserves this*, he told himself. *She deserves it for everything she's put my brother through. For everything she's taken from me.*

"Oh, sí," Diego grinned, twisting the knife a little further. "I don't think I've ever seen Artie so happy, sitting there in the square with the beautiful Celestina in his arms... ah, what wonderful music they make together!"

The men laughed again, and Esperanza stood up, her big blue eyes swimming with pain. Diego acknowledged her at last, trying to keep his face straight as though he had only just noticed her there.

"Ah, Isabella!" he cried. He always got her name wrong, deliberately, of course. He wouldn't want her to think that she was special enough for him to remember her name. "Has Artie not introduced you to his lovely Celestina yet? She's beautiful. He's been singing love songs all morning with her. He says that she's the new love of his life. Why don't you go and meet her for yourself? I'm sure you'll agree, they're the perfect match!"

"To Artie and Celestina!" cried one of the drunks, waving his beer mug in the air for a refill.

"Artie and Celestina!" the others echoed back, laughing as they drank.

Esperanza looked as though she wanted to say something, but emotion overcame her. She shook her head in agonized horror and backed away a few steps before turning and running from the taverna, her hands covering her face. Diego knew that he should feel bad, but he could not help laughing. The victory was small, but a victory, nonetheless. He even had the extra gratification of knowing that every word had been true; his conscience was clear.

"What's her problem?" one of the men asked. "She looked upset."

"I hope she was," Diego smirked, taking another sip of his beer. His head was humming pleasantly from the drink now, and he could hear his own speech slurring. The revenge had been petty, perhaps, but it felt *so* satisfying. It was good for her to see what pain felt like, for once.

"You know her?" asked the one who had been singing. "She's Dominguez' daughter, isn't she? Hadn't you better go after her, check she's all right?"

"No." Diego shook his head. "Believe me, she's not worth the time. Troublemaking little *puta*, that *Señorita* Dominguez."

"Dominguez?" growled a low voice from the corner. Diego couldn't see the speaker in the taverna's murky darkness, but he was too drunk to care who it was anyway. "That stuck-up little *señorita* been giving you the run-around, eh *Amigo*?"

Diego gave a derisive snort.

"Not likely," he sneered. "I wouldn't lower myself to chasing around after that stupid little *perra*. Saw straight through that one the first time I met her, and *that* was already one time too many."

His mysterious companion gave a low chuckle, and Diego caught a glint of gold in the dim light.

"Ah, like that, is it?" he mused. "Notice she left in a hurry. Your doing, I'm guessing?"

"*Sí* and I'd pay good money never to have to clap eyes on her again," Diego grumbled. It felt good to have someone to talk to who was on his side, for once. "That little witch has taken everything from me. My family, my dignity, my dreams. God, I'd give everything I'd ever owned just to make her go away and never come back."

The man grunted with amusement.

"Interesting," he muttered.

Diego nodded and turned to thrust his mug back onto the bar, gesturing to Pedro for another refill.

"And here's another thing-" he started, but when he turned back, he found that his companion had vanished. All that remained was an empty mug and the faint whiff of sweat and tequila.

CHAPTER TWO

Esperanza couldn't remember a time when she had felt more humiliated. Realizing that her face was wet with tears, she scrubbed at it with her sleeve, praying that she wouldn't bump into Artie *now* of all times. She wouldn't want that waste-of-space *músico* to see her getting upset over him. No, she wasn't upset over him. She was upset at herself. Angry that she could be so stupid as to fall for the charms of some two-timing, skinny little fool, with his stupid guitar and his falling-apart straw hat. She should have seen it coming, with the way those girls had fawned over him at the festival and that ridiculous love note she had found in the stables. Now one of the little *putas* had thrown herself at him, and he had revelled in the attention. Well, whoever this *Celestina* was, she was welcome to him.

Esperanza paused to catch her breath, leaning against a tree to steady herself. She smoothed her hand through her hair and lowered her heavy basket to the ground, willing her eyes to stop leaking.

Diego's words echoed through her head as he laughed with his friends. The way he had *smirked* at the stung expression on her face. The laughter of the men around him.

Diego always got her name wrong. Esperanza was sure he did it just to wind her up, although now she wondered if perhaps he really was confusing her with other girls. His smug voice and twisted smile, the feigned surprise on his face as he pretended that he had only just spotted her, all taunted her as she tried to stop her mind from replaying his words.

She covered her eyes, willing her mind to stop spinning. She should've known there was something amiss when she saw Diego smiling at her. Diego never smiled at her. She knew he resented the amount of time she and Artie had been spending together and how she apparently 'distracted' him from his songwriting. Artie always insisted it wasn't true, that she was his inspiration. Well, now it seemed she wasn't the only one. Esperanza, Isabella, Celestina... and goodness knows how many others. She couldn't believe how stupid she had been. Stupid, naïve, gullible...

"Esperanza! I've been looking everywhere for you!"

Oh no. She had spent the rest of her morning getting her groceries as quickly as possible, avoiding speaking to anyone and trying to make herself as unnoticeable as she could. She had even changed her route home, choosing to take the dusty, winding path down through the trees rather than walking along the main road so that she wouldn't have to see anybody. Artie was the last person she wanted to bump into, especially in this state. She brushed the tears from her cheeks, seized her basket and marched off in the direction of the farm. Artie, however, seemed oblivious to her desire to get away from him, lolloping towards her like an excitable puppy.

"Esperanza, wait! I've been looking all over for you. Where have you been? I saw Rafael making a delivery, he said that he dropped you off by the taverna. So, I thought you might come by the plaza, but you never came." He was chattering away, oblivious to the fury on her face. He finally looked at her, mistaking her glare for exertion. "Hey, can I carry your basket for you? It looks heavy. You should've waited for me to help."

"I don't need your help."

"I don't help you because you need it. I help you because I want to." Artie smiled, his eyes ablaze with affection, still blind to her icy glare. "I've got something to show you, look! Look what I got yesterday! It's not quite as good as the one I was after, but it's in great condition for second-hand. It's got a great tone, and look, the previous owner has hand-painted all these flowers on the-"

Artie's voice faltered as Esperanza swung around to face him, rage flushing her cheeks.

"Oh yes, Arturo. I've heard all about all the fun you've been having in the plaza. In fact, I suggest you return there as soon as possible before your fan club misses you. And you know what? They're welcome to you." She fought to keep her voice steady, but her words wobbled with fury. Her fists were clenched so tight around the handle of her basket that she was surprised it hadn't snapped in two.

Artie stared at her, his eyes confused and pleading.

"Esperanza, please, what's wrong? I thought- I thought-"

"You thought," she snapped. "Well, so did I. It seems that we were both wrong."

He flinched as though she had slapped him.

"Esperanza, please... *mi amor*... I don't understand. Have I done something to hurt you? Talk to me, let me put it right.

You know I'd do anything for you." His voice sounded high and frightened. He reached out to take her hand, but she snatched it away.

"Anything? Good. Then leave me alone. I never want to see your stupid face again."

Esperanza stormed away in the direction of the farm, keeping her head down so that he couldn't see the tears that poured down her cheeks. She didn't dare turn back to look at the figure standing frozen and helpless behind her, a forlorn look of pain and confusion on his face.

Acting, she reminded herself. The moment she was out of sight he would be back in the plaza, dancing with this 'Celestina' and enjoying himself as though she had never existed. Whoever this new girl was, she was welcome to him.

Half a mile more, and she would be home. Esperanza started thinking about what she would say to her mother. She certainly couldn't tell her the truth. One option was to feign illness so that she could hide in her room until she felt more able to face the world again, but she knew what Louisa's reaction would be; she would fuss over her, sending for the doctor and coming in to check her temperature every five minutes. It was the last thing Esperanza wanted.

She could always offer to do the laundry, which would at least allow her a bit of privacy and fresh air, sitting out by the river. But that secret clearing was now tarnished forever with the memory of Artie making her laugh with his silly songs, her heart fluttering as he stared at her with those soft eyes, his voice seeming to seep into her very soul. Maybe he was going back to sing to Celestina now. Maybe she would be made to feel the same way that Esperanza had felt then and would lose herself in those same beautiful chestnut eyes.

She had to stop for a moment to catch her breath. She had been walking fast, and the ankle that was still weak from her fall was starting to ache again. She pulled her boots off and threw them into her basket, leaning against a tree so that she could massage the ankle and pour a little water over the stinging blisters that had erupted on her heels. Then she emptied the rest of her cantina over her face, trying to wash away the evidence she had been crying. The water was warmer than she would've liked but still refreshing on her sore eyes and hot, tear-stained cheeks.

"*Buenos días, Señorita Esperanza.*"

Esperanza jumped and whirled around to confront whoever was addressing her, cursing herself for not paying more attention to her surroundings. She would never usually have allowed her mind to drift to the point where she failed to notice a stranger sneaking up on her, especially a man. Yet here he was. And, she realized with a jolt, he knew her name.

"*Buenos días, señor.* Do I know-" she stopped short as she caught sight of the man's face. "You! You've got a nerve, showing your face around here!"

Roberto Hernandez. Large, imposing and stinking even worse than usual of alcohol, he stood before Esperanza in his grubby greyish-white vest and filthy trousers that were worn through at the knees. He smiled at Esperanza through blackened teeth, his one gold incisor glinting in the sun. His eyes were narrowed with hate. However, she was not afraid; her anger towards him was too strong to allow any room for fear.

"It is good to see you, *señorita*. I've been waiting." His voice was a low growl, a mixture of amusement and venom.

"The only thing you should be waiting for, *señor*, is the next train out of this *pueblo*. You just wait until my father finds out that you've dared showed your face again here. He-"

"He wasn't the one I was waiting for."

Esperanza started as she realized the presence second man, slightly taller and thinner, standing in shade of the trees.

"Meet my brother, Bartoli. Where is that little brother of yours, señorita? Is he not with you? I was rather hoping to see him." The thinner man laughed, cracking his knuckles against the palm of his other hand. The sound made Esperanza's teeth hurt.

"You will stay away from my brother, and my father, too," she spat. "We all know what sort of a man you really are, and by now, the whole *pueblo* will know-"

Roberto and his brother laughed.

"Silly little *niña*. So naïve. It's not your brother we've been waiting for. It's you. So sweet, and young, and... alone."

Esperanza suddenly felt as though she had been plunged into ice-cold water. Her brain told her to run, but her legs seemed to have turned to lead. She couldn't move.

"I spent so long thinking about how to best get revenge on your father for the insult he dealt me. What sort of weapon I could use to hurt him most. And then chance delivered it right to me. His precious daughter."

Roberto lunged forward and seized Esperanza by the wrist. She screamed, grabbing the nearest thing from the top of her basket- her left boot. She lashed out at his face, the heel connecting with his cheekbone before he had the chance to see it coming. He snarled with fury, releasing her, but before she could run, two large hands grabbed her arms from behind and dragged her backward. She screamed again as Bartoli roughly shoved her back up against a tree, positioning himself behind her so that he could hold on to her wrists, twisting them until tears sprung to her eyes. Roberto's fist flew out of nowhere, connecting with the side of her face and stunning her. Her ears were ringing, and she felt him clap a dirty hand over her mouth, bending down so close to her that she could feel his hot breath on her face.

"You scream again, *señorita*, and you'll get another one of those. Nobody can hear you here. There's nothing you can do. Now be a good girl and do as you're told, and I won't make this any more unpleasant for you than it has to be."

He took his hand from her mouth and placed it instead on her knee, brushing the fabric of her skirt aside. Esperanza fought the urge to be sick as his fingers crawled up her thigh, his other hand snaking around her waist as he moved his body closer. His face loomed towards her, and she gagged at his sour breath as he forced his lips against hers.

Esperanza saw her chance. She bit down as hard as she could on his lip, jamming her knee up in between his legs as she did so. Roberto howled with pain, swearing as he doubled over. Esperanza tried to break free, but Bartoli still held her wrists from behind, twisting them with a hiss of anger. Roberto's face was purple with rage. One hand reached out and grabbed Esperanza by the throat, while the other he balled into a fist, swinging it back in preparation to strike.

"You'll regret that, you vicious little witch!"

Esperanza squeezed her eyes tight shut, bracing herself for the impact.

CRUNCH.

The hand disappeared from her throat. There was a cry of surprise from behind her as Bartoli released her wrists, throwing his arms up to protect his face from whatever was now standing in front of him. Esperanza opened her eyes to find herself staring straight at the lean figure of Artie standing over Roberto, who was crouched on the ground with his hands over his head. Large splinters of broken wood littered the ground, some sticking out of Roberto's hair, a handful of which Artie had grabbed from behind to keep him from standing back up. In his other hand, he held the long, broken neck of a guitar, the splintered end of it thrust into Bartoli's baffled face. Artie turned to her, his eyes wild with panic.

"Esperanza! Run!"

Esperanza tried to obey, but her legs had turned to jelly. Her skirts tangled around her legs, tripping her as she stumbled away from the trees, scrambling back towards the path on all-fours. She spotted her basket nearby and grabbed her remaining boot from it, unable to think of anything else that she could use as a weapon, but her legs were too weak with fear to hold her up, let alone fight.

"Help! Somebody, help!" she screamed in the direction of the farm, praying that someone would hear her. *Dios, please... someone, anyone....*

It took the brothers seconds to recover from their shock and overpower Artie. Bartoli wrenched the remains of the broken guitar from his hand, effortlessly snapping the neck over his knee and tossing it aside. Roberto, meanwhile, had managed to break Artie's grip on his hair. He seized the younger man by the front of his shirt, lifting him clean off the ground before throwing him sprawling on the dusty path.

"Esperanza... please... run..." Artie gasped. The brothers were approaching him slowly, circling like wolves. "Run now... *please...*"

"Well, if it isn't little Arturo." Roberto's voice was a low, deadly growl. "Once again poking his nose into matters which do not concern him."

Bartoli sniggered.

"You should've kept that guitar for playing in the plaza, boy, rather than wasting it trying to play the hero."

Esperanza felt as though the bottom had dropped out of her stomach. *Run*, her brain screamed at her. *Run, while they're distracted, go and get help, they're going to kill him...* But her body wouldn't move. She was frozen to the spot, powerless as the two men closed in on Artie.

"It's a shame, *niño*." Roberto crouched down next to Artie, grabbing him by his necktie and dragging his face so close that their noses were almost touching. "Interfering little snitch that you were, I will miss listening to your music in the plaza. It's tragic when the talented die so young."

Roberto struck Artie's cheekbone with his fist, sending him flying back into the dust. Bartoli drove a booted foot hard into Artie's ribcage. Both men laughed as Artie cried out in pain, his hands covering his face as he lay helpless on the ground, blow after blow smashing into his defenceless body.

The following minutes were a nightmarish blur to Esperanza as she watched with horror, tears streaming down her cheeks.

Do something, her head screamed at her. *Don't just sit there. They're killing him.*

Artie's cries turned to whimpers, his eyes closed, blood pouring down his face and soaking his shirt from a nasty wound near his temple. His face relaxed as he slipped in and out of consciousness, his breath coming in ragged gasps.

"Let me finish him."

Roberto held up a hand to his brother, who stepped away from Artie's crumpled body, dropping the bloodstained stone he had been using as a weapon. The larger man stooped down and rolled him onto his back, forcing Artie to look up at him through bleary, half-conscious eyes.

"Time's up, *músico*. You should've known better than to cross me. I warned you enough times. *Adios*."

Artie's eyes widened in fear as Roberto gritted his teeth and raised his fist above his head. Then Esperanza saw it–

the glint of silver catching the sunlight, shining in Roberto's hand. A knife.

"NO!"

Before she knew what she was doing, Esperanza scrambled forwards, throwing herself at Roberto with as much force as she could muster. She held tight to his wrist with one hand, trying to force the knife away from Artie, using her other hand to beat Roberto's head and face over and over with the heel of the boot she hadn't even realized she was still holding. Bartoli sprang forward and seized her around the waist from behind, hurling her to the ground, but not before she had managed to throw her head back hard against his nose with a loud crack. He lumbered towards her, and she prepared herself to aim a swift kick to his groin.

However, before he could reach her, he suddenly stopped. His eyes were fixed on something behind her, a look of sweaty panic passing over his face.

"Time to go, brother!" he hissed. Turning his back on her, he scrambled back towards Roberto, dragging him to his feet and away back towards the trees.

"There they are! Señorita Esperanza, hold on, we're coming!"

Esperanza was vaguely aware of her father's men charging towards her, armed with pitchforks, hoes, shovels and anything else they had been able to lay hands on. There were eleven or twelve of them, a few of them rushing to surround herself and Artie, others running into the trees after the fleeing Hernandez brothers.

"Señorita, you're bleeding, look at your hand..." Jorge was the first to reach her, but Esperanza pushed him away, struggling to her feet. She had not taken her eyes off the limp body on the path, lying crumpled in the dust. She stumbled towards him, pushing away the other men who were bending over him.

"Artie... no, please..."

Esperanza fell to her knees beside him and cradled his head in her arms. Her hand pressed against his chest, searching for a sign that he was breathing, a heartbeat, anything. His hair was orange with dust from the path, his face barely recognizable underneath layers of dirt and blood. His temple was still bleeding profusely, and there was already a large bruise rising underneath his left eye from where Roberto had punched him. She could feel the bones of his ribcage through his blood-soaked shirt and realized with a surge of relief that they were rising and falling irregularly with each painful breath. *He's alive*, she told herself. *He's hurt, but he's alive.* Her hand found his, and she raised it to her lips, kissing his fingers before holding it tight against her own aching heart. She felt him gently squeeze in return.

Hot tears spilled down her cheeks. She could hear the voices of the men around her, although she couldn't process anything they were saying. Someone was sobbing, and it took a minute for her to realize that it was her. A warm arm pressed itself around her shoulders, and Rafael's gentle, comforting voice rumbled in her ear.

"*Señorita* Esperanza. We need to get you and Artie back to the house. I've brought the cart, and we have sent a message back to your *mamá* to prepare her. Will you step away for a moment so that we can lift him into the cart? We promise we'll be very gentle."

Esperanza nodded. A strong arm helped her to her feet, which she remembered were now bare, and she felt sharp stones cutting into her soles. One of her boots lay beside the path from when she had been trying to fight Roberto, while the other was still over by the trees. As a few of the men lifted

Artie's limp form into the waiting cart, Esperanza noticed for the first time how her hand was stinging. Looking down, she realized she had cut it somehow- she guessed that Roberto had caught her a glancing blow with the knife as she was trying to wrestle it from his hand. Where was it now? Did he still have it? And more importantly, had he managed to use it on Artie while she was fighting off his brother? Esperanza felt sick again. She tried to take a few deep breaths, reminding herself that she would be of no use to Artie in this state. He needed her to stay strong.

Daniel retrieved her boots for her, along with the basket which still contained her shopping and something he had carefully gathered up in a blanket. Her heart sank as he brought it over.

"Lo... lo siento, señorita..." but what should I do with this?" He opened the blanket to show her the broken, splintered remains of a guitar. She took it, unable to find the words to reply.

"Ay, that is a shame." Rafael sighed, shaking his head. "He only got that yesterday. Someone had gone to the trouble of hand-painting it too. It was a work of art, that instrument."

"Ah sí, I saw him playing it in the plaza," Jorge added. "What a pity. It will be a great loss to him."

"It will." Rafael placed another blanket around Esperanza's shoulders and helped her into the cart beside Artie. "But at least it's replaceable. A guitar is just a guitar until the right fingers are playing it. You can decorate it any way you like, name it whatever you want, although I will still never understand why some sentimental *idiotas* feel the need to name their instruments. It will only become truly beautiful when a good mariachi is strumming it."

Esperanza numbly unfolded the bundle of broken guitar pieces in her lap, turning the splintered pieces of wood over in her hands. Among the wreckage of strings, tuning pegs and broken pieces of fretboard, a rainbow of coloured flowers glowed out. Vibrant yellow marigolds, blue forget-me-nots, pink roses with delicate green leaves… and there, ornately painted up the neck in striking letters of black and gold… a name. *Celestina.*

CHAPTER THREE

"Señora Louisa is not going to be pleased with this arrangement."

"Señora Louisa is not here."

Louisa had left a note to tell Esperanza that *Tía* Victoria had been taken ill. As the doctor was away on business in Santa Juanita, her sister had been summoned to look after her. She had left for the *pueblo* immediately, with strict instructions that Esperanza should continue running the household as normal in her absence. They must have missed each other by minutes, Louisa travelling by the main road while the cart had come up through the fields.

"I must protest, *señorita*. Señora Louisa will never forgive me if I leave you here alone after what has just happened. What if those men come back?"

Esperanza groaned with frustration. Her mind was still spinning. While she was grateful to Rafael for his concern, the longer he spent fussing over her, the longer Artie was lying there alone with nobody to care for him.

"Rafael, for the last time. I will remain here in the barn and take care of Artie. I will bolt the doors from the inside and will not allow anybody in until someone comes to tell me it's safe. I have even prepared *papá*'s shotgun, just in case."

"It still does not sit right with me, *señorita*."

"Whether it sits right with you or not, Rafael, my mother left instructions to say that I was in charge in her absence. And I am telling you, I am not leaving Artie. I believe I am the only one here who has any medical experience, unless any of your fellow farmhands have any secret healing powers they have been hiding? I thought not."

The old man sighed and shuffled his feet, and Esperanza felt a little guilty for being short with him. She softened her tone.

"Look at what they've done to him, Rafael. It's hurting me enough that he got into this mess trying to defend me. If he... he doesn't make it..." she tried to hide the emotion in her voice, trying not to show how scared she felt. She couldn't bring herself to use the word 'dies' aloud- somehow, it made the possibility more frighteningly real. She swallowed hard before continuing. "I'd never forgive myself if I hadn't done everything I could. Doctor Francisco is out of town, and Catalina with him. I'm the only hope he's got."

"All right, *señorita*," Rafael conceded. "I understand. You just promise me that you will keep this barn door bolted and barred the whole time we are gone, and you open it for no one unless they can give the code word that we agreed upon. *Sí?*"

"*Sí*," she agreed. "I promise."

"The other men have gone off in search of the Hernandez brothers, and they will not rest until both have been captured, I promise you that. I will take the cart down to the *pueblo* and find your *mamá* and your brothers, and I'm sending Daniel to take a message to the *presidio* to see if the soldiers will help us with the search. I believe the *comandante* is a personal friend of Don Raúl's. No doubt the Don will be prepared to pay a pretty penny to whoever catches the men who tried to harm you, especially if he thinks it may raise himself higher in your estimations."

Rafael's eyes twinkled at the stony expression on Esperanza's face. The last person she wanted to think about right now was Don Raúl, and clearly, he knew it. He was no more enamoured with the Dons and their snobbish aristocracy than she was.

"Don't worry, *señorita*. I will make some excuse to your mother," he assured her. "You take good care of him. Daniel has brought down everything you might need. I promise I will send word as soon as I hear any news."

"Thank you, Rafael."

Esperanza closed the barn door, barring it shut with a large wooden beam and sliding the heavy iron bolts into place. Nobody would think to look for her here; even if they did, they would never be able to get into the fortress that was her father's barn. All of the animals had been put out to pasture already and everything had been cleaned and swept that morning. Aside from the scratching of mice up in the rafters, all was quiet.

Gathering her courage, Esperanza walked slowly over to where Artie was lying on his bed of hay. Daniel had indeed left everything that she had asked for: bowls of water, blankets, clean cloths, bandages, food, an oil lamp, and even a small bottle of alcohol for cleaning wounds. There was a needle and thread, too, in case he needed stitching. Esperanza forced herself to ignore them, trying to push the thought from her mind.

She knelt beside Artie's limp form and placed a trembling hand on his chest, finding comfort in his laboured breathing. *No, it's not easy, but at least he is breathing,* she reminded herself. She had to try to shut off her emotions, just as she had done on that day when she had helped Catalina to treat the injured mineworkers. It was the only way to stop herself from breaking down, and then she would be no use to anyone. Artie needed her to hold herself together, at least until she had done all she could for him.

As long as it's enough, said the nasty voice in her head. *As long as it's not too late.*

She forced herself to focus, taking a deep, trembling breath to calm herself. His breathing seemed so painful; perhaps it would help if she removed his necktie. She fumbled clumsily with the knot, cursing her fingers for shaking. At least the fabric was red, so the blood didn't show up as starkly as it did on his once-white shirt.

Warm water for washing off the blood, cold for reducing the bruising, she reminded herself, hearing Catalina's voice in her head. Picking out a clean cloth from the pile, she soaked it, wrung it out and began to sponge away the dirt from his hands and arms, which thankfully seemed to have escaped with nothing worse than a few scrapes and bruises here and there.

Next, she moved on to the blood around Artie's temple. She traced the damp cloth down the side of his face, over his cheekbones and down towards his collar. For someone who had spent so much of his life as a malnourished child living on the streets, he really had turned out to be quite a handsome man, and Esperanza could feel her hands trembling as she stroked his jawline with her cloth. She remembered how sensitive he was around his neck and ears, thinking back to the day of the festival when she had absent-mindedly adjusted his necktie and he had crumpled like a ticklish child. *If he wasn't already unconscious,* she thought with a sad smile, *he'd probably have fainted anyway at what I'm doing to him now.*

The water in the bowl began to turn a brownish red as she continued her task, washing away any traces of blood and dirt from Artie's face and neck. He was starting to look more like the Artie she knew. Pale, yes, and bruised in places, but hers. She tenderly combed his hair with her fingers, placing a cold, damp cloth across his forehead to reduce the swelling from the wound on his temple. Then, taking a deep breath, she looked down at his chest.

Until now, it had been easy to tell herself that Artie's injuries weren't too bad. She couldn't help but remember, though, that for most of his ordeal Artie had kept his face and head covered. Most of those vicious blows had been delivered to his body: the fists, the boots, the stone. She couldn't tell through his filthy, bloodstained shirt how bad it was, but she tried to prepare herself for the worst as she took a deep breath and gently began to unfasten the first few buttons.

Her heart dropped.

Artie's collarbone was already turning a purplish-red, with bruising stretching almost from shoulder to shoulder. His soft skin stretched tight over his ribs, which were rising and falling awkwardly with each shuddering breath, a patchwork of bruising and dried blood. A large, weeping graze poked out from the hollow beneath his breastbone, disappearing down towards his navel. His whole chest was covered with tiny cuts and scratches, which Esperanza supposed had come from being thrown onto the path.

Shuddering at the memory, she wrung out another cloth and set to work.

What had he been thinking, taking on two men like Roberto and Bartoli Hernandez? Individually they were twice his size and strength, with plenty of experience in the field of violent thuggery. By his own admission, Artie had never won a fight in his life. What on Earth had made him think that he could take on either of them, let alone both at once?

He didn't, the voice in her head reminded her. *He wasn't fighting because he thought there was any chance he could win. He was fighting to save you.*

He had made the choice to fight for her, to buy her the time to get away, knowing that he was likely to die for it. He might still if he had internal damage that she couldn't see. And what did she do? Just sat there and watched.

Warm tears trickled down her cheeks and splashed onto Artie's chest. As gently as she could, she lowered her head to rest over his heart, listening to the feeble thudding against her cheek. What made her guilt worse, if that was even possible, was that before all this she had been angry with him. She had told him she never wanted to see his face again. If he had died during that attack, those would have been the last words he ever heard from her.

"Oh Artie, forgive me," she whispered into his chest, stroking the bruised skin stretching over his ribs. "What have they done to you, and all because of me? I'm so sorry." A sob escaped her. She turned her head to kiss him and felt herself breaking down. It was as though an invisible hand was squeezing her heart, to the point that it was physically hurting, and she said a silent prayer to every saint she could think of.

Today was meant to have been the day she told him how she really felt. She had planned out exactly what she wanted to say. How she wished that she could spend her whole life sitting by the river with him, listening to his beautiful voice singing only for her. How he made her heart skip when he touched her hand, how his smile could make her feel as though everyone else in the world had disappeared. She would do anything for the chance to see that smile again.

"Oh, Artie… you have to be all right. Please. You just have to. You are everything to me. I can't live in a world where you're not there." Her tears were flowing freely now. She kissed his chest, again and again, breathing in his soft scent, still stroking his bruised ribs with her fingers. She knew she ought to pull herself together, but she couldn't help it. Her tears pooled on his skin, and she kissed them away. "Artie, please wake up. I'll do anything. Please."

"Anything, *mi amor*? Then don't stop. I'm enjoying the attention."

Esperanza almost fell into her bowl of water. She looked up to see Artie's chestnut eyes staring blearily back at her, a gentle smile on his lips. His voice was weak, but his face was glowing. The saints had listened to her.

"Artie! How much of that did you – I mean, how long have you…?"

"Clearly not long enough. Please, continue saying such lovely things about me." He reached out a weak, trembling hand and touched her cheek, brushing away her tears. "I should get myself beaten up every day if this is the sort of reward I can expect from you, *mi amor*."

"Artie, this is not a joke," Esperanza scolded him, choking on her tears. She couldn't decide whether to kiss him or hit him for daring to make light of the situation. "You could have died today. There were points when I thought I'd lost you. How could you be so stupid, taking on two men like the Hernandez brothers single-handedly? What on Earth were you thinking?"

"I thought that was obvious, *señorita*." Artie looked up at her with those big, sorrowful eyes. "I did what I had to do to save you."

"I don't think they were planning on killing me."

"I know exactly what they were planning on doing to you. I couldn't allow it."

"So you thought that dying for my honour was a better idea?" Esperanza felt her voice rising. "What if you'd died, Artie? What would have happened then? They were going to kill you."

"Was I just supposed to stand there and let them do what they wanted to you? What kind of a man would that make me?"

"A *living* one, Artie! Which is something you are currently very lucky to be!" Esperanza stood and turned away from him, too overcome with emotion to stay still. "You think that my honour is more important to me than your life? You think that what they wanted to do to me today would've been harder to live with than losing you? *Idiota!*"

"You think that I'm an *idiota* for trying to protect you?" It was Artie's turn to sound angry now. "What about you? The last thing I remember was you throwing yourself at a mad, violent *cabrón* who was holding a knife!"

"What did you expect me to do?" Esperanza shouted, tears streaming again. "Stand there and watch while he murdered the man I- I-"

She turned away, the final word hovering unspoken between them. Saying it aloud was a step she was too frightened to take, even though she had known for a long time that it was true. Her heart was pounding so hard it hurt. She clutched at her chest with a loud sob, trying to stop her head from spinning.

"The man you... what? Esperanza?" His voice was barely a whisper. He reached out a trembling hand for her, trying to get her to look at him. "Please. The man you... what? Tell me."

"I think you already know. Don't make me say it out loud."

She had planned on telling him today, down by the river when they were alone. She had come down to the *pueblo* with every intention of taking him somewhere secluded, looking into his eyes and confessing everything she felt, but then it had all gone wrong. This wasn't how it was supposed to be at all, with them shouting at each other in her father's barn, both drenched in blood and tears. She let out another sob.

"Please, *mi amor*," he begged, his voice cracking with emotion. "I know the word I want to hear, but I'm too scared to hope in case I'm wrong. You're angry with me, and I don't even know why."

"I'm not angry." She knelt beside him again, her defensiveness melting away. His eyes were full of pain and confusion, every ounce of it undeserved, and she took his hand to soothe him.

"You were angry earlier."

"That was my misunderstanding." She shifted with guilt under his quizzical gaze, knowing that she would have to explain herself sooner or later. "I... I saw Diego this morning. He led me to believe that you had a new love. He said you'd been seen with some beautiful girl this morning in the plaza, holding her, singing love songs with her..."

"A girl?" Artie's face contorted into an expression of puzzlement. "What girl? Esperanza, you know that I would never look at any woman but you. We talked about this. I don't think I even *saw* any girls in the plaza this morning. I was just waiting for you and playing my new... guitar..." He stopped, a look of dawning realization crossing his face. "This girl I was supposedly with. Was she called Celestina, by any chance?"

"Yes. Artie, I'm so sorry. It didn't cross my mind that he could be talking about your new guitar, I thought that you-"

"You really thought that I would do that to you, Esperanza? Do you not know me better than that by now, after all we've been through?" He withdrew his hand from hers, placing it instead on his bruised chest with a grimace of pain. "Diego manipulated you. That is an inexcusable way to behave towards a lady, and he and I will be having words over it. But you… you should know better. I have always made my feelings clear to you, Esperanza, and have never given you a reason to doubt them. You are the only woman I want; you are the only woman I will ever want. What have I ever done to make you trust me so little?"

Esperanza lowered her head, her cheeks burning with shame. He sounded so hurt. The anger she could deal with, but his disappointment in her was far worse. They were both silent for a moment.

"Artie, I'm… I'm sorry."

He didn't reply. She tried to touch his shoulder, and he made a motion as though to shrug her off, grimacing with pain at the movement. He turned his head away from her instead, trying to hide the angry tears in his eyes. He really was upset with her. She felt a lump in her throat, and tears welled up in her eyes again.

"Artie." Her voice cracked, and she pulled away from him, unsure what to do. "I'm sorry. You're right, I was jealous and I should've known better."

He ignored her, refusing to answer or even look at her. Esperanza felt her heart shatter. He was right; he had never given her any reason to doubt him, but she had let jealousy get the better of her, and now she had ruined everything. This was all her fault. None of this would've happened if only she had given him a chance to explain rather than flying off in a rage. She didn't deserve his love or his forgiveness.

"Please, *mi amor*," she begged, tears rolling down her cheeks. "I can't bear seeing you like this. Look at me. Please."

Artie gave a little shiver.

"*Mi amor*," he whispered, echoing her words. His expression softened, his shoulders relaxing. "That's the first time you've called me that."

He tried to move, but a sharp pain made him stop and gasp, holding his ribcage. Esperanza made a small noise of pain herself, something halfway between a sob and a cry of fear. She was unsure what to do with herself, her desperation to comfort him held back by her fear of his rejection.

"I suppose in a way I should be flattered that you got so jealous over me," he grimaced. "Even if your rival did turn out to be made of wood." He laughed quietly, his laughter turning into a coughing fit which made him hiss through his teeth in pain, clutching at his chest.

Esperanza's resolve broke. She moved towards him, taking his hand, squeezing it while she ran the fingers of her other hand through his hair to calm him. His face relaxed with a shuddering sigh, his eyes closed. She stroked his bruised cheekbone, her heart fluttering as he nuzzled his face into her palm and placed a gentle kiss on her wrist. She was forgiven.

"You're going to have quite a shiner of a black eye tomorrow, *señor*," she told him tenderly.

"We will match then, *mi amor*," he retorted, reaching up to stroke her own bruised cheek. She had forgotten about that. "Did he hurt you anywhere else?"

"Only my hand, I think he caught me with the knife. It's a shallow cut though, it's really not serious, and I've cleaned and dressed it already," she finished quickly, seeing his eyes narrow with worry. "It's nothing compared to what he did to you. You just wait until the soldiers catch up with those *cabróns*. They'll be begging for their prison cells before I've finished with them."

"I don't envy them that," Artie chuckled, and his eyes met with hers. Esperanza felt a rush of warmth towards him. He was smiling lovingly at her again in spite of his pain.

"I think… I think you might have a few broken ribs," she told him, looking for an excuse to tear her eyes away from his gaze before she became lost in it. "I was just cleaning you up a bit before you woke. You've got a nasty graze on your chest that needs dealing with, too."

"Yes, I thought as much. Well, don't let me stop you. You just continue where you left off. I'll even pretend I'm still unconscious, so you can carry on saying lovely things to me." He closed his eyes, smiling. "Please, feel free to fuss over me as much as you like."

Idiota, thought Esperanza fondly. *Despite all this, he's actually enjoying the attention.* She decided to tease him a little, brushing his hair out of his face before tracing her fingers down his cheek over the sensitive spot on his neck. He took a sharp breath in and shuddered, just as she knew he would. Her fingers continued downwards, drifting over the bare skin of his bruised collarbone and down to his ribs, dipping her hands under the folds of his half-open shirt to stroke his chest. She glanced up to see that his grin had disappeared, replaced instead with a look she hadn't seen before. His face was relaxed but serious, his lips slightly parted, his breathing faster and heavier than usual. His hands, she realized, had grabbed handfuls of hay from the bales he was lying on, and he was clinging to it tightly.

"Am I hurting you?" she asked. He shook his head and swallowed, keeping his eyes closed, his fingers still clinging to the hay beneath him. She took her warm cloth and stroked it over his ribs, taking particular care wherever she thought it might be sore. She repeated the process on the other side, reaching inside the fabric of his shirt to get to his sides, stroking his bruised skin with both her cloth and her fingers. He trembled at her touch, his breaths turning to sharp pants as her hands explored. Whether it was due to pain or excitement, though, Esperanza couldn't quite tell.

"Artie," she said gently, "I'm going to deal with that graze now, all right? I'll need to clean it as the skin is broken. This... this may sting a bit. I promise I'll be as gentle as I can."

Artie nodded and took a few deep breaths in and out, a look of intense concentration on his face. Esperanza traced her hand back down his breastbone. She slowly unfastened the buttons of his shirt as far down as his navel, pulling the fabric apart to get better access to his injury. Artie was still fighting hard to steady his breathing, she supposed in anticipation of the pain. She tried to steady her own breathing, too, willing her hands to stop trembling.

Dios, if she ever got her hands on those men again, she would make them pay. She could see the dirt and even a few tiny stones still embedded in Artie's broken skin. As gently as she could, she wrung a little water from her cloth onto the wound, trying to clear as much of the debris as possible. Then she took a clean cloth and the bottle of alcohol, soaking it until she was sure that she could cover the whole graze in one go. It was going to sting, for sure, but at least she wouldn't be dragging out the pain for longer than necessary.

"Ready?" she asked, her voice hoarse. "*Lo siento, mi amor*, this is going to hurt".

"I'm sure I can be brave, as long as you promise to kiss it better afterwards," he winked back.

She smiled at him, bracing herself as she looked back down at the wound.

Come on, Esperanza, said the voice in her head. *Get on with it. It's not even your wound. If Artie can bear it, so can you.* Counting to three, she gritted her teeth and pressed the cloth against Artie's broken skin.

The effect was immediate. He gave a sharp yelp, arching back against his makeshift bed as the stinging pain seared through him like a hot knife. Esperanza had to use both hands to keep the cloth in place, fighting back her own tears. She knew that she had no choice; without cleaning, the wound could get infected, but still, she wished that there was some way she could suffer it in his place. It would be easier to bear than having to inflict such pain on him.

After what felt like several minutes, once she was sure that the alcohol had done its job, Esperanza removed the cloth, replacing it with a dry one and fixing it in place to keep the wound as clean as possible. Artie's contorted features gradually relaxed, his breathing laboured, and the moment she had finished securing his dressing, Esperanza took his hand and squeezed it. He pulled her close to him, sighing with relief that it was over. Her heart ached to see tears on his cheeks, and she gently brushed them away, running her hands soothingly through his hair and cradling his head in the crook of her arm.

"I'm sorry, *mi amor*," he laughed hoarsely. "Perhaps I wasn't quite as brave as I thought I would be."

"Today you fought off two men, each twice your size and both armed, knowing that they would probably kill you, and all to protect me," she answered quietly, bending to press her forehead against his. There was no point in trying to hide how she felt anymore. He had spent enough of his life without the love and affection he so deserved, and she had no wish to keep it from him any longer. "You are the bravest man in the whole of Mexico, and I love you, Artie."

Letting out a sigh of pure joy, Artie slipped one hand behind Esperanza's neck and pulled her face down to meet his. Their lips locked together. Esperanza felt as though her heart had exploded. Warmth spread through her chest, filling her with a wonderful tingling sensation all over. She felt his fingers entangling themselves in her hair, drawing her deeper into the kiss, his other hand travelling down her spine to the small of her back and pulling her tight against his body. She melted at his touch, one hand cradling his head, the other stroking his cheek, his neck, his shoulders. Her body pressed against his, every part of her seeming to take on a life of its own, separated from her brain, which felt as though it had blissfully evaporated. The rest of the world disappeared. It was just him and her and this moment. Nothing else mattered.

Her hand slipped down further down his side to his hip, feeling the warmth of his skin through the remains of his thin shirt, the jutting bone of his pelvis hard against her fingers. She felt him pull her even tighter to him, and he let out a quiet whimper, bringing her back to herself for a moment. Was she hurting him? She hadn't opened his shirt below his navel yet, or properly checked his sides for injuries- had she missed something? Suddenly worried, she broke away from the kiss and glanced down. A fresh patch of scarlet blood was soaking through the side of his shirt in an almost perfect line, about an inch above the length of rope he was using as a belt. *A knife wound.*

"No, no, no..." she panicked. "Artie, you're bleeding, please no-"

"Mi amor-"

Esperanza grabbed the front of his shirt, ripping it open so that the remaining buttons went pinging across the barn floor. She pulled the fabric from his waistband, frantically searching for the stab wound, almost knocking over the bowl of water as she sloshed the cloth over his bloodstained skin in her attempt to get a clearer view. She realized too late that in her panic she had forgotten to wring it out, and he was now soaked.

There was nothing there.

"Esperanza, *calme*! I'm not bleeding, you are- look!" Artie took her injured hand in his, showing her the bloodied bandage which had become unravelled. It must have loosened while she had been tending to his graze and then slipped off while they were kissing. She had been too distracted to notice any pain, but the new bloodstain on his shirt matched the cut on her hand perfectly. Realization broke over her like a wave, and she cringed with embarrassment as he started to laugh, winding the bandage back around her hand and securing it with a kiss.

"You're going to get me into trouble, *señorita*. What will your *papá* say when he finds my buttons all over his barn floor and realizes that his daughter has been ripping my clothes off?" He was laughing, but his voice was still breathless from the kiss, his hands shaking.

"I thought that Roberto had managed to use that knife on you," she croaked, feeling faint with relief. She lowered her head and kissed the hollow of his hip where his imagined wound had been. He exhaled quietly and shivered, his muscles tensing as her breath warmed his skin. "And now look, you're soaked."

She took a dry cloth and mopped the skin around his navel. His ripped shirt was hanging off his shoulders like rags. His trousers sat low on his slender hips, their waistband and rope belt now damp from the spilled water which rolled in droplets across his bare stomach. Esperanza traced her cloth over his navel and down towards the knot of his belt, catching the drops one by one.

Artie's heart was pounding so hard it hurt. His head was still reeling from the kiss, and now his breathing became more laboured with every touch, every new and exciting sensation, turning to gasps as Esperanza's hands crept down towards his belt. The teasing of her fingers dipping beneath his waistband sent a tremor up his spine that was too intense for him to bear, and he let out a yelp, catching her wrist with a trembling hand.

"¡Dios mío!" His voice was three octaves higher than usual. "Esperanza, please, you're killing me!"

"Lo... lo siento... was I hurting you?"

"No, no, mi amor. Quite the opposite." He flashed her a breathless smile and winked. "You underestimate your power over me, señorita."

Esperanza flushed with realization, an embarrassed giggle escaping her lips.

"Well, I'm glad it doesn't hurt."

"Ay, but it does. Here." He took her hand, placing it back over his heart so that she could feel how fast it was beating for her. "I think I need you to kiss it better again."

He tried to keep his expression serious, but his eyes were twinkling playfully. She couldn't resist. She climbed up onto the hay and cuddled in beside him, lowering her face to his until their noses touched.

"I love you, Arturo," she whispered, and their lips met once more.

THE MUSICIAN'S PROMISE – BOOK #2 (preview)

–THE MUSICIAN'S PROMISE SERIES–

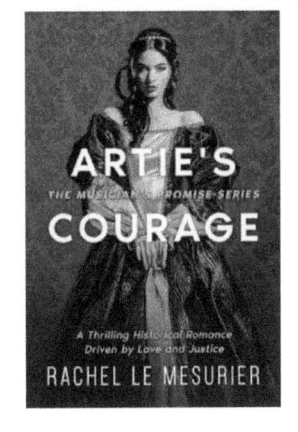

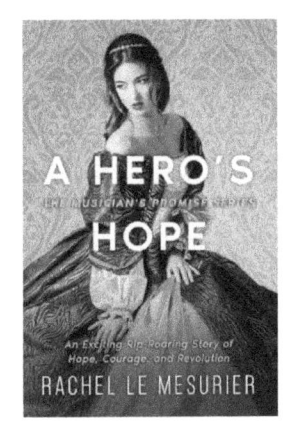

BOOK ONE:
ARTIE'S COURAGE

BOOK TWO:
A HERO'S HOPE

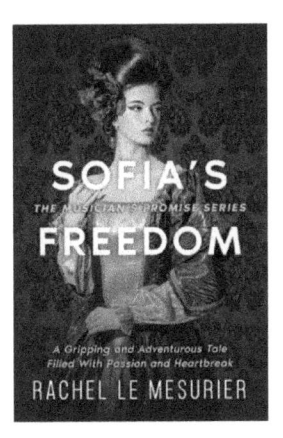

BOOK THREE:
SOFIA'S FREEDOM